THE Darkest SUMMER

The Darkest Summer

REBECCA J. GREENWOOD

SWEETWATER
BOOKS
An imprint of Cedar Fort, Inc.
Springville, Utah

ISBN 13: 978-1-4621-2094-9

Published by Sweetwater Books, an imprint of Cedar Fort, Inc.
2373 W. 700 S., Springville, UT 84663
Distributed by Cedar Fort, Inc., www.cedarfort.com

LIBRARY OF CONGRESS CATALOGING-IN-PUBLICATION DATA

Names: Greenwood, Rebecca J., 1980- author.
Title: The darkest summer / Rebecca J. Greenwood.
Description: Springville, Utah : Sweetwater Books, an imprint of Cedar Fort, Inc., [2017]
Identifiers: LCCN 2017029063 (print) | LCCN 2017038962 (ebook) | ISBN 9781462128334 (epub and mobi) | ISBN 9781462120949 (softcover : acid-free paper)
Subjects: | GSAFD: Regency fiction. | Love stories.
Classification: LCC PS3607.R4698 (ebook) | LCC PS3607.R4698 D37 2017 (print) | DDC 813/.6--dc23
LC record available at https://lccn.loc.gov/2017029063

Cover design by Priscilla Chaves and Katie Payne

Edited and typeset by Jessica Romrell and Nicole Terry

Printed in the United States of America

10 9 8 7 6 5 4 3 2 1

Printed on acid-free paper

To my love, Karl
Thank you for now and for eternity

Contents

Persephone gathered flowers over a soft meadow,
roses and crocuses and beautiful violets, irises also,
hyacinths, and the narcissus—a marvelous, radiant flower.
The girl reached out with both hands to take the lovely toy;
but the wide-pathed earth yawned,
and the lord Hades with his immortal horses
sprang out upon her.
He caught her up reluctant on his golden car
and bear her away lamenting.

Adapted from the Hymn to Demeter
Hesiod, The Homeric Hymns and Homerica
Translated by Hugh G. Evelyn-White, M.A., 1914

Chapter One

First Sight

FRIDAY, JUNE 28, 1816, MORNING

He first saw her in Hyde Park, a young miss with her maid taking a morning stroll. This would have been unremarkable except that it was raining and chill and no other young ladies were out.

She crossed the path in front of him, holding an umbrella over her pretty bonnet and pelisse, and her maid followed behind under another. He watched them till they were screened by trees.

Adam Richard Douglas, third Duke of Blackdale, was exercising Cerberus, his overeager stallion. The horse had been stabled for one day too many and became unmanageable, with a tendency to bite—hence the name—without activity, no matter that it was cold and wet outside. Adam would curse Cerberus for his folly, but having a mount that didn't mind the chill and damp was highly useful for a Scot and a soldier.

He turned onto Rotten Row. The stretch of waterlogged gravel and tan before them was clear. Adam let the stallion have his head, and galloped.

He felt the need of fresh air himself. He had been stifled in boardrooms and offices for too long. The fruitless and discouraging campaigning in the House of Lords, and the hours of social engagements in the evenings had drained him. He felt pale and listless. He was cursed with an unrelieved sick-room pallor.

It had been a miserable spring, and looked to be a miserable summer.

But yesterday . . . his hands tightened on the reigns as rage flashed through him. Jude and his philandering!

Yesterday, Adam had finished the distasteful job of cleaning up after yet another of his brother's sordid affairs. He paid for the young lady to spend her confinement in a comfortable Welsh cottage with an aunt, and then he had determinedly packed Jude and his disgruntled wife off to France before the girl's father had a chance to call Jude out and get killed for his trouble.

Adam had been so relieved to finally see the backs of them all.

He wished Jude and Henriette well of each other. He wondered if the French countryside would survive.

His brother, the war-hero of Waterloo, had gone through the bloody day with nary a scratch. Jude had come through the years-long conflict with Napoleon the best of them all, unlike Adam, and their other brother, Nicolas. Captain Lord Nicolas Douglas had been lost at sea. Why couldn't it have been Jude that was lost?

Adam stopped himself. That thought was unworthy of him. It was as it was. Nicolas was gone, and Jude, the libertine, remained.

Adam's wide-brimmed beaver kept most of the rain from his face, and the caped greatcoat kept him warm. He was almost used to being in civilian wear again, without the scarlet and tartan of his uniform. There was one thing to say about horseback riding in long trousers rather than a kilt: his knees were much warmer. Never let his men hear him say that—

His men. The few that were left.

The gunshots rose up in his mind, the boom of cannon fire, the screams of his men dying in the square around him, fellow soldiers propping up the one beside them as they were struck.

A flash of the cannonball that grazed his side, the fall from his horse, the agony and the blackness . . .

His breath hitched as pain flared in his side, and he pulled Cerberus down from his gallop. Trotting made it worse, and Adam cursed the lingering injury. It had a been a year since Waterloo, but his ribs still ached.

A groom exercising a horse gave him an odd look as he passed. The pain must be showing on his face. Adam controlled his grimace, brought Cerberus down to a walk, and turned off onto a side path to deal with the pain more privately.

The young woman was there, picking her way through a planted hillock. He slowed Cerberus to a stop to watch her.

The finely dressed young lady stopped at a clump of pitiful looking flowers and stooped down to look at them. She straightened, wrapped her skirts with one hand tightly against her body, and crouched gracefully. She managed to keep most of her skirts from the muddy ground.

But the lower half of her skirts and dark blue pelisse were wet and a little muddy. Apparently she had been doing this often, and was not always successfully saving her clothing. Her gloves were unfashionably dark and utilitarian looking, and he wondered briefly if he had been mistaken in taking her for a lady. But no, her pelisse and bonnet declared her a member of the ton, or at least a rich cit's daughter, as well as the presence of her maid, a soberly dressed middle-aged woman with a face twisted in disapproval.

The lady poked in the mud around the flowers with her gloved hand, and twisted to pass her umbrella to the maid, who held it over her. She plunged both hands into the mud, prodding and digging.

He wasn't close enough to hear their conversation, but half-reading the lady's lips, just visible under her bonnet's brim, he thought he caught the words, "should have brought a spade."

And her maid answered, "Fool's errand . . . you can't save every plant in the park. There are gardeners employed here, my lady. Even they can't save the plants. . . ." He heard more of the maid's words, since she wasn't bothering with a lowered voice.

Cerberus was nipping at the trampled grass under him while Adam watched this intriguing spectacle. The horse grew bored of standing still, raised his head, and nickered and pranced. Ill-trained beast. Adam controlled him with his knees and a hand.

The lady raised her head at hearing a horse so near her, and Adam caught full sight of her face for the first time.

She was beautiful.

Pale curls, wide-spaced eyes, small mouth, a pointed chin. An unusually long, straight nose, like a Grecian statue.

Lovely.

And young. He realized he was staring, and turned his gaze to the trees.

But he looked back a mere second later. The lady stood, her face flushed, and wiped her gloved and muddy hands against each other in attempts to clean them. She turned away, presenting him with her profile. It was enchanting, the resemblance to a Grecian statue even more pronounced when viewed from the side.

She glanced back at him, and he had the presence of mind to tip his hat to her.

He was making the lady uncomfortable. He firmly took control of Cerberus and urged him forward. He left the strange young lady to her gardening, and brought his horse to a canter.

He watched the lady from a distance whenever she was in view. He found himself discreetly following her.

She stopped at several more clumps of plants, shrubs, and multiple trees. She tore off dead leaves, and poked about, but appeared to become discouraged and walked off toward Grosvenor Gate.

He passed a park laborer, well bundled against the rain.

"Hello there, sir. Do you know the young lady who is walking there?" He gestured in her direction, the only young lady about.

"The one trying to do me job? Aye, milord, that's Lady Cora Winfield. A countess's daughter, who likes to claim herself a horticulturalist!"

Fascinating.

Adam dug in his greatcoat and flipped a coin at the man, who caught it deftly. "Thank you, my good man. You wouldn't happen to know where this young lady resides?"

"The Averill House in Grosvenor Square. A pleasure, governor." The laborer tipped his hat with a smile, shouldered his rake, and continued on his way.

Lady Cora Persephone Winfield trudged up the front stairs of their townhouse, and the door opened before her. Foley's impassive gaze took in her appearance—soaked skirts, muddy work gloves, and filthy hem—with only a tightening of the mouth to hint at his disapproval. Cora gingerly peeled off the sodden, dirt-caked gloves, and allowed Richards, coming in behind her, to loose her bonnet ribbons. Cora's cold-numbed and dirty fingers would only mangle them. The gloves hadn't been protection enough from the mud and pouring rain.

Richards removed Cora's sodden pelisse, and Cora sat down in the entry chair. Her half boots could not to be allowed into the house after what she had put them through this morning. Richards loosed the laces, and removed the boots gingerly. Cora felt her face flush in shame for all the extra work she had made for her maid. She kept her eyes downcast, but her chin up.

She could feel the disapproval coming from the two servants. She felt powerless to abate it. Mother would have just run roughshod, as she always did, but Cora itched under their disapprobation.

Mother would never have done something as vulgar as become muddy grubbing with water-logged plants in the plain view of everybody in Hyde Park.

That dark gentleman on the black horse had been staring at her. Her cheeks grew hotter with embarrassment at the memory. She had exposed herself. How many other gentlemen and ladies had been in the rainy park that she had not noticed? Would they all be ready to comment on her unladylike activities at tonight's ball?

When Mother heard of it, Cora would get another miserable scolding. Her shoulders wanted to hunch at the thought, but Cora forced them to stay back, her posture erect and perfect, as had been drilled into her from countless governesses, dancing masters, and finishing school matrons.

She shouldn't have bothered in Hyde Park. There was little she could do.

But the plants were dying!

They were drowning, waterlogged, and swampy. The rain kept coming down. There had been barely a dry day throughout England since May. The growth that had come out in the strangely cold and dark weather was now yellow and sickly. Some were rotting where they grew.

She'd tried to remove the damaged yellow and brown leaves from affected plants. But a strange fungus with reddish spots was starting to appear, and getting worse.

The army of gardeners for the London Parks couldn't do much to save them. And she surely couldn't. It had been futile—a wasted effort—that would now cause her and her servants even more trouble.

Perhaps if they slowly undammed the Serpentine, and dug ditches to direct the water . . .

Cora sighed, stood, and forced the problem of Hyde Park out of her mind.

In stockinged feet, she walked up the great staircase, hoping the softness of her passing would spare her mother's notice. But Richards had kept her own boots in reasonable order, and was still wearing them. Mother looked up as they passed her sitting room, and that was that.

"Cora, what in heaven's name have you been doing?"

Cora's eyes closed in consternation, and then turned to her mother with a sheepish smile, "I've only been in the park, Mother."

Mother stood and so did the gentleman and two ladies with her. Of course, Mother wasn't alone. Whenever was Mother alone?

Foley hadn't warned her though; he hadn't said a thing. He must be punishing her.

Despite the fact that morning calls shouldn't start till noon or one, there were visitors here. Cora glanced at the hall clock. Oh. It was noon. She had been in the park longer than she had realized.

Mother's two cronies, Lady Burrelton and Mrs. Winters, Cora felt safe to disregard. They would have catty remarks to say no matter how well Cora behaved. But the gentleman . . .

"I have managed to become quite muddy, so if you'd please excuse me." Cora tried to hurry past. She didn't want to face Lord Eastham, Earl of Soley, in her dirty, disheveled state. She would have thought her mother would have agreed.

"Cora! It is only our good friend and neighbor, Lord Eastham, and Lady Burrelton and Mrs. Winters. Please come in and greet them." Mother's loud voice was not to be ignored. Cora's cheeks flushed again, but she crept carefully into the room, keeping her steps small to hide the fact that she was shoeless, and wrapping her bare hands in her sodden skirts to hide them. She glanced quickly at her mother's face, and saw the moment she realized just how wrecked a state she was in. Mother's mouth tightened with anger and her eyes flashed, promising retribution later.

Cora tightened her own mouth, but curtsied politely to the ladies and gentleman, saying proper greetings. She could feel her skirts beginning to drip onto the Aubusson carpet, and cringed inwardly. "You will have to forgive me, as I am not quite fit for company at the moment. I did not realize the time."

"Oh, don't feel uncomfortable on my account, Lady Cora." Lord Eastham flashed her a mocking grin, wider than was usual for him. He was finding this amusing, she could tell. "I'm just paying a neighborly call, as I have recently come into town again after having spent some time in the country."

Cora's intention was to have gotten out of there as quickly as possible, but this news sidetracked her. "At your own estates, Lord Eastham?"

"Yes, there was trouble with some of the staff, and I had to get to the manor immediately."

"How is the weather? How is the wheat crop in the region? Does it look all right?" Cora hated being stuck in London every Season, instead of at the Grange, where she could be involved with the planting and growth of the tenant farmers' crops. She wanted to be home tending her own kitchen garden and the flower beds of the estate grounds.

Mr. Motley, rector and fellow horticultural enthusiast, kept her updated by letter on the local conditions, but he tended to be distracted by his own flower garden, and not notice how the local crops were doing to the detail she would like.

And he didn't write to her about the tenant farmers' troubles. She worried about Farmer Smith, with his weak leg, and only a daughter left at home. And the Wards, with Mrs. Ward dying in childbed after delivering twins, and how Mr. Ward surely was struggling to farm and take care of them. Things were likely not going well for all the tenants. Cora had heard of frost in May, and blight attacking the wheat and oat crops.

Lord Eastham wouldn't have any news of them, of course. But he had at least passed by some of their fields on his way to his own estate.

Lord Eastham raised his brows at her inquiry. "The weather is wet and unseasonably cold there, as it is here. The wheat crop, well, I confess I only glanced at it, but I don't think it was as green as it usually is in late June."

She wanted to press for more detail, but caught her mother's glare, and remembered that she was dripping on the carpet. Lord Eastham wasn't the type to have noticed or cared about the crops or the tenants who worked them, except if they weren't to get enough money to him. She might be being unfair to him, but he did give that impression. Blond, handsome, athletic, and dressed in the height of fashion, Lord Eastham was someone Cora had always found to be mocking her on some level whenever they met. He was her mother's favorite, so they met far too often.

"I apologize, Lady Cora, that I do not have more news to give you. So sorry to disappoint a lady." His half-smile made her feel like he knew her weaknesses, and would be happy to exploit them.

Lady Burrelton's grating voice intruded. "*The Times* assures us that the crops are doing just fine, my girl. No need to trouble yourself with it."

The Times was lying, Cora was quite sure. Her trip through Hyde Park this morning confirmed that. If the sun didn't come out soon, and stay out for a while, the nation's food crops were in danger.

"Thank you, Lady Burrelton," she said anyway, rather belatedly. She needed to get out of here. "It is a pleasure to see you, Lord Eastham. If you will all excuse me, I ought to be repairing myself."

"Of course!" Lord Eastham bowed graciously.

Cora caught her mother's scowl as she turned to go, and felt the various dagger-stares of the ladies' disapproval, and the Earl's mocking against her back as she carefully walked out, head in correct alignment with her spine and steps tiny.

Mother didn't stop her this time, and she made it out and up to her room without being waylaid again.

Dry and ensconced in his office with his London solicitor, Adam tried to focus on business.

The land permits for the canal from the main coal mine were at a standstill. Adam encouraged his solicitor to find solutions that wouldn't involve getting an act of parliament. This year's experience had convinced him that anything else was preferable.

The graceful figure of Lady Cora Winfield rose up in his mind, pulling him away from costs and expenditures.

He pushed the beautiful specter into the back of his mind, and inquired whether they had been able to engage Mr. Conniff, the renowned mine safety specialist, for August. Adam wanted to improve conditions in the mines now that they were his and not his father's, and had been pursuing a consultation with Mr. Conniff for his evaluation and recommendations.

He smiled in satisfaction when his solicitor confirmed Mr. Conniff was finally available. "Pay his travel expenses, and for his team."

The lady's softly curving lips pursed over vegetation in his memory. How would they look if they smiled? He wanted to see those lips smile.

What a foolish thought. He refocused on what his solicitor was saying.

His solicitor moved on to discussing the merchant fleet. The long war had caused several losses in ships, lives, and money, but it was beginning to be profitable once again. Discussing ships brought his younger brother Nicolas to his mind, a different sort of specter to torment him.

Nicolas would never retire from the Navy, and take over running the Blackdale merchant fleet for Adam, as he had hoped. Adam could only strive to make it strong in Nicolas's memory.

He pushed the image of Nicolas's laughing face out of his mind, and Lady Cora Winfield took the space once again. The countess's daughter who loved plants . . .

When they were finished for the day, and his solicitor shown out, Adam sighed, rubbed his temples, and gave up. He had to see her again.

He called for Malcolm. "Please find out all you can about Lady Cora Winfield, and her mother, the countess."

His valet raised a pale eyebrow over his heavy-lidded eyes, his long nose angled up. "Yes, your grace."

"And discover what next event they will be attending in town, and what it will take to gain an invitation for myself."

"Indeed, your grace."

Adam ignored his sideways look. His former batman would accomplish all he asked and more, he knew. He needn't feel embarrassed to be inquiring after a female. True, he rarely ever had, but still . . . Adam turned back to his ledgers to hide the ridiculous heat in his face. "Thank you, Malcolm, that will be all."

"Duke?"

Adam made an unnecessary notation with a dry quill point. "Yes?"

"On a separate matter . . ." Malcolm shifted his lanky form, and cleared his throat. Adam realized he was uneasy. How unusual.

"You've commissioned me to make sure life is comfortable here for Kate—Miss Douglas. And to inform you if any issues arise."

That caught Adam's attention. He sat up and focused on him. "There have been issues?"

"There was some . . . inappropriate talk on the servants' stairs this morning."

Adam scowled. "Who?"

"Now, I don't think it's necessary to give anyone their notice. It was just talk—" Malcolm held up a long-fingered hand.

"Such as?"

"Many of the town staff males have expressed interest in her, as happens. Miss Douglas has rejected them all, as is her wont."

Adam nodded.

"A few are disgruntled that she has turned down their advances, and this morning they insinuated that she is so far above their touch because she's under your interest and protection."

Adam grimaced, and squeezed the bridge of his nose. He could feel a tension headache coming on.

"I did what I could to dissuade them from that line of thinking, but what folks want to believe . . ."

"Yes. Thank you, Malcolm." Adam sighed. He supposed it was bound to happen.

Kate would hate it.

"Inform me if it gets too out of hand. Kate will let me know if it gets unbearable for her, but—"

"She might not, sir. She has her pride, as you know."

"True."

Nurse Anna's beautiful illegitimate daughter, his cousin Kate. She had practically raised him, assisting her mother in the nursery since she was a young child. "What to do about Kate . . ." Adam mused.

Kate had served his older sister Hester through her long maiden years as her lady's maid, and as an informal companion. She'd helped Hester through his parents' last years and made life better for her. Heaven knew he hadn't. He had been as far away as he could get, campaigning in the Peninsula.

But Hester had finally found love and married the parish minister. Adam had taken grim satisfaction in giving the portly, genial man permission to marry his sister, knowing how much his father would have hated it. The old duke had only considered rank in his daughters' suitors, and had not a care for their happiness. The thought of Hester's new position as Lady Hester Gilchrist, minister's wife, still made him smile.

Hester took Nurse Anna with her, and was about to add her first baby to the widowed minister's already full nursery of seven children by his first wife.

There wasn't room in the bursting manse for a lady's maid, despite Adam's contributions to its expansion. Kate had remained at Blackdale Castle.

But the castle wasn't safe for Kate with her mother gone from the nursery, so Adam had brought her to London, her skills wasted as she took on the duties of an upper chamber maid.

Malcolm shifted, "I know what could be done with her, she being the loveliest creature in all Scotland, and now all London, and all . . ."

Adam raised an eyebrow at that. "Malcolm." Adam let his voice be a warning.

The pale-haired valet grimaced. "I'll hold my tongue, your grace."

"Good." They'd had the conversation before, and it didn't bear repeating. "She'd make an excellent wife, though," Adam eyed Malcolm. "I could probably offer a dowry, see her comfortably settled with some respectable man, one close by so she could stay near to her mother . . ."

"Oh no! No no no, not me," Malcolm burst out, waving his hands, and his face flushing. It was the most lively Adam had seen him in a long time. He watched him in amusement.

"Just, not me." Malcolm deflated into a chair, his posture slovenly and defeated. He covered his face with his hands with a groan.

Adam couldn't help laughing. He'd brought his old friend to the point of sitting improperly in his presence. He sat back in his chair, pleased to have gotten one up on Malcolm. It was not easy to do.

"Though speaking of marriage . . . " The customary sly tone was back in Malcolm's voice, and he looked at Adam through his fingers, his hands still over his face. "Your grace, what odds would you like to lay on you finding a London high-bred lady who would be pleased by Miss Douglas's employment in your household?"

"Ho, Malcolm, who said anything about wedding a London high-bred lady?"

Malcolm raised his eyebrows, and Adam looked away.

"My sisters rather demonstrated that, didn't they? When they refused to take her after Hester married?" His younger sisters Jean and Caroline had written back with different levels of politeness, but with mutual unwillingness to welcome Kate into their households.

What would the lovely Lady Cora think of Cousin Kate?

"Cousin of the duke, and daughter of a slave?"

Adam gave him a warning look. "A freed slave, Malcolm, and a wonderful woman. Nurse Anna was more mother to me than any other, and I intend to do right by her and her daughter. I ought to prevail on her to retire, though I won't take her from Hester. But Kate . . ."

"Kate, the young and beautiful."

Adam rolled his eyes. "She's older than me, you do realize, Malcolm?" His valet was two years younger than Adam's own thirty years.

Malcolm coughed. "Doesn't matter." He ran his hands through his blond hair, dislodging his carefully styled waves.

"I trust you treat her with respect, Malcolm," Adam frowned. "Just as my entire household must treat her with respect, if they intend on staying in my employ."

"Oh, I respect her!" Malcolm flung up a hand. "Wouldn't dare not. She makes a man da—most uncomfortable."

"Yes, she has a commanding way. She'd be an excellent housekeeper, but her years aren't advanced enough for me to employ her in that position yet, not while I'm single." Adam shuffled papers and raised an eyebrow. "But if she were married . . ."

Malcolm sprang up, his dark eyes looking a little wild. "Well, I must needs get to your commission, your grace. Ladies must be investigated, and all."

"Malcolm," Adam stopped him with a word. Malcolm turned back with a grimace.

"I want my household to always be a safe place for Kate, Malcolm, as I've stated before. If this talk continues, I'm fully willing to replace staff, as I will in Scotland when we return."

Malcolm's narrow face softened. "I will keep my ear to the ground, your grace."

He bowed, and left.

Adam had long stewed over the issue of Kate. He didn't want London to be as bad as the castle had been. His ancestral home wouldn't be safe for Kate until Adam replaced his father's steward and butler. They'd be pensioned off as soon as he returned to Scotland.

He wanted a household free from cruelty.

It was locked.

Cora had only vaguely been aware that the door to the orangery had a lock. She jiggled the handle and pushed, but it remained firmly shut.

Only the housekeeper and her mother could possibly have keys to a room that had never been locked before. How was Mary to keep the brazier burning to keep the plants warm if the maid couldn't get in through the locked door?

What should Cora do? Could she pick the lock, like a heroine in a horrid novel? She felt around the flowers in her hair for hair pins, but then winced as the curling strands of her hair caught against her smarting fingertips. She let her hand fall.

A grim-faced Richards had dug out the dirt from around Cora's nails with rough determination, leaving Cora's cuticles raw. Her lady's maid had cut the nails too deeply, then slathered lotion thickly over Cora's hands to try to soften them. It made all the little wounds sting and left her skin red.

She needed to put her gloves on.

But what could she do to get into her orangery? She'd left a flowering *Strelitzia reginae*, a bird of paradise, close to a brazier to warm it, and it was time to move it away before it was damaged by the heat.

Of course, if no one could get into the orangery to maintain the coals, it wouldn't matter, would it?

Her mother was punishing her for Hyde Park this morning, and her dripping reception of Lord Eastham.

She felt like crying, or stamping her feet and throwing a rage. But rages had never been effective. Her mother viewed tantrums as ill bred, and would deny any wish that was expressed with too much feeling.

Cora squeezed her eyes shut, swallowed back her frustration and humiliation, and cleared her expression. It was time for dinner.

Cora would have to pretend to be unconcerned in order to get this door opened again.

Chapter Two

The Ball

FRIDAY, JUNE 28, 1816, EVENING

Cora sat against the plush carriage back and tried not to fidget. They waited, queued to exit their carriage in front of the Carterights' grand entrance. Judging by the length of time they had inched forward and then inched again, the Carterights intended a crush for their ball. Cora disliked a crush.

She stifled a sigh that would draw Mother's attention. Sir Merriweather, their escort for the evening, was chatting amiably with Mother about his recent visit to Paris, and thankfully keeping Mother's attention.

Cora wished to be back home at the Grange, with the freedom of country life and her gardens. But escaping from London wouldn't solve her problem.

Cora craved autonomy. If she married the right kind of man, she would gain some. She'd at least be out from under her mother's thumb, with a home of her own.

She'd begun this Season, her second, with full intentions to find a tolerable man and marry him. But it was drawing to a close, and her efforts were proving unsuccessful again.

Last year, when she had been presented at court to the Queen in a pink monstrosity of a dress with panniers, she had dreaded her coming-out ball. It would be miserable and crowded, with so many people she didn't know staring at her.

But she had been a hit. A few odd phrases from her, and she was an Original. With her fortune, she was elevated from a lovely girl to a diamond of the first water. A court of admirers gathered around her. She had tried not to let it get to her head, but all the attention had been a dizzying thing.

She was courted again this year, ringed about by hopeful young—and not so young—men. Her formidable mother scared away the obvious fortune-hunters, gamesters, and rakes, at least the ones of low enough birth that Mother found their vices unacceptable. If their rank was high enough, Mother didn't appear to mind. At least in Lord Eastham's case.

Cora had her pick. And she tried. She had run through being married to each of her suitors in her imagination. Several were amiable enough, she supposed.

She was twenty! And being treated like a child still. Her mother, locking the orangery! Just thinking about it brought up tears of rage and indignation to the back of her eyes, and she had to clamp down on her emotions and quickly think of other things, else she'd ruin her face for the ball.

She wanted to be an adult—a grown woman, able to do as she pleased. She needed to be in control of her own fortune.

"The rain this year truly has been abominable." Sir Merriweather said. "It is making travel dangerous. I have heard tell that Lady Nesbit's carriage was almost washed away in a flood only last week. And did you hear? Snow plagued travelers on the North Road. In June!"

"Yes, the roads are treacherous this year," her mother said. "My aunt Carston was intending to come to London to visit us from Newcastle, but the roads were so muddy, she gave up the scheme and went back home. I had a letter from her yesterday, and was most disappointed."

Cora felt a pang. It was sad to be missing great aunt Carston this year. She was one of Cora's more cheerful relatives. But she was getting old, and travel was hard on her.

"The riots! There have been riots in the countryside. Despicable I say!" Sir Merriweather sniffed. "Luddites and the poor over food prices.

'Bread or blood,' they say. They attacked a perfectly respectable family. Dreadful."

The price of bread was going to continue to rise, Cora thought, with the damage the weather was making to the wheat fields. Things needed to improve soon.

She felt as powerless in her own life as she was powerless to change the weather. Was there a way for her to gain control of her fortune and become independent? It seemed impossible. Her mother intended to turn Cora's portion over to her husband when she married. Anything further would only come at the death of her mother: the money, lands, and estates her mother owned would be hers—a considerable amount.

Mother did as she pleased, with all the autonomy any person could desire. She was a rich, high-ranking widow. Cora's father had died when she was young. Mother was much happier with him gone. It had been a marriage of rank with fortune, and her father had been much older than his wife.

She could do the same, she supposed. Marry someone old and indulgent, have a child or two, and wait for him to die.

She shuddered at the thought. How horrible to marry just to wish a man dead so she could have the autonomy of widowhood. And to leave her children without a father, like she had been left. She had had her Grandfather Averill, but still she had felt the lack.

It was a very lonely existence, in her eyes. Her mother filled her days with her pursuits and pleasures, and focused far too much of her attention on her daughter.

Maybe Cora should strive to get her mother married, and that would give Cora the freedom she wanted? Her mother would have someone else to focus on.

She almost laughed out loud at the thought, but caught herself just in time. Talk of misfortunes had brought up the late war, and her mother and Sir Merriweather wouldn't appreciate a giggle over their conversation of those of their acquaintance who had died at Waterloo.

The most sensible thing she could do would be to find an amiable and indulgent man who did not mind dirt under a lady's fingernails, and her spending a large part of her time in the succession houses and gardens. A gentleman farmer, then?

One she could like. And that her mother would approve of? That was an even more difficult case. There were several gentlemen her mother had shown a preference for, but none of those lords had interested Cora at all.

The one person Cora had felt a tendre for in her first Season, a kind-eyed young clergyman, Mama had squashed by cold looks and cold civility.

Cora had heard, through a friend, that her attractive parson had recently wed a nice rector's daughter. They would be happy in their snug parsonage forever.

She wanted to sigh again. She tensed her shoulders to keep in another sigh.

She would look carefully at each of her court again. Surely one in the group would suit her purpose? She must be missing something, mustn't she?

Their turn to depart the carriage finally arrived. The entrance to the Carterights' villa was crowded with people waiting to be announced. Her insides gave an unwonted shudder at the sight of all those people. It was still hard for her, even at the end of her second Season, to force herself into that crowd. But she stiffened her spine and raised her head. Maybe in that mob was someone with whom she could create the life she wanted.

The crush was appalling. Once they were announced, Sir Merriweather tried to politely open a way before them into the ballroom with excuses and pardons. He didn't make a dent. Mama lost patience and took the lead, her tall, imposing figure, and forceful personality able to open the way before her with a resonant, "Make way!"

Cora followed close in her wake, and Sir Merriweather scurried to keep up as the crowd closed in quickly after Mother's passing.

They finally reached a side of the ballroom inhabited with several of Mama's friends, and Sir Merriweather, satisfied that the dowager countess was situated to her satisfaction, reminded Cora of the dance he'd secured with her for later, and left them there. Cora's court noticed her arrival, and descended on her.

Adam walked down the stairs of the Carteright's ballroom after being announced, and greeted his hosts. He ignored the stares of the crowd. Famous or infamous he could hardly say, but his name was known, and they were all eager to see his face. He had been avoiding large gatherings since he arrived in London to avoid this.

The amount of finely dressed people crammed into the Carterights' was ridiculous. The silks and feathers made an intimidating wall as he moved beyond the reception line and into the ballroom.

The crowd opened in front of him, giving way to his passing, many staring as they moved out of his way. He schooled his face to be impassive, and stalked through the opening. The throng closed in behind him, and he resisted the feeling of being trapped that tried to seize his lungs. He heard his sobriquet being whispered through the crowd.

He fought the urge to scrunch his shoulders against the stares. His back itched. The tension arching through him made his ribs ache.

He breathed in and out, clenched his teeth, and moved forward until his path opened up at the dance floor. A line of couples were dancing a cotillion.

He moved around the curve of people that ringed the floor. Women and men moved back to allow his passing, and he heard sharp exclamations from those they bumped into to get out of his way.

This was unendurable. He walked too fast, trying to escape the throng, and find a less crowded place. He wanted to be stationary, where he could observe, but be less observed.

If he had gone to more social functions, they might be used to him by now. But he hadn't been able to bring himself to go through the torture of a ball before this evening.

He was caught up short by someone actually addressing him. It was Major Phillips in his best dress uniform. He was friendly and familiar. Adam eased under his greetings.

The major snatched a few friends from the crowd and introduced Adam to them. Adam was able to relax even more as a group around him made him less conspicuous than as the stalking Black Duke alone.

Later, Adam found a pillar that would partially obscure him. He stood next to it, and scanned the crowd desultorily. He could feel his brows furling into a scowl. He knew he looked forbidding when he let his face get that way. He forced his brows up and his face to smooth.

Then, at last, he saw her.

She looked young, almost a girl, though tall. Blonde curls bounced and her gown of pale pink swayed as she moved gracefully through a country dance.

Lady Cora Winfield.

Nonsensically, his heart began to pound against his ribs.

The dark gentleman was watching her again. Cora glanced in his direction, trying to see him without the gentleman realizing she had noticed his gaze. She didn't know him. Was he the gentleman from Hyde Park this morning? She couldn't be sure, as she had barely seen that man's face.

He had been staring at her most of the evening. He had yet to seek an introduction.

His intense stares were starting to irritate her. She wanted to stare back, boldly challenge his rudeness, but she couldn't. It wasn't a proper thing for a young lady to do. And, truly, she didn't want to be that forward. She was just tired of having his gaze creeping up her neck, giving her unsightly chill bumps down her arms and back.

But it was also thrilling, having this gentleman—dark, handsome, tall, and rather dangerous looking in black and red—focusing so much of his attention on her.

He stood alone and apart, the crowds around him leaving him an area of space despite the crush of people inhabiting the ballroom.

She turned her focus back to her court. Five gentlemen stood near, courteously vying for her favor, joking and ribbing each other. She often felt standing in a crowd around her and making her a toast was a game to them. Mother looked on them with a complacent eye.

But they were her options. She looked into each face, and thought what it would be like to be married to them.

Mr. Basil, with his loud waistcoat, weak chin, and debts. No, she would rather not.

Lord Charles, boisterous and old enough to be her father. Eh . . .

Mr. Yardley, his shoulders over-padded and his manners too eager. He was . . . a pleasant enough of a person.

Lieutenant Dean she dismissed without further thought. She couldn't stand his rude ribbing.

None of them had any interest in horticulture, and only listened to her with smiles of indulgence when she spoke of it. She had stopped speaking much.

No, she couldn't see a future with any of them. Not one of happiness and ease, in any case.

Captain Bowden was new, just introduced tonight. He was handsome, young, and had a mischievous grin over the red of his officer's uniform. He was an aid to the Duke of Wellington, he said, just up from the army of occupation in Paris.

He'd secured a quadrille from her for later in the evening, after supper, and had sauntered over to flirt with her between sets twice already.

The current set, a waltz, ended, and Sir Merriweather came to claim his dance. Cora looked at him in relief and some pleasure. He was an excellent dancer, and he was one of her mother's followers, not her own. It was safe to ask him if he knew who the dark gentleman was.

As she stood, she felt the dark gentleman's gaze on her once more. She took Sir Merriweather's arm, and when they had moved far enough away from the other men, Cora casually asked, "There is a gentleman in black with a red-embroidered waistcoat standing in the corner to our left. Do you know who he is?"

She risked looking directly at the gentleman. Their eyes met for the first time that evening. A thrill went through her body. He looked away quickly, as if theirs had been an accidental eye meeting of strangers across a room, instead of an interruption of his evening's intense focus.

Sir Merriweather paused and quaffed his quizzing glass, looking over the dark gentleman as people moved around them in the crowded ballroom.

"Oh, it's the Black Duke!"

Cora started at the epithet. "What?"

"As they have been calling him. It's Adam Douglas, Duke of Blackdale."

"Blackdale." She knew that name. "He was the one listed in the papers as dead at Waterloo?"

"Yes, he was discovered still alive on the battlefield a day later. How startling. But they'd already listed him among the dead, and it got reported everywhere. He was badly injured, of course. Seems he recovered."

She stared at the black-clothed man. Back from the dead.

"He's Scottish, and rich as Croesus. But almost his entire company was killed in the action. Some are blaming him for such heavy losses. I'm sure I don't know the particulars, not a fighting man myself."

As Cora and Sir Merriweather openly stared at the dark gentleman—a duke!—he turned away from them and walked down the room, joining a group of scarlet-coated officers in conversation.

Cora noted that they greeted him in a welcoming way, some with smiles, so his reputation among them couldn't be too bad.

But . . . the Black Duke had been staring at her! Her face flushed. She had no idea how to feel about that.

How awful to be left on the grisly battlefield. And to have your death announcement printed and reprinted in all the newspapers across Britain.

So many were killed at Waterloo. So many from this man's own Highland regiment. The only thing that made up for the harsh losses at Waterloo was that they had won.

Sir Merriweather led her forward, and they joined the dancers forming a set for the quadrille. They curtsied and bowed, and when Cora could take her attention from the steps, she looked in the direction of the Black Duke. He wasn't watching her anymore, but in conversation with the officers.

So she watched him.

Adam cursed himself for a fool and kept his eyes averted. She'd noticed. Of course she had. He had intended to be discreet, but his ungovernable eyes had returned to her again and again.

Lady Cora Winfield, Major Phillips had told him, was the only child of the Dowager Countess of Winfield, heiress of all her mother's considerable properties, and a diamond of the first water. She was in her second Season, and liable to be snatched up by any of the young gentlemen who were courting her.

His words affirmed what Malcolm had been able to discover, but the major offered what Malcolm could not—an introduction. "But to her mother first, of course. She's a dragon if you've ever seen one, and keeps a close watch on her young miss."

"Thank you, not right now," Adam answered. Not yet. He must evaluate more.

He watched her. Her light, graceful movements; her tall, lithe frame, small of bust but wide of hip.

There were other ladies here with figures more perfect.

He watched her golden curls bounce as she skipped in the dance, her smiles filled her face with sweetness. She smiled often when she danced.

When sitting out a set, she smiled less. She had a pensive, tense look. Almost worried.

Her laugh was rare, bell-like, and loud. It burst out of her as if she couldn't control it.

He thought it to be too loud for comfort if she was sitting next to a person. He preemptively winced for his ears, for when her laugh would rip the air next to him.

Wait. Stop.

No, she was not going to be next to him. He was not in London for a wife. If he wanted a wife, Edinburgh would be the place to go. A good, high-born Scottish wife was all he had ever considered for himself.

And there were plenty of such women with fine figures and quieter laughs in Edinburgh.

She was far too young. She looked like a girl. The major had said she was in her second Season. What, had she come out when she was fifteen?

He needed to discover her age. Some men wanted child brides—'moldable' as they termed it—but he had never been one of them. He desired a formed mind. An informed one. Surely she was too vacuous for him, this child who spoke little, and who only smiled when dancing.

He managed to situate himself during the supper hour so that he sat behind and to her left, where he could watch her profile as she ate. She was surrounded by her court of admirers: two officers, a lordling or two, and a few others that he dismissed.

He noticed her lack of female friends, and the presence of her formidable mother. The dowager countess was a large and imposing woman, still beautiful, but hawk-like over her fledging. He would have to step carefully around her.

But he was a duke. There shouldn't be too much trouble in that quarter.

The girl—Lady Cora, he reminded himself—didn't unbutton her long gloves and free her hands before she ate. She used a fork or spoon even for items that generally would be eaten with fingers. Unusual.

He would tug those gloves off, and hold her bare hands in his, when . . .

Stop. Rather precipitate his imagination was being this evening. He had yet to be introduced to the girl.

He left his chair quickly in the supper room and went to the card room. It was a bit thinner because of the supper hour, and he found Lord Eastham, his old schoolfellow from Eton, in need of a competitor.

During the first round, he casually asked if Lord Eastham knew the Dowager Countess of Winfield.

"Yes, quite well. Her principle estate is near mine. I attend her Harvest Ball every year." The blond man considered his hand.

"She has a daughter, Lady Cora?"

Lord Eastham looked at him with an amused gleam in his eye, and Adam resigned himself to the fact that there was no way to ask after a beautiful young heiress without drawing comment.

"Yes, Lady Cora, one of our brightest lights." Eastham shuffled his cards.

"She seems quite young?"

"Yes, and acts it too. But in actuality, she's twenty."

"Twenty!"

"Her grandfather died the year she was to be presented, and so it was put off a year for his mourning. She was nineteen when presented at St. James's. She managed to survive her first Season unwed—likely due to her mother—and is twenty now."

Not as young as she seemed. Twenty was a good age for a girl to get married. He couldn't object to twenty.

He was distracted from his card playing, and lost the hand. Lord Eastham watched him with a smirk, likely planning on how he could skin Adam for what he was worth with him in this state of mind. They began a new round.

"The dowager countess, of course, wants me for her daughter."

Adam's head snapped up. Lord Eastham was smirking at him as he laid down some cards, but Adam paid no attention to them.

Lady Cora would look well with the earl, golden blonds joining together and having golden blond children. His blood flashed hot and then ran cold.

Adam enunciated carefully. "Am I to wish you joy?"

"Not on your life." Lord Eastham threw back his head with a laugh. "I'm not interested in marrying Lady Cora, or any female. A wife would interfere in my pleasures far too much."

"You don't need to sire an heir?"

"My younger brother has three hopeful sons. The earldom is quite safe. Play?" He indicated the neglected boards.

Adam glanced at his hand, laid down, and didn't care that Eastham was beating him. "Why does the dowager feel you are the ideal husband for her daughter?"

That Eastham was a philanderer and a rake, known to keep concurrent mistresses in London and in the country, as well as a deep-playing gamester who could run through a fortune in a night; his reputation was well known. But he also had phenomenal luck, always seeming to win back his losses. He was a favorite with the Prince Regent and the Carlton House set, having kept Prinny afloat on more than one occasion.

Adam cataloged the man's virtues: rich, a famous whip, a perennial sportsman, a patron of the arts. The Dowager might overlook his profligacy for everything else Eastham could offer her daughter, though

Adam wouldn't be able to respect her if she did. His standards often differed from those of the ton.

"She's been intending me for her girl since the chit was in leading strings. She's not the most subtle of creatures, the dowager." Eastham snapped his cards together. "I think there are two reasons she wishes it. First," He laid down a card. Adam didn't look at it. "I would make her daughter a countess like herself. I think she feels anything less for her darling would be throwing her away."

Adam nodded. He could offer an even higher rank for the girl's mother to crow over.

"Second," another card, "our estates are quite close. She would be losing her daughter to a distance of only a few miles. She could visit daily. And I do predict that the dowager intends to."

Adam sat back. He would not be able to accommodate that. He had no desire to reside permanently in England. He intended to take his wife to Scotland, and in general, stay there. This could cause some challenges. Would he need to invite her mother to live with them permanently? Would he be able to stand that?

"Which is why I wouldn't take Lady Cora even if I did want to be leg shackled," Eastham fanned his cards. "She comes with her mother. A more interfering and demanding woman you will never meet. And, then, there's Lady Cora herself . . ." Lord Eastham paused, a pale eyebrow raised over his cards.

Adam stared at him, waiting for Eastham to speak. When he fingered his boards instead of answering, Adam prompted, "The lady herself?"

Eastham grinned, and looked over his hand at Adam. "Let's just say they call her an Original for a reason." He lowered his last hand, and was the clear winner yet again.

Adam was losing a substantial amount of money for this mix of information. "Care to elaborate?"

The sportsman sat back in his chair, smirking at his winnings. "How about I introduce you to Lady Cora, and you can discover for yourself? I will even dare to bypass the mother, and take you straight to the daughter. The dowager countess will forgive me anything." His teeth gleamed, and Adam decided that the earl was likely leading him into a trap. But it was a trap he wanted to be ensnared in.

"Thank you, I accept your kind offer."

Chapter Three

Introductions

SATURDAY, JUNE 29, 1816, AFTER MIDNIGHT

The Black Duke disappeared during supper. He had sat behind her, where she had felt his gaze and strove to appear unconscious of it. But the feeling had gradually eased, until she risked a glance back and discovered he was not there.

She watched for him everywhere and expected to see him at every turn as she came back from the lady's retiring room and moved to stand by her mother. He didn't appear.

"You've slipped your admirers, Cora?" Mother sat regally among her cronies, passing judgement on every gown and waistcoat that passed and the ladies and gentlemen who wore them.

"For a bit." Cora wafted tepid air into her face with her fan. There were no seats available around her mother, so she stood, watching the dancers. "They are all waltzing with other ladies."

"That is very ungallant of them, to abandon you during the waltz."

"Oh, I encouraged them. No need for them to miss the pleasure of waltzing just because I must."

Mother gave Cora a sharp look. She did not approve of Cora protesting her strictures in any way. The Dowager Countess of Winfield did not approve of the waltz and refused to allow her daughter to dance it.

Cora wanted to waltz. She disliked sitting on the sidelines for each of them, forced into conversation with her admirers.

She loved dancing; it was what made the crowds and uncomfortable socializing tolerable. Balls without dancing were dreadfully dull affairs.

"Still banned from the German dance, I see." Lord Eastham walked up beside her. His smile was mocking as usual, his blond brows quirked.

"Lord Eastham!" They exchanged courtesies.

"Frederick! You've come near the chaperones?" Mother's loud voice boomed out. "I am amazed."

"Yes, my lady," he bowed to her, "The thought did initially cause my poor heart to quail, but then I remembered your endless kindness to myself, and thought I might endeavor to draw near."

Mother clucked indulgently. Mother always softened when speaking to Lord Eastham.

"I have come because I know dear Lady Cora is unable to waltz, and so must be in need of something else to do." He turned back to Cora. "My lady, would you be so kind as to take a turn about the room with me? No dancing, I assure your ladyship"—to her mother—"just a friendly perambulation." He offered Cora his arm.

"Oh, go with him, Cora," Mother encouraged.

Of course. She had been throwing them together since Cora was sixteen, long before Mother had agreed to allow Cora to come out in society.

She took his arm, and they walked slowly through the crowds along the dance floor.

"I'm intending something wicked." Lord Eastham looked at her from the corner of his eye.

Cora's arm jerked, and she almost pulled away before she realized he was teasing. Surely he was teasing? "What a thing to say!"

"It's not truly wicked, but I'm quite sure it will annoy your mother."

"She can be most unpleasant when annoyed."

"True, true. But I will assure her it was all my idea, and she will forgive me."

She hid her discomfort. "I have to live with her, and you do not." Her orangery was still locked.

He laughed. "Come, gel, it won't be that bad!"

She shot him a look. "You give your word as a gentleman then, Lord Eastham, that any negative consequences of this will bypass me and fall on you?" She felt bold saying it.

"Gracious, child! I cannot control every repercussion! But I will endeavor to shield you, yes." He smiled at her.

"I suppose I will have to be satisfied with that. What is this horrid evil that you intend to commit?"

"Let us get to the other side of the floor and completely out of sight of your mother."

"Should my maiden heart be warning me that I ought to turn back now?" She felt that, maybe, she was holding her own against Lord Eastham. His worldly confidence and the decade of experience he had over her intimidated her.

"Perhaps, but I'm sure your feminine curiosity will overcome those warnings."

"You are right." She kept hold of his arm.

Progress was slow through the outskirts of the dancing couples. They wove through the milling crowd. When they reached the far side, he turned and led her under the raised orchestra balcony. The candles lighting this area were running low, and a few had winked out. It was darker than in the main ballroom, with its multiple chandeliers.

There were people around, including a group of ladies, sitting, standing, and talking to one another, so Cora still felt safely proper in this area. Nothing wicked.

A tall gentleman stepped near, a dark presence to her left. As soon as he moved in the periphery of her eye, she felt him, a force that pushed into her, like a solid wall, a rock, a mountain. He stood before her, filling her vision, and became a gaping maw, a chasm with a crumbling edge she would tumble down into. She would be lost, swallowed whole. A shiver of electricity washed over her entire body, and she let out a subvocal "Oh!"

It was the dark gentleman, the Duke of Blackdale. She stared at him in incomprehension, her mind racing over her body's reaction. She blinked rapidly, and forced herself to calm down. Another blink, and he was a man again—just a man, not an overpowering force.

But still, he was a man gazing at her with an intensity that made her stomach jerk and flutter.

Lord Eastham was still at her arm. She had no idea what her involuntary reaction had felt like to him.

He stepped away and said, "Duke, may I introduce Lady Cora Winfield?"

She glanced at Eastham's face. He had turned watchful, the teasing gone. Cora had no idea what her face showed. Panic? She swallowed and schooled her features.

"Lady Cora, may I introduce Adam Douglas, the Duke of Blackdale?"

She curtseyed and the duke bowed, his gaze not leaving her face. "It is a pleasure to meet you, Lady Cora."

His voice almost caused her to wobble. It was deep and rich—a beautiful voice. "Likewise," she said. It came out breathy, barely audible.

She was being ridiculous. She inhaled and forced herself to be rational. "It is good to meet you, your grace." She focused on his chin—strong, clean shaven, with a cleft—and avoided his eyes. "Have you been long in London?" There, that was proper and civil.

"Several months."

She was drawn to his eyes again. They were blue, very blue, the dim light of the candles surrounding them catching in their depths like hot blue flames. His hair was black, thick and cropped short. He wore a black cravat, an unusual affectation.

"I do not think I have seen you about before?" She was sure she had not. She looked away again, those eyes too much for her.

"I have been in town on business for several months, but I haven't been very social in the evenings."

His skin was pale, showing red in his upper cheeks and in his ears. Was he blushing? She swallowed and searched for a topic of conversation. "Where are your principal holdings, your grace?"

"Scotland, in the Highlands, along the coast, off the Firth of Lorne."

"You are from Scotland, then?" She looked up, and those eyes caught her again.

"Aye, born and bred." And she heard it, or he let it slip through, the Scottish burr amid his carefully cultured public school English. Her breath caught in her throat.

She searched for something more to say. "Do you come to London often?" Her face was burning, she had no idea why. Her heart pounded, and her stomach twisted in knots. Was she scared of him? Was he frightening?

She wasn't sure. All she knew was she wasn't comfortable near him.

"No, not often."

She looked down once more and didn't raise her head again. The conversation ground to a halt.

The music of the waltz ended, and the crowd applauded.

"Are you engaged for the next dance, Lady Cora?" Her name in his voice seemed to tug at her, to draw her near.

She planted her feet. "N-no." She stumbled in her words. "The next is a waltz as well." She looked at his waistcoat, black with red embroidery. Twining vines and fruit. "I do not waltz."

"Her lady mother does not approve of waltzing." The mocking tone was back in Lord Eastham's voice.

Her face flamed again and she shot him a look. He didn't have to say that. He didn't need to reveal to this intimidating man that she was so ruled by her mother.

"I see," the duke said. "Are you free for the next set that is not a waltz?"

"I apologize, your grace, but that set has already been claimed." She suddenly felt weak and fatigued. She needed to disengage, to have solitude. The night was endless, this conversation unbearable. "It has been lovely to make your acquaintance, your grace."

She almost looked up into his eyes again, but stopped at his mouth.

It was wide, with well-formed lips, an unusually red shade in contrast to his pale skin. His lips were parted slightly. She couldn't look away from his mouth, and the space between his upper and lower lips. His mouth curved in a quick half smile.

"And the next, Lady Cora? Would you do me the honor of dancing with me this evening?"

She found her weight was on her toes. She was leaning in toward him. She quickly swayed back onto her heels, and jerked her gaze to the floor.

He would touch her in a dance, any dance, even if it was gloved hand on gloved hand. She couldn't, she shouldn't. She should refuse him, claim the headache that was building behind her eyes.

"Yes, the next after. I thank you, your grace. If you would excuse me." She curtsied, and moved away, but didn't pick up her feet enough, scuffing her dance slippers along the parquet floor. She corrected her posture and her footing and walked away, keeping her head high and level, alignment precise.

She was halfway back to her mother before she remembered Lord Eastham. She'd left him without a thought or a glance.

Served him right to be snubbed. He'd introduced her to that . . . that man.

But she slowed and glanced back. He was behind her in the crowd, making his way to her side.

"I . . . I'm sorry," she said lamely, when her reached her.

"No need to apologize, child. That was most entertaining."

Irritation flared in her. She glared up at him.

"Oh, there is the look! Enchanting! No, don't stalk off. I know I'm being abominable." He chuckled. "So diverting." He held out his arm.

She didn't want to take it, but did.

"After your dance with the duke who has yet to be introduced to your mother, you should dance with me. It will soothe her ruffled feathers."

She squeezed her eyes shut. She had agreed to dance with the duke. There would be consequences, like electricity, static shocks, and her mother's indignation.

"Yes, that would help," she agreed.

"I believe it will be a waltz. Perfect."

"Oh! You!" She almost jerked her arm out of his again, but he held her hand fast with his other, keeping her there. She didn't like it.

"Calm, Lady Cora. It is late in the Season. Your second Season, no less. What better way to end a glorious spring? And completely overshadow the very decorous cotillion you shall dance with Blackdale?"

She glared at him, lips pursing. "I think adding disobedience to indiscretion would incense her enough make my life a misery for weeks. No, I thank you, Lord Eastham, but no."

"You know that the only way she will acquiesce to your dancing the waltz would be for me to offer to dance it with you. And once allowed the first time . . ."

Insufferable. "You are likely right, Lord Eastham. How galling. If I had considered it before now, I would have begged you to ask me, just to pull her to that concession. However, you had thought of it before, hadn't you? And refrained, just to see me miserable?"

"Oh, never miserable, child!" he interrupted.

"It's been a form of humiliation, Lord Eastham. And now you only offer to alleviate it when it will cause double the mischief! So, no, no, I thank you, no. I will suffer the last waltzes of the Season as I began it, a restricted wallflower."

She quickened her pace, and Lord Eastham, holding onto her arm, was forced to keep up with her or be dragged along.

Adam watched Lady Cora until she disappeared into the crowd. Lord Eastham's tall golden head remained visible, and Adam saw that he had caught up with the lady and would escort her properly back to her mother. Eastham had smirked at him after she had fled and said, "A successful introduction, your grace!" and had gone after her retreating form.

Adam's brows pressed together. She had stumbled. She had not been at ease. The longer Adam had talked to her, the more uncomfortable she had become, until she was near running to get away from him.

Was he so frightening?

She had blushed, but she had trembled and swayed as well. Was he to be encouraged or put off by this?

She hadn't rebuffed him entirely, however. She had agreed to a dance. He would take that dance, no question of that.

He waited as the second waltz ended, and the next set, a quadrille, began. Lady Cora was escorted to the floor by an officer. She looked tense. Her movements were less light, though still skilled. She wasn't enjoying the dance anymore. She had stopped smiling.

He watched her with concern. Did she feel ill? Was it her partner? Was it him? Did the thought of dancing with him next make her feel ill?

Surely not. They had just been introduced. He didn't always come off well on first acquaintance, he knew that. She would get to know him, and she would be fine.

He stood on the edge of the dance floor, the crowd around him a bit thinner this late after midnight. The quadrille ended, the dancers clapping in appreciation of the orchestra. The musicians were still going strong, having had several breaks and a good supper. A cotillion was next. His first dance with the Lady Cora Winfield. Her previous partner, the officer, took her arm, preparing to take her back to her mother and her court of admirers.

Adam stepped onto the floor and approached them. "No need, sir, I am the lady's next partner." He held out his hand for her to take. She looked at it, and quickly up at his face, and then down again. A blush bloomed on her cheeks.

The young officer protested, but the lady spoke. "Thank you, Captain Bowden, it is fine. Thank you for the lovely dance." She let go of the officer's arm, and held her hand out in front of her body, pausing before Adam, staring at his hand in its black kid glove. Her long gloves were creamy white, and clung tightly to her hands and arms, outlining their elegant shape.

Her previous partner left. Adam scarcely gave him a thought. The lady posed in front of him seemed about to take flight. She was on her toes, angled slightly toward him, and to his left, as if she couldn't decide whether to take his offered hand, or to flee.

Adam held very still, every detail of this moment sharp and focused. He could count every lash on her beautiful downturned lids, number the few light freckles that dotted her flushed cheeks. Her lips were parted, a lovely pale pink.

Her eyes raised, and he was startled to realize that they were a luminous leaf-green, like the youngest leaves of new spring. His breath caught in his throat.

He had no idea what expression had taken over his face—wonder?—but the lady moved a half-step closer, and put her hand in his.

Her hand was warm. He could feel the heat even through two layers of fine leather. His were cold, despite the crowded ballroom, and his body wanted to come closer to her, to feel of her warmth. The slight weight of her hand felt right in his. He allowed himself to draw a bit closer to her, carefully judging the distance. He was vaguely aware of the other dancers queueing up on either side of them, and how they must be an object of interest to their neighbors.

He let out his breath slowly, and felt himself relax. Here she was, with him, where she ought to be.

"Thank you for this dance, Lady Cora Winfield."

She didn't say anything, but tilted her head and nodded. She looked calmer than she had before.

The music began, and he snapped back to an awareness of their surroundings. He led her to her place in the set, and strode to his in time to bow, and begin the dance.

He looked into her eyes as they turned around each other. He reluctantly pulled his gaze away when he ought to pay attention to the other lady in their set, bowing. He took Lady Cora's hand, and turned. They parted, danced singly, then came together, and linked arms to turn and promenade. Energy raced through him where their bodies touched. He had never felt so charged, so electric from dancing with any other woman, not from the ballrooms of Edinburgh to Lady Richmond's ball in Brussels the night before the fateful days of Waterloo.

They didn't speak. The energy between them filled the silence. He looked away from her only when the dance required. The flush stayed on her cheeks and intensified, running down her neck as the dance progressed. On the turn they stood out, she kept her eyes on the floor, breathing more heavily than the dance warranted. But as they joined the set again, he caught her eyes once more and held them captive with his own.

Too soon, the dance was over, and they were clapping politely to thank the orchestra. The musicians were to take a break, and come on again in fifteen minutes. They put down their instruments and stood in the musician's upper gallery.

Adam moved to Lady Cora's side, and held out his arm to her. She looked down the room, toward where her mother sat. He followed her gaze, and saw that the dowager countess was standing, looking at them. The expression on the woman's face was not pleasant.

"Your grace," Lady Cora turned to him. "Would you do me the honor of being introduced to my mother?"

His stomach clenched. "Of course, Lady Cora. It would be my pleasure."

She took his proffered arm, tucking her hand into the crook of his elbow. The heat of her body permeated the layers of cloth between them, diverting his thoughts.

He reigned in his emotions, and turned toward where her mother was reigning in state.

She stopped him. "Please take me to Lord Eastham first. We must beg his assistance."

Lord Eastham stood languorously to their left, watching them through his quizzing glass. What did she need from him?

"Of course, my lady." He led her there.

"Lady Cora, you've come to take me up on my offer of a waltz?" Lord Eastham looked at her with amusement.

"Of course not, my lord. I am here with a better plan."

"Indeed?"

"Yes, would you do me the honor of coming with us, and introducing the Duke of Blackdale to my mother?"

The quizzing glass dropped. "Surely now that you are acquainted, you do not need an outsider to introduce the duke?"

"Yes, I feel that I do. Your presence would be most appreciated, Lord Eastham. It would be a shield over us all, would it not be?"

"Ah." What appeared to be long-suffering resignation settled on Lord Eastham's face. "Then lead on, my lady. I will do the honors, as you've requested."

Adam raised an eyebrow.

"Let us beard the dragon in her den." Lord Eastham threw this over his shoulder as he strode through the crowd. Adam and Lady Cora followed behind.

Lady Cora made a tsking noise at his statement.

Dowager Countess of Winfield watched them approaching from her chair, surrounded by the other chaperones. She held herself like a queen on a throne, ruling over her court.

She was a fine-looking woman not quite into her fourth decade, deep bosomed and tall of stature, gowned and turbaned in gold silk with burgundy. Her wide-set eyes and grecian nose were like her daughter's, but her eyes were slitted and her nose imposing. Her hair curled a rich copper untouched by gray, and she wore heavy jewelry of gold and topaz.

Her wide mouth was pressed into a hard, jagged line, and her eyes glittered at them through narrowed slits.

Yes, the dowager countess was not pleased.

As they reached her, Lady Cora's hand squeezed his arm once, and let go. "Thank you, your grace." She curtsied, he bowed, and she moved to her mother's side, turning to face Adam and Eastham. The dowager countess harrumphed under her breath.

Lord Eastham stepped up to her and bowed. She raised her eyebrows at him. He turned back to Adam.

"Duke, may I introduce Lady Winfield, the Dowager Countess of Winfield?"

Adam bowed.

"Lady Winfield, may I introduce your ladyship to his grace, the Duke of Blackdale."

The dowager countess deigned to stand and curtsy shallowly.

"It is a pleasure to meet you, Lady Winfield," Adam said.

"The new Duke of Blackdale. You have quite the look of your father."

Adam froze, his blood running chill. Lady Winfield's eyes slitted further.

"Were you acquainted with my late father, Lady Winfield?" His words were stiff and his jaw felt tight.

"Yes, I was acquainted with him. Though we were not friends, by any stretch of the word."

Adam could do no more than nod tightly. His mind raced, memories and conjectures and scenes of terror bludgeoned through his mind.

Under what circumstances had Lady Winfield known his father? He had been a reasonable man among the upper classes of society, outside of his own family. He had been careful among those with power and influence. Adam would have expected a countess to know nothing about how his father was with those who weren't able to fight back.

But the coldness in her eyes said she knew something of what his father had really been.

"I knew your mother," she said. "Well, at one point. We corresponded multiple times over the years."

His mother. He swallowed down the bitterness that rose at the mention of her. What had his mother told her friends over correspondence? Something of the truth, it seemed, from Lady Winfield's expression.

"I see," was all Adam could say.

The dowager released her glare, and turned to Lord Eastham in a dangerously friendly manner. "And you, I suppose, Fredrick, are who I am to thank for introducing my daughter to the Scottish Duke of Blackdale?"

"Yes, your ladyship, I am the one to be thanked." He bowed with a quirked lip and an elaborate gesture toward himself.

"I will have to find an adequate way to reward you, Fredrick. You may start by ordering our carriage to be brought round. My daughter is drooping and it is time to depart."

Adam glanced at Lady Cora. She straightened in response to her mother's comment, but he could see she was worn down.

"Yes, thank you, Mother. I'm feeling quite done for the evening."

"Then I will go directly." Lord Eastham bowed and departed.

The dowager looked at Adam once more. "Tell me, Duke, do you consider yourself as taking after your father in taste and inclination?"

Adam's entire body hardened at her words. "No, your ladyship," he said through clenched teeth. "I most certainly do not."

She looked at him in equal hardness and tilted her head. "As you say. We shall see."

His veins ran cold with icy rage. He needed to get away from this woman before he did something he would regret. He bowed stiffly, but then looked over to Lady Cora.

She was watching him, her beautiful face strained with concern. Was that fear as well?

He forced himself to relax and bowed more graciously to her. "Thank you for the dance, Lady Cora. It was a pleasure to make your acquaintance." He meant that with all his heart.

He walked away, forcing his fisted hands to relax. He would leave as well, but after the ladies. He would not risk another meeting with them tonight.

On the drive home, Mother gave Cora a tight-lipped smile. "How pleasant to have conquered a duke, my love! I hope you enjoyed your brief flirtation. But he is completely ineligible."

Cora blinked at her mother through her fatigue. The night had been wearing. "An ineligible duke, Mama?"

The smile twisted. "He's Scottish!" She waved a bejeweled hand. "Even being a Scottish peer does not make up for the fact that his lands are hundreds of miles from the those that will be yours someday. Your lands cannot be so neglected. You would not be able to watch over them properly from Scotland." She sat back against the squabs. "So, completely ineligible." She spoke with finality.

Mother's words rankled. Cora didn't stop to consider why. "I suppose an Irish peer would be worse?"

"Oh indeed, child! But Scotland is bad enough. He's a fine flirtation for an evening, but I think you ought not to encourage him further. Men like that don't take well to hearing *no* if they've received a few tacit *yes*'s."

Cora couldn't call the strained and unusual exchanges she'd had with the duke "flirtation." There had been none of the light teasing, or back and forth pleasantries many of her court engaged in to try to win her favor.

She didn't enjoy "flirtation." It was such a strain, always trying to think of witty things to say.

But Mother never seemed to notice that Cora enjoyed flirting much less than Mother did.

Chapter Four

Nowhere, Everywhere

SATURDAY, JUNE 29, 1816, LATE MORNING

The duke was not among the callers who paid their respects the next morning.

Cora waited for him with a tight knot in her stomach, and caught her breath at the sound of every carriage that stopped in front of their townhouse, or each ring of the doorbell.

All the rest of her dancing partners from the night before visited. But he did not.

She swallowed her disappointment, and chided herself. Had she even liked him? Their introduction had been . . . awkward and uncomfortable.

But their set had been the most charged dance she had ever engaged in. A charged cotillion, of all things!

Amid the cut hothouse flowers her callers had brought, she found a potted plant that had not been there before, a *Viola odorata*, sweet violet. She picked up the little pot with its pretty purple blooms, and breathed in their sweet fragrance. A few breaths and the scent was gone, lost from her nose. But the violets, they would last. She would come back later to smell them again.

A quick discussion with Foley revealed they had been delivered by a florist's boy at 9 o'clock, but there had been no note. Only "For Lady Cora" stated by the deliverer.

A thrill of excitement raced through her. The other flowers that callers brought were all cut and in water. Yes, they were lovely, but this was better.

At afternoon tea, she politely asked her mother if the orangery might be opened?

"No, it will remain shut," were her mother's clipped, decided tones. "You have spent too much time there this Season. You have only a few short weeks left of London. Perhaps you can spend them with clean nails and soft hands."

Cora clenched her work-damaged hands in her lap and bit the inside of her cheek to keep herself from saying anything.

Mrs. Winters and Lady Burrelton tittered behind their tea-cups. Cora flushed and kept her eyes downturned.

That night, at the King's Theatre, they enjoyed the *Marriage of Figaro*. During the Countess's aria, chills went down Cora's arms. She tore her gaze from the stage, and saw him in a box across the theater. The Black Duke. He was watching her. She jerked her head back to the action on the opera stage.

But she kept finding herself drawn back again, turning her head toward him, watching him watching her. Then, from what she could make of his expression from that distance, his brows drew together and shadowed his eyes. His face became forbidding.

Cora realized her mother was scowling at him. The duke looked away, and disappeared from the box before intermission. He didn't visit their box during the break, unlike Captain Bowden, who brought refreshments and cheeriness, or Mr. Basil who fetched her fan and fawned.

His box stood empty the rest of the performance.

The next morning, sitting in their pew at Grosvenor Chapel, she happened to turn around, and there he was, across the aisle, and a little behind. Face solemn, listening to the sermon, not watching her.

He owned a villa in Kensington, on the other side of Hyde Park, she knew. Yet here he was, at their chapel in Mayfair. His eyes locked with hers.

She swung back around before Mother could notice her distraction, and bowed her head, hoping her deep bonnet rim would hide her heated cheeks. She didn't let herself look round again, and when Sunday service was over, he was no longer anywhere to be seen.

But she looked. She kept her gaze moving over every pew, and around every corner as they walked home. She clenched her fists in frustration.

She caught her mother in private. She was still locked out of her orangery, and the plants had been neglected for three days. This couldn't go on.

"Please Mama," she begged, "allow Mary to keep the brazier going in the orangery. The plants will suffer in this chill. And she needs to get in to water them!" She clasped her hands in front of her, turned up her face, but kept her eyes downcast. "They need daily maintenance, Mama."

"Fine," Mother snapped. "Mrs. Weller has a key, and will allow Mary to enter and maintain the plants."

"Thank you, Mama."

"And then she will lock it after. You are not to attempt to enter, Cora. I will have obedience in this."

Cora's stomach twisted, but she said, "Of course, Mama."

She snuck out to the gated garden in the center of Grosvenor Square, aching to plunge her hands into the soaked soil. But she kept her gloves on, and stood decorously under her umbrella, visible to every front window in the square. She breathed in the wet coolness of the leaves, and enjoyed the squelching crunch of the sodden gravel under her feet.

Adam caught sight of her walking in the Grosvenor Square Gardens.

He hadn't expected to see her out. He'd driven onto her street with the half-formed intent of staring at her townhouse windows from across the square. It was better than staring at the four walls of his study.

Why could he not get this girl out of his head? Why did just looking at her cause his heart to beat faster in his chest? What was it about this young woman that consumed his every thought? He had spoken to her once, had shared one dance. Why did his heart thrum in his chest with an ache to be near her?

She walked alone, umbrella over her head in the chill rain of the afternoon. Where was her maid? It was a gated garden, but this was London.

As he watched, she approached a tree, stroked its leaves, and seemed to examine it. She moved onto a small bush, tenderly inspected it, and continued to a clump of planted flowers. In an action that appeared thoughtless, she drew off her gloves, and pressed her bare fingers into the soil around the stems.

He couldn't help but smile. This lady had a passion and single-mindedness that went beyond propriety and social expectations, to the focused devotion of a calling. She cared, deeply, for her plants.

How would she respond to a man if she loved him? With this same single-minded focus? This tender care?

Warmth flooded his body at the thought, filling him with a glowing heat.

He wanted that. He wanted love and attention like that so badly it was a physical ache in his chest.

To be touched. To be loved. To be cared for like she cared for her growing things. He would thrive under her touch, planted solid like an oak, roots thrust deeply into the ground, branches spread wide.

He had never felt such a love in his life. He craved it like a hunger.

His chest expanded with air. He breathed so deeply his healing ribs gave a twinge. With that sharp pain, he was brought back to his present reality.

Her mother didn't approve of him; she had made that clear. A gentleman ought to retreat, ought not to encroach against a mother and guardian's wishes.

But he wanted her, Lady Cora, the sweet and beautiful, the woman so full of tenderness and compassion she displayed it openly, thoughtlessly.

He ached with it.

His horses snorted, and moved restlessly. They had been left standing too long in the rain.

He circled the oval garden. The hood over his phaeton protected him from the rain, but kept blocking her from his view as he circled. A tree came between them as well, and he wanted to rush the horses past.

He kept them at a decorous pace, only half-watching the road in front of him.

It was good it was a rainy Sunday afternoon, and few were out.

She came near to the fence, examining a plant there. In his circling, he drew parallel to her, closer than he had before. She looked up, and saw him.

Her eyes widened. He drew up his horses and stopped near her, turning in his seat to keep the eye contact.

"Your grace!" She called out to him. She came to the fence.

His heart leaped. Without conscious thought, he was down from his perch in the phaeton, dragging his reins with him. Where was his groom? He hadn't brought a groom. He hadn't wanted extra witnesses to his lovesick behavior. Curse his folly.

The reins were long, thankfully, and he was able to draw near. He reached her, staring down at her upturned face through the dark posts of the wrought iron fence, into her beautiful eyes.

She blushed, and looked down, her bonnet obscuring her eyes. "Oh, forgive me, I shouldn't have—"

"No!" He caught himself, and gentled his tone. "No, the pleasure is mine, Lady Cora."

Her eyes raised once more, luminous in the diffuse light. The rain came down on his high-crowned beaver, struck his caped greatcoat. Though the railing separated them, the soft pinging of the rain on iron and cloth gave a feeling of privacy to their conference.

He had to force himself to give proper courtesy. "How do you do, my lady?" He bowed, tipped his hat.

"I am well, thank you, your grace." She curtsied. "And you?"

"I'm . . ." He had to stop, and swallow against a dry throat. "Very good, thank you." His throat tightened, his stomach roiled with sudden nerves. "Lady Cora, it is . . . wonderful to see you again."

Her mouth curved in a small smile. "It is good to speak with you again."

"Yes." He could hold her eyes no longer, and looked down. She was hiding her hands in the skirt of her pelisse. They must be muddy. He smiled, and looked back into her face. Her cheeks were pink.

He wished to kiss them, to feel their softness under his lips, for their heat to warm him. He found himself leaning down, bringing his face closer to hers.

Curse hat brims and fence posts.

"Lady Cora! My lady!" A strained voice reached them, and he backed away, surprised at this new craving that was shaking his control. It would not be appropriate to kiss her in any fashion. Not yet.

A middle-aged woman was rushing toward them, still tying her bonnet ribbons, wearing only a house dress, not even a cloak. He recognized Lady Cora's maid from the park last week.

He was reawakened to the staring eyes of every window in the square, each holding a possible witness to his conversation through the fence with Lady Cora. They were in sight of her townhouse, and had been noticed.

"My lady!" the servant huffed, panting as she reached them. Her look was very disapproving. She straightened her bonnet and closed her mouth primly, holding in a scolding, he was sure. She kept her eyes away from Adam, so she didn't see his mouth twist. The interruption was perhaps fortunate. He chided himself for thoughtlessly entertaining premature inclinations. He must not be so hasty.

"Lady Cora, it was good to see you." He tipped his hat again.

"You as well, your grace." She curtseyed.

He couldn't interpret the expression in her eyes. Was it regret? Regret that she would get a scolding as soon as he left?

He remounted his phaeton, his horses moving restlessly. But he caught her gaze before he flicked the reins, and held it as long as he could.

He drove away, and let out a breath.

What did he care for parental grimaces? Mothers and their selfish disapproval, their weak manipulations? He clenched the reins. He would not let what some mother wanted keep him from his own happiness.

Daughters must leave their mothers, and cleave unto their husbands. And the husbands must cleave to them in return. A spike of joy struck him at the thought.

He would do as he desired. He would pursue her. He would win her.

Monday morning another potted plant arrived. An *Iris latifolia* with glorious, deep purple petals. This time, it had a note. "For a lady of flowers."

It was unsigned. But surely it was from him?

Cora hugged the pot to her chest. She rearranged the sideboard in the breakfast parlor to display the irises in the overcast morning light.

Captain Bowden arrived on the heels of the delivery boy, his eyebrows raising at the lingering blush on her cheeks from the note. He was much too early for their scheduled ride in Hyde Park.

"I most painfully apologize that I must cancel and be away, fair Lady Cora. Duty calls." He gave his most mischievous smile, tossing his dark waves out of his face. "The Duke of Wellington has arrived in town from Paris, and I am being called upon to rejoin his staff."

Cora couldn't fathom why his statement warranted a mischievous look. "Of course, Captain Bowden. Thank you for coming to let me know."

His grin widened at her statement, doubling his look of self-satisfaction. "I knew you would understand, lovely creature. I will return to reschedule, and will pray that the day I am able will soon come." He bowed over her hand.

Was it a game to them, Cora wondered, to the ones who acted like Captain Bowden? Who flattered her with obvious insincerity? A joke to make her the talk of town with all their attention?

"But before I go, how are your plants, Lady Cora?"

She looked down. Her orangery was still locked. Cora could see through the glass that most of her plants were fine. Mary watered them, and kept the brazier warm, but Cora was still banned.

She did not speak of it to her callers, however. It was too humiliating. Thankfully, not all her plants were in the orangery.

"The cyclamen is improving." She offered. "*Cyclamen persicum*. It has been suffering from the chill, but I've moved it to the morning room, and hope that with more southern exposure, it might be coaxed into blooming again. If the sun would appear, it might. With all this rain . . ."

His smile had become a smirk. He was indulging her interest, but not actually interested.

"And the asters are budding." She ended, lamely. *Aster amellus.* She was quaint and provincial to them, that was it. Pretty enough, definitely rich enough, that they tolerated her eccentricities with smiles and nods. And didn't pay attention to her words.

She closed her mouth, gave a smile that did not perhaps reach her eyes. She thanked the captain for letting her know of his new circumstances. He took his leave.

Sir Merriweather accompanied them to Covent Garden that night to see *Romeo and Juliet,* Miss O'Neil performing. The newly married Princess Charlotte was also there with her handsome Prince Leopold. Cora watched her with interest. Cora and her mother had attended some of the wedding festivities. How was marriage for the elusive princess?

The crowd also wanted to know, and called out to Princess Charlotte, wanting her attention. Mother tsked at their rudeness. "Let the gel enjoy the play."

Cora felt attentive eyes on herself. She scanned the rowdy crowd and the boxes across the way.

There he was, in a box a level below theirs. He was watching her again. Butterflies fluttered through her stomach.

She swallowed, and nodded her head to him, giving him a smile. His expression lightened. He smiled and bowed in return.

Her heart pounded in her chest. She turned back to the action on the stage.

But he stayed in his box. They exchanged glances, and looked away. He didn't disappear.

At the intermission, he came to their box. Her heart caught in her throat as he stood in the doorway, his tall frame filling it.

He wore his black neckcloth today with a brilliant sapphire pin. Its blue fire matched the fire in his eyes as he looked at her.

Mother was cold, but not openly rude to the Duke of Blackdale. Cora's heart thrilled as he came near her.

They engaged in polite conversation. Mr. Basil dominated the box as he chatted about his latest purchase of a fine high stepper of a horse, touching her on her arm to keep her attention. She hadn't noticed when he came in.

Lord Eastham entered, greeting them all. He gave the duke a smirk, a bow to Cora, and took a seat next to her mother.

The duke was quiet, observant. He watched the men, he watched her mother, and he watched Cora. She wanted to speak with him, but didn't know what to say. Her tongue felt thick in her mouth. She swallowed against the lump in her throat.

Sir Merriweather turned to her. "Don't you find it odd, Lady Cora? Prince Leopold comes to one of the greatest plays by our greatest playwright, acted by our greatest actors, but look at him! He's been reading a book all evening!"

Cora had scarcely noticed the prince after she'd felt the Duke of Blackdale's eyes on her. She stumbled around for something polite to answer. "Oh, well, perhaps it's the Shakespearean language? It may give him trouble. It is so different than the modern tongue. The prince is German, you know?"

The duke stood solemnly next to a curtain, distracting her with his silence. Her arms broke out in chills. He was so close, his presence like a cool weight.

Soon intermission was over, and the men took their leave. The duke bowed over her hand, murmuring something—she hardly knew what—and exited.

Cora collapsed back into her chair, exhausted by all the emotions that had been racing through her.

Why had he just stood there?

But as Romeo and Juliet died, preferring self-destruction over separation, she felt him watching her. She clutched her hand to her chest and swallowed.

A potted *Crocus longiflorus*, the long-flowered crocus, with lilac buds just beginning to open and reveal their fragrant orange centers, was delivered promptly at 9 o'clock with a gust of cold wind.

The unsigned note:

"This bud of love, by summer's ripening breath,
May prove a beauteous flower when next we meet."

She caught her breath, and wrapped her shawl around her shoulders more tightly.

She tucked the note away before her mother could see it to ask, and went to check on the orangery. She peered through the glass. Were the coals in the brazier still warm?

Would summer ever come?

The Carltons' musicale that evening was tolerable. The young ladies performing were skilled enough, and none made mistakes so obvious that she wilted in sympathetic misery for them.

It was both a shame and a relief to only be in the audience this year. She could carry a tune, but found practicing a bore, and performing a horror of nerves. After last year's less than stellar performances, Mother had stopped insisting she pursue music.

So she sat among the spectators, surrounded by gentlemen of her court who paid too little attention to the performers, and too much attention to her.

The duke was here tonight. Would he only watch, yet again? Would he act on that note? Would he do anything to bring a bud of love to flower?

He sat on her periphery, where she could not watch him without being blatant. As the evening drew on, he didn't appear to be watching her anymore. He was, merely, there. And she was vitally aware of it.

After the performances it happened that she was sitting alone, her mother speaking with friends across the room, her court having dispersed to various places, some with promises to return. He came to her then and spoke with her.

She grabbed at this chance. "Have you been sending me the potted flowers, your grace? That have been coming unsigned?"

"Yes." He answered, his eyes burning down into hers.

Her heart was pounding. "Thank you, they are beautiful. I like them very much."

"It is my pleasure, Lady Cora."

Mr. Basil returned then with glasses of ratafia. She felt powerless to get rid of him. The duke bid his leave, and she watched him go with frustration tugging at her chest.

Chapter Five

Orangery

Wednesday, July 3, 1816, morning

Wednesday morning a *Rosa chinensis minima* arrived in a pretty painted pot. A miniature Chinese rose bush of brilliant red.

The note was still unsigned, but the handwriting was the same. She studied it in the hallway, away from her mother's eyes. The letters were neat and precise, with long, almost spiked ascenders and descenders.

The note said:

O my Luve's like a red, red rose,
That's newly sprung in June

It was July, but she would forgive him that. It felt like October outside.

Others had spoken poetry to her before: more verses from Robert Burns, some Shakespeare, and select words from Lord Byron. It had never felt as sincere to her as these scant lines did.

She tucked the note into her bodice, near her heart, next to the lines from *Romeo and Juliet.*

That night Cora and her mother attended a supper party at the Basils'.

Despite the intimacy of an event with less than twenty people invited, the duke was there. Would he speak more than a few words to her? If he didn't, she felt like she might scream.

But Mr. Basil clung like a leech to her side, sitting next to her at supper, and staying by her through the short card party afterwards.

He was a tall and gangly young man only a year older than herself who wore loud waistcoats and shirt-points high enough to obscure his weak chin. He was too desperate to be attractive. His family needed money, she knew. She felt bad for him. But every day his attentions grew more pointed, and her interest grew less.

She tried to gently discourage him, "I do not want to monopolize you this evening, Mr. Basil, and cause you to neglect your guests. As host—"

"Oh, they're my mother's guests, Lady Cora! I'm merely here to fill out the numbers! I'm free to spend my time as I like. I'm very happy here."

He tried to take her gloved hand. He had taken to kissing it like he was a macaroni from a generation ago. She, as politely as possible, tugged it away from his lips, clasped her hands together, and turned to Captain Bowden on her left. She asked him how the Duke of Wellington was faring?

She was making a fourth at whist, sitting between Captain Bowden and Mr. Basil. Mr. Basil's sister, Miss Fanny Basil, was across from her, and also paying Cora far too much attention. Cora knew her insincerity, and it grated. Last Season, Cora had overheard Fanny talking about her, calling her "That bluestocking farm girl." It had stung. Cora had shrugged it off as jealousy and resigned herself. She didn't have many friends.

But tonight, Miss Basil was toad-eating, excessively friendly. As they played several rounds of whist, Captain Bowden won three times, and Cora won twice. Captain Bowden wouldn't have let her win, but the other two . . . she was sure her wins were because the siblings were trying to get her to win. She wasn't a skilled card player. She didn't care enough about it to pay the attention it required to excel.

She eyed Captain Bowden to see if he had noticed the oddness of their game. He had on his characteristic mischievous smirk, and his eyes twinkled at her over his fresh hand.

Oh, he knew.

"Lady Cora," Mr. Basil said, "you've visited our orangery here at the townhouse, haven't you?"

"Yes, it is a lovely one. I congratulate you, Mr. Basil."

"Thank you. My mother has recently acquired a rare species, an Oriental persimmon. I'm sure you'd find it fascinating, if you'd like to come with us and see it."

Finally, something interesting this evening! "Oh! A *Diospyros kaki*? I'd love to!"

As soon as that hand was done, and the finals tallied—Captain Bowden winning again—they bid thank you to Captain Bowden, and Mr. and Miss Basil escorted Cora down a hall to their orangery. It was dusk, and the hallway was dark enough that the well-lit orangery could be seen through the uncurtained windows. The orangery was a lovely large room glassed in on three sides. It jutted into the Basil's small London garden.

The approach was charming, the lit branches of the orange and lemon trees shining through the fading night. They turned a corner to reach the door, and entered to see the exotic new addition.

The fruit tree was in a place of honor in the center of the room in a large painted pot, but it was not very healthy. Leaves were drooping and browning, and the red-orange fruit was rotting where they grew.

"Oh," Cora cried. "It has suffered in transit." She rushed to the yellowing persimmon tree and began examining leaves. "Did you transfer it immediately after it arrived? Must have, it's in shock. Let me help."

She took stock of the room. "Do you have some clippers? These dying leaves should be clipped off to give the plant leave to focus on the main trunk and branches. And we need a fertilized infusion. I've never actually nurtured a *Diospyros kaki* before, but I'm sure . . ."

Cora spotted the gardener's cabinet and opened it in search of tools. She reached for a large pair of clippers. She noticed her gloved hands and recalled herself. She was in someone else's home, and at a social event. She needed politeness and permission. She turned back and looked at the siblings with her hands clasped in front of her.

"Oh, forgive me. I got overexcited. Would you mind if I use my limited expertise to help your fruit tree?" She asked as demurely as she could as she bounced on her toes. She wanted to spring into action.

The siblings looked bemused.

"Of course, my lady, we only wish to please you." Mr. Basil gestured with his hand.

"Thank you!" She spun, stripping off her fine gloves, and grabbing the clippers, noting that the cupboard contained a fertilizer mix that might be helpful and watering pails.

She began judiciously pruning, cutting away failing twigs, and freeing up the plant to focus its energy where it was needed. Maybe some of the fruit could be saved. The ones ruined she plucked off.

"Do you have a rubbish pail to place the dead fruit in?"

"Ah . . . yes, here," Mr. Basil handed her one, and she placed it on the floor, tossing mushy and brown fruit into it.

Here and there were a few ripe and healthy pieces of fruit, soft but not discolored.

"There are some here that should be edible! Do you have a pail?" She found one, and pulled it over. "For the good fruit. Can you get sugar and water for me? That would help." She left the hard ones that looked healthy but unripe.

"I will fetch some!" Miss Basil cried.

"Thank you."

Cora vaguely heard her leave the room, and shut the door. This branch here was hopeless. She clipped it. Another rotten fruit. She plucked it with her left hand, the clippers in her right.

"At last, we are alone!"

Cora was swung around violently. Arms pressed her face into a starched cravat. "What—?"

"I love you passionately, my darling!" Mr. Basil cried.

She flailed her arms for a second or two, trying to get away without injuring him with the heavy metal clippers, or smooshing the overripe fruit into him.

Why was she trying to protect him? The man was embracing her without her leave!

He loosed his grip on her enough to grab her hair, yanking her head back. It hurt. "Ow!"

He crashed his mouth against hers. Their teeth jarred against one another. She cringed, and managed to swing her left hand up. She smeared the rotten fruit into the side of his face and into his ear.

"Yuhgh!" Mr. Basil let go.

Cora stumbled back from him. She caught herself, and lifted up her clippers in both hands, the messy and the clean, to ward off further attack. She sucked on her teeth with her lips and tongue to sooth the sharp ache that had shot through them at his attempted kiss.

She found her voice. "What do you think you're doing, sir?"

He had his fingers in his ear, shaking his head to get the liquid out of his ear and splattering over-ripe persimmon juice everywhere.

He stared at his hand, coated in red pulp, and down at what he could see of the mess that had been made of his clothes. He looked over at her, mute shock over his face. The red juices had run down, and were soaking into his high shirt collar, making it droop on one side. His cravat and his yellow and violet embroidered waistcoat were splattered and stained. "You—you . . . my new waistcoat is ruined!"

"Yes, that is particularly sad." She considered it. "That is lovely embroidery. Do you know how long it takes to do that fine of work? Hours and hours. Quite miserable work, I assure you. Perhaps if you dye the entire thing in brilliant red—vermilion or carmine should do the trick—it might be saved? Maybe an improvement, even."

She was babbling. The shock, she supposed. Back to the important subject. "Never-mind the waistcoat! You, sir, are lacking in principles!" She shook her clippers at him.

"Indeed, they both are," a deep voice made them jump and look toward the entrance. The dark duke was there, entirely in black, with a hand gripping young Miss Basil's arm.

"I am returning Miss Basil to her proper place as chaperone." He forced her into the room. She had a horrible scowl on her face, and walked stiffly. He took her over to a padded bench. "If you would please sit down, my dear." His guiding grip didn't give her a choice. She sat.

He turned to Cora and her erstwhile lover, and his mouth twitched.

Her mouth twitched in response.

Oh, no, she mustn't giggle, she really mustn't. She swallowed a laugh that almost burst out with a rough choking sound and cleared her throat.

The duke kept ahold of himself admirably, only that slight twitch betraying him at all. He focused on Mr. Basil who was looking at him in horror. The Duke of Blackdale's face took on the sternness of solid stone.

"Mr. Basil, you ought to be called out for your night's work."

Mr. Basil's face blanched of all color except the red smears.

"But as you are far beneath my touch, and not worth the bother that would come when I inevitably killed you . . ."

Mr. Basil swayed and looked liable to faint.

"The lady has already defended and avenged herself quite admirably, I feel. Do you agree, Lady Cora? Do you think you have properly punished the interloper?"

"He's foolish beyond belief, but doesn't deserve death. Debtor's prison and deportation, perhaps." Saying that barb was rather satisfying.

Mr. Basil gave out a squeak of misery.

Cora lowered her clippers. She stood tall and faced Mr. Basil. "Which might happen, because I am not going to marry you, Mr. Basil. I didn't mind you in my court, but no more. I and my mother will never return to this house as long as it is in your possession." She glanced at Fanny. "You and your sister . . ." her stomach felt trembly. "Fanny intended to bring an audience to witness our being alone, and you . . . embracing me. You wanted to force me to marry you?"

"I found her leaving this room and heading to the drawing room, likely to call over some witnesses." The duke gave Fanny a cold look.

"Mrs. Nesbitt and her daughter, I suppose?" Cora sighed. "More than one ill-fated match has been forced by their malicious gossiping. Well, you were mistaken in this instance." She took a deep breath, and felt calmer. "I would not have been forced by scandal into any match."

Fanny made a noise of disbelief.

"Indeed, Fanny," Cora raised her chin. "My mother will never make me marry where I do not wish. If I had a father, mayhap he would force me, but I barely knew my father, and I know my mother disliked her marriage enough never to make me wed where I do not desire." Cora gave a small smile. "She's told me so herself."

Fanny looked away from her, and sat, her face sullen.

Mr. Basil started babbling, "My apologies! My feelings overwhelmed me!"

"Enough, sir." The duke commanded. "I suggest you leave now, and go change, before any of the rest of the company sees you in that state."

Mr. Basil looked down at himself once again. "Yes, you are right, yes, of course, must change. . . ."

"Soak it all, or give it straight way to your valet to soak it, and you might be able to salvage your clothes, Mr. Basil." Cora couldn't help adding.

"You are very kind." Basil seemed to come to himself, and straightened and bowed, "Good evening, Lady Cora. Your grace." And he walked out stiffly.

Cora stood, vitally aware of the duke's presence and her hand covered in fruit slime. And the tree, only partially cared for. "Fanny, did you get that sugar for me?"

Fanny flushed and gave her a wrathful look. "No." She snapped out.

"Oh." Cora felt deflated.

"You need sugar?" The duke asked.

She flushed. "Yes, sugar water can help transplant shock. The roots have been damaged."

She looked between the tree and the duke. "If you will pardon me, your grace, I would like to finish doing what I can for this fruit tree."

His eyes crinkled a tiny bit, and his mouth did that almost imperceptible twitch. "By all means. How can I assist you?"

"I need water. The roots ought to be well watered."

"And you desired sugar for sugar water?"

"Yes, thank you, if you please."

"Right away, my lady." He moved to the door.

"If you will not be needing me . . ." Fanny rose.

The duke turned back. "Sit down." It was the command of an infantry colonel.

Fanny sat.

He quieted his tone, but not the authority in his voice. "Unless you think arranging a scandal between Lady Cora and myself would be a proper revenge, sit still. While we could test Lady Cora's theories on how far her mother would stretch her tolerance for scandal, it would be better to not. I will return in a moment." He left.

"Well, I never!" Fanny burst out.

Cora tried to ignore her as she evaluated where next to trim, but she could feel Fanny's glare boring into her.

"This is an expensive tree," Cora tried to lighten the mood. "You should be able to sell it again. But it would be best to wait till it's recovered some, or you won't get as good of a price. It won't fruit again for several months, but if you wait till it flowers, that might be enough to make most of your money back on it."

Fanny looked ready to explode.

Thankfully, the duke came back then.

"I caught a footman, and have ordered a tea tray, and a bucket of water. Will that be adequate, Lady Cora?"

"That should work well. Thank you, your grace."

The Duke of Blackdale came over to the tree. Though its drooping leaves separated them, Cora could feel his presence pulling at her.

Cora trimmed smaller branches. She was trying to lower its size by a third, without damaging it so badly it lost hope and died. It was an art.

"You care much for plants."

"Oh, yes, they are my main passion. And have gotten me into trouble more than once. They used my weakness against me quite well." Cora flushed again at how easily she was lured and distracted. "I can be too single-minded, I suppose."

She snipped. The sap was sticky, almost a gum, and her dress wasn't faring well. She was leaving quite a mess for the gardener to clean the next day.

"How did you come to be here and rescue me, your grace?" She asked, attempting to be light in her speech.

"I will admit to you that I followed." He spoke low. Cora looked at him and his eyes were burning into her once again. "I did not like that you were with him, no matter the chaperone."

Cora's stomach fluttered and she couldn't look away.

"The windows make this quite a fishbowl at night. I could see into the room clearly," He gave a self-deprecating grimace. "When Miss Basil left you alone with her brother, I caught up to her. I'm sorry I was not quick enough to keep you from being assaulted."

"Oh, well," Cora turned to her clipping again, embarrassed. "I didn't even think when she left. I was too focused on this poor tree. Thank you for your quick action and understanding."

"I did little. You had already rescued yourself. Soft fruit to the ear. I shall remember that next time I'm in battle." He smiled genuinely, and Cora smiled back.

Fanny shifted on her bench, probably enraged at being ignored.

The tea tray arrived. The two footmen, one with a tray and the other with a bucket of water, looked wide-eyed at the mess on the floor, their mistress, the duke, and the lady trimming a tree in evening dress. But they schooled their features and set the tray next to Miss Fanny.

"Thank you, please put the bucket right here," Cora indicated the gardening table.

Once they had left, she asked, "Fanny, could you please make some sugar water for the tree? Just dump the sugar in the teapot, that should do it." Fanny gave her a glare, but reached for the sugar bowl.

Cora washed her sticky hands and the clipper in the bucket. Some mud and juice wouldn't hurt the tree when she watered it. She tried to keep her dress from being splashed, though flying juices and gummy cut branches had already reached it.

She shouldn't be doing this in a fine evening gown.

"Oh dear!" Fanny's voice rang out, "I'm afraid I thoughtlessly added the tea leaves to the pot as well. I have ruined it for the tree. How clumsy of me."

The duke gave Fanny a cutting glance.

"Oh, that's fine. The acidity in the tea will help the soil." Cora's hands were dripping. "Is there a tea towel over there?"

The duke left her side, and fetched it from the tray. Fanny's face was a dark mask.

The duke brought the towel to Cora. "Thank you." She blushed to be so served by a duke. But as she reached for it, he caught up her hands in the towel. She sucked in her breath and stared into his handsome face.

Gently, he dried her hands. She felt her face flush even deeper, mortified. She swallowed down bile that rose up in her throat. Her bare hands! Rough, with scars and small cuts, the nails and cuticles hopeless. Five days locked out of her orangery were not enough to transform her hands into those of a lady.

"Ah, my suspicions are confirmed."

She couldn't look into his face.

"The answer to the mystery of why you never remove your gloves in company." His voice was soft and low. "Even when it is inconvenient not to do so."

Her mouth tightened, her back stiff with mortification. She wanted to snatch her hands back, but he held them firm.

"Lady Cora," he bent down, and moved his face into her view, catching her eyes. "Your hands are a wonder and a delight."

What?

"They are the hands of a lady of talent and passion."

Her breath caught in her throat, and his eyes captured hers once more. He bowed over her hands and released them. She held them in the air between them, too bewildered to move. One side of his expressive mouth raised in a small smile.

"Miss Basil, is the tea ready?" He fetched the pot. Cora blinked rapidly, and took it from him, her breath coming fast.

She poured the tea and sugar concoction into the bucket of water to cool it, then poured the water over the base of the tree.

She had done all she could for it.

"I apologize for the mess on the floor," She told the stiff-faced Fanny. "But if I attempt to clean it, my skirt will be ruined past recovery, I'm afraid."

"I'm sure the Basils' gardeners will be happy to clean it tomorrow." The duke said. "Are you done, Lady Cora?"

Cora found her gloves, and gratefully put them on again. "Yes, your grace."

"Then I shall escort you and Miss Basil to the ladies' retiring room, where you can repair yourselves from your evenings' exertions. Miss Basil." He held his hand out to Fanny. She moved stiffly, her tight mouth working.

The duke held his arm out to Cora, and she clasped his elbow with wonder. Had he really said that? Had he really meant it? Her heart was full in her throat.

Adam released Lady Cora at the door of the lady's retiring room, loathe to let her go. But he held onto the manipulative creature on his other arm as Cora disappeared into the room. "Miss Basil, a moment."

She glared up at him.

"If I hear a word of scandal or gossip connected to this, I will make things very unpleasant for your family. I have connections with all the banks and money lenders in the city. Debts can be called in, and debtors' prison is a reality. Do I make myself clear?"

She wrenched her arm out of his grasp. "Understood." She turned and stalked away.

Anger tightened in his gut. What that scoundrel and his sister had tried to do to Lady Cora . . .

But oh, she had been glorious! His love, the woman he would marry. She was perfect. A delight, a joy. How she'd smashed that fruit into the blaggard's ear!

Adam grinned at the door that Lady Cora had disappeared behind. A maid walked by with towels over her arm, and gave him a wary glance. He realized his presence at this door would look inappropriate.

He wiped his face, murmured, "Excuse me," and headed back to the drawing room.

He swallowed, and approached the dowager.

"Lady Winfield."

She gave him her customary cold, forbidding look. He ignored it, and leaned over to her ear. "Your daughter is in the ladies retiring room.

She could use your assistance." She stiffened next to him. "She is whole, but she has had a fright."

The dowager gave him a sharp look. He bowed, and moved off to stand by the fireplace.

The dowager's mouth twisted, but she bade leave of her friends, and strode out of the room.

Mother was appalled. She wanted to declaim the Basil's outrageous behavior loudly to all their guests, humiliate their mother, and storm out. Cora grabbed her hand. "Mama, no, it's been smoothed over. Please, let's just leave and never return."

"And the duke, he had a hand in it?"

Cora flushed. "In rescuing me. He caught Miss Basil and brought her back into the orangery, and made her stay."

"Humph." Her nostrils flared. But Cora watched in relief as she controlled her anger, and straightened with a snap of purpose. Mother inspected Cora. "Your dress is destroyed. We must go home to change before we go to Almack's."

Cora felt a wave of exhaustion go over her body. "Must we attend tonight, Mama? I'm feeling tired after—"

"Of course we must. It is the last time we'll attend this Season, and we must bid leave of the patronesses."

"Last time? Are we going home soon?" Oh, that would be such a relief. This chill Season had been never-ending, with its cold, indoor confinement, and its endless, endless social events. To go home to her gardens!

"We will leave soon, yes, but not for home. We've been invited to Sir Merriweather's house party in two weeks."

"Oh." Cora had to force her shoulders to not roll forward from disappointment and fatigue. Sir Merriweather was kind and well-meaning, and not a suitor of hers, so a least that was a relief. She did not want to be around pursuing men at all. She kept her eyes downcast, but she could feel her mother's narrowed gaze on her.

"Come, Cora, we will get you home, changed, and off to Almack's!"

Chapter Six

Almacks

WEDNESDAY, JULY 3, 1816, EVENING

Was it a waste? It had taken a personal effort for him to secure a voucher. Would she come here tonight after the rough events of the earlier evening?

There was still a clear space around Adam as he stood in the crowded assembly room, but it was a smaller berth than at the Carteright's ball last Friday. Perhaps the voucher and the greeting that patroness Princess Lieven had given him when he arrived had calmed some of the ton's uneasiness around him. That could be a benefit from attending Almack's tonight, though it hadn't been his purpose.

He was here for the chance to dance with her again. If she didn't arrive soon, he would retire, and hope Malcolm had sniffed out her next activities.

But there she was! The voucher was not a wasted effort. She moved through the room, her steps gliding in contrast to her mother's solid footfalls ahead of her. She was now gowned in soft white gauze embroidered in lavender sprigs, looking even more beautiful than earlier in the evening, if it were possible.

He watched her, his mood lightening with every step as she progressed into the room.

She looked up, and their gazes locked from across the assembly hall. Her mouth opened, and a rosy hue bloomed on her cheeks. She looked away, but her eyes returned to him after a moment. He felt a smile tug at his lips. He bowed, and she nodded in acknowledgment.

Several men descended on her like circling vultures. He would bide his time and wait till they had cleared before he approached.

He was here! Burning energy raced down her veins. Despite her former fatigue, she would not, could not, cry off dancing tonight, not when she might have a chance to dance with him.

More of Cora's usual court gathered around her. She smiled at them and tried to not look pained. Mr. Jordan, with his fashionably disheveled hair, Lord Snow with his wild eyes, Lieutenant Dean with his over-padded shoulders and too eager manners. Sir Merriweather joined them, and her smile turned more genuine. He was not desperately pursuing her. He was safe, as the others were not.

The next dance was soon secured by Mr. Jordan, the second by Lord Snow. The third would be a waltz. If the duke did not come soon and ask a dance of her, there might not be any sets left for him. She looked over at where he stood. Several ladies were being introduced to him by the master of ceremonies. Mothers and daughters. She dragged her eyes away from him surrounded by other females. Yes, he was a handsome, available duke. Mamas would be interested, despite his dark moniker. The Black Duke could pursue any lady he wished.

She swallowed, and determined to save the fourth dance for him. If he did not come and claim it, she would sit it out, proclaim the headache that was building behind her eyes, and beg Mother to allow her to leave.

Captain Bowden appeared at her side, and was dismayed when she told him the next four dances where spoken for. "But not the waltz, surely?"

"The waltz is claimed by Mama, to be passed at the sidelines, as you've been informed previously, Captain Bowden." She couldn't help the snippy tone of her voice. It rankled. And Lord Eastham, he who could convince Mama of anything, refused to come nigh the doors of Almacks, so the possibility of his asking Cora to waltz and therefore convincing her mother to allow it was off the table this evening.

Captain Bowden's mischievous smile suffused his handsome face, his eyes twinkled at her, and he turned to her mother. Cora's back tensed. What was this reckless young man about to do?

"Lady Winfield! How lovely you are this evening! I understand that Lady Cora does not waltz. But you, dear lady, do you waltz? Could I beg the honor of giving you a turn around the floor?" His grin was wide and full of charm.

"I certainly do not, young man!" Her mother proclaimed. But a smile played over her mouth, and she tapped him on the chest with her fan. "As for Lady Cora—"

Cora turned toward her mother, her breath caught in her throat. Mother looked like she was considering. Was she? Would she?

Mother's eye was caught by something beyond Captain Bowden's scarlet-coated form. "Is that the Duke of Blackdale there with Princess Lieven?" Her voice had chilled.

The captain turned, following her gaze. "Yes, Madame, I believe it is."

Mother's mouth worked. Then she sat back, her spine straight and head imperiously erect. "As for Lady Cora, she also does not waltz. For now." She snapped her fan.

Hope deflated from Cora's chest in a long exhale.

The current set ended, and Mr. Jordan came to claim her hand for her first dance of the evening.

There was joy even in a country dance. As she moved through the lively steps, she felt herself lighten.

The dark duke had yet to come near her this evening. He danced with a lady she did not know during the second set, and they passed each other as they moved down the room in the fast Scottish Reel.

In the glimpses she could catch, he looked a fine dancer. Maybe a bit stiff, but his timing appeared excellent.

But now she sat at the wall, away from her mother's entourage, watching the couples whirl in the waltz. Three of her court sat near, chatting over her.

The duke was not dancing, but stood alone across the room, looking stern and imposing, his brows drawn. Why did he not approach?

Maybe the duke would not while other men sat near, giving her their attention. As she cast quick glances in his direction, she caught him looking their way, the scowl darkening his eyes.

She had to rid herself of her court.

The vultures never left. Adam ground his teeth.

What, was it beneath his dignity to speak to a woman others spoke to? To court a woman others courted?

He wanted to speak to her alone! And not have to compete with the pretty speeches of others. He cursed his folly, but still stood immovable, his stomach in a tight knot.

Mr. Jordan was easy to encourage off. Lord Snow a little more difficult, but she flattered him that the other young ladies were missing his excellent dancing, and he shouldn't deprive them.

But Captain Bowden was full of attentions this evening, and declared himself content to spend the waltz at her side. A quick glance at the duke revealed he had moved several steps forward at the leaving of her two companions, but the width of the room still separated them.

In desperation, Cora asked the captain to fetch her some lemonade. He left, finally, with a gallant speech of his pleasure at doing her bidding.

Cora locked eyes with the duke.

He flickered in and out of her sight, the dancing couples blocking her view of him, and then revealing him, a strobe of visual stimulus. Her breath caught as he walked forward several more steps. Her brain swam with the revolving movement of the couples and the swirling music as she tried to keep her eyes on him.

Another couple passed before him, and he was gone. She had lost sight of him. She sucked in her breath, realized she had been holding it, and looked down at her hands. She inhaled, trying to calm her spinning head.

"Lady Cora." His deep voice washed over her.

He'd finally come. "Your grace."

"May I?"

"Of course."

He sat beside her. Cora looked at him with wide eyes, a small smile pulling at her lips. He was here.

"Have you recovered from the ordeal of the early evening?" Concern warmed his voice.

"More or less. I've felt worn out by it, but . . ."

"But what, my lady?"

"I was happy to see you here, sir, and decided my megrims were not so severe as to warrant leaving." She looked down, nervous from her bold speech.

"Thank you." His voice was deeper with emotion. "I am here only for you." She raised her head. His brilliant blue eyes burned into her. Her heart pounded in her throat.

Oh, his speech was bolder.

"Lady Cora, may I have the honor of the next dance for which you are still free?"

Her smile could not stay controlled now. "The next dance has been reserved for you, your grace. The quadrille. I'm so glad you finally came to claim it."

He raised an eyebrow, and his eyes sparkled. "Reserved for me! I'm glad I have come in time to claim it as well!" His hand moved toward her.

"Lemonade for the lovely Lady Cora!" Captain Bowden strode up, brandishing small cut-glass cups. Cora sat up, stifling her grimace. That had been too short. The duke's eyes shuttered into their severe mask once again. Captain Bowden glanced between them.

She stood, and the duke followed. "Your grace, has Captain Hugh Bowden been introduced to you? Captain Bowden, the Duke of Blackdale."

"A pleasure, sir!" the Captain bowed with a smart click of his heels. "We've fought on the same battlefield, but I don't believe I've been introduced before."

"Captain Bowden," the duke bowed, his face even more severe. "It is good to make your acquaintance."

Cora sat, and the men followed, each on the either side of her. The captain handed her a glass, proclaiming regret that he had only brought two. "And I've already sipped from mine, your grace, unless you should wish it." He lifted the glass and an eyebrow.

The duke waved a hand in negation.

The waltz needed to be done, and soon. Adam wanted his quadrille with Lady Cora, and to pull her away from this popinjay of an officer.

The man was too smooth, too charming, too handsome. And he appeared to be playing everything for a lark.

Adam ground out one-word answers to the officer's questions, and sat next to Cora, aching to sweep her up into his arms, and away.

She turned her glass in her hands, her eyes on it. She seemed to be wilting between them.

"Are you in mourning, your grace?" the captain asked. "You seem to favor black."

Impertinent fellow. "Not formally. I honor the dead of my regiment." His mouth twisted. "And it suits my humor."

Lady Cora had perked, and was watching him with blinking interest. He let a genuine smile touch his lips as he met her gaze.

Finally, the waltz ended. The next set was his. Adam held out his hand to Lady Cora.

"I believe it is our dance, my lady."

She smiled at him with a sweetness in her eyes that took his breath away.

They stood, winded, at the bottom of the set. His side ached. He held himself rigid to conceal it.

Her eyes were beautiful and bright.

Conversation. He must converse with her. "What potted flower would you like to be delivered tomorrow, Lady Cora?"

"Oh!" She smiled. His heart thrummed. "Please, surprise me! They've all been so lovely."

"Have you found good places to put them all?"

"Of course! Though the best place I can't get to—oh!" She fell silent, and looked as if she wished she hadn't spoken.

What was this? "You can't get to the best place to put the flowers?"

Rose suffused her cheeks, and chagrin her face. "We have a lovely orangery at Averill House. I use it for everything, from *Citrus aurantifolia* to *Ananas comosus*—key lime to pineapple—but . . ." Her mouth twisted, she raised her head, but kept her eyes downturned. "But I am currently banned from it."

His brows lowered. "Banned? Why? How?"

"By my mother."

Anger kindled in his gut. The woman was cutting into Lady Cora's happiness.

"She feels I let it distract me from what is important. She's locked it, and refuses to let me tend my plants there." Her mouth tightened.

"And what is more important than your plants, Lady Cora?"

She let out a short laugh, "Thank you, sir, for that kind phrasing. Mother thinks everything is more important than my plants, but most especially, it is important to her for me to behave as a proper lady should."

"Ah." He cast a glance toward the dowager. She was watching them, a scowl on her face. He slitted his eyes. "I have found, in my experience, that mothers are either too over-controlling and protective, or they aren't protective enough." He felt his own mouth twist in a grimace.

He glanced at Lady Cora, and she was frowning at him with a pinched crease between her eyebrows.

He smoothed his expression. "I am sorry your mother is so interfering of your pleasures, Lady Cora."

She gave a wan smile. "Thank you, your grace."

He fidgeted with the edge of his glove. "In Scotland, at the castle—Blackdale Castle, my principal seat—we have an orangery."

"You do?"

Adam could not bring himself to look at her as he said the words, his heart and his stomach too full of trembling to allow it. "Yes, and an old conservatory, in addition to succession houses, and various flower gardens, and . . . many more could be constructed or arranged, should the future lady of the house wish it."

He swallowed. "She would have free reign to do as her heart desired." He slid a look to her upturned face. Her eyes were wide, her mouth parted. He held his breath.

She closed her mouth, and downcast her eyes. "How happy your future duchess will be, your grace, if she is a lover of plants." She angled away her body, disconnecting from him.

No! Why was she turning away? "My fervent hope is that she will be."

She studied him, questions in her eyes, but it was time to rejoin the set, and they were caught up in the dance once more.

He had hinted at marriage, hadn't he? That had seemed to be what he was saying. He'd offered gardens to his future lady!

She'd been offered gardens before, of course, by various suitors. Some from those she knew would only be able to acquire those gardens with her dowry. The Duke of Blackdale, by all accounts, was very rich. If he had gardens, and offered more, they were his to give.

She felt light-headed, and not just because of the steps of the dance.

Mother opposed him. And her word was Cora's law until Cora came of age next year. For longer after that, if Cora needed the money Mother would only offer to a marriage that she approved of.

The duke shouldn't need that money.

Cora watched him. What would it be like to be married to this man?

The dance ended. Adam offered his arm to his beautiful, light-footed lady, and relished her nearness as they walked toward her seat.

She had gone quiet and distracted after his veiled offers. But as he looked down at her face, she turned her blooming cheeks to him and a slow smile lifted them, her face radiant with light.

His heart throbbed in his chest. She was glorious. His love, the woman he would marry.

He covered her gloved hand with his on his arm, and tucked her in as closely as he dared.

Where had her chair been? There.

The dowager stood before the seat Cora had vacated, snapping her fan in her palm. Her expression was forbidding.

Several of Lady Cora's suitors, the carrion birds, were ranged near: the overly pretty officer, and several who Adam had not noticed further than as physical impediments to Lady Cora.

He was loathe to let her go. He wanted to dance a second set with her, and a third. Announce to the world that this was his intended bride. Give them a waltz as the fourth, monopolize her every step, scandalize them all.

Especially her dragon of a mother.

But he returned her. He paused before the dowager, still holding firm Cora's hand on his arm, and let the dowager see them, standing before her, and before all, as a couple.

Only then did he turn, bow over Lady Cora's hand, and release her. "Thank you for the pleasure of the dance, Lady Cora."

"The pleasure was mine, your grace." She curtsied.

"Lady Winfield." He bowed to her mother.

"Duke." Her curtsy was so shallow as to be nonexistent, her head barely inclined in an nod. "Cora, we leave after the next set. There is much we must do tomorrow."

Cora raised her eyebrows. "Has something come up, Mama?"

"Yes, we are leaving town on Friday. I have decided we will spend some time at the Grange before our—" She stopped, and gave him a sharp look. "Our summer engagements begin. We will only have tomorrow to put the house in order before it is shut up for the Season."

Adam grew cold. His mouth tightened. She was taking her away.

"Oh!" Cora sounded surprised. "But you said—" She stopped. "It would be lovely to spend some time at home, Mama."

"Indeed, child. Now, does not Captain Bowden have your next dance?"

And soon Lady Cora was gone, whisked away from him by the officer. Adam bowed stiffly to the steely-eyed dowager, and left without a word.

Chapter Seven

His Addresses

THURSDAY, JULY 4, 1816, MORNING

She was leaving tomorrow. He had to act now.

He took extra care over his toilet, hassled Malcolm over the closeness of his shave and on the set of his hair: short cropped and combed precisely forward a la Caesar, his side whiskers long but sharply trimmed. None of the wildness currently in fashion for him.

For his cravat, he chose white today, representative of purity and optimism. Also symbolic of death in Oriental cultures. His mouth twisted at the irony of that.

He chose an emerald stick pin. Reminiscent of her eyes, though hers were lighter.

His morning dress was of buckskin breeches, fawn waistcoat, black coat, and black Hessian boots shined to mirrors. His phaeton was waiting downstairs, Charlie Coachman grumbling at being relegated to groomsman, rather than coachman, with this vehicle.

He viewed himself with a critical eye. It would do.

Malcolm did an excellent job, both of his valet duties, and his information gathering. The ladies were at home to visitors this afternoon, and had been receiving quite a few, according to Malcolm's remarkable network of informants.

"Well?"

"Yes, your grace?"

"Am I acceptable?"

"Of course, your grace!" Malcolm pretended to be insulted. "If you are not found acceptable to the lady's mother, it will not be by any fault of dress."

"Thank you, Malcolm. And thank you for all your extra work. I greatly appreciate it."

Malcolm let his slow, lazy smile reveal itself. "You've paid well for it, your grace."

"Worth every penny, as usual, Malcolm. Now, we'll see if all the attention was enough."

"Good luck, your grace."

"Thank you."

And Adam left to face destiny, his stomach in knots.

Adam was shown into the drawing room, but was informed the ladies had just retired from morning calls to rest before their evening's entertainments, and that "the dowager countess will not be home to visitors for the rest of the afternoon."

"Please take my card, and let the dowager countess know the Duke of Blackdale requests an audience."

"Yes, your grace."

The officious butler left him cooling his heels for fifteen minutes. He knew the time exactly, as he checked his pocket watch every five minutes and forced himself not to fidget.

Several of his potted flowers were in the room. He touched a leaf on the crocus. It was in full bloom. The one he sent this morning wasn't here.

Done with waiting, he left the room, ignored the footman, and went down a connecting hall. He had a vague idea where the orangery might be in the dowager's townhouse.

There it was, and there she was.

Lady Cora Winfield stood surrounded by lush plant life, a smock protecting her dress, her hands bare and plunged into dark soil.

He watched her for a few moments. She transferred seedlings to larger pots, and arranged the pots on the floor and on terraced tables.

The room was illuminated by cloud-filtered sun, and warmed by a brazier. She looked luminous in the refracted light, her pale hair falling in careless ringlets from a fetching upsweep.

His flower of the day, a pink *Hyacinthus orientalis,* was near her side. He'd been sure to get the Latin designation from the shopkeeper.

His heart swelled in his chest. Here was the lady of his choice, a bright flower of loveliness, grace, caring, and originality. And thoughtlessness and single-minded determination.

She had defended herself from unwanted advances with over-ripe fruit and clipping shears. She had been glorious. And she hadn't paid attention to the cattiness of Miss Basil, taking it all in stride in her single-minded determination to save their abused fruit tree. He let the smile he had wanted to show last night spread over his face.

What a wonderful creature she was, his lady. She would be his happiness, he knew it.

He took another step into the windowed room, and she looked up, startled.

"Oh!" Her vibrant green eyes widened at the sight of him, her dirty hands flew out of the soil, and into the folds of her smock, specks of damp earth scattering around at her abrupt movement. A fiery blush wreathed her cheeks, and her eyes lowered. "My lord duke." She curtseyed, awkward with her hands so covered.

"Pardon me, my lady," he bowed. "I'm being intolerably rude. I left the drawing room without a by-your-leave."

"Oh, come in, I suppose. Or not . . ."

"I think it will be fine, with the door open, and so many windows." He stepped further into the humid room. "You are in your orangery."

"Yes, because we're leaving, Mama agreed to let me arrange things here for our departure."

"I am glad." He smiled at her.

She gave an answering smile, but it was wan, and didn't reach her eyes.

He realized that her face wasn't serene, as he thought it had been. Her cheeks were streaked with half-dry tears, and her eyes were bright because the green irises were ringed with red from weeping.

"My lady! You have been crying." He moved closer to her in concern.

"It is nothing. Tears of frustration." She covered her face with her muddy smock to wipe it, and streaked her cheeks with mud. "Oh dear, I've made it worse, haven't I?"

"Yes, you did." He pulled out his handkerchief, very willing to sacrifice it to this cause. "Here, let me. Do you have fresh water?"

Tears swelled in her eyes. "Oh, this is silly," she sniffed, hurried over to a basin in the corner, and poured water from the ewer. She washed her dirty hands and face, and came back fresh and smiling politely.

He put the handkerchief away, disappointed that he hadn't had the chance to use it. "May I ask why you were crying, Lady Cora?"

She sighed. "Mother's announcement last night started a cascade. All the suitors who have been courting me, and a few others that really haven't, decided they must all act quickly. They all came to ask for my hand today. It's been a trying morning."

Adam stiffened. All of them? "And what has been the result?"

"Thankfully, Mother turned several away as unsuitable, or not quite up to her standards. The four she allowed through as acceptable enough . . ."

Four? Panic tried to rise up in Adam's throat and he swallowed it down. He had not felt threatened by her attentive court before—much—but the possibility of her being stolen away from him before he could even declare himself gripped him. His eyes locked on Lady Cora's. His breath arrested in his chest.

"I had to listen as graciously as I could, and . . ." Her eyes were wide. Her recitation was too slow. Adam stood frozen. Why would she not just say it?

She swallowed. "I turned them all down." She finished in a rush, and turned back to her seedlings. "It was difficult to dash the hopes of four men in the space of less hours."

She'd turned them down. He could have swayed in relief, but didn't allow himself. "None were in consideration?" His voice was rough with strain, and he swallowed again to clear it.

She let out an unhappy laugh. "Oh, I've considered. Weighed options, evaluated, imagined, asked questions . . ." Her hands grew still. He studied her profile. "None who've yet offered have been quite what I feel I want for my happiness."

She looked at him, a quick dart of the eyes, and then looked down on her plants once more with a sigh. Her shoulders rolled forward, and tears looked about to fall afresh. He reached out a hand, but withdrew it as she shook herself and straightened again.

"So." She became brisk and matter of fact. She gathered two pots and moved them to a low shelf. "Yet another Season ends, and I am still unwed." She bustled about, cleaning up the mess of plants and dirt.

He probed. "Did you wish for different, my lady?'"

"Yes." She kept her back to him. "I started the Season with firm goals and a resolution that I'd find someone acceptable, and that I would accept him. But, when faced with my final options this morning, I couldn't. It's too important and too permanent to . . ."

"To settle?" He finished for her.

"That is an unkind way to state it, but yes."

"And now you prepare your plants to be without you again."

"Yes. I am always having to leave my plants." She scooted a small pot into alignment with its neighbors. "I start them, or continue the process, cultivate while I am here, and then have to leave them to others. Sometimes when I come back, they have thrived. Sometimes, they are dead and gone." Her face was sad. "I have to always be willing to let them go. Else I would just be very unhappy." She placed another pot on a low table and stepped back. "I do what I can for them, leave them in a good place, and let go." She analyzed the placement, and nodded. "It is the best I can do for them."

"Would you like a place you wouldn't have to leave? A permanent spot of ground that you could cultivate all year round, yours alone?"

A sad smile tugged at her mouth. "That'd be an unwise hope, I fear. Under my mother, and most any husband I might marry, I will always be called upon to leave my plants. And to leave them to others."

"I would give you such a place. Several such places, to do with as you pleased."

She sucked in a breath and looked at him with wide eyes.

"Will you consider me, my lady? Have you considered me?"

Her mouth trembled. Her bottom lip retreated, and her eyes grew bright with unshed tears. "I—I cannot. I have, but I cannot."

"Why not, my lady?

"I—I'm sorry, your grace. My mother . . ."

She took control of herself, and clasped her hands in front of her body. Her chin raised, and her eyes reached the level his throat. She stopped. "Oh! you're wearing a white cravat today." Her voice was full of surprise.

Irrelevant. "Yes, my lady, I am. Your mother?"

"She doesn't think you are suitable, your grace." She said it low, almost a whisper, her face drained of color. She twisted her hands together.

"I . . . am not suitable." Adam's mind stuttered over this strange, foreign thought. "It may be . . . hubris to say, but may I ask in what way I would be considered unsuitable?"

"I'm afraid, my lord duke, that it is because all your holdings are in Scotland."

"Because I am a Scot?" Anger burst through him.

"Because your principle seat is hundreds of miles from the land that will be mine one day. Mother feels I should not be that far away from our land. It cannot be properly cared for by an absent mistress." She spoke quickly. "That is why, sir, and that is only why. It's not because of anything to do with yourself."

"Just my ancestral seat, the definition of who I am and all my responsibilities in life. Nothing to do with me at all." The words came out harshly bitter.

"I . . ."

"My lord duke."

An officious male voice cut into their argument. The butler had found him. Adam spun to the servant standing stiffly in the doorway, and barked out. "Yes?"

"Her ladyship the Dowager Countess of Winfield will see you now, your grace."

Oh, she would, would she?

"About time." He turned back to Lady Cora, who stood still, her face stricken. He couldn't . . . He bowed stiffly. "Pardon me, Lady Cora."

He turned with military precision and followed the butler out the door.

As he walked, Adam strove with internal violence to gain control of himself.

If he was to convince the dowager that he would be a good husband for her daughter when she had already decided against him, he must be polite. It would be better to be openly engaging, like his brother, who seemed to be able to win anyone to his side, especially females. Or like Lord Eastham, whose indifference paired with flattering words seemed to draw the ladies in.

But he was none of those things. He had control and politeness, and that would have to do.

The butler went in before him, and Adam took calming breaths. His ribs hurt and he could feel a headache forming at the back of his tense neck.

"The dowager countess will see you, my lord duke."

Adam entered the gold-toned lady's sitting room with barely a glance at his surroundings.

The Dowager Countess Theresa Averill Winfield sat on a settee, but rose when he came in. A rich cap covered her copper hair, and her day dress was of burnt orange.

She was tall for a woman, taller than her daughter, with strong features and a wide mouth.

It was pressed with disapproval.

"My lord Duke of Blackdale. I have risen from my couch to meet with you this afternoon out of respect for your rank, but it has been a trying morning, and I wish to be through with this conversation quickly."

Adam felt rigidness take over his body, leaving him still and silent as she continued.

"You are here to request the honor of paying your addresses to my daughter, the Lady Cora Winfield, are you not?"

This statement, barely a question and with no form of politeness, made him want to deny all intentions and leave immediately. But that would be counterproductive, if anything could be productive in this situation. He forced his stiff neck to nod.

"I'm afraid I must inform you that I do not feel you would be a suitable husband for my daughter, and that I must refuse my consent."

She ended with resolution, as if that was all there was to say. Silence rang through the room.

Adam dragged his voice out of his chest. "May I ask your reasons for refusing your consent, my lady?" His men would have seen how dangerous a mood he was in. But this woman did not seem to realize it.

"You may," she stated. "The first and foremost reason is that of your principle seat and all your land holdings being in Scotland. Lady Cora is my heir, the only child of the Averill line. She will inherit extensive holdings in East Anglia, lands my family has cultivated for generations. They ought not to be neglected by an absentee mistress, to fall into carelessness and abandonment.

"If she is hundreds of miles away, bearing children and not able to travel, she will not be able to do otherwise. It would fall to stewards, and not have the careful oversight of the true mistress. The Averill lands should not be relegated to second and third thoughts and distance."

Adam breathed out. This was a valid concern, and he had some answers for it. "Roads are improving every year, as are communications. She would be able to visit more easily than previous generations have. And she would not need to look after her lands on her own. I would help her as well."

"Yes, I assumed you would give such a response. And that a duke would not consider my family's lands as a deterrent, when so many of your lands scarcely see your personal oversight, I'm sure."

He stood silent. The lands had been overseen by stewards for years. Adam had continued to soldier, despite having come into his title. But he had begun to step into his role with full attention and diligence after Waterloo. The stewards were finding him now an attentive and exacting landholder. And some had found themselves replaced.

"But I have additional objections to your suit. I have looked into you, Duke, and I know of your family and estates. I have several objections on that score.

"You are very rich, with the majority of your wealth coming from coal mining. My bright child of flowers and sunlight to be associated with dark coal mines, and soot? No, the mind shudders."

"I would not ask her to go into the coal mines, Dowager Countess."

She sniffed. "Clean and wholesome farming by tenants is the right way for the landed nobility to gain our wealth. I do not approve of anything else."

Adam gave her his coldest stare. "Indeed. But not all land is arable, my lady. Do you object to sheep as well? The non-arable lands are extensively used by shepherds. Wool and mutton are not quite wholesome enough for you, I am sure."

"They are not, if by non-arable, you are referring to the so called 'modernization' of the Highlands. The Highland Clearances? I know for a fact that your estates were involved." Her eyes gleamed with malicious triumph. "How do you justify that, Duke? Tenant farmers thrown off lands they've been on for generations. It is abominable. I do not condone such actions, and I know my daughter will not as well!"

Adam's stomach twisted. Yes, many Blackdale tenants had been cleared off their lands and left homeless. It was still happening elsewhere in the Highlands. "My father was involved in that. His death put a stop to it on Blackdale land, and I will not continue. I oppose it as well." It wouldn't happen again wherever he had control. But in many cases, the damage was done. The tenants were gone.

"Your wealth was gained from coal and the misery of your tenants, but also, much came previously from the horrors of the slave trade."

Anger stirred in Adam again. "Previously, madam. We do own a merchant fleet. In my father and grandfather's day, those ships were involved in the slave trade. But that aspect has been abandoned. We no longer deal in slaves."

"But slavery still touches your life, does it not, Duke? Do you not have several negroes on your estate in Scotland, and have even brought some to London?"

"Yes, madam, I have former slaves in my employ. They are fully paid and well treated."

"My daughter has never been touched by such matters."

"She lives in England, my lady. If she has eaten sugarcane, she has been touched by the slave trade."

The dowager countess ignored this. "And then there is your brother."

"My brother? Of which brother do you speak, madam? The lost and lamented sea captain, or the war hero?"

"The hero, of course, the one who has been gallivanting around London since the war, proving himself the most dangerous rake to ever cross the path of susceptible females. I know of at least two by-blows he has helped foist on respectable men, destroying those marriages, and two other young ladies he has ruined. He has humiliated his wife and made a laughing stock of several respectable men. You, sir, when you marry, will have to worry about the virtue of your wife whenever your brother draws near her, but that wife will not be my innocent daughter!"

Humiliated anger swirled in Adam's stomach at this hit. His brother Jude's escapades were a source of frustration and chagrin. He was paying for the upkeep of two of Jude's castoff women and their bastard children already. He was sure that had been hushed, so Lady Winfield must have information on two others he hadn't been aware of, likely because he hadn't needed to be applied to for money on their upkeep. They were legally the children of the cuckolded husbands, despite they not being the fathers.

"What can you say to that, duke?"

"Little, madam. He is as you describe." He could not leave it at that. "But I would shield any wife of mine from Jude's philandering."

"He would likely see that as a challenge."

The thought of Jude touching Cora . . . Adam swallowed down the bile of rage that rose in his throat. He'd kill him, hero of Waterloo or no. Adam closed his eyes to regain control of his emotions, breathing in through his nostrils. "Are you quite done, my lady?"

"I have two more reasons, sir." She seemed to pause, and consider her words for once. "There is the issue of Waterloo."

She dared speak of it! "Waterloo?" His voice was a low whisper.

"Your regiment, my lord duke, was nearly decimated. Some of the heaviest losses in a battle of heavy losses."

The screams of his dying men rose around him, the panic seized his stomach once more. The blood, the booming shots, the impotent terror of being left on the field, the rain on his parched and broken lips, the ruddy mud seeping into his woolen uniform . . .

"Yes, Madame."

"I cannot imagine how an officer could allow his men to stand still under such bombardment, and not retreat. Their position was surely not worth all of their lives—"

Adam moved with a jerk, stepping dangerously near her with fists balled. He caught himself before he touched her, his mouth curling into a snarl. "My men died."

Mere inches separated them now. Her eyes were wide, but her jaw was set, and she did not look away.

He must answer her. "I have thought long, have analyzed, what I could have done differently. But Wellington himself has not questioned me on the results of that battle. The causes are known, just as they were unpreventable at the time.

"I was hit, Madame, grazed by a cannonball. I fell from my horse and was knocked unconscious. My men thought me dead. One lieutenant was already dead, another died soon after. And the order to retreat never reached them. They held that position because they thought it was vital. The soldiers were too inexperienced to know that they should break and fall back. They came under heavy cannon and rocket fire. It ripped through them."

He backed away from her, the panic of waking buried under the bodies of his men, soaked and sticky from their blood threatened to overwhelm him. He blocked it from his mind, carefully filling his chest with air and exhaling slowly. His lungs worked, there was enough air, his ribs were healed. They only twinged a little.

He calmed enough to finish what he was willing to say. "I knew nothing of this until I awoke to lucidity hours later."

He walked over to a flowering plant on a side board. The petals were yellow, the leaves long. One of Lady Cora's, he was sure. It was lush and beautiful, like the lady herself. The lady he was being denied.

"Whether that will satisfy your ignorant prejudice on matters of the battle, Lady Winfield, it does not matter. You've made yourself very clear." He looked over at her. Her lips were pursed and scowling.

He turned to face her once again. "Ah, but you had one more complaint against me, did you not? I shall not deny you a final opportunity to insult me."

She narrowed her eyes at him.

"I bring up the continued issue of the character of your father."

The calm Adam had won fled from him. His back stiffened to steel. His jaw strained.

"I knew something of your father's temperament and actions from your mother, but only a little. I appealed to your mother's other friends, who corresponded with her more closely than I. Their reports, if true, and even tempered by years, are shocking. Brutality to servants, and harsh treatment to his wife and children."

"My father is dead." Adam's voice was slow and lethally quiet.

"Brutality in a sire often repeats in the children, your grace. In sons especially."

"Enough," Adam whispered.

"You are the very image of your father."

"That is enough." Adam's spine trembled and a sharp pain ripped through his chest and arm. He clenched his hands to stop their shaking. "I have heard enough."

"Then you fully understand, my lord duke, why I will never allow my daughter to marry a man such as you. My every feeling as a mother forbids it."

"You are mistaken in my character, madam. I am nothing like my father."

He felt his face tighten as he struggled to control his expression. "I will prove it now, to myself if not to you, by leaving immediately. "

He turned away from her and walked out.

A door banged. Rapid thunks of fast steps came from the stairs. Cora stopped her pacing, and went to the library window. The front door slammed. The duke's tall black-coated form rushed down the front steps of the town house and paused at the empty curb side.

A chill rain was falling, and for the last hour, the Duke of Blackdale's groom had been circling his phaeton around the square to keep the horses from suffering.

The duke stalked around to meet it across the square. He was bare-headed and handed. He hadn't stopped to allow the butler to retrieve his hat and gloves. The rain was hitting his short cropped black hair as he half-ran though the storm.

He leaped into the carriage without letting his groom slow for him.

She watched the phaeton pass by the front of the townhouse. The duke kept his eyes forward. His face was terrible, a strange mix of tight strain, rage, and despair. She blinked. Surely she had misinterpreted his expression?

The carriage was past, and he was gone.

Cora's stomach was shaking, a spasm of tension and distress. She felt sick. She wiped her clammy hands on her skirt, and discovered they were shaking as well.

She went to the sitting room. Mother was standing at the window, staring out. Had she watched the duke's flight from their home?

"Mother, what did you say to him?"

She turned to look at Cora, her face tight. Then she turned away, and began pacing, back and forth across the room.

"I should tell you, should I not? So you know my reasons?" She turned front then back. "I refused my consent to his paying his addresses to you."

"Because his lands are so far away from the Averill lands, right, Mother?"

"I have more reasons than that. They are damning. And I will tell you them." She stopped, stood still. "In addition to being a Scottish nobleman, most of his wealth is from coal mining, not agriculture. And his family has previously been involved in the slave trade and the Highland Clearances, all abominable practices. And his brother is a dangerous rake that I do not want near you."

"Oh, Mother." Cora's heart was sinking into her stomach.

"And I spoke of the decimation of his regiment at Waterloo."

"Oh, Mother, you didn't! He was gravely injured at Waterloo! They thought he was dead!"

"So he said. And then I brought up his father."

"His father?"

"I have made inquiries. His father was a brutal, unprincipled man." Mother faced her. "Men often become like their fathers, Cora."

Cora sat down. "Did he have an answer to that?"

"He claimed he was not like his father, of course."

"I see." Cora buried her hands into her hair to relieve the tension in her scalp, and yanked at the pins.

She stood and paced a few steps. "Was that necessary, Mother? To bring up all those painful things and throw them in his face?"

"Yes, because they were my reasons. The location of his lands alone would not be enough to deter a duke from what he wanted. Now, he should never approach you again."

To never have him come near her again. Cora's eyes burned.

"I think, Mother, that you were brutal." She turned, and fled the room, ignoring Mother's shocked "Cora!" behind her.

Chapter Eight

Abduction

Adam reached Blackdale House, his head shamefully bare, and mobilized the household. "I am leaving for Scotland in the morning."

He left instructions for his traveling carriage and baggage to be prepared for early departure, and for the rest of the servants to close up the house and follow in easy stages with his cattle. He then went up to his room with the intention of getting dead drunk.

He made it through two glasses of scotch before his spinning mind slowed to a form of brilliant clarity.

He was not his father. But if that woman—he almost spat, but restrained himself—expected him to behave as a son of his father would . . .

He should oblige her.

He rang for Malcolm, and composed a list of vital purchases he must acquire before the shops closed for the night.

Malcolm held the list of items with two fingers, staring at it like it threatened to ignite his world with uncomfortable inconvenience, which, Adam reasoned, it would.

"Is this not a bit drastic, your grace?"

"It is expedient."

"Well, I suppose half the ton will pretend to be shocked but actually think it quite romantic, and you'll be forgiven in a year or two."

Adam turned to the fireplace and stared into the blaze. "Romantic. Quite."

After Malcolm left, Adam went down and spoke more frankly to Charlie Coachman. Adam trusted him to go willingly along with anything his duke proposed to do. Adam gave him specific instructions for the following day.

And then Adam went to find Kate.

Friday, July 5, 1816, morning

Adam shifted against the padded back of his large traveling carriage, his ribs aching. The back of his head pounded and pulled with the tension of his restless night. He had planned and stewed, had second thoughts and reversals till around three in the morning, when he had finally fallen into a desperate sleep.

But he had made his decision, and had set his plan in motion. Now he only had to accomplish the steps.

On his lap he held a cluster of white narcissus in a sturdy pot. He had ordered it a week ago, and it had arrived this morning. He had intended it to be the next gift in his courtship. Now it was a key part of his plan.

The scent of the flowers was strong, a deep, heady perfume. They filled the coach with their narcotic aroma, and muddled his thinking.

Malcolm slitted his eyes at him from the backward-facing seat. The batman turned valet was already snoozing, or pretending to, pointedly ignoring Adam's restlessness in the seat across from him.

Adam watched the street out the window. His stomach was a tight knot. He straightened his legs out, and cocked them back into right angles at the knees. They were passing by Hyde Park.

Unexpectedly, the carriage turned into one of the entrances, and went down the drive. Adam frowned and called out to his coachman, "Charlie, why did you turn into the park?"

"You're going to see the young lassie, aye, your grace? I spotted her; she's walking in the park."

She was? Adam swung back and forth between the windows, searching for her. Ah, there she was! Walking on a path in a pelisse and blue cloak, bundled against the chill, a bandbox under her arm.

"Thank you, Charlie! Pull up near."

Adam scanned the vicinity. Where was her maid? She looked quite alone.

What was this? Some strange blessing from God? Unlikely, with what he had in mind. But still, there she was.

"You didn't expect her here, your grace?" Malcolm was wide awake now.

"No, but I'll take it."

Adam put the potted flowers in their crate on the floor at his feet, and joined Malcolm in closing the curtains in the carriage. Adam pulled out a velvet bag. It contained a few key items. He pulled from its confines three freshly starched white cravats. He ignored Malcolm's confused "Your grace?" at the sight of them.

The coach stopped.

Adam took a deep breath to compose himself, opened both carriage doors wide, and jumped down out of the coach.

The air outside was shockingly chill for July. Autumn was here and summer had never come.

Lady Cora Winfield was walking with a distracted air on a trail adjacent to the carriage path. She hadn't noticed his carriage or him coming from it.

He left the carriage doors open, and walked toward her.

"Lady Cora."

She looked up at him, her delicate mouth a small O of surprise. "My lord duke!" She curtsied. He bowed and tipped his second-best beaver, never taking his eyes off her face.

Her nose and cheeks were reddened in the cold, but additional color flooded her cheeks under his regard. His heart beat faster and his shoulders relaxed a small amount as he reached her. Her presence seemed to excite and soothe his body at the same time. He felt a small smile of wonder reach his face at how standing near her made him feel happier.

He wanted to never leave her side. If his plan was successful, he should be able to accomplish that.

"This is unexpected, meeting you here." She faltered, looked confused, and started again. "I was actually coming to see you."

"You were?" He was surprised.

"Yes, to return to you this." She held out the band box, a plain one, white with a blue trim around the lid rim. He looked at it in confusion.

"I'm sorry, we don't have any boxes for men's hats at our house, so I put your hat and gloves in one of my bandboxes. I realize it's odd. But you left them, you see, and no one returned them to you." She broke off.

His heart filled with gratitude and love for this young woman. She was kind, his lady, and she cared about him enough to return these things to him. He felt his heart fill as he lifted his hands to take the offered bandbox from her.

She had been coming alone to see him.

"Thank you, Lady Cora, I am grateful." He moved to her side, and walked forward. She automatically fell into step with him, bringing them closer to his coach. "I was coming to see you as well."

"You were? But the servants would not have let you in, that's why I was coming alone, I . . ." She dropped off in embarrassment.

He quirked a smile. "I thought they might not. But I hoped to entice you out anyway. I have a gift for you, another flower."

"Oh?"

"Yes, a narcissus. Particularly, a *Narcissus papyraceusm*, as you would likely call it."

"Oh, a paperwhite! How wonderful!"

"The nursery owner told me it's of a rare variety, with a sweeter scent than most paperwhites. And he trained it to be shorter, of a height more appropriate to the indoors. It's in my carriage now, if you'd like to see it."

"I'd love to." She smiled.

They walked forward together and reached his carriage. Malcolm handed out the potted narcissus to Adam. He presented it to Lady Cora.

"Oh, how lovely!" she looked at it in delight, and took the pot into her gloved hands. Her attention was caught by the multiple blooms.

Adam gave a glance around. There were no people in their vicinity of the park on this cold morning, and Charlie Coachman had presciently positioned the coach near a stand of high bushes that would obscure the view of the coach from distant onlookers. The coach itself blocked the views from the street.

Adam caught Charlie Coachman's eye and gave him a nod. He tipped his hat with a returning nod, and controlled the restless horses.

Adam handed the band box up to Malcolm. He took it with a quirk of his head.

Lady Cora buried her face in the blossoms. "Oh, it smells lovely! Definitely sweeter than paperwhites often smell."

Adam moved to stand behind Lady Cora, judging her size and weight. She wasn't a small woman, so he would have to be careful, swift, and use all his strength. He braced himself for the pain that was about to come from his ribs, focused his mind and readied his body.

"The scent of paperwhites is contended, actually," she chatted. "Some people love it, and others think it doesn't smell good at all. I'm fortunate to love the smell. I think—"

He reached around her head and clapped his hand over her mouth. He stooped, encircled her ribcage, pinned her arms, and lifted her body. With the side of his knee, he swept her legs out from the ground, and in a smooth continuous movement, kept his leg going upward to step directly into the carriage. Her extra weight almost over-balanced him to fall back, but he pushed against his supporting leg and barreled forward, half falling onto the seat with his burden tucked into him.

Lady Cora gave a muffled scream. Malcolm closed the doors with haste.

Charlie Coachman yipped the horses into motion, and the carriage gave a lurch. It settled into a steady, town-appropriate pace. Adam had given him strict instructions to drive normally in town to allay suspicion.

Adam's burden was squirming and fighting his hold.

"Malcolm!" His voice was tight with the strain. She was kicking, and wildly shaking her head, trying to fight her way out of his hold. "Bind her feet with a cravat!"

"Your grace?" Malcolm voice was shocked and dismayed. Adam had to convince him to help him quickly.

"Paris, Malcolm! Like Paris!"

"Paris." Malcolm muttered, but did as Adam asked. He skillfully held her skirt-tangled legs together from the side, restrained her kicks, and bound her legs above the ankle.

She screamed against Adam's hand, opening her mouth as wide as she could against his large hand. He tried to keep her delicate lower jaw clamped shut, but she soon had her mouth open despite his efforts, and tried to bite his hand. He released her mouth in time to save his palm from being mauled. She got out several loud screams. He held her upper body better with two arms, and constrained her as she bucked against him, but screams from a carriage on a London morning would draw attention.

"A gag, Malcolm," he said through clenched teeth.

Malcolm gave a curse, but grabbed the next cravat, and knelt over them. He got the cravat wrapped around her head and around her mouth like the expert at trussing that he was.

As soon as her screams were gagged, Adam used one hand to clench her wrists together and urged Malcolm to use the last cravat. His valet tied her hands together in front of her. Not the most secure way to tie a prisoner, but Adam was kidnapping his bride, not arresting a traitor to the crown.

He hoped to keep her as comfortable as possible in the circumstances.

The fight left Lady Cora's body. She collapsed in limp exhaustion against him, wheezing through the gag.

She was crying.

Of course she is crying, Adam Douglas. She has been horribly treated.

Malcolm sat back in his seat. They all panted into the sudden quiet of the carriage interior. His eyes were wide, staring at Lady Cora. Adam supposed Malcolm was staring at what he had just done.

Adam would have to make it up to him somehow, this loyalty into criminal activity.

Adam's ribs were screaming in pain, strained by his wrenching effort. His every breath in and out hurt, but he fought through it, needing the air. Lady Cora's limp weight was pressing on his ribs. Adam caught his breath, and gingerly moved her off him, and onto the seat beside him. He moved over and turned to see her clearly.

Her hair was a mess, pulled and straggling in wild wisps around her head. The gag was stretching her face in uncomfortable ways, and likely pulling at her hair.

Her hands twisted in their restraints, still fighting though the rest of her body had given up.

He forced himself to look full into her face. Tears streamed from eyes that were shut tight. Shuddering sobs wracked her body.

He had done this to her. A lance of pain went through Adam's chest.

It was necessary. He cooled his heart, straightened his spine, and spoke calmly. "Lady Cora."

Her eyes flew open with a look of blazing, murderous rage. She gave a several syllable shriek against her gag.

His gentle lady of flowers could look murderous? Fascinating. He filed that away to be considered when he had greater leisure.

"Lady Cora, please do not be afraid." His voice was calm and chill. He couldn't afford to warm it. "We will not harm you. My intent is not to harm you."

She gave another muffled holler through the gag, but he kept talking. "I am taking you to Scotland. You will be as well treated as we can afford while still accomplishing our goal of getting you to Scotland."

She looked bewildered through her rage, and gave a sound comprehensible as "Why?"

He hesitated. This was not how a man wanted to propose to his bride. It would be better if she were feeling less murderous toward him when he brought up their marriage.

Would she feel anything but murderous toward him ever again?

Of course she would. Adam forced the thought back. "Be assured that you are physically safe, and will not be hurt . . . or," he stuttered, glancing at her legs, "or violated any further."

She shrank away from him, trying to tuck her legs against herself. She got as far away from him as she could in the small, confined space. Her face was full of shock and betrayal.

Adam took her expression into his mind and locked it down. He would examine it all later, and feel it more fully. He clenched his jaw and forced his expression into a controlled mask.

Chapter Nine

Words

Friday, July 5, 1816, morning

Cora could not believe this was happening to her. Her body ached, exhausted from the fruitless fight she had waged. Her saliva was soaking the gag that pulled her mouth tight and immovable. She could taste the starch in the linen as it lost its crispness. She wheezed though the gag. Her nose was stuffed and running from her uncontrollable crying. She was crying! She was so angry!

The man who had smiled at her so kindly, the man who had looked at her with gratitude and with what she had thought was love, was gone. In his place was a cold monster with hard eyes.

He was cool and clinical. His jaw was tight. She looked away from him, and refused to look at him anymore.

He was sitting next to her, close, too close in the confines of the carriage. He was turned in toward her, and his knees kept touching hers. She drew away as far as she could.

He had trapped her, confined her with his arms and body. She was tied, snared, helpless.

The gag was pulling her hair in the back. Her hairpins were digging into her scalp. The ties around her ankles were tight. She pulled against the ties on her wrists, twisting, trying to get her hands free.

Scotland! To his home? Why ever for? He didn't need her money; her mother had been sure of that. He didn't need an heiress to marry. Why was he doing this?

Her hair was falling into her face, and she couldn't move it. Her nose was clogged and running from her uncontrollable sobs, but she couldn't wipe it, she couldn't reach her handkerchief. She looked at her bound hands. White linen. A cravat.

She couldn't speak, not to be understood. This horrible gag!

She sniffed, trying to keep mucus from running down her face and into her gagged mouth. The thought of it brought fresh tears into her eyes, and made the runny nose worse. She stared at her linen constraints. She could wipe her nose on them. But to do that in front of his man! He was still looking at her, she could feel it.

"Here, my lady."

A white handkerchief was put into her hands. She looked up. It was the servant who had bound her. Her eyes widened, but she moved the handkerchief to her face with her bound hands. She blew her nose forcefully and wiped her face with the linen. She took a long sniff through her nose, so grateful to be able to breathe.

"Thank you, Malcolm, I didn't realize—thank you." The duke said.

She stared at her feet, and noticed dirt smeared on her hem. The narcissus!

She sat forward, and searched in the dim light of the curtained windows for the poor flower. It had fallen from her hands in the struggle. There was the pot, on its side, its contents spilled onto the floor. Their struggling boots had ground in the dirt and scattered it on the carpeted floor. Where was the narcissus?

She gave a muffled cry of dismay when she spotted it, stems half-crushed and on its side, its bulbs pitifully exposed.

"Oh!" The duke followed her gaze. "The flowers."

"Your grace, I shall—" his servant began.

"No, let me." The duke held out a hand to keep his servant in his seat, leaned down, and picked up the pot. Cora watched with wide eyes as he moved onto one knee and scooped the dirt back into the pot with his black gloved hands. He picked up the fallen flower with an appearance of gentleness and care.

He sat back, and balanced the pot between his black-breech-clad knees. She wanted to take it from him, and use her expert care to try and save the flowers, but her hands were tied and her mouth was gagged. He dug and rearranged the dirt with clumsy fingers. He planted the bulbs back into the soil, and patted the earth around the bent and bedraggled stems. He did a better job than could be expected from a duke and a kidnapper.

He held the pot out to her, "Are my efforts adequate, my lady?"

She didn't look at his face—couldn't look at it—but she inclined her head. He pulled the crumpled handkerchief out of her fingers. She felt bereft without it. Her dismayed protest locked in her throat. He placed the flower pot into her bound hands. His right hand rested against hers for a second before withdrawing. His touch burned with cold even through the double layer of their gloves. She shrank away, and pulled the flowers in close to her. The pot's weight calmed her slightly, and tears pressed behind her eyes once more.

"Could some water be of benefit to the flowers, my lady?" The servant asked with what she normally would have interpreted as gentle politeness, but now had no basis of judgement to know anything. She had lost her foundation. Her roots were ripped from their bedrock and lay exposed on shifting sands.

She lifted her head, and gave him a slight nod. The servant opened a carriage basket and pulled out a water skein. He reached across and trickled water on the soil around the damaged flowers. It was enough. She stopped him by straightening a few of her fingers.

"Thank you, Malcolm." the duke said.

She pushed the pot down between her skirted legs and held it tight with her knees. The carriage jostled and bounced through London's streets. She pushed at the bulbs in the soil with her finger tips to arrange them more perfectly, trying it keep her elbows in close. She didn't want to brush against the duke. She ripped off the most damaged of the stems, leaves, and petals, all that were too destroyed to recover. Her shoulders relaxed slightly as she cared for her flowers.

"Your grace, we are reaching the crossroads where Kate is waiting." More light from the cloudy day outside entered the carriage as the servant, the duke's valet from his clothing, checked outside through the curtains.

"Good," the duke said. "Help her in as quickly as you can." He twisted, took out a carriage blanket and reached over Cora. He draped it over her legs. She pulled back, tucking the flowerpot into her chest to avoid being touched by him.

The blanket was red and black plaid, probably a Scottish tartan. She stared at it. Scotland. He was taking her to Scotland. Surely not because he wanted to marry her. Reasonable men did not kidnap their brides, not outside of melodrama. And in melodrama, kidnappers were villains to be vanquished.

He had wanted to marry her yesterday. Mother had refused him in the most insulting way Mother could manage. Her mother was capable of insulting people very thoroughly. This man was a duke, almost the highest rank in the land. He was surely used to getting his own way.

Was this revenge against her mother for her insults, pure and simple? Ruin her daughter and dump her somewhere public for her mother to discover her? Ravish her and make sure it was reported in all the news sheets?

Cora cringed at that thought. He said he wouldn't 'violate' her further. But what was a word of honor to a kidnapper?

The servant, Malcolm, was looking through the curtains.

"Help her in," the duke said.

The carriage slowed to a stop, as at a curb.

"Yes, your grace." Malcolm moved to open the carriage doors.

The duke swung around to face Cora. He leaned in close, and took her face in both of his gloved hands. Cora pressed back as far as she could into the velvet padded seat-back. He moved his face toward hers until there was barely an inch between them. Cora's eyes unfocused. He was too close.

What was he doing? Was he going to kiss her? Where would he kiss her, on her horribly stretched lips, around the soggy gag?

"It will be alright." The duke's hot breath hit her face with each syllable.

Chills erupted up Cora's back and neck, and raced under each of his gloved fingertips as they held her face. He was so close. Cora's breathing sped, too much for her nose. She tried to breathe through the gag again, a terrible humiliating panting. She was panicking, the pounding of her heart almost blocking his low whispered words.

"I will not harm you. No one here will harm you. I give you my word that you will not be harmed, Lady Cora."

The carriage rocked with the entrance of a new passenger. The duke's face filled her field of vision and his hands kept her face still and directed toward him. He continued to speak words that Cora didn't hear.

The light had brightened with the opening of the carriage doors, and dimmed now again as they closed. The duke moved his face back from hers, and she could see his jaw was tense and his eyes were tight. They burned into hers once again, like they had when they had first met. He let go and turned away from her, sitting back in the seat beside her as the carriage moved forward once again.

Cora tried to calm herself.

The new occupant was a woman. She was dark-skinned and strikingly beautiful. The woman stared at Cora with wide eyes, and her hand jerked to her throat. Her full mouth tightened.

Cora squeezed her eyes shut and pressed her face into the padded side, tears oozing through and wetting the velvet. She couldn't stand to look at these horrible people any more.

"My lord duke," the woman's voice rang through carriage, cold and imposing.

"Paris, Kate, like Paris," the duke said.

"Paris." She sounded angry.

"Yes, Paris."

A silent tension took over the cabin. It almost pulled Cora away from her padded side to see what was happening.

"As you will, your grace," the woman finally said. Her voice was low and rich, with a Scottish burr.

The tension lessened, and they traveled in silence for a few minutes. Cora focused on inhaling and exhaling through her nose.

"Lady Cora." Cora jerked at the sound of her name from the duke in his deep, formal voice. "Lady Cora." he repeated again, more softly. She lifted her head slightly.

"This is Kate Douglas. She will be your lady's maid."

What?

"She is to make sure you are cared for, and comfortable, and properly accompanied and chaperoned."

Cora turned wide eyes on the beautiful, intimidating woman. She noticed for the first time her dress, which was conservative, dark, and high-necked, in line with servant's traveling garb, with a plain bonnet and black ribbons. The woman, Miss Douglas, looked on Cora with a severe, expressionless gaze. There was tension in her ram-rod posture.

But Miss Douglas gave Cora a nod, a bending of her long, elegant neck.

This exotic creature, to wait on her? Cora suddenly missed her own dear Richards. She had been her lady's maid since Cora had left the schoolroom. Richards might have been more loyal to Mother than to Cora, but she'd been tolerant, and had brushed her hair through many a bout of young tears. What Cora wouldn't give to have her here now instead of this intimidating woman.

"And this, of course, is Mort Malcolm, my valet, and former batman. He has been with me since the Peninsula." The duke's servant gave her a nod as well, his eyes half lidded. It appeared he had decided to be at his ease.

"Kate's mother was my nurse, and Kate helped keep me in line with her mother," It sounded like the duke smiled, but she wasn't looking at him. "She was lady's maid to my sisters before their marriages. I know she will care for you well."

The carriage gave a turn, and sped up, the horses having been urged to speed. Mr. Malcolm looked out between the curtains.

"We've reached the Great North Road."

The road to Scotland. A long journey, several days in good weather. The weather hadn't been good lately.

Cora didn't know whether to wish for horrid weather to slow them down, or fair, so that this journey would be faster. She squirmed. There was an itch behind her back she couldn't scratch, the pins and tied gag were still digging at her scalp, and she was getting thirsty from her tears and the linen in her mouth sucking all her saliva away.

Was she to endure this misery for several days?

"My lord duke." Miss Douglas's voice filled the silence.

"Yes, Kate?" The duke's rich timbre answered. He sat so close that Cora thought she could feel the vibrations of his speech over the vibrations of the carriage.

"If I am to serve my lady, may I begin now? Her hair is in disarray, and I'm sure she could be made more comfortable."

There was silence for a few seconds. Cora lifted her head. Miss Douglas's gaze was direct at the duke. She raised her eyebrows at him.

"Of course, Kate. That is a good idea. Let us switch places." The duke rose, and stooped over. He waited on the side next to the door, as Miss Douglas rose, and took the duke's place at Cora's side. The duke was now diagonal from her. She kept her eyes away from him and felt her body calm some with this increase of distance between them.

Miss Douglas pulled a hairbrush out.

"Here, my lady, if you sit up, but keep turned away, I will brush and redress your hair."

Cora did as she asked, and was surprised at the gentleness of her touch. Miss Douglas eased the askew pins and let Cora's heavy hair hang loose. The removal of the pins was such a relief, Cora felt a few more tears leak from her eyes. The brushing was calming. Miss Douglas eased her caught hair out of the gag's knot without loosening it, and was careful not to tug on the gag as she brushed. Truly, she was amazing, with the bouncing of the carriage, to work so patiently and carefully.

A tension, a prickling, ran up the right side of Cora's neck. It was the duke's gaze, she knew. And she blushed to have this man see her in so vulnerable and intimate a position as her hair down and being brushed.

Silence reigned in the cabin, and Cora felt the focus of all present on her. She slid her eyes to the side, and was relieved that the duke's valet appeared to be sleeping. One less, at least.

Her curly hair bushed around her.

"True curls, lovely," Miss Douglas said. "I look forward to properly caring for your hair later, my lady, with water, and oil, and a comb. We should barely need the hot tongs. But this will do for now."

She deftly controlled Cora's unruly hair, twisting it in what felt like a simple style, and repinning it.

"If you'll turn toward me now."

Cora did. Miss Douglass's jaw tensed and flexed at the sight of Cora's face. Cora was sure she looked hideous: red, blotchy, tear-streaked, puffy, and her mouth stretched and horrible from the gag.

Miss Douglas said nothing, but deftly took out a handkerchief, wetted it with a skein, and wiped Cora's face clean of dried tear-salt. She combed out Cora's fringe, wetted it, and reshaped the curls around her face.

"There," she said, then frowned, her mouth tense. "Wait, one more thing." She took out a pot of emollient lip balm, and swiped it across Cora's stretched lips with a careful finger. The lip balm eased some of the strain on her lips, and Cora looked at her with gratitude. Her eyes threatened to fill again, but she forced the tears back, not wanting to ruin the semblance of comfort Miss Douglas had achieved for her.

"Now, relax as much as you can." She gave Cora a tight, strained smile. It made her strange, beautiful face look friendlier for a brief moment. "We have a long journey ahead of us."

Cora obeyed, sat back, and closed her eyes.

After several minutes of silence, Miss Douglas asked, "Where is my lady's bonnet?"

Cora realized she had no idea, and hadn't noticed its absence. She looked, alarmed, around the carriage interior, but did not see it.

"I'm afraid it was knocked off in the initial . . . action." The duke said. "I don't know if it made it into the carriage at all."

"That is unfortunate." Miss Douglas said.

"Aye," the somnolent valet said, his Scottish accent slow and languid. Mr. Malcolm was not as soundly asleep as he had appeared. "Milady's blue-trimmed poke bonnet, left forlornly in the mud of Hyde Park."

His eyes slitted half-open, and he gave Cora a lazily, sardonic look. "A morbid message for the dowager countess to discover. Fortunately, there are two equally ravishing bonnets in my lady's trunks, purchased yesterday by myself in preparation for this journey."

Cora stared at him. He purchased things for her yesterday? This abduction was well planned?

"I do hope they will be to your taste, Lady Cora. I have often been complimented by ladies on the exquisiteness of my taste."

"Indeed, Mr. Malcolm?" Miss Douglas's voice was cold. "How thoroughly did you prepare for my lady's needs without any input from a lady?"

"Oh, I had the input of several ladies, Miss Douglas. I think you will find milady is well supplied when you open the trunks this evening."

Cora could feel Miss Douglas bristling next to her. "Tooth powder?"

"Yes, and a selection of toilet waters, and—"

"Thank you, Malcolm." The duke cut him off. "Kate, if you discover anything vital for the comfort of Lady Cora missing, we will endeavor to purchase it on the road."

"Thank you, your grace."

Silence reigned. It felt that hours passed. Cora tried to sleep, as that or staying miserably awake were the only alternatives.

They didn't stop to change the horses.

"My lord duke, I respectfully request that we stop in a secluded area where we can speak privately," Kate said.

Adam roused himself from his stupor, and looked at Kate. Her face was stony and her eyes recriminating. He checked his watch. "We will not be changing horses for another two hours. We will be pausing to rest and water them for fifteen minutes soon, I'm sure, in a likely village. We are taking the first two legs with this team. They are mine, and I know they can handle it."

Her eyes glittered at him. "Indeed, your grace. Then when we stop to water the horses, and hopefully to water ourselves as well, I request to speak with you alone."

"Lady Cora should not be left unattended."

"Then we will bide in sight of the carriage door."

He had put off this conversation long enough. It must be faced. "All right, Kate."

He stretched up and knocked on the hatch, "Charlie Coachman, turn off to the side in some private lane and give us a pause, sir."

"Aye, your grace," he answered.

Adam went back to carefully not staring at Lady Cora, with her misery-filled eyes and horribly gagged mouth, as they waited for the coach to turn off the main road. She clutched the flower pot, buried her face in the padded side of the carriage, and was silent.

Charlie Coachman pulled the lathered blacks up in front of a small copse of trees that would provide some shelter.

Adam opened the carriage door just wide enough to step out. The area was private, he could see no people out on this miserable July day, and the carriages and carts passing on the Great North Road were distant enough that travelers wouldn't be able to make out the details of their group.

His legs needed stretching after their several hours of sitting. But first things first.

Charlie Coachman climbed down off his high seat, and started checking over the horses. They were lathered, needing rest, and water.

"I can't keep them standing for long, your grace." Charlie told Adam.

"This will be quick." Adam assured him.

Kate followed him out, stepped away from the carriage a distance, and looked at him with glaring expectancy.

Adam faced the carriage to keep an eye on the door, and braced himself for her onslaught.

Kate's face darkened and her eyes flashed with righteous indignation. "I thought I was assisting in an elopement, not a kidnapping! Why did you do this? What is the point of this horrible ordeal you are putting this poor lass through? You claim that you love her?"

Adam had promised himself that he would not get angry at Kate. He had known she would not approve of his actions, and he had deceived her. He drew in a breath, and pushed down his defensive anger.

"I do love her."

"Then why did you kidnap her? Does she not love you?"

"She hasn't had a chance to love me yet. Her mother—"

"It doesn't matter about her mother. You've killed any love she might have begun to feel. Now all love is dead, and you are forcing her to marry you anyway."

"No, love is not . . . I will not . . ." He stumbled over his words.

"Kidnapped and forced. Like a slave. You are treating the woman you claim to love like a slave."

Adam's sight went dark, then red. He spun, and stalked away before he lifted his hands to her in rage. He must never lift his hands in rage.

The mud under his feet sloshed. He stood, sightless, and felt the torrent of emotions racing through his veins, the sharp stab of panic that arched through his chest, and into his ribs. His breathing hitched. He took control of his diaphragm, forced a deep and even rhythm. His stomach cramped with nervous tension. He straightened his back and sucked in his gut to stop it.

"Thank you, Miss Douglas, for so thoroughly speaking what I was thinking," Malcolm's voice made Adam want to hunch his shoulders. He resisted.

"This is a private conversation, Mr. Malcolm." Kate's voice was cold.

"And I am joining it. Our illustrious employer, Miss Douglas, has decided that the only way he can gain the lady of his dreams is by stealing her. He did not consult with us about it, obviously, or perhaps we would have been able to dissuade him before things had reached this pass. Though it appears Charlie Coachman knew our duke's plans."

"Yes, I knew he would go along with anything I requested of him." Adam said.

"Such loyalty, through all folly." Malcolm's voice was acid. "I suppose it's a compliment to ourselves, Miss Douglas, that he realized we would have opposed him if he had explained his full purpose."

"Indeed. I'm ashamed that I've gone along with this as far as I have. Lord Adam," Adam tensed as she addressed him as she had as a child, her four years older than him, and in charge of keeping him and his siblings out of mischief. "You must return Lady Cora to her mother."

"No."

"I cannot support you in this, Lord Adam. I must decline."

"And resign?" He turned back to her. "You will leave Lady Cora here with men, unprotected by any female companionship?"

"I cannot assist you in forcing a woman to marry you, sir."

"I will not force her."

"Oh, you will not? That's a fine speech. How will she have any choice? You are ruining her."

"Not if you stay. If you are here, I am merely escorting Lady Cora and her maid to her sick aunt's side. We can say that at every posting house, and all will be fine."

"Her sick aunt's! And what do we tell the good people about the gag in her mouth?"

It began to rain. Cold plops of water hit Adam's face and he blinked and grimaced at the sky. "The gag is a problem."

"You could do the same as sensible kidnappers," Malcolm said, "and threaten her with a gun or a knife to keep quiet."

Adam gave him a cold look. "No."

"Do you have any blackmail you could use?" Malcolm continued. "A licentious letter that will ruin her mother in the eyes of the ton if published? Something that could induce her to stay quiet?"

"Of course not."

"There is ruination, of course." Malcolm shifted his weight and lifted a hand. "That if her predicament became widely known, she would be ruined, and would have to retire quietly to the country, living unwed and alone forever." He gave a humorless smile. "Or else marry you, which might be worse."

Adam narrowed his eyes at him.

"It might need to be that, Lord Adam." Kate grimaced. "But she cannot stay gagged and trussed any longer. She needs food and water, and to relieve herself, my lord duke, in case you have forgotten that your perfect lady is a human with basic earthly needs. She will need to be seen at posting houses, and get out and stretch her legs. If you keep her in this animal state the entire way to Scotland she will hate you forever, and no amount of fine jewels and being addressed as 'your grace' will change that she was forced like a slave into a life she did not want." Her voice was chill and hard. "You had said your purpose had been to remove your family from the slave trade, my lord duke."

Adam rounded on her, his eyes wide and his hands clenched so tight they trembled. Kate looked at him with unflinching eyes, the outrage of her negro slave parentage blazing though her regal bearing.

Seconds burned long as Adam struggled with her words. "So what will you do, Kate?" His teeth ground together.

She remained quiet for several moments. "I will stay with my lady. I will protect her and serve her. She is innocent. But you must release her from her bonds, and find some other way to keep her from running from you and crying foul. Stop forcing her."

The rain was making them thoroughly wet, dangerous as they were traveling. Adam turned away from her. "I will think on it," he said. He grimaced, and sighed. "Unbind Lady Cora and assist her. We will leave in five minutes."

He stalked off in another direction to find chill relief.

Chapter Ten

Release

Friday, July 5, 1816, morning

Lady Cora's maid was the first to notice she was missing.

Her lady had gone to bed early the last evening with the headache, and at 9 a.m. she still hadn't rung for her maid. The dowager planned on leaving for the Grange that day, and Richards needed to get on with the packing. She went upstairs to check on Lady Cora.

The bed was empty, unmade, and her mistress's nightgown was draped over it. In her dressing room, her pink-sprigged day dress with pin-able drop front, a dress her mistress could get into unassisted, was gone, as were her blue walking boots, her blue leather gloves, her navy-blue pelisse, her warm dark blue woolen cloak with sable trim, and her blue-trimmed poke bonnet.

Her mistress had dressed herself for walking.

Richards checked the orangery. It was empty. She looked out the windows into the garden. It was chill, raining, and also empty.

She ran out and checked the Grosvenor Square Garden. Her mistress was not to be found.

The upstairs chambermaid confirmed that Lady Cora had been in her bed when she had come in at 7 a.m. to dress the fire in milady's room in the unseasonable cold of the morning.

Richards checked with the footmen, the butler, the housekeeper. Were any of the servants not at their expected posts? Had any seen milady leave? She checked in the stable with the grooms, in case.

None had seen milady leave.

She mobilized the household, in case milady was in an obscure place in the house or around the square. She wasn't found.

At 9:40 a.m., Richards braced herself, and went to the dowager's room.

In the unexpected solitude of the empty carriage, Cora pulled the gag off, ripping a few caught hairs away from her scalp with a grimace. She worked her jaw and lips against dead tingles to bring feeling back to them.

She looked out the window again. The duke and his servants were still talking. She tugged at the knot at her wrists with her teeth.

No, they weren't talking. Their words were heated. There was anger in the duke's face. They were arguing.

The dark-clothed figures of the duke and his two servants were far enough away that she couldn't hear their conversation except for a few disjointed words, but the duke was angry, and so was Miss Douglas.

Then, pure rage filled the Black Duke's face. Cora's body tensed like a taut string, muscles knotted in painful fear. What if he hit Miss Douglas?

The duke spun away, and stalked with heavy steps away from his servant.

Cora waited, breathless.

He was furious, but he didn't lash out. He didn't hit.

Their discussion continued. It calmed.

He wasn't happy, but he didn't yell.

Mother thought that the Duke of Blackdale was the type of man to lash out at underlings.

Watching him, his tall body and broad shoulders tense with restraint, Cora's back muscles relaxed. Her free mouth dropped open, and the knot escaped from her teeth.

He controlled himself.

She blinked and shook herself. She should attempt her ankles. Maybe she could run. She bent low, twisted her trussed hands, and tugged at the tight knot that bound her ankles. She worked at it. It didn't loosen.

The carriage door opened, and Cora sprang back up, her eyes wide and body filled with fear again.

Miss Douglas was at the door, her intimidating face calm as she viewed Cora's efforts to free herself.

A ghost of a smile passed over the dark woman's features. She entered the carriage, and untied Cora's ankles and hands.

They were on the road again, and Cora was much, much more comfortable.

As comfortable as she could be in a crowded carriage, being carried against her will to a location she did not desire, with rain pouring down hard on the windows. It was almost like being back with her mother, except very, very different.

Mr. Malcolm handed her a crate to hold and protect her narcissus. More improvement.

Miss Douglas pulled out a basket of food for their luncheon, and Cora devoured the cold cheese, mutton, and bread, and drank her fill.

Must keep up her strength.

The meal was silent, and Cora relaxed in the quiet.

"Lady Cora," The duke's deep voice sent her back knotting once again. "If you will agree to it, in the posting houses and in company on this trip, we will say that I am taking you to your ailing aunt, accompanied by your maid. An unexceptionable reason, and one that will protect your reputation."

Cora's eyes widened, but she kept her gaze on the duke's knees. If she didn't agree to this, would they tie her again? She must keep her freedom of movement if she was to escape. "I have a great aunt Carston who lives in the north of England. That would do as a story until we pass where we should turn off for her home near Newcastle."

Protecting her reputation was important, and if she helped them trust her enough, if she saw an opportunity, she could be able to slip away, as easily as she had often slipped away from maids and chaperones in the past. Or if she was free to show her face in the posting houses, she could cause a scene there and seek rescue in that way.

"That would be excellent. I thank you."

She risked a glance up at his face. His expression was almost tender again. She looked away and clenched her teeth and her fists. She turned back with determination and looked him in the eyes.

"My lord duke, why am I here?" she demanded. "I do not think you are in need of my money, are you?"

"No!"

"So you are not an adventurer, seeking a rich dowry, or simply a kidnapper, seeking ransom?"

"Of course not! My lady, I . . ." He swallowed. "I apologize that this is not as I would wish this conversation to take place. I spoke to your mother yesterday . . ."

"Yes."

"I requested your guardian's, your mother's, approval for me to pay my addresses to you. She refused me." He wasn't looking at her.

"Yes." Cora stared at his face, his high cheekbones, and the heavy brows that hung low until they peaked unexpectedly outside the corners of his eyes. His chin jutted into a sharp point from his triangular jaw, a cleft striking through the tip.

He was thin and pale, as from illness. His war wounds might still pain him.

Was it a handsome face, she wondered? She had thought it handsome before, but now . . . A distinguished face, indeed, a commanding and aristocratic one. His pale skin and jet black hair were a shocking contrast to his brilliant blue eyes. He was all black, white, blue . . . and red. The red of his lips, shapely but not full, drew her eyes.

"I could not accept your mother's answer. I know you are not of age, and therefore cannot marry without your guardian's consent in England." He sat back, straightened in the seat, and gazed at her with his piercing eyes. "So I am taking you out of England."

Cora's mouth dropped open. He was—he did—he was intending to marry her! He hadn't asked her yet! She had not said yes, she hadn't had a chance to refuse or deny. He stole her, and tied her up! Outrageous!

Ire rose up, and made her bold. "So, sir, I assume we are going to Gretna Green. And there you expected to untie me, ungag me, put me before the blacksmith and his anvil, and that I would say yes? Yes, I'll marry my kidnapper and tormenter? Taking me out of England, my lord duke, will not change the fact that I have not given my consent. It does not matter where we are, in Scotland, in England, in France, over the anvil or at a church. If I say 'no,' when asked, we will not be married. And I shall say no!"

Cora was leaning forward, panting through the anger that constricted her lungs. "So what will you do now, then? Drug me? Hold a pistol to my back when we are at the anvil? Douse my wine so that I am compliant?"

His face flushed. "No, I will do none of those things. I am not so dishonorable as that."

"Honorable! Kidnapping is honorable?"

His mouth tightened and he remained silent.

She sat back, and stared at the curtains over the window beside her. "Have you considered, my lord duke, that I will be of age in one year? You could have plied your suit for a year, and after that year I might have said yes, and we would not have needed my mother's permission."

"I do not have time for that."

"You don't have time?"

"Yes, I need to be back in Scotland, attending to my lands and my people. They have been left masterless for too long, to the great detriment of all. I would not have come to London at all this spring if it hadn't been unavoidable. But I could not risk leaving you to your suitors and your overbearing mother for a year. I would lose you."

Cora's mouth opened and closed. "You could not know that I would not refuse them and still be free next year."

"I could not know that you would not. Every indication was that you would accept one just to get out from under your mother's thumb. And I could not be here to make sure I was the one you chose, especially since your mother had refused me, and therefore would block me and interfere at every turn."

Cora looked away from him. "She could not block a duke so well as, say, a poor parson, or an adventurer."

"I'm sure she would endeavor and prevail, my lady."

Cora couldn't answer that. She grabbed onto her next objection.

"All right then, sir, you had an interfering mother, and a short window of time. You could have done as every other conniving rake does, and seduced me into running off to Gretna Green with you. Young ladies are often going against parental wishes because an attractive man made love to them. You could have tried that. You did not need to kidnap me!" She sat back, and tilted her chin up. Let him find an answer for that.

His face became stony, with two bright spots of color over each high cheek bone, and he looked away from her. "I am not . . . a rake."

"So all men say, but many still manage it."

"I am not well versed in the arts of . . . flirtation and seduction." His fists clenched. "No, it's not that I am not versed, I've seen many an example . . . I just . . . I am not good at it. It is not in my nature, I am afraid."

You were doing fine enough for me. The words were on the tip of Cora's tongue, but she bit them back.

Mr. Malcolm let out a snort of laughter. She started. She'd forgotten that he and Miss Douglas were there. Her face burned. What a conversation to be having in front of servants!

"Allow me to add my testimony to that, milady." His Scottish accents gave his languid voice an odd drawl. "Our lord duke has had plenty of fine examples of the art of seduction, from myself for one—"

"Malcolm," the duke's voice almost growled.

But Malcolm continued, giving his master no mind. "And from his youngest brother, renowned throughout England and Spain for his triumphs on the battlefield and in the bedroom—"

"That's not a recommendation to either ye nor he!" Miss Douglas snapped out.

"And from half his grace's regiment, all who were more successful with the ladies during the war on the continent than our dear duke."

Cora watched Mr. Malcolm with fascination. What strange servants the duke had! Very free with their words and their opinions. And such language in front of her, who was usually shielded most annoyingly. How refreshing!

She decided to not be embarrassed to have this conversation in front of them. She felt lighter.

"If he had only applied to me, Lady Cora," Mr. Malcolm continued, with an arch and flirtatious manner. "I could have coached him through his wooing, and your regard most assuredly would have been won."

"Because you know, always, exactly what to say to any lady at any time, of course, sir." Miss Douglas's voice was dry.

Cora gave Miss Douglas a wide-eyed look.

"Thank you, Malcolm, enough." the duke said. "My talents do not lie in that direction, and I did not want dubious assistance."

Cora pushed her gloved hand against her mouth. She had a most inappropriate urge to giggle. She glanced at the duke, and he had paused, his mouth open, and was staring at her with an arrested expression. She glanced away with confusion, and there was silence in the carriage for a few seconds.

"So," Miss Douglas started with a brusque tone. "We are at an impasse. We are still headed up the road to Scotland, which is the duke's wish, but when we get there, Lady Cora has said that without the coercion of poison, befuddling alcohol, or the threat of bodily harm to force her, she will not be saying yes to marriage to the Duke of Blackdale. The duke has assured her that he will not force her in this way, any further." Cora looked at her in amazement, and glanced at the duke. His expression had darkened, but he did not interrupt his maidservant. "Therefore, when we arrive, Lady Cora and the duke will stare at each other over the anvil, and nothing will be accomplished."

Cora blinked.

"Or, at the next posting house, Lady Cora could raise a hue and cry." Malcolm stretched out his long legs, invading Miss Douglas's space. She shifted her skirts to avoid him with a scowl. "Miss Douglas and I would be arrested for kidnapping a lady, and likely either hanged or deported, while the duke would wriggle out of it because he is a duke."

"Don't forget to mention Charlie Coachman, who was the only servant in this cursed enterprise who knew that this was to be an abduction." Miss Douglas turned to Cora. "Lady Cora, I want to assure you that I thought I was assisting in an elopement, not in an abduction. I would never have gone along with it in the first place if I had known."

Cora looked at her wide-eyed. "Then why did you, Miss Douglas?"

She looked down and away. "Because Lord Adam has had my loyalty and my trust since he was a boy." She looked toward the curtained window beside her and didn't say more.

The duke made a noise, and Cora swung her head to look at him. He was watching Miss Douglas, his face white and mouth tense.

A strained silence took over the carriage until Mr. Malcolm drawled, "Deuced dark in here. Now that our lady is no longer trussed up, we could open these curtains." He sat up, swished the one nearest him back, and tied it open with a deft movement. Cora blinked in the sudden light. She joined him by opening her own curtain and tying it back, happy that she could use her hands to do this simple task.

The world outside the window was cloudy, the sun weak. It was cold, but the rain had slowed for a moment.

Kate opened hers.

Only the duke's window was still curtained. He looked at Cora with an unreadable expression.

He opened his curtain.

The greater light hitting his face showed the strain he was carrying. Cora wondered at it, this man who methodically kidnapped the woman he wanted to marry, but had the loyalty of such intelligent servants, and allowed them to openly speak their minds and opinions.

He was an enigma.

She remembered something. "What is 'Paris' in this situation? You spoke of Paris?" she asked the group of them.

"Oh, Paris." Malcolm drew it out in a sigh.

"No, Malcolm, we shall not speak of Paris at this time." the duke stopped him. And Malcolm obeyed, shutting his mouth and half-lidding his eyes with a semblance of lazy ease.

"We are coming up on a posting house, and that is good. I can feel how the horses are flagging. We've pushed them hard enough, and it's time to change them out." The duke gave her a sharp glance. "Lady Cora. You did not willingly start this journey, and if you choose to, you could raise a cry at this posting house, and have this trip curtailed.

I ask that you don't. Please come with me to Scotland. I won't tie you up again."

He looked at her with steady eyes, and seemed to hold his breath, waiting for her answer. Cora felt anxiety grip her stomach. He wanted an answer now. He wanted her word. If she gave it, would she not be able to try to escape? Would she find herself facing the anvil in Gretna Green? This was far too fast to be making a decision like this! If she went, was she agreeing to marry him? She was not going to be agreeing to that now, definitely not.

But she was intrigued. This journey had just gotten interesting. He fascinated her. She wanted to see more of him, to see if, maybe, in a year perhaps, she would say yes.

If she did raise a cry, it would damage his servants, who she was beginning to like, despite everything. And she would never get another chance to study this enigmatic man, who admitted to be a poor flirt, but had the gall to kidnap her.

She would be taken home to her mother, to spend another year in her gardens and her fields, but also under her mother's thumb even more than before, after this scare. And then another Season, with lackluster approved gentlemen yet again. None else had come close to her heart, or sent so many chills and thrills down her body as this man had.

But he'd had the criminal arrogance to abduct her! And her mother . . .

"My mother!" Cora startled them all. "My mother is going to be—has to be—livid and terrified and, oh my!" Cora's mind filled with gruesome imaginings of what her mother might do.

"That is why we are moving as swiftly as we can." The duke gave her a steady look, like he would deal with her mother, but was avoiding it till, what? He was married to Cora and her mother was powerless?

Cora stared at him. She didn't want, she couldn't want . . .

But . . .

If she went home now, would she ever see him again?

No, it would be all over—his heady attention, his intense focus—gone. She would never be near him again. A strange ache hit her chest at the thought.

Her mother would ensure it.

Cora's hands clenched in her lap.

She'd never know if . . . If he and she . . . That bud of love . . .

He wanted to marry her. Her breath caught in her throat.

"We've reached the town; the posting house is in sight." Miss Douglas said.

Cora turned to the window, seeing the cottages and shops roll past. Her time to consider was up.

Without taking her gaze from the window, she said, "Miss Douglas, will you please find one of those bonnets that Mr. Malcolm claims to have purchased when we pull up? I will look odd without one."

"Yes, milady."

"The kind duke is escorting me to my great aunt Carston's in Newcastle on his way back to Scotland. Will someone please inform Charlie Coachman of this, so we can have a consistent story?"

"Aye, milady." Mr. Malcolm said.

Cora kept her eyes on the window. "Your grace, I am not agreeing to marry you over the anvil." She took a breath in. "But I am agreeing to go along with this journey for a while, to see . . . to see what happens." She tilted her chin up in his direction, but did not look at him. "It may be best if you do actually take me to my great-aunt's."

The coach drew up to the posting house, the ostlers coming up to the team, and they heard the coachman call for special care, "They've been hard-driven, and this is the duke's own team."

Mr. Malcolm got out, letting down the step, and Miss Douglas followed.

Cora gave the duke a sideways glance, to judge his reaction.

Then she turned her head fully and caught her breath in her throat. His eyes were burning at her again, blazing with hot blue fire. She saw hope and joy there, and it stole her breath.

He lowered his head in a nod of acknowledgment, not taking his eyes off of hers.

Cora's head started to swim, and a buzzing began around her ears and the back of her head.

She vaguely heard Miss Douglas ask Mr. Malcolm where in the trunks the bonnets might be, and the duke finally broke his eye contact with her. She sucked in a breath, and realized she hadn't been breathing.

He glanced back, and murmured an "Excuse me, Lady Cora," and exited the carriage.

She breathed heavily, in and out, and wondered what she had agreed to put herself through.

She was staying. She was coming with him.

He felt lighter than air, and ready to take on anything. He promised the ostlers a sovereign each if his team was later picked up by his groom in perfect condition, and encouraged them to walk them till they were cooled. He asked that their best team available be hitched up for their next leg of the journey north, slipping extra money to the ostler who handled the exchange of funds.

He went into the tap room and ordered hot tea for his party, paying generously.

The money and the ducal seal on his carriage, a calculated risk, were working their charm. He judged the team brought out for him to be high quality, and the tea was delivered quickly, bypassing several already waiting.

Lady Cora emerged from the carriage, wearing a fetching bonnet of creamy velvet and silk flowers. It appeared Kate had done what repairs she could to the creases and travel stains on Lady Cora's pelisse and gown. All traces of her ordeal were erased, her eyes flashed and her sweet, pointed chin lifted as she walked into the taproom, Kate behind her in somber black.

She was ravishing. He felt a smile—a grin—threaten to erupt over his face. There was his darling lady.

No, not his. The thought struck him like a hit to the gut. She wasn't his yet. This type of thinking was what had led him to steal her, and that had been . . .

Not a mistake. A calculated risk. But his calculations had not factored in all the effects the abduction would have on Lady Cora. How horrible it had been to see her tied and gagged and weeping. That had been . . . awful.

But here she was. She was coming with him for now. He had a chance.

The ladies retired to refresh themselves, and he went out and took a brisk walk up and down the street to stretch his legs and ease the ache in his ribs.

Chapter Eleven

Bored

FRIDAY, JULY 5, 1816, MORNING

The dowager had gone out last night to enjoy a last salon and supper party, leaving her daughter to her megrims. She had come home late, and was languidly enjoying her morning tea and instructing Masterson, her maid, on her packing.

She did not take the news of her daughter being missing well.

She sent all the servants who could be spared to discreetly search the streets, and her daughter's favorite haunts: the lending library, the botanical gardens, the Tower of London menagerie—though that had been only a youthful fascination—and all the public parks and gardens in the vicinity.

The dowager countess waited an hour for reports back, all negative, before mobilizing her secretary to begin inquiries, less discreet, at all the houses of Lady Cora's friends and acquaintance. This brought the young men, those who had hung on her daughter's sleeve all Season, to the house, and from there, out to search.

She sent her secretary to the residences of each of the young men who had offered marriage and been refused yesterday.

Mr. Basil, who had tried one more time and hadn't gotten past the doorstep, had drunken himself into a stupor and was still abed.

Lord Charles had caroused all night and had just dragged himself home when the knock came to his door.

Lieutenant Dean was found at Jackson's boxing saloon, working off his aggression with rough science.

Mr. Yardley was at his tailor's, adjusting the fit of a new coat.

Mr. Jordan was only found hours later, having sought consolation with a new mistress.

And the Duke of Blackdale, the most distinguished and most insulted of milady's suitors, had left to return to Scotland that morning. His house was still being put up by his servants, but they all assured the dowager's secretary that the duke had left in the early morning in his crested traveling carriage accompanied by his coachman, his valet, and a maid. A footman hired for the Season, and annoyed to be looking for another position with little warning, insinuated the maid was one of the few that could handle the duke, "if you know what I mean."

The secretary brought all these tidings to the dowager, with attempts at discretion in wording that the dowager trampled on, as usual, until she got the raw information out of him.

She paid close attention to the news of the maid who went with the duke, and considered it with furrowed brows and pursed lips.

Mort Malcolm sauntered over to Charlie, catching him before he headed into the taproom.

"Lady Cora has decided that we are taking her to her great aunt Carston's in Newcastle on our way home to Scotland, and be sure that's what you tell anyone who asks."

"Oh-ho!" Charlie's craggy old face broke into a smile.

"Yes, she's decided to give him a chance, which I will have to chalk up to Miss Douglas and I's flattering devotion to his grace, because he has not been choosing well how to win a bride."

"Likely she does want to be a duchess, despite her mother and," he thankfully lowered his voice, "the kidnapping. I knew the good duke would pull it off."

"She hasn't said yes yet." Malcolm cautioned. "So be careful how you phrase it, when you are asked."

"Never fear, Malcolm. But we'll see him prevail with the lady yet."

Malcolm left him to his restorative drafts and gossip in the taproom, and followed Kate with his eyes as she walked behind Lady Cora, who was looking quite fetching in the velvet bonnet he had chosen for her, if he did say so himself, which he did.

But Kate . . .

If only he could dress her as she should be dressed, like the lady she ought to be with her regal bearing covered with silks and jewels.

But if she didn't have the blood of her slave mother running through her veins, if she were instead the legitimate daughter of her father, the duke's uncle, she wouldn't look twice at a valet.

There was a life she could choose, a different one where she would be draped in jewels and furs—a life in the demimonde. But she didn't want that life. She chose to live obscurely and simply as a housemaid in a country estate . . . and chastely. No kisses on the stairs, no quick tumbles. She'd rebuffed his every attention, his every attempt to win her favor.

She'd said no. She didn't like him. She snipped at him whenever her dignity would allow it.

Why couldn't he get her out of his head?

So instead he snipped back, and wallowed in frustrated obsession with the most gorgeous creature he, a feminine connoisseur, had ever seen.

At first, he had thought she must be in love with her cousin the duke, a reasonable assumption. He had watched their interactions, seeking signs and markers to prove his theory. But they hadn't come. There was mutual regard, caring, and respect, but to his disbelieving eye, no desire. They trusted each other, and Kate was often the duke's closest confidant in his household after Malcolm himself, but they were not attracted to each other.

Malcolm had thought this should help him, then, with her. He was close to the duke, so was she, if that wasn't a wedge, then it should draw them together.

No such luck so far.

Maybe she was jealous of his closeness to the duke?

Bah.

He abandoned his fruitless thoughts and went to buy himself a beer.

As the afternoon stretched, silence reigned in the carriage. Adam resigned himself to taking the rest of the trip sitting backward next to Malcolm, rather than next to Lady Cora. She seemed more comfortable that way. He was at least able to face her this way and watch her. He tried to be discreet. He kept his eyes on the landscape the majority of the time, and snuck surreptitious glances at her when he judged it safe.

Lady Cora held the potted narcissus on her lap and watched out the window. Rain hit the closed window glass. The heady scent of the flower filled the carriage.

She shifted, resettled her feet, and Adam shifted. She sighed, and Adam had to keep himself from sighing as well.

A few minutes later, she shifted again. Every movement drew his attention like a beacon. It was excessive. She wasn't as restful of a person as he had thought. Could she not sit still? Must she squirm like a child?

He was intensely aware of her. He had thought that was the love, the infatuation he had been feeling for her. But her constant movement might drive him mad. He couldn't concentrate on not looking at her if she kept moving like that.

Her feet shifted, and his eyes were drawn to her trim ankles in their half-boots. She adjusted her grip on the flower pot, then bent down and put the narcissus back into its crate. She sat back up and fiddled with her gloves. He stared at her hands, small for her height, with tapering fingertips, clad in tan kidskin gloves. Her every movement was elegant. But it was continual. She didn't stop fidgeting.

The rest of them had no trouble sitting still. Even he, with aching ribs that needed adjustment far more often than he liked, didn't move as frequently as this girl.

Malcolm snoozed, his expertise at sleeping anywhere at any time being admirably displayed on this trip. Adam contemplated trying to sleep. Lady Cora stretched her neck, and he moved his gaze back to the window. No. No sleep for him.

Kate sat still and stately, more ladylike than the lady, her hands demurely clasped in her lap, her darker skin contrasting with her white cap and the collared white tucker under her black dress. Kate had no trouble staying still for long periods of time.

Bored, bored. She was so bored. Who knew being abducted and rushed to the border for a forced elopement could be so dreadfully dull? Cora had nothing to do, and no one was talking. They all sat like statues, Mr. Malcolm sleeping again, Miss Douglas sitting still and serene. And the duke . . . he was mostly still. Except when she would catch his eyes watching her. Different parts of her, not always her face. But it was his eyes that moved.

His brows were drawing down, deeper and deeper into a scowl.

What was making him unhappy? Was it boredom as well? Cora had never been in such a quiet carriage. She'd often wanted quiet when she was traveling with Mother, who brought along guests and hangers-on to keep her entertained, or at least talkative maids, but now that Cora was experiencing the opposite, she longed for some conversation.

Could she start a conversation? Cora rearranged her feet and ran through polite conversation starters in her head. What if she just burst out with some?

So, atrocious weather we are having. Do you think the cold is caused by all the strange sun spots that have been marring the sun? That's what some of the papers have said . . .

Or, Princess Charlotte's wedding in May, hadn't it been so very romantic?

Or, I'm so happy for Princess Mary, finally getting married at forty! Mother and I had invitations to some of the wedding festivities, but it appears we won't be going . . .

No, no talk of weddings.

Better to be grim. Did you hear of the volcano that erupted last year on the other side of the world? A Mount Tambora in the Dutch East Indies. Two weeks of spewed ash and lava, and so many people dead.

And speaking of many dead last year, how was the battle at Waterloo?

If she were bold, she could ask the duke all the questions she had a burning curiosity to know the answers to. What did happen at Waterloo? Lots of your men died? How were you injured? How long was your recovery? Are you all right now?

Her mother might burst forth with uncomfortable questions like that, but Cora could not. What if she spoke up, and was met with cold stares from the duke or his servants?

No, she couldn't. She was the abducted one; they needed to talk first. She should ignore all of them instead and stay in her mind.

She bent, lifted the narcissus pot again to her lap, and stared at its soil in the watery light from the window to judge its moisture level. It was fine. She spotted a petal that was discolored, and plucked it off. Done. There was only so much you could do with one plant. She wished she had many more to keep her busy, but that was impractical in a carriage.

She lowered the pot again to her lap, and sighed.

"Lady Cora," the duke spoke. His voice sounded clipped and sharp.

Words being said aloud! She looked up at him with eagerness. "Yes, duke?"

His mouth hung open for one second, and then closed. His scowl deepened.

Adam had no idea what to say. Lady Cora's pointless movements were driving him mad, and her name had just burst out of him.

Her look of relief and the expectancy shining in her beautiful eyes blanked his mind. What could he say to her? Was he to entertain her? He couldn't entertain her. She had had an entire court of admiring young men filling her ears with pretty compliments for an entire Season, and she hadn't found any of them to her liking, she had said. He could not begin to compete with that. He stared at her, dismay tightening his stomach.

She looked away, her face falling into dullness once again.

His hand clenched.

"Lady Cora, would you like something to occupy your hands?" Kate. Oh thank you, Kate. "I am ill-prepared, and only have some mending—"

"Yes, please!" Lady Cora said.

Adam looked at Kate as his savior as she pulled out her humble mending box, and set a white shirt on Lady Cora's lap. She accepted it with a look of gratitude.

Silence overtook the carriage again. Lady Cora bit her lip, and poked the needle through the fabric.

Mort held back a snort. The poor girl. Having to go to such lengths to ease her boredom. The duke was truly pathetic in matters of courtship. Mort should assist him . . . but he felt disinclined. His back tensed with anger at his grace's actions today.

This foolhardy kidnapping endangered Mort, yes, but he was sure he would be able to slide out of prosecution, if it came to that. He clenched his hands. However, this scheme endangered Kate as well. No one had better lay a finger on Kate in connection with this horrid farce. He forced his hands to relax and resumed watching the beautiful lady's maid through his lashes.

She was trying not to stare as Lady Cora mangled her mending. Kate's famous aplomb was being tried. Mort bit back his smile.

The Dowager Countess of Winfield listened as Mr. Yardley, a denied suitor who was still devoted, begged to be given a task to do. She set him to tracing the progress of the Duke of Blackdale's carriage, and asking at the first posting house the duke stopped at about the state of his carriage and all passengers. Then Mr. Yardley was to send word back to her.

At 2:00 p.m., news reached her that Lady Cora's blue-trimmed poke bonnet had been found in Hyde Park, the ribbons tangled and covered in mud and rain. It had been trampled on, and tumbled about, but was assuredly in the park, and not blown in from elsewhere.

Chapter Twelve

Levee

Friday, July 5, 1816, afternoon

"Your grace," Miss Douglas's voice interrupted Cora's focus on her stitchery. "Have you heard recently from your sister, Lady Hester? How go things at the manse?"

Oh, a conversation opener! Cora lifted her head, and caught the furled-brow look the duke gave his maidservant. His sister was in a manse, the home of a minister of the Church of Scotland?

"I haven't received a letter since the one last week, so I assume things go along as they had before."

"How holds her health? When is her confinement expected?"

"She's been hale most of her pregnancy. Cheerful. Not due till September, as well you know, Kate."

"Thank you for the kind reminder. And the minister, he remains in good health?"

"Hearty, as usual, from her last letter." The duke looked irritated with this line of questioning. Cora blinked in interest.

He noticed her gaze, and she cast her eyes back down to her poor stitching.

"Lady Cora." His voice was gentler. "Have I told you much of my family?"

Cora looked back up to his face. "No, I know very little, Duke. Your sister is staying at a manse?"

"Lives there. She married the minister of our parish last year."

A duke's sister? Married to a minister? How was that even possible?

"She's my elder sister. She was a maiden for long years, but fell in love with the widowed pastor, and is now happily adding another child to his nursery."

"Did she marry without your consent?" The question escaped before Cora could bite her tongue.

A smile teased the duke's mouth. "No, I gave my consent with alacrity. Was glad to finally see her happy."

Cora blinked at him, and then closed her hanging mouth.

"I'll admit to you, Lady Cora, that part of my pleasure in saying yes was how much my father would have hated it." His smile went bitter. "My father was a duke of the traditional school. He would have despised this match for his daughter."

"Oh. And you didn't consider it a duty to his memory to oppose a match he wouldn't have approved of?"

His eyes shuttered, and the smile vanished. "No, his memory does not deserve honor."

Silence overtook the carriage.

Cora looked back to her stitches. They were rough and uneven. She would have to rip out all of them. "She's happy with her pastor? Lady Hester?"

She risked looking into his face once more. His hard features softened. "Yes, I believe so. Very happy."

The tension eased. "You have other siblings?"

"Yes, Lady Caroline, a year younger than I, is married to the Marquis of Stacey. She has only one daughter, and I believe she is as overbearing and hovering over her one chick as any mother hen."

Cora grimaced in sympathy, and caught a slight uplift in the duke's mouth at her expression.

Cora wanted to know everything. She pushed through the flutter of nervousness in her stomach. "How did that marriage come about, Duke?"

"My father arranged it." His face hardened, but he continued. "The year after our mother died."

"How did he not arrange a marriage for Hester?"

"He offered Hester first, I believe, to the marquis. But the marquis was more interested in Caroline, so Father allowed that. Hester had taken over hostess duties for my father for several years at that point, and he was comfortable keeping a biddable daughter at home to run the household."

"But your mother had just passed away?"

"Yes, my father and she were separated. She stayed at the Edinburgh estate, and Hester remained with Father at the castle."

Oh. Sad.

"How is Lady Caroline's marriage?" Cora's heart thumped. It wasn't a polite question.

He looked at her for a moment, but answered. "Cold, I believe. Occasionally contentious."

"My sympathies."

"We aren't close."

Cora looked down and set another ill stitch.

Mr. Malcolm spoke. "And Lady Jean married the same year as her sister, did she not, your grace?" Cora had thought Mr. Malcolm was asleep, but his dark, heavy-lidded eyes were sly and half-open.

The duke gave him a grimace. "Yes, she married the English Earl of Kingsley's heir that year, soon after Caroline's marriage."

"Eloped." Mr. Malcolm popped the last syllable, gave her a look with a lift to the corner of his mouth, and closed his eyes once again.

Cora turned wide-eyed to the duke. He gave his manservant a glare. "Yes, she eloped. Father didn't arrange it or approve it. He was in a rage for weeks. I was happily not there; I was heading for the Peninsula by that time. But he calmed. The family was noble, though impoverished. He paid off her husband's debts and allowed Jean her dowry."

"How has her marriage fared?" Cora's stomach tightened.

"Not well, she never writes but to complain. Her English lordling is a spendthrift and philanderer. My sympathy is not strong. She made her own bed."

Miss Douglas spoke up quietly. "She was sixteen. She eloped to escape." Her eyes were downcast. The duke shut his mouth. The carriage was quiet for several moments, only the patter of the rain outside, and the creak of the leather traces imposing on the pause.

"Did you assist her, Kate?" The duke's tone was low, but not hard. There was gentleness in his expression.

"No, she was not one to confide in me." Miss Douglas gave an almost-smile. "But Charlie Coachman, she turned to him, and he helped her reach her lordling's side. They had his friends as witnesses, and it was done."

"My father must not have learned of Charlie's hand in it, or he would not have stayed in his employ."

"No, those of us who knew never spoke of it. We knew what would happen if we did."

The duke nodded. He turned to his window with a contemplative look in his eye.

"Lady Jean," Miss Douglas said, "has two children, a fine home to live in, and a brother who is more generous than her father was." She gave a small smile to Cora. "But she will complain."

"Generous!" The duke gave a scoffing noise.

"Ah, you forget, your grace. Lady Hester does confide in me. She has told me what you have done for Lady Jean."

The duke gave a huff, and turned his gaze out the window.

Sir Merriweather, just getting out for the day, heard at his club that Lady Cora had gone missing, and that all were speculating that she eloped with the Duke of Blackdale, though she took no luggage—"wouldn't need to, rich as Croesus, that one, buy her all she needed fresh"—and her bonnet was found ominously tumbled about in the park.

He went immediately to the dowager.

"My lady, I was coming home this morning and around 8:30 or so, I was driving by Hyde Park, and saw the Duke's carriage turn into the park. I thought it was quite early for a promenade, but didn't think any more about it, till I heard of Lady Cora being missing, and how her bonnet was found there."

The dowager clutched her hands to her bosom. "He took her! My child has been abducted by the Black Duke!"

A duke—a Scottish duke, but a duke none the less—had stolen her daughter.

The dowager dismissed the idea of Bow Street. They wouldn't be enough to save her daughter from a dastardly duke. Her own status, as lofty as it was, might not be enough. She needed to go higher.

Lady Winfield dressed in her finest and most imposing: with turban, ostrich plumes, and the ancestral jewels draped about her person—she missed once again the Winfield jewels that she had had to give up to her husband's nephew, the new earl, upon his marriage—and went forth in search of high ranking allies.

She was a strong believer of going straight to the top. She set out for Carlton House immediately to appeal to the Prince Regent.

"You have a brother, Duke?"

A dull pain rose up in Adam's heart. "Brothers. I had two. But Captain Lord Nicolas Douglas was lost at sea during the war."

"I'm sorry. A great loss."

Adam gave a nod of acknowledgment. He had tried so hard to protect Nicolas as they grew up. It hadn't been easy. Nicolas was high spirited, and with his fast temper, he'd run afoul of their father more than once. Adam had spent much effort to shield him, to make sure he reached adulthood, only to lose him so young to the sea. A waste.

But so it was, with the storms of the ocean, and the storms of battle. So many dead and wasted.

"But watch out for the living one." Malcolm's snide comment cut through Adam's sorrow. He gave him a glare, but Malcolm paid him no mind. "The duke's brother Lord Jude, the young hero of Waterloo. He's a first-rate rake. Quite dangerous. I'm sure your mother warned you about him?"

Kate's face pinched in disapproval. "Mr. Malcolm, that's no way to—"

Was Malcolm trying to ruin things for Adam? He was used to his snideness in private, but talking this way to Lady Cora was beyond toleration. "Malcolm!"

"Does she not need to be warned, Duke? If she's to become a part of the family, you'll want her inured to him well before they meet, aye?"

His unrepentant manservant slouched further into the padded back of the coach, looking satisfied with himself.

Lady Cora was blushing, and shifted in her seat. She glanced up at Adam's face, and looked away. Her blush drained to paleness. His face must look forbidding. He closed his eyes, pressed his fingers into the tension headache building in his temples, and schooled his features.

"My brother Jude is a dangerous womanizer." Adam conceded. Yes, he wanted her wary, no matter the outcome of this trip. "He's . . . very charming."

"I wouldn't even call him charming," Malcolm said. "Just big and braw and boastful. It's sad so many women fall for his overbearing ways." Malcolm leaned forward toward Lady Cora. "But you are an intelligent and discerning young woman, Lady Cora, and I'm sure you will not be swayed by his attentions." He gave her a raised eyebrow.

She widened her eyes at him, her mouth dropping open.

"Mr. Malcolm." Kate gave a sharp rebuke. "This talk is most inappropriate."

He sat back, a pleased smile on his face, and gave a wave of his hand. "Forewarned is forearmed."

"If we are speaking so plainly," Kate's full mouth thinned, "Then I'd say careful to not make it a challenge. Lord Jude rarely heard the word no growing up, and I'm afraid he doesn't hear it well now."

Adam clenched his teeth, the vision of Jude approaching Lady Cora with lustful eyes overtaking his mind. A hot flush of anger rushed through his veins. "I'd kill him."

Lady Cora gasped, and the vision yanked away, replaced by the horrified expression on her face.

Shame immediately doused the fires of rage. "Your pardon, my lady. I should not speak so. But if he ever comes near you—" Adam covered his face with his hand, and breathed in and out to calm his mind.

On Pall Mall, the dowager's coach was stopped by guards.

Yes, the prince was in residence, but today was his grand levee, with all the royal dukes and many high ranking noblemen in attendance.

Females were not welcome.

The dowager gritted her teeth, and directed her driver to the Archbishop of Canterbury.

Mr. Basil, his head pounding from his hangover, his persimmon-stained waistcoat ruined, was humiliated, rejected, deeply in debt, and desperate for money. He saw another chance for the reversal of his fortunes. He took a shot of whiskey, hired a hack, and started off to Scotland to rescue the lady from the duke.

How dare that dastardly duke steal the heiress! He didn't even need the money!

"You said Lord Jude was big and braw, Mr. Malcolm?" Lady Cora's voice sounded curious. "I don't suppose the duke's brother was Lieutenant Lord Jude Douglas of the Royal Horse Artillery? Very tall, blond, blue-eyed? A large officer? Only a little older than me? A booming laugh?"

Adam's muscles tensed. Lady Cora knew his brother Jude.

"Aye, that's him. He was with the Third Battalion of the Royal Horse Artillery during the Peninsular campaigns. You've met him, my lady?"

"Nothing so formal. I was a part of a group of girls that met him and some of his fellow officers during my last year at school. He turned the heads of most of the girls." Her eyebrows pressed together. "One of my schoolfellows fell so completely in love with him she wrote sonnets. He seemed to reciprocate. At least, I heard they had managed to sneak away together more than once. Then a few months later, she left school unexpectedly. The rumor around the school was that she was with child."

"What was her name, my lady?" Kate asked.

"Miss Diana Ashby."

"Of the Pickton School? You attended there?"

Lady Cora nodded.

"Yes, Miss Ashby. How well I remember." Kate's mouth twisted. "The rumors were right. Lord Jude was back on the Peninsula when her condition was discovered, as was Lord Adam. The old duke was abed, soon to die. The pleas of the girl's parents fell to Lady Hester. She paid for Miss Ashby to be taken to Ireland out of her own pin money, and the child was placed with a family."

"Oh, my goodness." Lady Cora sighed. "Diana wasn't a friend to me, but I would not wish that on anyone." She looked down.

"Hester wrote me of that." Adam said. "I was able to reimburse her, and there have been other moneys spent. If it was an isolated incident . . . but it is not. I was able to insist Jude marry Henriette, his French wife, the next year, when we were both in Paris. It took the combined wills of myself, the girl's family, and the girl herself to bring that marriage about. But now . . ."

"Those he seduces don't even have the hope of marrying him. He's well and truly leg-shackled already." Malcolm said. "But still it happens. So be wary. Aye, my lady?"

Lady Cora looked incredulous. "You all seem to be concerned I would be in danger from this libertine. But I assure you, he didn't turn my head when he was a bachelor, and he surely won't now. I have a repugnance for such behavior." And she turned up her elegant nose.

Adam could not help but smile. The knot of tension in his stomach eased some.

The dowager countess imposed her might to gain audience with the archbishop. He heard her story, felt for her loss, but was uninterested in attempting to dissolve a marriage made in Scotland, "if it was uncoerced, of course."

If it were coerced, it might still need a ruling from Parliament before it could be dissolved, as it was a contract made by a duke.

With a glare, the dowager countess set out to again attempt the Prince Regent.

"How did a duke's heir come to be an army officer on the Peninsula? Seems most unusual."

Adam sat back against the velvet squabs, and laced his gloved fingers together before him. "I was army mad since I was a boy, but of course my father wouldn't allow it. I attended Oxford at his insistence, but the year I reached my majority, my mother passed away, leaving me with a sizable inheritance that was completely under my control. I had the funds and the legal right, and he couldn't stop me. I purchased a commission, and was in the Peninsula fighting Boney as fast as the army could get me there."

That inheritance. He had used to say that it was the greatest gift after life itself that his mother had given him—the gift to kill or be killed with his king's blessing. His mother had given him little else.

"How did you find it, Duke?"

"War is killing, death and dying, illness and dismemberment. The gloss and glow wore away quickly." He was blunt, but he still woke mornings with the stench of the corpses of friends lingering in his nose.

"Then why did you stay? Why continue?" Lady Cora's eyes were cautious. Or was that compassion in those green depths?

"Besides a determination to never see my father again?" His lips stretched taut over his face. "What was left was duty. A duty and a job to do in defending king and country. Napoleon was intent on conquering the world, and we were to stop him." His lips twitched. "And we did, twice."

"Thank you," Yes, that was compassion in her eyes. Adam felt his heart warm under the softness of that gaze. "For helping to make my world safe."

As time went on, Cora found herself almost at ease asking the duke questions, for he answered them. He was kind and courteous once again.

"When did you come into your title, duke?" Cora asked.

"Three years ago. I had heard my father was ailing, but I was on the eve of a battle when word came that he had died. My men needed me, and the campaign was intense, so I stayed and fought. I didn't make it back to London for my presentation till the next year, after Boney was on Elba."

"And you did not sell out of the army then? How did you come to be at the Battle of Waterloo?"

His mouth twisted. "I was encouraged to go home, but I didn't wish to. I went to Paris, and was there when Boney escaped and started heading there with an army. I got out of the city and made it to Brussels in time for me to take over a regiment in need of a colonel, and we prepared to meet Napoleon's forces again." He spread his hands. "Then Waterloo."

"I understand you were injured at Waterloo? Are you quite recovered?"

"A few minor twinges left, that is all."

"That is good."

Cora was a poor seamstress. Her former governesses would be astounded to see her at work at the despised activity, but they wouldn't be impressed with the result.

The afternoon wore on with bone-jarring jangling and jostling that the fineness of the duke's carriage couldn't overcome. Cora found herself gazing out the window, exhausted from the hours on the road, the mending forgotten on her lap. Several more days stretched ahead of them. She sighed at the thought. Maybe she should put up a fuss at the next change, just to get out of the length of the trip to Scotland.

But then she'd have to go back to London. Another coach-ride. She sighed.

"My lady, is there any way I could assist you?" Miss Douglas's face was serene, but over the afternoon Cora had caught a few of her dismayed looks at Cora's dismal mending.

"Here, Miss Douglas." Cora handed the white linen back to her. "Thank you for lending me the use of it. And please rip my stitches out when not in my presence, to spare my blushes."

Mr. Malcolm, slumped in his seat with his eyes closed, let out a low guffaw that turned into a snore. Cora eyed him askance, but caught the duke's upturned mouth, and turned to the window, trying to keep embarrassed amusement off her face.

"You own coal mines, Duke?" was her next question.

"Extensive coal mines near Edinburgh. They were my mother's. She brought them into her marriage."

"And your principal seat is Blackdale Castle?"

"Yes, in the Highlands, along the coast, off the Firth of Lorne. The castle was built in 1650, but has been extensively renovated and added to."

Prinny, corpulent, well groomed, and having suffered from parental tyranny in the marriage department for decades, had already heard the story going around London of the lady, the duke, and the lady's mother. He had given his slightly inebriated opinion to those in earshot that he was sure the maiden had eloped with the duke, and that he wished them joy.

When the Dowager Countess of Winfield tracked him down at his post-levee Grand Dinner, the Prince Regent was dismayed to be faced with this pinnacle of high-bred maternal rage, and did his best to avoid, and when that failed, put her off.

So the Dowager Countess went to the Duke of Wellington.

"What I'd like to know, what has been niggling my mind, I have no business asking. But I will anyway." Mr. Malcolm's heavy-lidded eyes slid over to Cora, and she waited as he paused in his question. Anything could come out of his mouth. "Why was Lady Cora," he nodded to her, "coming to see the duke this morning, unchaperoned? His grace has said he did not arrange it."

Cora felt her face heat, and she avoided the gazes of the duke and his servants. "I was coming to return the duke's hat and gloves, and . . . ," she swallowed, conflict running through her veins, leaving her hot and chilled in turns, ". . . to speak privately with his grace."

"What did you want to speak to me about, my lady?" The duke's voice was gentle.

"First," she forced herself to talk, "I intended to apologize for my mother's treatment of you, your grace. She can be most . . . harsh."

She risked a glance at him. His face had hardened, but he nodded.

She swallowed down the tightness in her throat, and pushed past the nervous clenching of her stomach. "And then, I was going to say, I was intending to say—" She rushed the rest, she just had to say it, to get it out. "—When I sneaked out of my mother's home to go see the Duke of Blackdale, I was going to tell him . . . that I turn twenty-one next March. I will be of age, and can marry where I will. If you will be patient, and if you do not need my mother's money, because she will not give it, but if you will be patient, if you are still interested and unattached next year, you could ask for my hand . . . could ask me then."

Silence reigned in the confines of the coach. She found herself breathing rapidly, and forcing back the stinging press of tears in her eyes. "And then, in March, I would be able to give my own answer, of my own will, freely, and with full power to act on it."

Her eyes were drawn back—riveted—to his again, his burning blue gaze wide, his jaw working.

"And would that answer have been yes?" His voice was deep, like it had been dragged out of him from a painful place.

She pulled her gaze away, and clenched her hands in her lap. "I . . . I don't know anymore." She would not cry. She would not.

Miss Douglas let out an exhalation, and turned her face to her window.

The Iron Duke, brilliant victor of Waterloo, had recently arrived in London, having come up after a year of leading the army of occupation in Paris. He was, conveniently, a guest of honor at the Prince Regent's dinner.

The Duke of Wellington had heard the story that was circulating around the ton of how the countess had insultingly denied the former Colonel Douglas, Duke of Blackdale, to pay his addresses to her daughter, and how the young lady had the next morning gone missing, her bonnet found stripped of its owner in Hyde Park, where the duke's carriage had also been spotted.

He listened with attentive sympathy to the dowager's maternal woes, and the lack of support she had experienced among the heads of state and religion.

But his grace also knew his grace the Duke of Blackdale rather well. Blackdale had been unusual from the start: an heir to a great house who insisted on becoming a soldier, bought himself his own colors when he came of age, and marched off to war with determination and grit. Wellington had plucked him out of the officers' ranks, had him spend time on his staff, helped him gain his promotions and regiment, and used him as a Scottish spy in France.

He knew Blackdale as a controlled and honorable man, strictly just, unafraid to deal out harsh punishments if they were warranted, and to do the job, no matter how ugly.

He also had a cold temper.

If he had been denied the lady of his choice in a way he did not feel was just, he might have decided to take her anyway.

The Duke of Wellington did not approve of stealing gently bred young ladies and forcing them to marry against their will, and so he said he would support and help the dowager if it turned out the young lady had not eloped willingly.

Captain Bowden, one of the Duke of Wellington's staff officers, stood near, and listened to the dowager's recital with noises of shock and dismay.

"Bowden, do you know the young lady?" the duke asked.

"Yes, your grace. I was introduced to her a week ago."

"Will you go after them, Bowden? Find the duke, and discover if the young lady is with him. And, shall we say, the nature of their relationship?"

Bowden snapped a salute and flashed a grin. "Yes, sir! I will start out immediately."

The dowager had to be satisfied with that. She went back home to stew in indignation and await reports.

The only way to know that, yes, they truly were in July, was that the sunlight lasted until 9 o'clock, though hidden behind clouds. As the sun went down, a brilliant yellow and red blaze, gorgeous in color, suffused the sky.

Lady Cora's face in the golden-red light coming through the curtains was beautiful. She was a fire creature of exquisite structure, the soft curves and planes of her face illumined, and her eyes glowing. Adam, contentedly sitting across from her, couldn't keep his gaze off her. She was so beautiful, this fire fairy. She was holding her narcissus again. It seemed to be looking healthier than after its ordeal this morning, at least a small amount. He could hope. Its blossoms had taken on an omen of herself in his mind. If they recovered and prospered despite the damage, then there was hope that she would recover, and forgive as well.

She kept her eyes focused on the passing fields and the setting sun, and didn't seem to notice his ardent regard. Until he caught her looking through her lashes sideways at him. Oh, she had noticed.

Kate sat primly in the seat next to her, her hands folded in her lap, watching through the window as well.

Malcolm beside Adam kept his legs stretched out as far as Kate's legs would allow him to. He irritated Kate intentionally, Adam knew. He picked at her every chance he could. Adam mentally shook his head at Malcolm.

His eyes were drawn back to Lady Cora, she who was beautiful, and not yet his. Through their conversations of the afternoon, he'd begun to hope. She was not yet easy, but had been becoming more relaxed as the day had passed.

Deep, heavy clouds sat on the edge of the horizon, encroaching on the beauty of the sunset. As the sun disappeared behind the hills, the wind picked up. It began to rain hard.

Captain Bowden set out for Gretna Green at 11 p.m., after gathering his supplies, taking leave of a lady or two, and boasting of his errand for the Iron Duke to his brothers in arms. He hired a hack, and started off in high spirits through the drizzling dark.

Chapter Thirteen

Torrent

Saturday, July 6, 1816, 2 am

The rain came down in sheets. It hit the windows of the carriage, cold winds buffeted them. The temperature in the coach, which had been comfortable in Cora's pelisse and gloves all day, plummeted. She could see her breath in a pale cloud in the dim light coming from the carriage lanterns outside.

Thunder rolled in the distance, and lightning lit the outside. A flash and instant boom of a strike hit close to them. The horses whinnied, and the carriage jerked with their alarm.

She felt horrible for the post boys and Charlie Coachman outside, experiencing the full onslaught of the elements.

"Your grace, this isn't good." Miss Douglas's voice was almost drowned in the sound of the torrents hitting the roof.

"No, it isn't," He answered. He pulled out his pocket watch and checked the time. "It's a quarter after two. I had not planned to stop, but that may not be possible if this continues."

Their progress slowed to a crawl. They all sat tense, watching the windows as sheet after drenching sheet hit the glass.

Cold droplets struck Cora's face as Charlie Coachman opened the hatch, and yelled down to the duke.

"Your grace, we can't proceed in this, and it don't look likely to let up!"

"I agree, Charlie!" He called back, turning to kneel on the seat, and bring his face closer to the hatch. "Find the nearest hostelry, and we will stop for the night."

"Aye, milord duke!"

The hatch shut, and Cora relaxed some at the thought of a bed, safety from this storm, and an end to this crazy, interminable day. She hoped they would find an inn quickly!

The hatch opened again. "Your grace, the boys say the closest inn is small, but should have room. It's off the main road, but we should be able to reach it in ten minutes, even in this downpour."

"Sounds good, Charlie, let's head to it!"

The road changed from the wide and well-traveled avenue of the Great North Road, to a smaller and tighter lane through trees and fenced fields. A few shapes that might be dark cottages passed by her window. She felt isolated in the pounding noise of the rain and the rumble of thunder.

Lightning illumined the worried face of the Duke of Blackdale, the long ordeal of the day made worse by this onslaught.

The drumming outside escalated into pings and clatters. The horses whinnied in alarm.

"Hail." Mr. Malcolm said, and grabbed the leather strap hanging nearest him.

Oh my. Cora followed suit. She squeezed the strap that hung near her face with her hand, and clutching the flower pot in its protective crate with her other.

The hail was small, it pinged against the painted wooden roof of the carriage. The men outside shouted at each other. The carriage lurched and stopped and lurched again. The sound of the hail worsened. The pieces were getting bigger. No longer small, bead-sized rounds of white ice, they became pearls, and then coin-sized, then the size of figs, plummeting down and pummeling the horses and men outside.

The horses panicked.

The carriage lurched again, and then accelerated, shaking with the wild running of the horses. Cora screamed as the carriage skidded and planed, swinging uncontrollably around a bend as the team plunged and bucked all efforts to control them.

Then they were falling. Cora felt herself suspended in the air for one second, and saw the face of the duke, eyes wide in horror, in a flash of lightning.

In the slowed rush of seconds before they hit, Cora felt arms grab her roughly, wrap around her body, and turn her. The carriage crashed onto its side.

Her hip hit half on the padded side of the carriage, and half on the window frame. She felt a sharp pain, and heard the oomph as her weight came down on the person who had put themselves between her and the side.

They slid. Glass shattered underneath her. She felt her skirts tug, rip, and tear, and pain burned through Cora's leg. She cried out.

The carriage stopped. They panted in still silence for a second before the carriage lurched, grating against the ground. The horses were screaming, struggling against each other and their traces. Cora screamed as well, pulled her leg away from the grinding ground, and buried her face against the warm body underneath her. The lurching continued for several minutes as the men outside worked in dark and hail to cut the horses loose from the toppled carriage.

The sound of the hail lessened, and the softer sound of rain resumed. The carriage finally stopped moving.

The chest under hers rose and fell unevenly, his breathing rough with a strange catch and gasp. One lantern remained outside, the light fitful and flickering over the skewed interior of the carriage.

Cora lifted her head. The duke looked up at her, his face pale in the strange, shifting light. He lifted a trembling hand and stroked her face.

"Are you all right?" His words came out in a rough croak.

"I think so. Bruised, and my leg . . ." she whispered. His breathing was labored, she was hurting him. She struggled to sit up, to find a place to put her knees and hands that would not dig into him.

"Shhh." He stilled her with his hand against her cheek. It was warm and strong, a soldier's hand, an officer who rode long hours in the saddle.

"I'm hurting you."

"Only a wee bit. Here, let me." His body shifted under hers and pushed her as he sat up. He rearranged her limbs till she wasn't digging into him. Her face flushed hot. She was now decidedly sitting on his lap.

"Kate, Kate, are you all right?" the voice of Mr. Malcolm called above them.

"I'm fine," Miss Douglas's voice came from right beside Cora. She had fallen on the padded side, right where Cora would have been if the Duke had not pulled her to him.

"Your grace!" Mr. Malcolm called. "Your ribs! Are you all right?"

The duke coughed, and groaned. "I think—" he broke off hoarsely, "I think they are only bruised. No new breaks."

"Thank heaven," Mr. Malcolm's was fervent. He dropped down near them.

The carriage door above them opened. Cold rain fell on Cora's head as one of the postboys looked down on them.

"Are you all right in there?" The man called.

"Just bruises, we think," Malcolm called up.

"Good," the man said. "We've got a broken arm out here, some bad bruising, and even worse, one of the horses has broken its leg."

"Oh, no!" Cora cried out, her voice joining several other cries of dismay.

"We are going to shoot the horse. Recommend the ladies stay in the carriage until it's all over."

"Wise idea." the duke croaked out. "Malcolm, why don't you go out and see if you can assist in anything. I will stay here with the ladies, and catch my breath."

"Yes, your grace." Mr. Malcolm stood. He paused, and turned his face back to them. "You're sure you are all right, Kate?"

"Och aye, am fine," she answered testily.

"I'm sorry I didna catch ye, Kate," he said, worried sincerity in his voice.

"You couldna have caught me, ye daft man! Go do as you are bid and get that door closed!"

The rain was soaking Cora through her pelisse.

"Aye!" He scrambled up and out, and swung the door closed with a bang.

Cora moved to get off the duke, but his arm on her waist stopped her. "My darling, are you sure you are all right?"

His darling? Her mind shuttered to a stop. His face was near hers, and he tightened his hold on her, bringing her even closer. She forced her brain to start working again. "My leg hurts."

"Which leg?"

She indicated her left leg with her hand on his. He reached down and felt along her leg. She started at the touch. Goodness!

Then his hand reached the sore spot. She hissed in pain, and scrambled off him, his arms releasing her. She crouched against what was normally the carriage floor. He pulled up his legs to give her room, and leaned against the roof.

She pulled off a glove with her teeth and felt along her leg, finding the pelisse ripped and skirts wet, perhaps from the rain. When she found the spot that hurt, where the glass and gravel had caught her, she pulled her hand back wet. Her fingers looked black in the darkness of the carriage. She raised her hand, trying to catch any of the light from the lantern outside.

"I think I'm bleeding," She felt calm.

The duke let out an alarmed groan, and scrambled toward her. "Show me?"

Cora straightened her leg with a grunt and grimace. "Here," she indicated her lower thigh, above the knee. "It's a bad scrape, I think."

He tried to examine her leg, moved fabric out of the way. "Light, I need light."

"I will seek some, your grace," Miss Douglas said, moving to stand.

"Wait, not yet, Kate." The duke stopped her.

Cora had been distracted from the awful whinnies coming from outside the carriage. She realized now that some of the tension in her shoulders was from the horrible sounds of pain coming from the wounded horse.

She heard a man's voice call "Clear!" and then a shot rang out, loud and appalling in the dark.

"Oh, no!" she cried, and felt her shoulders grabbed by the duke. He pulled her into his chest once again, and she buried her face into his neck, dry sobs wracking her lungs.

His hands rubbed her back, and she gasped. His spicy scent flooded her senses.

"Shh, my darling, my bonny lass, shhh." He murmured into her ear. Sweet words tumbled from him, his voice rumbling in his chest, vibrating into her rib cage. They throbbed into her heart. Her breathing hitched. Such wonderful words! She wanted to stay here, and continue being touched and spoken to so lovingly.

How inappropriate! She laughed, a quick burst, sounding more of panic than humor. He released her, but brought his hands up to her face once again, stroking her forehead and cheeks. "Better?" he asked.

She nodded rapidly, not knowing if she could handle any more of his affection without losing her sanity. She felt on the brink of two opposites. Her mind urged her to run from him, to get away. Her heart told her the opposite: to fall into him and never let go.

This day had been too much. In self-preservation, she pulled away from him, and clasped her hands, clutching them in front of her as a barrier. Then she remembered the blood on her hand, and looked down at it in dismay.

The duke looked at her hands. "Now, I could use the light, Kate."

"Aye, your grace," she answered, her voice steady in the dark.

Cora heard her movements as Miss Douglas stood, and she fumbled with the carriage door latch above her. It opened, Malcolm appearing above them.

"Thank you, Mr. Malcolm. Lady Cora is bleeding, and we need a light in order to assess the damage."

"Right away, Miss Douglas." His voice was formal and cool.

The light was brought, and as the duke looked over her leg, she realized his breathing had normalized. Then he moved, twisted, and it hitched once more.

Her falling on him had hurt him.

She felt numb, cut off, overwhelmed by the events of this day that never ended. Her abduction this morning, being tied and gagged, the harrowing storm, the crash tonight.

And then to be touched with gentleness, and spoken to with the tenderest words of love any man had ever given to her, even among all her persistent suitors.

She was a stripped tree, bare of leaf and many branches, exposed to the cold wind. She crouched and wrapped her arms around herself to contain the chill.

A lantern arrived, and it was determined that she had a bad scrape on her outside thigh. They needed to clean the glass and gravel from it, rinse and bandage it. Miss Douglas set to work in the light of the lantern with a bodkin and a water skein. Cora gritted her teeth against the pain of Miss Douglas's ministrations.

The duke gave a soft sound of dismay. "Oh, your narcissus, Lady Cora." The pot had been tumbled and overturned yet again. The crate had lost its lid, and now in the light of the lantern, they could see that the dirt was smeared all over the velvet upholstery, and was turning into mud where the pounding rain outside had gotten in with each opening of the carriage doors above them.

The pot was still in the crate, though its soil had been tossed all throughout the cabin. The duke worked to gather the soil that he could, and he put it all together in the pot again, setting the poor bulbs back into their now-inadequate soil.

He placed the pot into Cora's numbed hands. Her fingers were too cold to be dexterous. She pulled off her remaining glove, and attended to the damaged plant. Several flowers heads were crushed, but, somehow, the majority of the stems had survived their second ordeal.

She ignored what was happening to her leg as best she could until Miss Douglas poured wine onto the wound. Cora couldn't keep back an indrawn hiss. It stung.

"Let it work, my lady, and then I will rinse with water, and it will be better."

Miss Douglas produced a bandage and plasters. She bandaged Cora's leg, and declared herself satisfied.

The duke had left at some point. Cora hadn't noticed. It was much less cramped in the overturned carriage now with only Miss Douglas and herself crouching on the padded sides, avoiding the wet and broken window below them.

They were informed a carriage was coming from the inn a half-mile off.

The sideways walls of the carriage were closing in on Cora. Her lungs seized. She couldn't get enough air. There wasn't enough air in here.

The doors were drip, drip, dripping along their seams, the water falling into the center. She had to stay away from the cold water. She felt like she was drowning, surrounded, crushed in this horrible cabin.

Cora's narcissus needed more earth. She needed to get out of here and get more soil for her flowers. She didn't care that the cold rain was still pouring down outside.

She needed to get out.

She rose into a half-crouch and reached up to fumble with numb fingers with the latch of the carriage door.

Through a muffled buzzing she heard Miss Douglas say, "My lady?" She said more, but Cora didn't hear her. She managed to unlatch it, and pushed, pushed so hard, and broke the seal of the pooled water over the door. It came down on her in a wave. The door flew up and open, crashing down on the other side with a bang. Cold air hit Cora in the face and she sucked in a fresh, sharp breath. The rain came down on her, freezing, on the edge of ice, like sharp needles of cold pain on her skin. But she gasped and sucked the air through the sleet and coughed as some water got into her mouth. She lowered her head and was able to breathe normally.

"Lady Cora!" Malcolm, his hat drooping in the rain, and his coat bundled around him, ran toward the carriage when he saw her. "Stay in the carriage, my lady, it's miserable out here."

"No—I need—I need—" she stuttered, her lips numb in the cold. "I must get out of here!"

Mr. Malcolm stared at her with wide eyes. He didn't do anything to help her! Anger flashed in her. She reached up, and searched for handholds. She would pull herself out. But her hands couldn't find a grip, they slipped and didn't clamp down with her numb fingers.

Then the duke's hands were there, grabbing her by the arms, and pulling her.

"Malcolm, Kate, help me."

Kate pushed her up from behind, and Malcolm grabbed another arm, and they got her out. The duke's arms were around her, easing her feet to the sodden ground.

Her leg was burning with pain, having flexed and been hit in her mad scramble to get out of the carriage. She hissed, and the duke's arms tightened around her, stealing her breath. No, no, she couldn't.

She pushed away from him, and he let go. She stumbled back, panted, felt wild and unhinged.

"Are you all right, Lady Cora?" he asked.

"I—I—I'm fine. I'm fine now." She endeavored to engage rational thought. She could breathe, she was out of there, it was all right. Her leg hurt, and she was cold. Her head was bare, the rain pummeled her scalp, her hair plastered to her face and neck. She flexed her fingers, trying to get feeling into them.

Where was her narcissus? It was on top of the carriage, being drowned in the cold rain. She stumbled over to it and took it carefully with her palms, her fingers not responding.

Her teeth were chattering, a strange, uncontrolled scatter clatter.

Then Kate was there with her crushed velvet hat, putting it on her head and tying the ribbons. And putting her woolen cloak over her shoulders. Wool, that was good in the cold rain. She wrapped it around herself, and buried her face in the still-dry inside lining of soft flannel. It was warm, and she clamped her jaw down against further chattering.

Kate was bundled in a cloak as well, her hat also crushed from the carriage accident.

Cora looked around with wild eyes. The horses had been led off, the men coming and going, a crowd of men came from the village to help.

She saw the poor, pitiful shape of the dead horse. Someone had covered the body with a horse blanket, and she was grateful to them.

She held the flower pot close to her body under the cloak. It needed more soil.

She looked down at the hail-strewn ground around her. She spotted a promising stick. Her feet were numb. She slipped, almost fell from the fallen leaves that slicked her path. She bundled her ripped skirts and cloak around her legs, and squatted onto her heels. Pain flared from the horrid scrape on her thigh, and she groaned.

"Lady Cora?" someone asked. She ignored them.

She picked up the icy stick, and began to dig in the ground with awkward movements. She went below the litter of decaying leaves and into the dirt beneath. After a few minutes, she's gathered enough soil to replenish the pot. She tried holding the clump of muddy soil in her hands to warm them, but her hands were too cold to make much difference. She arranged the soil around the plant by feel, little light reached her from the lanterns around the accident site.

She brought the pot into her huddled body, hoping her core still retained enough heat to keep the bulbs alive.

She stayed there for several minutes, balanced on her heels, water rising around her as her booted feet sank into the sodden ground. Hailstones, fallen branches, and leaves clogged the earth around her. The trees above were stripped of their foliage.

A carriage finally arrived to rescue them. The ladies entered with relief, dripping wet and shivering. Kate instructed the luggage to be freed from their overturned carriage, and loaded on the carriage they were transferring to.

It was warmer in the carriage, out of the rain, but they were so soaked that Cora still shivered and huddled to conserve her body heat.

They reached the small inn. Cora was numb with exhaustion. She blinked in the light of the entrance way, and moved her stiff body slowly.

Kate requested towels and several kettles of hot water, and a tea tray—"Just tea, thank you"—brought up to their room.

Once there, Cora was too tired to be self-conscious in front of Miss Douglas as she undressed her, rubbed her down with towels warmed by the fire, and wiped her face, hands, and feet with hot wet facecloths. She wrapped her round with blankets, twisted a towel into a turban over Cora's soaked hair, and handed her hot tea. Kate investigated the trunks to find out what was in them. She emerged with an unfamiliar white flannel nightgown, embroidered with whitework, lovely, expensive, and appropriate for any young lady.

Cora vaguely heard her exclaim that "Mr. Malcolm has better taste then a body would think!"

She pulled it over Cora's head, careful not to displace the towel holding her wet hair. Cora realized that Miss Douglas was still in her own soaked traveling garments when her wet skirt brushed her.

"Oh, you are . . . still cold, Miss Douglas." Cora felt her word slur with tiredness, but couldn't fight it.

"I'm fine. As soon as you are in bed, I will attend to myself."

She checked the bandage on Cora's leg, clucked over it, rubbed Cora's hair next to the fire, and bustled about, running the warming pan under the bedclothes. "These sheets are questionable, but they are well aired, and now they are warm."

And she directed Cora up the steps into the high bed. Cora laid down with a sigh of pure relief.

Her limbs ached as they thawed. Her hip hurt, likely a bruise. She lay and hurt and wondered if she would ever feel good again. Miss Douglas finally stripped off her own sodden garments, and readied herself for sleep in the trundle from under Cora's bed.

When Miss Douglas blew out the light, the banked fire glowed dimly in the dark room. The rain poured and pounded on the roof of the inn, a new cadence, different from the pounding on carriage roofs. Finally, Cora was able to sleep.

Chapter Fourteen

Morning

Saturday, July 6, 1816, 5 AM

Adam woke with a gasp, sucking in air, his chest heaving. He threw open the bed curtains, and stumbled out of the tangled sheets onto the cold floorboards.

How had those curtains gotten closed? Malcolm would never! He knew better. He knew Adam needed air moving about him, space around him as he slept.

Adam welcomed drafts, craved open spaces and bracing breezes. He could not stand to be hot, stifled, airless.

Adam stood, panting, letting the chill of the room outside the bed curtains seep into his bare feet, and cool the clammy sweat on his brow and neck. His heart slowed.

He turned, and studied the curtains. The ties had come loose. They were old and worn out. The curtains had fallen closed in the night.

He wanted to rip them down, get rid of them. It was still dark. He wanted more sleep.

But it wouldn't be polite as a guest in this sorry inn to further destroy their second best room.

Instead, he bunched, twisted, and loosely knotted the curtains. He poured himself a glass of water from the ewer on the washstand. He was parched.

He splashed his face, fumbling in the dark room. He didn't want to bother with candles and flint. He leaned, dripping, over the washstand.

Sleep. He needed sleep. And to get that dream out of his mind.

The screams rose up in his ears again. The moans, the cries for water. The terrible dryness of his own throat. He could not stand to be thirsty any more. Would not allow it. He must have water, must quench his thirst.

The feeling of dead bodies, dead friends, covering him, burying him. Sticky, congealed, stinking blood in a pool around him, soaked into the ground like grisly rain.

Adam woke the second time to dull aches that sharpened as he moved. His recently healed ribs were bruised again. It would slow down his interminable recovery. It had been almost a year since Waterloo and the cannon shot that had grazed him. A year since so many of the men under his charge died.

Two hundred and twenty-five. That was the number.

The aching sore on his heart flared. He made himself think the number again, and to feel the ache.

He could list the names, they were branded into his mind with sharp clarity, able to be called up at any time and read out, each of them.

Gerald Macleod

Sam Ogilvy, dedicated and grizzled soldier.

Clarence Smith, so young—too young to be in a battle such as that . . .

He stopped himself. There were other things he must do that day. He lived, as so many of them did not, and he had a future to secure.

He was determined to secure that future, the happiness he wanted. To have the love he had never before been granted. He craved the depth and intimacy that a wife well-chosen was said to bring to a man's life. He wanted it deep in his bruised bones and in his aching heart.

Lady Cora could give him that love, couldn't she?

He had chosen well, he knew it. But she pushed him away last night.

A natural reaction to the events of the day. Being abducted, tied, and gagged that morning by him, a prisoner confined, and then the traumatic crash. She had been shocked and panicked.

That crash! And her injury. She was under his care, and she had been hurt. Guilt ate at the edges of him.

But it had been an accident. Nature had unleashed itself on them, and she had been hurt.

He needed to gain her trust again. He had to overcome her natural aversion to these traumatic circumstances by kindness and whatever love she would let him show her. He would give her all the freedom of movement he could afford to give her.

Which was a problem. He still needed to get her to Scotland. He couldn't afford to give her much freedom at all.

He groaned, and rolled out of the lumpy bed. He'd insisted on the innkeeper giving Lady Cora their best room. Their second best wasn't impressive, but it was swept, and it was better than many accommodations he'd suffered through in the Peninsula. And infinitely better than bivouacking in the freezing rain outside.

He stood still for a moment, letting the pain and stiffness of bruises and damaged ribs pass over him like a wave, and then forced his body to move.

He needed to get them on the road.

Cora awoke with a clear mind, an aching hip, and a stark recollection of the wild events of the day before. She lay there, aware of Miss Douglas moving in the room, but not wanting to stir.

How did she get herself into this situation?

Yesterday morning, she had wanted to talk to the Duke of Blackdale before she left London with Mother. She'd had the nominal excuse of his gloves and hat needing to be returned to him. Dressing herself and sneaking out of the house after the housemaid had made up a fire in her room, but before Richards was up to serve her, had been tricky, but doable.

But the abduction! It had been horrible. Really, what was the duke thinking?

And why was she going along with it?

A knock of a breakfast tray arriving, and news that the duke wanted to leave in an hour motivated Cora to rise and get ready for another miserable day of travel.

Miss Douglas took out three gowns from the trunks the duke had provided. Awkward and improper to wear gowns purchased for her by a man who was not a relation, but her walking dress and pelisse were well and truly ruined by last night's accident. Cora didn't have a choice.

They were surprisingly lovely and practical traveling gowns. Cora chose the lavender one to wear for today. Miss Douglas helped her into it, and then pinned and tucked to perfect the fit. Cora ate breakfast as Miss Douglas stitched.

"Lady Cora," Miss Douglas began, and stopped. Cora looked up from her toast. "I want to assure you again that I thought I was assisting an elopement, not a kidnapping. And I—" Miss Douglas glanced at her, but then averted her eyes again.

Cora waited for her to go on, her feelings a roiling mix.

"I am willing to assist you in leaving and heading back to London. I have some money, and we could take the stage or the mail, if you want to leave without confronting the duke. Or if you are willing to confront him, and tell him you will go no further, I am sure he will provide funds for us to go back by post. I would accompany you, and make sure you were safely brought back to your mother."

Cora watched Miss Douglas, her beautiful face, her dusky skin, and her proud bearing. She was willing to betray the duke and help her. Cora's heart warmed.

But she frowned. "I ought to, oughtn't I?" With this opportunity, Cora really ought to . . . She pushed at a dry crust on her plate. "I ought to insist, and if he resists, cry foul and cause a huge scene. Should have yesterday." She looked down at her tray of mackerel and toast. She took a sip of tea and thought about oughts, naughts, and possibilities.

How did she feel? She was away from her mother, and there was a sense of freedom in that. She was on an adventure. She was heading to Scotland with a handsome and intriguing man.

"Thank you, Miss Douglas, for the offer. I will . . . consider it."

The way the duke made her feel was dangerous, heady. His attention made her head spin and her breath quicken. She ought to leave and go back to London where it was safe and restricted.

But . . . she didn't want to.

She swallowed. "I think, for now, I will go along with this adventure, and see where it takes me." She set down her cup with a clink. "But Miss Douglas," Cora caught the maid's eye. "Thank you for the offer; that was very honorable for you to do. Will it still stand, if later in the trip I decide I do need to get away from this situation?"

"Oh, aye, just say the word, and I will help you leave, my lady." Miss Douglas's eyes were relieved. She sat up even straighter.

Cora nodded. "Good. And you may have noticed, I'm generally a poor traveler." Cora smiled wanly. "I really don't want to get into a carriage again."

The dowager had had enough of waiting.

The report from the duke's first change of horses reached her late, in an almost illegible letter dashed off by young Mr. Yardley. The servant he had sent back to deliver the letter was a bit more intelligible in his report.

The duke had pushed his own team further than was prudent, and hadn't changed horses until two stops were past. There, they had left the dangerously spent team, and taken a fresh. The passengers had reportedly been the duke, his manservant, and a maidservant and a lady whom the duke was escorting to an ailing great aunt in Newcastle.

The lady had been seen and matched the description of Lady Cora.

Young Mr. Yardley, discovering this at the posting house, had dashed off the illegible letter to the dowager, given it to his servant, and had hired a horse. He had ridden after the duke and the lady he was 'escorting.'

The duke had her! He had her daughter!

Lady Winfield paced up and down, driven mad by inaction. Soon her supportive friends and rivals would come to console her, keep her company in her time of need, and to snipe behind her back.

She must act!

Lord Eastham arrived, finally having heard the story after having been out of town for a day. He entered, proclaiming himself shocked and dismayed.

"You! You are the one who introduced them!"

"I confess I did."

"And mostly to cause mischief!"

He remained silent, but they both knew she spoke true.

"You must fix this!"

"How?"

"By going after them. He must be heading to Gretna Green. He must expect pursuit, and it's the closest point. There he will force her to marry him!"

"Surely not, they will not marry an unwilling bride, even over the anvil. She only need say no."

"Beaten, coerced, a gun to her back! He will do it, he with his black heart."

"I can't imagine, no, Lady Winfield, he loves her. He would not beat her."

She paced, wringing her hands. "What was his father? A brutal man, by all reports! I have heard tales. Servants, underlings, even his wife and his own children! Beaten. And what is he? A soldier and an officer, surrounded by death! How can you know what he will do with my daughter in his power?"

Lord Eastham's face was white and strained. After a long moment, he said. "I will go after them."

"Good! And I am going with you." She swung about, throwing open the doors to her breakfast parlor, and finding a maid, two footmen, and her butler waiting outside.

"Lady Winfield!" Lord Eastham burst out in dismay.

"You!" to the maid. "Tell Masterson to pack my bags. I am leaving for Scotland immediately." Her skirts flared from her high-waisted gown as she pivoted back to the earl. "What is your vehicle? Covered carriage or phaeton? Who are we taking?"

"I was intending on taking my phaeton with only my tiger, to travel the lightest and the fastest."

"Excellent, an open carriage. I will sit beside you, and take the reigns if you get tired."

"Madam! A lady in an open carriage, in this weather? All the way to Scotland? And you will not take the reigns!"

"I am an excellent whip, as you know, Lord Eastham. Enough of this discussion, we must act! Go get yourself ready. My kitchens will pack food, but you must dress warmly, make sure you have adequate supplies and money, and bundle up your tiger, it's remarkably cold outside for July. And raining."

"I have noticed, Lady Winfield." His answer was dry and a scowl marred his beautiful face.

But he did as she commanded.

The coach was beyond repair.

Adam negotiated with the innkeeper for the vehicle that had picked them up, and prevailed.

He went to check on the postboy who had broken his arm. He gave the man three sovereigns, and let him know that Adam would pay his lost wages until he could get back to work. Adam also paid for the horse, giving them a letter to go to the postmaster on how to contact his solicitor.

That taken care of, he went to see Charlie Coachman.

"I'm sorry your grace, so sorry, the horses got out of my control, and the lassie was injured—"

Adam shushed him. "It was hail, Charlie, no one could have kept control of their team in that onslaught. They were being stoned, and so were you all. How are you feeling?"

"Bruised, milord duke, but otherwise hale—" He coughed, "Eh, otherwise hearty, your grace."

"Are you healthy enough to continue on?"

Charlie insisted he was. He proclaimed insult at the idea of him staying here to recover, and a substitute coachman sought.

Assured, Adam asked him to be ready in an hour to go, and what vehicle they would be taking.

Adam left him to his recriminations and his breakfast, and went inside to dash off the letters to his solicitor that were needed to wrap up this business before he could get them on their way.

There was no private parlor to let, so he ate his breakfast in the tap room with most of the rest of the village, and left Malcolm to fuss over trunks and clothes in the second-best bedroom.

He was sitting there when Lady Cora came down with Kate. She was wearing an unfamiliar traveling dress of lavender, a pelisse of dark rose, and a hat trimmed with pink flowers. All Malcolm's acquisitions, he was sure. His valet had done good work. She looked fetching.

She was holding her pretty little flower pot, the narcissus looking better than it had last night. His heart warmed to see it.

He got up and walked to them as they reached the bottom of the stairs. Coming closer, he could see the faint bruises under her eyes. She was still exhausted. Yesterday had been an ordeal for them all, but especially for her.

They exchanged bows and curtseys, and he stepped closer.

"Lady Cora, are you well enough to travel this morning? How is your leg? Are you all right?"

She smiled faintly at him. "I'm well enough, your grace. I'm just a little worn out."

"Are you sure? We can, I can . . ." he trailed off. He really couldn't. He couldn't delay much more, they risked pursuit catching up to them. And he couldn't leave her here, not without ripping up his every chance of happiness. He refused to be parted from her now that he had seized her.

But she was tired, and probably hurting.

"I never travel that well, you know," she gave a small laugh. "I like being there, or planning on being somewhere, but the actual travel between, I'm often miserable during."

He frowned in concern. "You do not get sick in the carriage, do you?" She hadn't complained of that yesterday.

"No, not generally. I dislike the confinement and restriction, the lack of activity." She gave him a small wry smile. "If you, with your connections and abilities, could find a way to spirit me to your chosen destination in an instant, your grace, I'd be much obliged."

He felt his lips upturn in response, a warm glow suffusing his chest. She was wonderful, adorable. He loved her.

"I will get working on that immediately, my lady. Though I apologize, that we only have a second-hand carriage and job horses right now to get us on our journey."

Chapter Fifteen

Mud

SATURDAY, JULY 6, 1816, AFTERNOON

Their forward progress had slowed. Cora glanced out the window. The rain was a steady drizzle, and they seemed lower to the ground than usual.

Mud. The road was thick with it. Churned, tracked, rutted, and, from the pace of the horses, miserable to pull through.

"With the state of these roads, we're going to need to change horses every five miles rather than every twenty." Mr. Malcolm observed, awake for once.

"That may prove to be so." The duke looked through the window with a grimace.

"What are the tolls for, but to keep the roads from getting to this state?"

"What are you expecting, Malcolm, miles of paving stones? Cobbles?"

"That sounds good. Or gravel; that could also work."

"The rain just keeps coming down," Cora said. "I worry about the nation's crops. Overwatering can kill. The roots drown."

"The weather is very strange this year. And most inconvenient." The duke gave a wry upturn of his lips. "You have such pleasure in your plants, Lady Cora. Have you been so since a girl?"

"Yes, since a very young child. It began with flowers; I loved them. And my interest was fanned by fruit and berry picking." Cora remembered indulgent nurses during berry season at the Grange, her mouth and hands covered with sticky red juices. "Till my grandfather gave me my own potted flower to care for. And soon my little potted garden grew, and I had taken over the conservatory."

The duke smiled. "I look forward to showing you the gardens at Blackdale Castle. They have been only under the care of gardeners for the last year."

She looked at him, not sure what to say. Longing rose up in her heart, soft and persuasive over the loud objections of her mind.

The carriage jerked, slid sideways, stopped, and sank several inches. The cabin settled down at a tilt. The horses strained and whinnied, the carriage rocked, but they didn't move forward. Despite the four horses, they were mired and unmovable in the mud. Completely stuck.

"We need to get out of the carriage, and lighten the load," the duke said.

"If we must." Mr. Malcolm gave a grimace.

"Else be here forever."

Malcolm let down the step, made a face, and exited the coach, squelching sounds coming from his steps. The duke followed.

Cora moved to the open door, and looked down at the yards of mud surrounding the mired carriage. The mud was past the horses' fetlocks. She judged the distance to where the ground might become solid again to be a rise of hill with a copse of trees twenty yards away.

She had dealt plenty with mud, but usually close to home, where other pairs of half boots were available, and baths, and multiple servants to take care of the mess.

The men were in tall hessian boots, much better for slogging through mud. But hers would fill, the mud deep enough to overflow the top of her half boots. She didn't relish the thought.

The duke reached out a hand to her. "Lady Cora, will you allow me to carry you to higher ground?"

"Oh! Are you sure, Duke? I'm not—" Blushing, Cora stopped herself before she said 'not light.' She was her mother's daughter, which meant she was not a tiny, slim miss. He was a tall man, with broad shoulders, but on the thin side. Not as thin as Mr. Malcolm, who was lanky and slender boned, but the Duke looked like a powerful man who had lost muscle from illness. She remembered his catching her last night, and how it had hurt his war injuries in the process.

"I'm sure I can save you from a thorough coating of mud over your half-boots, if you will trust me."

Trust him? She really ought not. But he looked at her with those serious blue eyes, and she moved forward. He swept her up in his arms, leaving her breathless. Her injuries from last night twinged, but the pounding of her heart as his arms supported her outshined any aches. Her arm snaked behind his head, careful not to dislodge his tall hat.

"Are you settled, my lady?"

She nodded, not daring to speak more. He took a deep breath, turned, and stepped though the calf-high muck. Each step sunk low, and sucked at his feet until he freed them with a squelch.

She could tell he was straining, and once he wobbled. She clutched at him with a gasp, but he righted, and kept going forward with a clenched jaw. He deposited her gently on the mud-free rise to the side of the road. The soaked ground squelched under her feet, but didn't suck her down. His arms lingered on her, and he looked down at her with burning eyes, his breath rapid from his exertions. Cora felt her pulse quicken, a pounding in her ears. He backed away, tipped his hat, turned, and waded back into the muddy road.

Malcolm watched the duke with his fair burden, and held his breath as they threatened to fall and land in the mud. When the duke successfully traversed the treacherous road, Malcolm turned with a grin to Kate. She stood in the doorway of the carriage, watching Lady Cora and the duke with anxiety in her dark eyes.

"You surely would like to spare your ankles as well, Miss Douglas?"

She raised her brow at him.

"I would be happy to take you over to the side of the road in the same way."

She looked him up and down, and her beautiful mouth twisted. "No, Mr. Malcolm, I am not interested in such a conveyance. My ankles will just have to suffer."

That stung. She was tall, but not as tall as he, and he was strong!

A nearby postilion watched her, and came forward with a smile, "Miss, I would happily take you over."

Malcolm felt his hackles rise, but strived to hide it. The man was shorter than him, but stockier.

The other postboy whistled, "Me too, miss, anytime!"

Malcolm glared at him, "Careful, sir," he said with all the upper-servant haughtiness he could instill in his voice.

Kate turned her finely-shaped nose up at them all. "Thank you, sirs, but no."

She gathered up her dark skirts, revealing a length of worsted-stocking covered leg. Malcolm wanted to shield her from the eyes of the workers who were staring at her, but held still, keeping his hand out to assist her down. She grimly stepped down the carriage steps, ignored his offered hand, and squelched into the mud. She paused at the bottom as she sank into the muck, and Malcolm saw the mud rise to above her half boots and seep in over the top. He could see the shudder go through her body. But that was all the acknowledgment she gave to the discomfort of the cold wet slime, and with her back ramrod straight she squelched and squished over to the rise to join Lady Cora.

"Kate!" Adam raised his brows at Kate's labored progress through the mud.

"Oh, Miss Douglas, your boots!" Lady Cora cried.

"You should have waited for one of the workers or Malcolm to bring you over, Kate." He frowned at her.

"Your pardon, sir, but I chose not to accept their kind offers."

Adam watched the prim tightness on her face, and had to stifle a smile. "Kate, I can't have you catching your death from wet stockings because of pride. Next time, I will take you over the mud myself if you can't stomach the other men."

Kate started, and looked over at him with wide-eyed outrage, "Oh no, sir, that would never do!"

"Will it not? Then accept Malcolm at least."

She sniffed, her gaze downcast and her mouth tight. Whatever was Adam going to do with the two of them? "I'll have the trunks brought over. You are to put on dry stockings at least, Kate, and do what you can for your boots."

"Yes, your grace, of course."

Adam kept his gaze on her, and was amused to realize she was blushing. Her stance became straighter and her expression even more prim, but that didn't hide the deep dusky pink her skin was becoming. She had mud squishing in her boots, and only her pride to blame. He glanced down at Lady Cora, and their eyes caught. She'd noticed Kate's blush too, and her eyes twinkled at him. For Kate's sake, they both pretended they hadn't seen.

One of the postillions came with Adam's trunk. "Set it here, never mind the wet. Malcolm, will you bring Miss Douglas's bag? Thank you." Malcolm arrived, already carrying it, along with one of Lady Cora's trunks. "Lady Cora's trunk on top of mine, thank you. Would you like to sit on them, Lady Cora?"

She glanced at it, and blinked at him. "I suppose."

He reached over and took her by the waist, and lifted her—stifling a grunt; his ribs ached—onto the piled trunks, higher than most comfortable seats.

"Oh," she said, and blinked down at him.

His eyes slid to her lips, rose-bud pink and sweetly shaped, directly at his eye-level. He realized his hands still encircled her waist, his arms running alongside her long thighs. He swallowed, forced himself to release her, and turned away.

Maybe those postboys needed an extra hand?

Kate grumbled over her shoes, standing barefoot in the wet grass, and ruining a towel cleaning them. Cora watched her with sympathy, but was glad it wasn't her this time who had caused yet another lady's maid to slave over a pair of muddy half-boots.

After the trip they were having, Cora was almost comfortable with Miss Douglas, which amazed her. She wanted to ask her probing questions, to find out more about them all, and their unusual relationships. She ought not to intrude on a servant's privacy, but . . .

Cora screwed up her courage. "Miss Douglas? May I ask how you came to be in the employ of the duke?"

Miss Douglas flashed her a look, and turned prim. But she answered. "My mother was the duke's nursemaid. I assisted her, and have continued in the family's employ."

"Assisted? He said you were only four years older than he?"

"Four were enough years that that I was able to make him mind when he was small." A smile softened her expression. "His younger siblings even more so." She set a boot, passably clean now, on the ground, and started on the other. "I am pleased to be a lady's maid again, Lady Cora. I have been in a household lacking a lady since the duke's eldest sister married."

"You did not seek another position?"

Miss Douglas turned her face away. "My mother is devoted to the family. She's nursemaid to Lady Hester now. She will remain with them, and so I will remain near her. And there is safety in Lord Adam's household. Things are much better now."

"Better now?"

Miss Douglas turned her solemn eyes back on Cora, and seemed to evaluate her. "The situation was not good under Lord Adam's father, the old duke. He was a harsh man, though I ought not to speak ill of the dead."

She bent her head over her shoe. "Lord Adam is a much better man, despite what he did yesterday. He is unfailingly just, and often kind. I wish . . ."

Cora's chest was tight. She watched the men struggle with the carriage. The duke was down there, getting mud-covered and straining with the post-boys and Mr. Malcolm, Charlie Coachman at the horses' heads. Miss Douglas watched them too.

"You wish?" Cora prompted her.

"It's not my place to say this, Lady Cora, but—"

"Please, speak freely."

"I wish this was a true elopement. I am bitterly disappointed that it is not. Lord Adam has been, before, most deserving of the love of a good woman—a good wife, and to have a good family. He needs it. And I fear he has ruined all by his impetuous pride. This fool's act." Miss Douglas whipped at her shoe with the filthy towel, handling it roughly, her full lips pressed together, her nostrils flaring, and her voice tight with anger.

She rounded on Cora. "Tell me the word, and I will help you out of here, Lady Cora." Her eyes blazed, and she stood tall, twisting her towel in clenched hands, an avenging Fury. "I was born as a slave, and though my mother and I were freed when she stepped foot onto Scottish soil with me as a babe in her arms, I've been faced with the idea of slavery my entire life. It was my mother's life, and her mother's. I would hate a man forever who forced me into it now. Forced me to do anything unwillingly."

Cora gulped, and almost shrank back. But she looked into Miss Douglas's fierce eyes and strengthened her spine. "Thank you, Miss Douglas. That's . . . thank you. I greatly appreciate your offer, and your explanation of your feelings."

Now curiosity burned hotter, and she pushed through all her reticence. "How did your mother come to be in Scotland, Miss Douglas?"

"The duke would likely prefer me not to tell you."

She didn't speak again for several moments, and Cora was tied in knots of suspense. Miss Douglas's mouth screwed up in repressed anger again. "But I don't know if he warrants that much consideration. And you deserve to know what you are being forced into."

She finished with her shoe, placed it down, and dug in her traveling valise.

"I apologize if it is shocking to your tender ears, my lady, but my mother was Lord Percival Douglas's favorite mistress."

Cora blinked.

"Lord Percival was in charge of the Blackdale sugar plantation in the Caribbean. He wasn't very wise, I'm afraid, and ran it into the ground. Lord Adam's father, the old duke, ordered his younger brother to come back to Scotland. He refused to board the ship without his mistress. And she refused to come without her suckling baby girl, his daughter."

Cora's mouth was hanging open. She had to remind herself of countless deportment lessons to close it.

"He was a wastrel, and a soft touch, it seems. Mother tells me she could always charm him. I only have vague memories of him as stinking of rum, and being very affectionate. He would pick me up and twirl me around." A soft expression came over her face, and she was twice as lovely as she was before. Then she hardened into business-like control again.

Cora tilted her head at Miss Douglas, and stared at her with wide eyes.

Miss Douglas moved over behind the pile of trunks, and Cora twisted on the top to follow her.

"He died before I was very old, leaving my mother with another babe, my brother. The old duke didn't like his brother's former-slave mistress hanging around the castle idle, so he hired her as nursemaid for his newborn son, and she stayed in the nursery thereafter, caring for each of the Douglas children. My mother loves babies. And children. She loved us all." Her face was soft again as she spoke of her mother. She held two pairs of fresh stockings in her hands, and stared down at them.

"Here, sit next to me to put those on, Miss Douglas."

A flash of gratitude from her normally guarded face left Cora feeling warm. Miss Douglas hopped up on the top trunk, and set about wiping down her feet, and donning the stockings, a double layer.

She grimaced as she slipped a foot into a damp boot.

"Where is your brother now?"

"Johnny is a groom. He loves horses. He's helping raise the duke's prize cattle in the Lochelys estate. I only see him when he makes it over to the castle to visit Mother."

A sudden cheer went up from the men. Cora swung around again to look. The carriage was free!

They pulled it forward, out of the low, mud-locked patch of road, and up to a solid section.

Cora's mind spun with all Miss Douglas had told her. She knew little of slavery, and less of mistresses. But Miss Douglas was a Douglas indeed, the duke's cousin from the other side of the blanket. And she spoke freely, the unusual closeness of a devoted family retainer, and an oddly placed relative. She had the duke's trust and consideration.

The duke walked behind, chest heaving with his exertions, covered in mud splatters on his buff trousers and white shirt-sleeves. His eyes turned to her, his color high. His brilliant blue eyes blazed, despite the overcast day. Cora's heart sped in her chest. He was gorgeous.

Energy raced through her limbs, and Cora hopped down from her high perch. Breathless but full of sincerity, she said, "Thank you, Miss Douglas, for sharing all of that. And I appreciate your willingness to assist me to escape greatly. I . . ." *I want to kiss that man.* "I think I will go on, for a while longer, at least." Her cheeks warmed, but she gave a decided nod to Miss Douglas, and turned to face the duke as he walked toward them. He had re-donned his coat, and looked almost respectable again, if his mud spattered breeches and caked top boots were ignored.

"Ready to go again, Lady Cora?"

"Yes, Duke, I am." She smiled at him, and he paused with an arrested expression. She almost lost the smile at the look in his eyes—amazement?—but he held out his arm to her, and she took it, thrilling at being close to him.

The sun showed its face from behind the clouds, and the day warmed. The mud-coated men climbed onto the outside of the carriage for the afternoon's travel, leaving Cora and Miss Douglas to spread out in the carriage cabin, open the window glass, and enjoy feminine conversation over a cold luncheon.

"What was the duke like as a boy?"

"Dutiful. Occasionally stubborn. He was a good lad, solemn, but considerate. I fear the war has changed him."

"To be like his father?"

"No! Well, no, he has not beat anyone or thrown anything . . . but he is hard—harder than he was before—and grim."

"What happened at Waterloo, Miss Douglas? Do you know?"

"Indeed, I do. I helped nurse him in Brussels."

"Were you there for the battle?" Cora raised her eyebrows.

"No. When Lady Hester learned of her brother's injury, she set out immediately for Belgium to be by his side. I accompanied her, along with the minister, now her husband. My first trip out of Scotland." Miss Douglas smiled.

She grew serious again. "But the duke . . . he was not found till the day after the battle. His men thought him dead, among so many others. When he was finally rescued from the battle field, he languished on death's door for weeks. He had broken ribs, severe bruising, and a concussion. He developed pneumonia, and one of his lungs collapsed. He was not expected to live. All this, and the cannonball had only grazed him. A little to the left, and he would not be here at all."

Cora exhaled at the horror of the thought.

"When we reached him in Brussels, they had him in a crowded chateau. Mr. Malcolm had been doing what he could for him, but it was not till Lady Hester sat by his side that he began to recover. She is a gentle, caring lady. They are close."

Cora smiled. It was good to hear that at least one of the duke's family was kind and cared for him.

"Thank you, Miss Douglas, for telling me."

"If you would like to, my lady, you may call me Kate. As the family does."

Cora felt honored. "Thank you, Kate."

Mr. Yardley stopped at every posting house, asking after the duke. When he didn't hear about him for three stops, he backtracked and cast a wider net. He discovered the carriage accident, and the new equipage.

But as stops progressed, and the duke in his new carriage stuck to the Great North Road, Mr. Yardley realized that all his stopping and asking was slowing him down.

He cursed, and started skipping stops.

Chapter Sixteen

Berries

SATURDAY, JULY 6, 1816, AFTERNOON

What would happen when they reached Scotland? Cora tried to imagine it. They would enter Gretna Green, and he would take her to the blacksmith's shop. There, over the anvil and in front of the infamous blacksmith, she would say . . . what? 'No, thank you. But thank you for the nice trip across the country'?

Perhaps then they'd go to the closest inn and stay there until her mother's emissary caught up with them.

Cora winced. She shouldn't be so foolish as to suppose her mother would wait in London and only send an emissary. Lady Winfield was not one to sit idly at home. She would be coming after them now, hopefully with a gentleman she'd pressed into attending her, and not just with a groom. Perhaps Sir Merriweather, poor dear.

Then, when her mother reached Cora, Mother would be horrified when she discovered that Cora had never really tried to get away. Mother would scold and rage, and they would go home.

Cora would be ruined in the eyes of the world. Unless the story hadn't been spread around, and the tale they told at the inns and at the posting houses—that she was just being escorted by the Duke to a relative—was allowed to take hold, and wasn't supplanted by something more salacious.

But her mother wasn't known for her discretion.

No, Cora had to err on the side of the whole world knowing everything: that she had been kidnapped, had chosen to go along with it, and then hadn't married her kidnapper, a handsome, rich, and eligible duke.

Why had she gone with it, again? Because it was an adventure, and this fascinating man wanted to marry her, and she wanted to see how it played out?

Because after the initial kidnapping, he had treated her honorably, and provided an amazingly competent maid for her who he treated almost as an equal. That had intrigued her.

A droplet splashed her through the open window. Rain started coming down, and they closed the windows quickly. After several seconds of downpour, the carriage halted and shook. Kate and Cora exchanged glances, and Kate rejoined Cora on the forward-facing seat.

The duke and his valet reentered, splattering droplets from their clothes. "Excuse us, Lady Cora, Kate."

She appreciated that they appeared to have been able to remove most of the mud from their boots in the hours they had been outside in drier air. She found a smile on her face as the men settled themselves, until the duke caught her gaze, and his eyes burned brightly into her. She turned back to the window and felt her cheeks heating.

But the blush faded and a worried frown settled on her face as she thought through the implications if her situation being known. If it was, in the eyes of the world she would be ruined unless she married this man before her.

Now, her mother wouldn't force her to, she knew that. So instead, they would go home to the Grange, her maternal grandfather's principal seat, now her mother's, and there she would live quietly and in disgrace the rest of her life. She would likely never marry, but instead she would be able to stay with her plants, flowers, and fruit trees, and to tend the fields of the Grange, Greenlake, and Averillshire, the properties that would one day be hers. She would be excluded from all society, but would be able to focus on her work, the growing things that made her so happy.

She wouldn't be interrupted by the yearly London Season. She had cursed it more than once, to have to go and dress and do the pretty among London's high society right during planting season.

She'd be able to do those experiments in modern concepts of agriculture written about in the botanical journals, like crop rotation. She wanted to try leaving fields fallow every seven years, like in the Bible. When one wasn't there at planting time, setting up unusual experiments was difficult. She would not mind never being stuck in London during the planting season ever again.

So, really, ruination would help her get what she had wanted for years.

But . . . it wouldn't get her out from under her mother's thumb. Instead she would always be a spinster under the control of a tyrant of a dowager.

Cora had tried so hard to find a man she could respect to marry this Season.

It had fallen flat. Except for the duke.

The countryside passed before Cora's window without her seeing it.

The duke had made her nervous. But he hadn't mocked her interests and eccentricities. He distracted her, made her thoughts linger on him. None of the approved others had come even close to touching her as the duke had.

So she had two choices.

Live the curtailed life of a spinster, happily tending her plants, but never marrying, never growing her own family. Her womb would be bare and lifeless. She would never have the children she had always expected to have, wanted to have. Even as a child, she had tended her little potted garden and her dolls, mother to all.

To ever be treated as a maiden, even when well past the age of maidenhood? What a miserable thought. She'd been tired of 'maidenhood' in her first Season, always surrounded by chaperones and bounded by rules and decorums. If she married, those would be lessened.

Oh, she did want to get married!

Cora brought a hand to her mouth as a terrible thought occurred to her.

Would her being ruined curtail her mother's enjoyment of the Season as well? That would be horrible. It was her mother's favorite thing, what she planned for all year, and what kept her going. The whirlwind of social events, seeing and being seen, gossiping and ruling, walking among the highest levels and most influential people of British society. Her mother, when deprived of that, was a miserable person to be around.

Mother had had to forgo the Season when grandfather had died in Cora's seventeenth year, putting off her coming out, and giving Cora the most enjoyable and free April and May she had ever had. No London! No nurses, tutors, governesses, and dancing/drawing/pianoforte masters! It was her gardens all day until evening. It had been glorious, and she had felt a little guilty that her beloved grandfather's passing had brought her such joy.

Mother insisted on Cora dressing like a mourning lady in somber black finery in the evening and joining her for their quiet family dinners. Those meals had been long and tedious, her mother often in a glum and snappy mood with so little to distract her attention. It was always a relief when the parson and his wife were invited to dine, which was often, as it directed her mother's focus away from Cora during more of the meal.

Their restricted time of mourning had been so unexpectedly wonderful for Cora, but it had been everything that was dull and lifeless to her mother.

So, another point in favor of marriage. Cora's ruination wouldn't get in the way of her mother's social enjoyments. If Mother had to avoid all polite society ever after, she would be a nightmare to live with. She needed people and things to do, and people were what she chose to do.

Cora was fine without people. Well, at least, she preferred a small group she knew well and was comfortable with.

That was hard to find in London, where she ostracized herself from the other young ladies through her general thoughtless oddness, and because of jealousy. It was lonely in London.

So, all right, she would marry.

And it appeared that she had only one choice of partners now. This man, this duke, Adam Richard Douglas.

Her eyes turned to him again. The Duke of Blackdale, attractive, fascinating, at turns cold, awkward, and kind. She watched him.

To be a duchess, that would be interesting. She would get even more attention than she had as daughter of an earl, and an heiress with a comely face, figure, and bank account attached to her. But at least she would not be a prize on the marriage mart anymore.

Of course, she ought to not discount that there were desperate gentlemen who would not mind her ruination as long as they could get their hands on her dowry. But those would be the type to be glad of her ruin, as it would put some power back into their hands. They would feel less indebted to her wealth, and hold their rescue of her over her head throughout the rest of their lives.

That type of man as her husband, with power over her person . . . Cora shuddered at the thought.

But the duke, he didn't need her money. He seemed to want to marry her, Lady Cora Winfield, not her fortune. Because he'd be marrying her without her mother's permission, he would never see any money from it.

Mother would likely will the money to Cora's children in a trust, though the lands went to Cora alone. She would control them, just as mother controlled them now.

She had always been pleased with that. She need not marry if she did not want to.

So, she could marry, she wanted to marry, but did not need to for financial reasons. Only for comfort, for children, for freedom . . .

Would this man give her freedom?

He hadn't started out well. That abduction, it had been horrible. She had never been subjected to such confinement in her life. She had hated it. He had done that to her. By all rights she should be running away from him, and back into her mother's arms.

But he'd redeemed himself somewhat since then. When he'd been angry at Kate, and hadn't retaliated. He'd stomped and paced, but he hadn't yelled or raised his hand. That was when Cora had begun to relax. And then Kate had untied her, and Cora had stayed.

She needed to discover if this man were a man she could marry and live with happily. Else, she should run back to her mother and a life of curtailed but quiet spinsterhood.

What could she do to determine whether he was a good man to marry?

Learn more of him and see him in a wide range of situations. Traveling was providing the range, that was for certain.

He'd been cold and domineering, then conciliating, and if not repentant and apologetic, then he at least seemed unhappy that she was miserable and wanted to fix it.

She stared at him, his thick black brows, his remarkably red lips.

There was the physical to consider. Was she attracted to this man? She contemplated touching those lips with hers.

Would the red of his lips transfer to hers, like eating berries left a stain? She imagined it. She licked her lips, and considered the taste she might experience if she kissed him. Sweet? Perhaps not. He wasn't a sweet man.

A savory red kiss.

She felt a fiery blush expand from her cheeks and outward till her ears burned.

She wanted it. She wanted to try. She determined to try. She would find a way to kiss this man and see what it was like.

Her lips parted. His lips parted as well.

She looked up to his eyes. The duke was staring back at her, his eyes blue flames. He was across from her, so close yet so far in the confines of the carriage. Not a word had either spoken in an hour, but he had noticed, he had seen in her face the ardor in the turn of her thoughts. Her heart leapt into her throat. Her blush deepened and then fled, leaving her cold. She tore her gaze back to the window with a gasp. She tried to compose herself and calm her racing heart.

What must he think of her?

Captain Bowden found himself flagging, having ridden hard all night and half the day. He approached the next posting house and smiled with satisfaction as he spotted the mail coach in the yard. It was heading north. Perfect.

He got himself a ticket and climbed aboard, packing himself in next to a rough workman, and a lad and his mother. He smiled at them winningly and fell into a grateful sleep as the roughly rocking vehicle kept him headed in the right direction at a clipping pace.

The rest of the afternoon was steady travel, occasionally slowed by skidding mud. Night fell, and so did the temperature. It plummeted until Cora could see her exhalations hovering white in the air.

The edges of her window were frosting. She stared at the creeping white patterns—it was July!—and noticed white flakes falling outside. "Snow!"

"Snow? What?" Malcolm started up from his doze, and Kate gave a startled noise.

"Surely not!" The duke stared out his window, and groaned. He removed one of his black leather gloves, and rubbed at his eyes with long, strong fingers. "This weather! It's a curse! A plague."

Malcolm went back to heavy lids and a laconic drawl. "Just know that all that faces us must surely face our pursuers as well."

"One can hope." The duke lifted the hatch, and called out, "Charlie! How goes it?"

"As long as it stays light and doesn't start to sleet, we should be fine, Duke!"

"Thank you, my good man. Let us know if conditions worsen."

"Aye, your grace."

A half-hour further, and "Your grace, I'm sorry, sir, but it's sleeting."

The duke acquiesced to stopping.

"But if it clears later, we shall head out again. We can't afford to stop for the night until we reach Scotland."

Cora suppressed a groan. She wanted dinner and a bed. Her bruised hip ached, and the scrape from the accident twanged whenever it was pressed. She hoped the snow continued so she wouldn't have to spend the night sleeping fitfully on Kate's shoulder through the jostling dark.

A quarter of an hour later, Cora's cheeks stung as wind gusted ice into her face. They rushed into the blessedly warm interior of a respectable inn. The duke secured rooms and a private parlor. How promising!

Then he said, "Would you join me for a late supper this evening, Lady Cora?"

Cora's mouth dried. "It would be a pleasure, your grace."

In her room, all tiredness fled. Cora and Kate pored through the trunks of clothes Malcolm had secured. There were two evening gowns. Cora chose the pale green with pink rosebuds because it spoke of spring and summer. Chill lingered in her fingers and toes as she wrapped a lovely rose shawl around herself with gratitude.

At eleven o'clock, Adam, un-muddied and in fresh evening clothes, white satin knee breeches and black cravat, waited for her to join him in the private parlor. The overly alert innkeeper and a tense manservant stifling his yawns waited on them.

The innkeeper apologized profusely for the simpleness of the fare, and Adam began to wish he had changed to traveling incognito. But he didn't want to ask Lady Cora to go by anything other than her rightful title, and a duke escorting a lady drew less comment than a mere mister. So he stayed the duke.

The annoying obsequiousness of the innkeeper was driven from his mind as Lady Cora descended the stairs. She was the most beautiful creature he had ever beheld. Her cheeks bloomed rose pink under his gaze.

He had best control his eyes in front of others.

He seated her himself and waited with impatience for the innkeeper and his man to withdraw.

The food was simple but adequate, and he was starving. He noticed Lady Cora ate heartily as well.

"I had an excellent conversation with Kate today, Duke."

He paused, his soup-spoon at his mouth. "Indeed, what did you speak of?"

"Many things. She told me some about your family, and about herself."

He had to tread carefully.

Lady Cora seemed to gather courage, and said, "We spoke a little about your father." He put the spoon down, his appetite fled. "I've heard little of substance about his character—"

"You've heard he was not a good man." His tone was too sharp.

Her eyes widened, and her mouth paused over restrained words. "Yes, that is what I've heard, but—"

"And that is the truth. He was not. Forgive me, Lady Cora, if I desire to leave it at that."

She lowered her eyes. "I see; as you wish." They resumed eating in silence.

He swallowed, tension twisting his gut. He had to propose a new subject of conversation, he had to—

"My mother, she—" Lady Cora spoke, and his body tensed further. "She claimed a man with a bad father, forgive me, Duke, that such a man would grow to not be a good person as well." She glanced at him and away. "So I ask you, Duke, are you a good man?"

Adam sat frozen, eyes unseeing, staring at the table. A lump had swollen in his throat. He spoke through it. "I don't know. I hardly know." He closed his eyes, and swallowed the lump down. "I try to be a just man."

"Just?" Her voice was gentle. "All justice? Do you have mercy as well, duke?"

He removed his hands from the table, and gripped his knees. "I know little of mercy."

"That is sad. All justice, and only justice, can be very harsh."

"I have known much that is harsh in my life." He lifted his gaze. "Perhaps," He sank into her gentle green eyes. "I could be taught mercy."

P*lease, Cora, show me mercy.* His heart thrummed in his chest. *Teach me gentleness.*

The proprietor entered with a quick knock, delivering a spread of meats and breaking their locked gazes. When he finally left again, Lady Cora launched into questions about his sisters and their children. Adam eased. These he had no trouble answering: the names of Lady Hester's seven step-children and their activities, more about the one on the way, Lady Caroline's daughter's age, "Eight, I believe," and details about Lady Jean's two children.

They were nearing the end of the course when she said, "And your mother?"

"My mother." So much not to say concerning his mother. He was almost as loath to speak of her as he was of his father. "She passed away several years before my father. I was at Oxford at the time."

"I'm sorry, that must have been so difficult, being away. Did you only hear of it after she had passed?"

"I had received word that she was ill, but couldn't"—didn't want to—"get away from my studies in order to rush to her bedside. The next missive to reach me contained the news."

"How awful. I can't imagine." Her face was full of sympathy.

His heart twinged, and he suppressed it. He had not cried when he had heard the news, but he had cried later—bitter, hollow tears, walking dangerously alone with his bayonet through the darkness of the Spanish countryside—the night after his first battle. Then he had finished and done. He had gone back to his men and the other officers, face and heart as stone.

He hardened them now once again. "Do not trouble yourself." He half-smiled, and spoke with irony. "We cannot all have such a close relationship with our mothers as you have had."

Cora's face froze, her eyes wide. She looked away from him, red spots glowing high on her cheeks. She put her hands in her lap, and stared at the table. That wasn't a pleased blush. Adam clamped down his mouth. His words had been too much, too bitter and mocking. He had to apologize. "That was—"

"I am close to my mother, my lord duke. Yes, she is sometimes . . . difficult. But she is a good woman who loves me, and has tried to bring me up well. I love her, your grace, and I ought to honor her."

"I apologize, Lady Cora, I meant no disrespect. It is a blessing to have a good woman as a mother."

"And you didn't, Duke, is that what you are saying?" Her eyes were soft but discerning, seeing into him.

"I—" hadn't wanted to go into the complexities of his mother. "I wouldn't say she wasn't a good woman. She . . ."—abandoned him, didn't protect him—"lacked courage in some things, I fear, and it put a strain on our relationship." He looked away, took a sip of wine, and didn't know where to focus. The unrelieved tension of the last few days pressed into him as a heavy weight. His whole body ached, each muscle overused and tight. A spasm in his back made him control his expression with severity.

He wanted to be in Scotland with his lady, and this interminable trip to be over. Curse the weather!

Cora regarded him with her arresting green eyes. "I'm sorry you were hurt by this lack of courage in your mother, and that it brought bitterness into your connection with her." Her sweet face was full of compassion. He put down his glass and drank in that look. He basked in it like the sun. His back relaxed.

She reached forward with one hand, her glove tucked up and away for eating for once, and grazed her warm fingers over his cold ones. He caught at her hand and held it, the warmth in them sending spikes of heat through his arm.

She flushed and her breathing rate increased.

"Duke?"

"Yes?" It was almost inaudible. He had little breath in his lungs.

"I have been contemplating our situation. Pondering what I want, and what I ought to do."

His heart spasmed, fear clenching his gut.

"I haven't decided yet, Duke. I'm not sure . . . but I do know what would help me to decide. I'd like—" her face flushed. She lowered her eyes.

"Anything. Name it, my lady."

"I would like it if you would kiss me, Duke."

His breath caught in his chest, his heart sped.

"It would be an . . . important experience, and assist me in making my decision." Her lashes raised, and her green eyes glowed at him.

He stood. The chair scraped loudly over the floorboards, and he was striding around the table before his brain had fully processed that he was moving.

She stood at his approach, her eyes wide, flicking between his face and away. She scrambled to put her napkin on the table, and twitched at her skirts.

He caught both her hands, the shock of the contact going through him with a thrill. "My lady, Cora, may I?"

She swallowed, nodded, her lips parted. He stooped and claimed them.

Her lips were soft against his, her breath warm.

His heart seemed too full in his chest. It pounded at his ribs as if it would leave a bruise on the inside.

He wanted to take her in his arms, to hold her tight, and bury his face in her neck. But he controlled himself, and kept their hands between them.

One more kiss, tender, full of all the love he could manage to pass through his lips and into her, and he withdrew.

Her eyes were heavy-lidded, and fluttered up to look at him. "Oh," she breathed.

There was a knock at the door. They sprung apart. The proprietor entered, bringing more wine and asking if they wanted anything further. The mood was shattered, and Lady Cora excused herself.

Adam watched her retreating back with hope rushing through him.

Cora wanted to race to her mirror and study her mouth. Had she caught the color from his lips through his kiss? Were her lips stained like from the berries of summer in the field, plucked from the vine? Raspberries, red gooseberries, currants? Or from her orangery, the exotic, difficult-to-grow pomegranates, the seeds lush, red, and vibrant?

She stifled a giggle, but it bubbled up her throat like champagne, and escaped. She rushed up the last few steps to her room. She shut the door, pressed her back to it, and clutched her hands to her chest. She pushed off, and twirled, her arms outstretched. She waltzed across the small room and to the small mirror.

She fumbled, lit a candle, and stared at her lips. Were they redder?

She couldn't keep them still. They stretched into a wide grin, flashing her teeth. The giggle rose up again.

Oh, that had been . . . that had been so marvelous!

Wonderful.

Two kisses.

She wanted to kiss the duke—Adam, she wanted to kiss Adam again.

And again. And again.

Chapter Seventeen

Through the night

Saturday, July 6, 1816, evening

Mort nursed his ale. He watched as Kate stood from her empty plate and disappeared into the hall that led to the stairs and the rooms upstairs.

Two men stood after she'd passed them—the two who had bothered her earlier. Their expressions made Mort's blood chill. He abandoned his tankard and followed after, his brows drawn.

He heard a cry. It was Kate. He ran.

The scene he found sent a wash of hot rage through his innards.

One man rolled on the ground, groaning in pain, clutching his groin. But the other held Kate from behind in a bear grip, pinning her arms. She struggled against him, kicking, but couldn't connect.

Mort slammed his fist down on the connection between the man's shoulder and neck. The villain's knees buckled and his arms lost strength. Kate scrambled away.

Mort grabbed the blaggard by his despicable neck, and threw him into the grimy wall. Mort's dagger was in his hand and he pressed the blade into the man's throat. "Be still, or die." Mort snarled.

The man froze, his yellowed eyes wide and round. He cursed, puffing the noxious smell of cheap alcohol and rotting teeth into Mort's face. "The doxy's yours, then? Not willing to share?"

Mort twisted his grip on the rotter's neckline, digging his knuckles into his Adam's apple, and pressed the knife closer. "Your next word will draw blood."

He risked a look over at Kate. Her face was ashen, but she stood solemn and wide-eyed, her arms clutching her ribs.

The man's friend rolled and groaned, still prostrate on the floor. Kate had got him good. Mort smiled with unholy humor and the man he held swallowed and started to pant shallowly, his eyes darting.

"Drink has blinded you, sir. You have accosted a virtuous woman." Mort spoke through his gritted teeth. "You're the lowest scum of the earth, and not worthy to be the sludge she wipes off of her shoe."

Raised voices came from the tap room. Their altercation had been noticed. From the corner of his eye, Mort saw Kate turn and flee up the stairs.

"Sirs! What is this?" The proprietor bustled toward them.

Mort gave the villain another shove against the wall, and snarled into his face, "You do not know how close you were to death this evening, sir." He let him go and backed away, palming the blade to hide it from view.

The man slouched, gripped his knees, breathing hard. Then with an angry grunt, clearly telegraphing his intent, the lily-livered swine charged Mort, and took a swing at him. Mort ducked and with a satisfied smile, fisted the dagger again, and drove the butt of it into the man's padded gut. He let out a bellow of pain, and dropped. Mort flipped the knife up into his sleeve, and gave the wide-eyed proprietor a bow. "Just finishing up here."

Charlie rushed out of the tap room and joined them in the hall. "Malcolm! Ye needing help, man?"

"Thank you, Charlie. I think I have it in hand."

"What happened?"

"They propositioned Kate in the tap room. When she refused, they followed her out, intent on having their way never mind her nay."

Charlie's grizzled face twisted, and he slammed his fist into his palm. "I'll blacken their daylights m'self," he growled.

"Now, sirs, if the men made an honest mistake—" The proprietor made placating gesture.

Mort felt his vision darken, and his fingers itch to pull the knife again. Charlie rounded on the portly man, "M'lady's abigail, mistaken for a light-skirt? Ye daft blaggard! The duke will have yer hide!"

"Now now!" The fool's eyes widened in alarm.

"Go find the duke, Charlie, he should be in his private parlor. I'm going to check on Kate." Mort didn't wait for Charlie's acknowledgment, but turned and resisted kicking each of the groaning men on the ground as he passed them. He sprinted up the stairs two at a time.

Cora dozed on the bed, still dressed in evening finery, when the door flew open. Cora bolted upright and blinked at Kate, who slammed the door and bolted it. "Kate?"

Kate whipped around and looked at Cora with wide eyes, her breathing heavy.

Cora slid off the bed. "Kate! What's wrong? Are you well?" She went over to her and took Kate's hands.

"I'm fine. I'm well." But the trembling in her hands belied her words.

"Come, sit down, Kate." Cora drew her to the bed, and sat down with her. "What has happened?"

Kate gave a harsh laugh. "Men happened. It isn't the first time." She pressed the palms of her hands into her eyes. "But that foolish man! He's going to get himself killed! Or deported!"

"Who?"

"Malcolm! He defended me! With a knife!"

Cora's mouth dropped open. "Is he all right? Are you all right?"

Kate sniffed, and her eyes overflowed. "I can only assume so! I ran!"

Cora found a handkerchief for her, and put an arm around her shoulders. "That is very sensible, Kate. I'm so glad you came here immediately. And have locked the door." Cora thought of how unlocked that door had been, and apprehension rippled up her spine.

Kate gasped with shuddering sobs. "I—I got one of them, but I couldn't get the other! If Malcolm hadn't come—" She curled into herself even more. "I still feel his hands on me!"

Cora encouraged her to lie down, and stroked her back as she gave way to tears.

A pounding on the door made Cora jump. Kate give a small cry.

"Miss Douglas! Lady Cora! Are you in there?" Cora couldn't tell the voice through the muffling of the heavy door. The handle rattled.

Cora scrambled off the bed and stood in front of the door, alarm running through her. "Who is it?" she called.

"Lady Cora! It's Malcolm! Is Kate with you?"

"Yes, she is!"

"Is she well? Can I come in?"

"No!" Kate cried softly, her voice strangled with tears. She sat up, wiped her face, and straightened her dress.

"She's whole! And no, you may not!" Cora stood between Kate and the door. No one would get by her!

"Kate, talk to me! Are you all right?"

"Go away, ye daft man!" Kate yelled at the door. She stood shakily, strode to the washstand, and poured water into it from the pitcher.

"Kate, I'm so glad! I'll stand guard at your door. Don't fear!"

Kate scrubbed at her face with water and didn't answer. Cora looked between her stiff figure and the door.

"Kate?" His voice was almost plaintive.

"We would appreciate that, Mr. Malcolm!" Cora answered. Kate whipped around and gave Cora an accusing look. Cora raised her eyebrows at her. "It would help us feel safer, thank you!"

Kate's mouth tightened and her eyes widened against further tears. She dried her face, and sat in the chair next to the washstand. She held herself still and straight, her hands clasped tightly in her lap. Cora watched, her heart aching for her.

Rage ran through Adam's chest and clenched in his stomach. He strode through the upper hall, Charlie following behind. Adam had banished the proprietor from his sight.

He came to Malcolm standing at Lady Cora's door, his face grim. "Are they both in there?"

Malcolm nodded curtly.

"How are they?"

Malcolm grimaced. "They've only spoken to me through the door. It is bolted tight."

Adam raised a brow. "Good." He gestured for Malcolm to give way. He obeyed with a tight mouth.

Adam stood in front of the door, and took a deep, controlling breath. He knocked.

"Who is it?" Lady Cora's voice.

"Lady Cora, it is the duke. May I speak to you?"

There was a long pause. "One moment."

The bolt slid back, and her wide eyes peered through a crack in the door. She took in the three men outside her door, and opened it a little wider. "Yes?"

"Is Kate—Miss Douglas—is she whole?"

Lady Cora's head turned back to the room, and then she nodded. "She is whole. She's had a bad scare."

"Yes, I understand. And I will not tolerate such treatment of her. Charlie Coachman tells me that the sky has cleared and the moon, such as we have of it, is out. We are leaving."

Her eyes widened. "But—" Then she closed her mouth, and nodded. "Very well. We will pack up once again."

"Malcolm will not leave your door until you are ready, and he will assist you in taking down your trunks."

"All right."

"We leave in twenty minutes. I'm sorry for this alarm and all that has happened, Lady Cora."

She nodded, her face solemn. He searched for more to say. He wanted to see Kate for himself, assure himself she was uninjured, but he wouldn't push himself into their room. He would see her soon enough. He nodded to Lady Cora, and she shut the door again. He waited until the bolt slid home again.

"Your things, your grace?" Malcolm took his place in front of the door again.

"I will commandeer that manservant from earlier. Things won't be packed as you would like, but it will be fine, Malcolm."

He grimaced, but kept to his post.

Cora, dressed in traveling clothes once again, hurried down the stairs with Kate and Mr. Malcolm. Her whole body ached from the jostling of two days on the road, the healing scrape on her leg pulled, and her bruised hip twanged in painful protest with each step.

Night travel. Cora did not approve of it. But back into the bouncing misery of the carriage she went.

The sky was clear, and the air sharp and chill as they left the hateful inn. The welcome sight of the gibbous moon and stars overhead calmed her.

Settled and swaying down the road once again, Cora pressed for more details. "Was anyone injured?"

"No blood was drawn." The duke answered. "But the scoundrels will be feeling it in the morning."

"Kate incapacitated one herself. She was brilliant." Mr. Malcolm said.

Cora blinked in surprise. "Really? How did you do it, Kate?"

"I wish not to speak of it."

"You should teach Lady Cora, Kate." Mr. Malcolm's face was in deep shadow. "She could use a few defenses against kidnappers and the like." His voice was dry. Kate shuddered beside her, and Cora linked her arm into Kate's, seeking to give her solidarity and comfort.

"Malcolm." The duke's voice held a warning.

Kate let out a pained-sounding laugh. "Yes, she does. Perhaps I shall." She squeezed Cora's hand. "A good skill for a vulnerable female to have. But it wasn't enough tonight."

"Two against one is more than most can handle. You did excellent, Kate." Mr. Malcolm's voice had warmed.

Cora felt Kate stiffen. "But you, Mr. Malcolm! That knife! What were you thinking?"

"What? Me dagger was very effective, Madame. Why do you complain?"

Kate leaned forward, loosening Cora's grasp on her arm. "This isn't the war, this isn't Paris. You could be hanged or deported if you'd killed one of them!"

"In defense of a lady!"

"A lady! What jury would look at me and hear that plea?"

"That knife stopped him right quick, Kate, and I would do it again."

She sat back with a noise of disgust.

"Paris again!" Cora exclaimed, feeling bold in the darkness of the night and violence of the last hour. "What happened in Paris?"

The other occupants of the carriage went silent. Mr. Malcolm shifted in his seat.

The duke gave a long sigh. "While Napoleon was on Elba, Malcolm and I were sent to Paris to be a Scottish duke and his valet enjoying the freedom of the city freed from war. We were actually there as spies. Well, Malcolm was at any rate, I think I was just his cover."

"Spies." Cora breathed it out.

"We were to watch the populous, sniff out any Bonapartist plots to dethrone King Louis XVIII again, and do what we could to foil them if any came to light."

"And were there any?"

"Oh, a few. But when news of Napoleon's escape from Elba reached us, we gained details of his march through France, the army he was gathering, and came across some additional vital information that we needed to get to the Duke of Wellington. We were discovered in our attempt to escape the city with our intelligence by, let's say, a passionate, Bonapartist lady. We were forced to tie her up and take her with us."

"No!" Cora said.

"We dropped her off, still trussed, in a town several miles outside of Paris. Unbeknownst to us, her manservant had been tailing us, and once reunited, they pursued and caught up with us once again. Unfortunately, they intended to kill in order to stop us. Malcolm was forced to kill the manservant."

Cora gasped.

"The lady we carried with us, and delivered as a prisoner of war to Wellington's camp when we reached Brussels." Only the outline of the duke's face was visible in the refracted light from the carriage lanterns. His eyes were dark hollows under his heavy brows. He spread his hands. "And that is why I knew Malcolm was skilled at trussing up a lady. And why I was reluctant to explain. I am sorry if this frightens you."

"Oh." Cora said in a small voice. She blinked against the darkness of the carriage, and shook off all apprehension. They had been at war. "Thank you for finally telling me."

Mr. Basil, his shirt-points wilted beyond recognition, his hessians scratched irreparably, shivering and missing his valet, was still dressed finely enough that he came under notice of highwaymen as he rode his hired hack through the night.

He made it a third of the way to Scotland before he was held up with a blunderbuss shot into the air and the words "Stand and deliver!"

He dragged his sorry self, stripped of jacket, boots, waistcoat, watch, purse, and mercifully thrown a horse blanket to ward off the chill rain, to the nearest inn, where they called the constable, took pity on the poor robbed fool, and let him sleep by the fire that night.

He had to write to his mother for assistance, having no more money. He got no further in his pursuit of the heiress.

She was an odd one anyway. Glad to be rid of her.

Lady Winfield and Lord Eastham, with his young tiger well-muffled in the back of his phaeton, the top raised to give some protection from the rain to the driver and his passenger, found the roads wet and cold.

The first day was long and arduous, but Lord Eastham controlled each successive change of four well, and the post boys hopped on and off with respect for the driver, and eyes rolling at the snippy, cross lady who bickered with the earl the entire way.

It began to snow.

The phaeton upset, and broke its axle. They trudged through the slush to a local inn, where they were forced to wait the night. The dowager paced and stomped, but the next morning Lord Eastham succeeded in hiring a job cart. It got them to the next change, where there was a carriage for hire, and the lady was stuck by herself in greater comfort, but with no one to snipe at, as Lord Eastham insisted on continuing to drive. He sat with his tiger in the driver's box, and they pressed on.

Captain Bowden couldn't stand the mail coach any further. There had been a few delays, a horse had lost its shoe mid-post, and it was bone-jarring and crowded. He hired another hack, and started out again, refreshed and rejoicing in the crisp air.

Adam took over for Charlie at 3 a.m., allowing him to rest in his place inside the carriage. "I can control a coach and four, and well you know it. Now get some rest."

Charlie was too exhausted to complain further about impropriety.

As Adam drove through the deep night, images of the war consumed his thoughts.

The face of Mr. Smith as his sneer changed to horror, and then to tear-streaming begging as the lashes hit his back. One, two, three . . . ten, eleven, twelve . . .

Adam had stood firm, and watched. It had been a just punishment, but his stomach had roiled nonetheless.

The men had tested him when Adam had first arrived as a freshly commissioned officer. A duke's heir, a sprig of the nobility, they expected him to be coddled and weak. They'd pushed him, tricked him, tried make his life so miserable that he would run back to Papa Duke, and sell out. Few duke's heirs joined the army.

He had stood firm. Proved he would enact all justice, full punishments, full discipline. All that was required by law for an officer of the crown to do when disciplining his men, he did.

They learned.

After a few months, the rabble-rousers were subdued. By a year, he had one of the most disciplined forces in the Peninsula.

The good men respected him. He knew it, and it gave him the courage to continue to stand strong, to never to act in anger, to never act in rash emotion, never lash out, or punish beyond what was required by law and justice. Never to seek petty vengeance.

He listened to the reports, investigated every charge, questioned witnesses carefully. He didn't take accusations at face value. He discovered if a crime was as it appeared. More than one time, he revealed the truth when a rival was digging a pit of lies to trap another soldier.

His stern justice put the fear of pain into the roughest of his soldiers, but it was his strict justice that earned the respect of the good men under his command. His company respected him, followed him. His men's excellent behavior on the battlefield and off gained him commendations, and the attention of the great men of the army, including the Iron Duke himself.

Adam always acted honorably.

He was not acting honorably now. His hands tightened on the reigns.

Clouds covered the moon, and he slowed the team in the deep darkness, the lanterns not showing enough of the road ahead for his comfort.

The discipline of Adam's men didn't get them the medical care they needed, or the food and supplies to keep them fed and healthy. On the Peninsula, illness was what did them in more than battle.

Dysentery ripped through their ranks. He lost more men to it than to battle wounds.

Mr. Smith of the first lashing fell to dysentery a year later. And MacRay, whom Adam had saved from an unjust flogging two months before. So much death.

When Napoleon had finally been sent to his first island exile in 1814, Adam had been relieved to see the end of war.

His father was dead. He was the duke. He returned to Edinburgh for a time, but the bitterness of his childhood plagued him there. He soon wanted away again.

He'd been glad to take the War Office's request to spy in Paris. He'd enjoyed the city, and the cloak and dagger intrigue of feeling out the tenor of the people and watching for dissent.

When Adam reached Brussels after Napoleon's escape, he'd been put in charge of a Scottish regiment with inexperienced officers.

Then Waterloo.

He'd been hit in the fourth hour.

He slowed the spent team to a stop in front of the posting house. The postboys jumped down, and the next team was brought out. Adam climbed down to check on his passengers. Charlie awoke as Adam opened the door, but Adam waved him back. Malcolm appeared asleep, but Adam knew to not trust that.

Lady Cora slept, her head resting against Kate's shoulder. Her sweet sleeping face calmed Adam's misgivings. Yes, he wasn't being honorable, but to have her in his life was worth any dishonor.

Her eyebrows furrowed over her closed eyelids. Adam frowned. He watched her in the light streaming from the posting house lanterns, waiting with apprehension for her brow to clear again.

Kate looked up, her eyes bloodshot but alert. Adam's concerns for his cousin resurfaced. "Kate, how do you fare?"

"Well enough, your grace."

"Are you recovered?"

Her lip quirked humorlessly. "It was not the first time I've had to fend off unwanted attention. I will survive."

"I'm sorry, Kate."

Unwanted attention. His chest tightened, and his eyes were drawn back to Lady Cora. The grimace was still in her brows. She was not happy in her sleep. He clenched and unclenched his hands. He needed to get her to Scotland. There, things would resolve, things would improve.

He didn't have a solution for the problem of Kate, however. He needed to find a good place for her, where she could be safe and secure. Was there a place where she could be happy?

A quick glance at Malcolm revealed his valet's eyes were slitted, watching Kate.

Was there hope for Kate's happiness and protection in that quarter? Would Kate allow it, if Malcolm could be brought up to scratch?

Adam retreated back to his lonely perch, driving them inexorably to Scotland. It was his home again, and the land of his hope. He wanted this over and done.

Chapter Eighteen

Scotch Corner

SUNDAY, JULY 7, 1816, EARLY MORNING

Captain Bowden reached the Scotch Corner at 3 a.m., and after begging a late supper to warm himself up at the posting house, hit the road through the Pennines, relishing a challenge.

Cora jostled awake. They halted at another change. The sky was brightening outside.

Charlie Coachman snoozed inside the carriage across from her, next to Mr. Malcolm. She needed to walk about and relieve herself. She shifted carefully, not wanting to wake their put-upon coachman for her own comfort, he needed his rest. She touched Mr. Malcolm on the arm. “Could we take five minutes at this stop, please?” she asked softly.

Mr. Malcolm opened an eye. She’d discovered that though he could sleep anywhere, he always reacted quickly when roused. He gave a nod. “Step outside. I’ll inform the duke.” He kept his voice low as well.

She didn’t want to wake Kate either, though Cora supposed she ought. Kate was, amazingly, slumped into the padded squabs, and seemed to be sleeping soundly.

Mr. Malcolm opened the coach door, lowered the steps, and exited, holding out a hand to assist her. She dismissed the idea of waking Kate, and stepped down.

There were wide cultivated fields all around, and the cool light of morning filtered through mountainous thunder clouds above them. The air was charged with the power of the storm overhead. Her breath chilled before her, but her heart was calmed by the fresh beauty of the stormy morning around her.

On the packed dirt of the posting house's drive, she looked up into the driver's seat and found the duke's gaze on her. His eyes seemed like dark holes, the lightening sky not illuminating them. His face under his tall hat was grim. Or just tired.

Despite everything, his dark eyes still burned when he looked at her, restrained passion behind his furled brows, and hollowed, intense eyes. He watched her, and Cora watched him, arrested for several seconds.

Mr. Malcolm gave a "a five-minute break for the lady," and the duke nodded.

Cora pulled herself away, and entered the posting house. Finding a lady's retiring room, she noticed the unusual sparseness of people at this posting house this morning.

Oh, it was Sunday.

Troubled, Cora washed her face and hands, and felt a bit more like a person again.

The duke was in the main room waiting for her when she emerged. She approached and spoke softly to him. "It is Sunday morning, Duke."

"Yes?"

"We really ought not to travel on Sunday, sir."

The duke gave her a lifted brow. "My lady, we are rushing to the border. Sunday travel is expected."

He spoke low, but she glanced around, not wanting their exchange to be overheard. Her face flushed. The proprietor was watching them, but shouldn't be close enough to hear. No others were in their vicinity. "If we were not rushing to the border, but instead you were escorting me to my great aunt's . . . we ought to rest on the Sabbath."

"But we are past that fiction, are we not, my dear?" His face was a controlled, polite mask.

She balled her fists into her skirts, her face hot. She looked away from him. "Are we?"

He took a step closer to her. The coldness of the night air clung to him and pulled at her exposed skin. She felt even hotter where the chill reached her. "We are under pursuit. We cannot afford a day of rest."

She looked up, and his hollowed eyes caught her again. She couldn't look away.

"After we reach the border, and there, when you give me your answer . . ." His lips were the brightest spot on his pale and shadowed face. They drew her eyes. "If you wish, after we can rest a day before going on to Glasgow, and then to Blackdale Castle, my chief estate."

Her chest was tight, her body stressed from this low-voiced confrontation.

"And if my answer is *no*, duke?" She looked at his eyes, and then his chest, and then his brows. They were lowered, his eyes shuttered.

"If so . . ." He did not continue.

"If so," she answered for him, "we will wait for pursuit to catch up with us, and I will rejoin my mother. But only in Gretna."

His jaw worked. "Only in Gretna." He dragged out.

Tea, and warmed bricks for their feet arrived, and the conversation was over.

They reached the Scotch Corner before 8 o'clock, and Adam breathed a sigh of relief. Scotland was in reach, a full day more only.

"How is the summer road? Is it still safe? Any reports?" Adam asked the ostler at the Scotch Corner Inn as they changed the horses. The Summer Road had been clear and easy two months ago when they had taken it on the way to London, but with how the weather had been on this return trip, he wanted to take no chances. The route through the North Pennines could turn out to be foolhardy if their current luck was holding. Adam was loath, however, to take the longer Winter Road around the high hills if he could avoid it.

"We've had heavy rain, your grace, but the drovers haven't been complaining, should be safe enough." The ostler, the same he'd met several times on this route, assured them.

"Thank you, sir." Adam tipped him, and turned to Charlie Coachman. "How are you feeling?"

He was looking haggard, but stiffened his spine. "Well, your grace! And I know this route as well as I know any other. Been over it near fifty times."

"Safe in dark and rain?"

"We'll persevere! Must get to Scotland, sir!"

Adam clamped him on the shoulder. "Thank you, my good man."

"Lady Cora, we've reached the Scotch Corner."

Cora roused out of her doze, and blinked at Kate, her mind fuzzy.

"This is the point where we will leave the Great North Road and head Northwest for Gretna. If we were to take you to your aunt's in Newcastle, we ought to stay on the Great North Road."

Oh.

"If you want to do as we've been saying, and actually go to your great-aunt's, then you need to speak up immediately."

Wide awake now, Cora gulped.

"We'll have to put pressure on Lord Adam if you want to do it. But I'm sure you could convince him." Kate spoke earnestly and low. Malcolm appeared to doze, as usual, but Cora thought she detected a change in his breathing pattern.

Great-Aunt Mrs. Sophia Carston in her manor outside of Newcastle. Cora hadn't seen her in a year. Should she insist? Should she show up at her aging aunt's doorstep with a duke in tow?

"Ask him to court you properly from your Great-Aunt's."

Cora blinked at her. "Court me properly? That's a thought." He hadn't done much properly, had he?

Despite the ill sleep of the night before, when Cora stepped out of the carriage in front of the Scotch Corner Inn, she felt energy fill her limbs. The sun was shining through the large gaps in the clouds above.

"Kate, I need a walk. Will you accompany me?"

She was walking away.

"Lady Cora! Where are you going?" Adam tried to keep the alarm out of his voice.

She turned back, her elegant nose upturned, bright spots high on her cheeks. "I am going for a short walk."

"A walk?"

"Yes, a quick perambulation to restore feeling to my limbs. Kate is with me, and we will soon return." She didn't wait for his yay or nay, but turned again and disappeared into a lane edged by tall bushes, Kate behind her.

Adam's gloves creaked as he clenched his fists.

The sun was bright, and she drank it in, turning her face up toward it. There had been so little of the sun seen lately.

They walked through empty lanes beside cultivated fields.

Cora couldn't resist anymore, and with a relieved sigh, improperly pushed her bonnet back to hang by its ribbons against her neck.

Her freckles would come out, but she welcomed them. She craved the warmth of the sun; her bones ached for it. She had been so cold on this journey. She wanted to bake it in, let it warm her through.

Cora walked, Kate trailing behind her in silence. The wind wasn't biting, the sun was out, and the world felt hopeful. Cora sighed and felt more relaxed than she had in days. More at peace.

And realized she wasn't thinking. She refocused her mind on her options.

Spinsterhood . . . scandal, forever being stifled under her mother . . . perhaps isolation with her plantings, which would be the only good benefit…

Marriage to the duke . . . babies, the marriage bed—Cora almost came to a halt at that thought—influence over ducal estates, more land to play with, if the duke wouldn't mind . . . Possibilities . . .

And the duke himself, Adam Douglas . . . handsome, enigmatic, and desperately in love with her?

That silver birch was lovely. *Betula pendula.* And oh, was that watercress in that pond?

Their kiss last night . . .

I have already made my decision, Cora realized.

She stopped, and swayed, her knees weak.

Oh, yes, she wanted more kisses, and babies, and to discover all that marriage entailed. And Adam Douglas . . . she was attracted to him, he thrilled her, fascinated her. And she might even like him.

She liked his unusual servants, she liked his height, and strength, the breadth of his shoulders. His arresting, burning blue eyes, his beautiful red lips, his distinguished nose. His calm intensity, his authority, his presence that slammed into her when he came near.

Now, if she could trust him to give her the freedom she wanted.

Out of all the men she had been around these past two Seasons, he had fascinated and attracted her the most.

She wanted to marry him.

She would marry him.

Over the anvil, in Gretna Green, she would marry Adam Richard Douglas, the Duke of Blackdale.

A laugh rose up in her throat again, and she bent forward and clapped her gloved hands over her mouth. She glanced back, blushing, to the calm Kate, then laughed outright. Kate raised her eyebrows with a small, answering smile.

Cora couldn't hold her limbs still anymore and ran down the lane. She skipped, then ran again, grabbing up her skirts, hopping over puddles, and splashing through others.

She felt so free.

"Lady Cora!" She heard Kate call. She ignored her for several more yards, and then slowed, panting, and turned with a hop to face toward the maid she had left far behind. She grinned at Kate's dignified pace. No running for her.

"We ought to not go too far," Kate called.

Cora caught up her skirts, and ran back to her, laughing. She grabbed Kate's hand. "Kate! It's famous!"

"What is famous, my lady?" A smile was curling her mouth.

"I'm going to marry him!" A fierce joy rose up in Cora as she said the words, and her face flamed with more than the heat of her exertions.

The smile left Kate's face, and was replaced with hope, wonder, and worry. She searched Cora's face with intense eyes. "Really? Are you sure, Lady Cora?"

"Yes, pretty sure." Cora gripped her hand tighter, then stepped back. She still didn't know if he would give her freedom, how much autonomy he'd give her. "But let's not tell him."

"No?"

"Engagements are very binding, you know." Cora searched her mind and her heart. Her heart was sure, pretty sure. But her mind had concerns. "I reserve the right to change my mind. I will tell him in Scotland if I still want to marry him by then. Perhaps I'll tell him over the anvil." She couldn't help grinning at the thought.

Kate gave a small cry, her hand over her mouth, and tears swimming in her eyes. Cora's eyebrow's scrunched. "Kate?"

"I'm . . . I'm so glad, Lady Cora." Her shoulders were curling in, her perfect posture marred by emotion. Cora put her hand on Kate's shoulder. "This has been . . . awful. I've been praying so hard." She sucked in a breath. "If you'll marry him, despite all he's done, how utterly villainous . . ." She pulled out a handkerchief, and wiped at her eyes. She pulled back from Cora's touch, and straightened herself again. "He's a good man, truly. I care about him. And I think you will make him so—" sniff, "—so happy."

She wiped one more time and put the handkerchief away. The fierceness came back into her eyes. "And he'd better make you happy, or Mama and I will have to do something drastic!" She gave a decided nod, turned, and started marching back down the lane.

Cora's heart was full. She swung her arms, skipped to catch up with Kate again, and matched her stride. They walked companionably down the lane.

"Are you sure you aren't just relieved that no kidnapping charges will be brought to you and Mr. Malcolm if I marry him?" Cora asked mischievously.

Kate gave her a look. Cora grinned.

"Yes, that is also a part of it," Kate sighed. "Though we aren't going to be sure of being free of that until everything is settled with your mother. She could still bring him before parliament."

"Hm, yes. Let's get going. She's probably coming after us right now."

But there were a few things Cora wanted from the duke.

Adam paced across the inn yard. She should be back by now. Though the weather was fine for once, Charlie Coachman was walking the horses, never liking them to be kept standing.

Cora and Kate appeared, and he stilled. There was a look in her eye . . .

She was beautiful and fresh, and came up to him with bouncing blonde curls and bright eyes. He stared down at her, drinking in every aspect of her, his heart burning.

"Duke? May I speak with you privately for a moment?"

His stomach tightened. "Of course." He bowed.

She moved to the private lane she had just emerged from. He followed. He noticed Kate only stood and watched them, a small smile on her lips.

His heart started pounding.

They were alone and shaded by bushes when she turned back to him.

"My lord duke." She curtsied.

"My lady Cora." He bowed.

She took a step closer to him.

"Your grace, thank you . . ." Her eyes were intense, but her mouth was soft. "for last night. For the kisses." She looked away, then back up at him. He didn't dare blink. "They gave me much to think about." Her mouth quirked up. "And I've realized, sir, that I do believe that there is something you have been intending to ask me. Now would be a good time, if you would so please."

Adam blinked at her. She was looking at him boldly, expectantly. His heart was in his throat. He swallowed it down. "I assume, my lady, that you are referring to . . ." He had to swallow again. "The issue of matrimony between us?"

There was a strange light in her eyes. It made his stomach clench. "Yes, Duke, that is what I am referring to."

His heart was pounding like mad. He should make speeches; he should win her . . . His mind was blank. The silence between them lengthened as he scrambled to find what he should say. It was taking too long. The lady had asked, he must act. "Lady Cora . . ." He must speak! "Would you do me the honor of accepting my hand in marriage?"

There. It was asked. His head felt light. He sucked in a breath, and tried to calm his heart.

"Thank you for asking me, Duke." The light was still there. "I appreciate the honor of your request being offered to me, and I will consider your suit." She gave a curt nod.

He barely kept himself from gaping at her. That was her answer? What did that mean? "Consider?"

"Yes, I will consider your offer until we reach Gretna Green. I will then let you know what my decision is."

Desperation seemed to take hold of him. "You could not let me know your decision now?"

She quirked a maddening uplift of her beautiful lips. "No, I offer a better option, sir." She tilted her head, looking up at him. "You have been remiss in your courtship of me thus far, Duke. You have the rest of the trip to Scotland—one day—to court me and win my favor."

He did gape at her now, his heart failing. "I am not good . . ." She lifted an eyebrow at him. "Not good at courtship, my lady, as I have explained, previously."

She grinned. He gulped. His mouth was dry. His hands were sweating in his gloves.

"My dear sir, all you need do is seek to please me. I'm sure you can manage, if you put your mind to it."

His mind was blank. His face was hot.

She moved nearer to him, and stood close, so close. Electricity seemed to arc between them, sending a jolt into his stomach at her nearness.

She inched forward, closer, and closer, then darted up onto her tip-toes, and kissed him, quick, in the corner of his mouth. He was too startled to move his head, or try for more. A frisson of bright joy went through him at the contact of her lips.

She moved back just as quickly, and he blinked with shock. His heart was pounding. A strange uplifted curve shaped her lips.

She snapped into action again. "Now, the next thing you can do to please me is to get us on the road. I do believe my mother is in hot pursuit of us as we speak. She would interfere with your courtship of me dreadfully, so I would like to keep our advantage." And she strode past him with a businesslike gait, reminding him of the dowager countess more than she ever had before.

He gulped again.

Cora settled back in her seat, and nearly purred with contentment. His face when she'd given her terms! She thrilled with feminine power. Oh, she would marry him. But she wanted him to work for it.

The carriage door shut. Adam was still outside. She frowned in confusion, and the coach shook with a heavy body climbing to the driver's bench. Charlie Coachman was already in place, she knew.

She exchanged looks with Kate. Malcolm raised an eyebrow, and the coach started off.

She almost gasped aloud as disappointment flooded her. How would he please her from outside the coach?

Frustration and annoyance surged. That man!

As the morning drew on, Cora tried to distract herself from the horrible lack of attention. "Mr. Malcolm, do you never sleep at night, to allow for all the sleeping you do during the day?"

He lifted an eye-lid, and answered. "Just an old campaigner's skill, my lady. If I am not driving or riding, I am very happy to sleep."

"This allows you to spend your free hours in dissipation, sir?" Kate asked in a deadpan voice.

"You wound me, Kate. I have been ever so righteous this trip. No ladies besides yourselves for company, little drinking, almost no gambling."

"You haven't had time. We are on a mad dash to the border, after all."

"If I had the desire, that would not deter me."

Cora watched them, fascinated. They barbed and parried. She was horrible with this type of flirtation. She wasn't witty, and never could come up with teasing remarks in the moment. Anything cutting and antagonistic just made her uncomfortable. Was this what Adam thought she wanted from him? What he claimed he was unskilled with?

She didn't want him to flirt like this. She wanted . . .

He wasn't even trying. She sighed in disappointment.

At the next change, he checked on them. "Such a fine day," he said, and climbed back into the driver's seat once again.

They opened the windows, and enjoyed the wonders of the scenery as they went up hill and down dale. The Pennines were beautiful, and Cora had never traveled them before. But the view was soured by her irritation at the duke.

Even Malcolm soon abandoned them, joining the duke on the driver's box, as Charlie climbed down for a quick respite.

Kate asked Cora for the details of what had happened when she conversed with the duke, and Cora gave them in a low voice, the triumph she had felt earlier now sour in her stomach.

"I think you scared him off for a bit. But he's committed. He should come around soon."

Adam had retreated like a coward.

The day was fresh, and the Pennines were beautiful. They trudged up the hills, and made up for lost time running down into the valleys. The speed and the clear weather helped lift his soul from the frustrating delays of the last few days.

He wished for Cerberus. A good pounding ride through these hills would loosen the tension in Adam's joints. But dragging the stallion behind them on this dash to Scotland, no matter how braw of a warhorse Cerberus was, had not been practical. Adam's grooms would bring him up. He would miss the ill-mannered beast until they arrived.

He could hire a hack and ride beside the carriage . . .

Adam was still being a coward.

He had no idea how to please her. He'd wracked his brain the last two changes. Even spoke of it to Charlie.

"Well, in my experience, your grace, women like to be admired, like to be desired, like attention, and like to get what they want. That last one the most."

What did she want? Pretty speeches? The few lines of poetry he had already presented to her had been carefully considered and long agonized over. Adam groaned.

Clouds closed in overhead and it began to drizzle. But what was a little rain to Scotsmen and four stout British horses?

At the Scotch Corner, Mr. Yardley found the ostlers too busy to talk to him. He didn't need to speak to them anyway. He had the duke's direction. He kept on the Great North Road, heading to Newcastle. He'd find the young lady at her great aunt's, where he was sure she'd be so grateful to be hearing from someone sent from her mother that she'd fall into his arms.

Rain pounded down, but he knew the ardor of his heart would keep him through the cold chill.

Chapter Nineteen

Filthy Waters

SUNDAY, JULY 7, 1816, MORNING

It was eleven o'clock and raining steadily before the duke left the driver's seat and retook his backward facing seat. He pulled his top hat over his eyes and appeared to sleep.

Cora was starting to resent him. He hadn't attempted to do anything to please her since she'd told him she wanted him to. No courtship, less consideration. She wanted to pound her feet, and yell, "I was going to say yes, you horrible man!"

Instead, she held back tears. She watched the rise and fall of the hills around them, and held her narcissus for comfort.

After a brief luncheon at noon, Cora became aware of the intense feeling of his gaze on her. She glanced in his direction, and yes, he was watching her under the brim of his hat. She looked away, and felt her cheeks redden.

Why was she looking away? He was the one who needed to change how he was behaving! She swallowed, tensed her stomach, gathered her courage, and turned her head back toward him.

She stared at him straight back.

She didn't try to not blink, she just looked at him, and refused to look away. She tried for calm impassivity. She couldn't tell if she succeeded.

His eyes widened. Then his brows lowered in grim puzzlement. He looked away, but soon looked back.

His gaze sharpened in intensity, his mouth softened, and his eyes began to burn. The barely leashed desire was there again, blue-stoked coals behind his eyes.

They closed, and he slumped in his seat, an expression of weary defeat on his tired face. His demeanor softened, and for the first time in what felt like hours, he spoke to her. "Lady Cora, may I beg leave to displace Kate, and take the seat next to you?"

Cora blinked, glanced at Kate, who'd raised an eyebrow, but sat forward, nodding consent.

Cora said, "That would be fine, duke."

As Kate and the duke maneuvered in the confines of the carriage, Cora clamped down on the thrill of excitement that went through her. She would await what he would do.

She was vaguely aware that Malcolm was giving Kate an inappropriate grin, and she was flashing him a disdainful look as the duke settled next to her. Cora decided to ignore them both. They were trusted servants, and Cora needed to converse privately with this man she thought to marry.

He took off his hat, and placed it on his knee, clenched his hands together, unclenched them, and finally looked down at her.

"Lady Cora, how are you?"

"I am fine. You?"

"Tired." Full honesty was in his voice. "Conflicted."

"What about, Duke?"

"I have not . . . have not done this well. None of it."

Yes, he hadn't, but she didn't want to discourage him by agreeing out loud.

"I'm afraid I am at a loss on how to go on. Or even start."

His hands were uselessly on his lap, when they could be better employed.

She could laugh, or cry, but she gathered her courage instead, and took off her travel-stained gloves. "Let me help you, then. May I take your hands, Duke?"

His eyes widened, "Yes, my lady, of course." He presented them to her, long-fingered, elegantly masculine hands. His fine leather gloves were damaged from controlling the reins for hours last night. She, amazed at her own boldness, drew the gloves off, tugging at one finger at a time till they gave way, and released his hands. When they were free, she took them in hers, bare skin to bare skin. He caught his breath. Her heart pounded, her cheeks warmed, and chills were racing up the backs of her arms under her pelisse sleeves.

His hands were strong, lightly callused, and smooth, but there was nothing soft about them. Hers were rougher than a lady's should be. She'd mistreated them forever, plunging them into dirt whenever she could. Her nails and cuticles were never in the healed smooth state they should be. But right now, they felt feminine, small, and soft as she put her bare hands in his.

She looked up at him, and there was color in his face, soft warmth, and tenderness in his eyes. Their fingers entwined, and he held her hands softly.

She shifted in her seat, drawing closer to him, so that their sides touched. The length of her leg nestled next to his, and as the carriage swayed, they rocked together in unison, becoming even closer.

"There, that is a good beginning, Duke."

"Call me Adam." He spoke abruptly. "Please."

Oh, she was being so bold. Wanton? It didn't matter. "Adam." She lifted one hand from his, and placed it over her heart. "Cora."

"Cora." He smiled, a warmth in his beautiful blue eyes that caught at Cora's breath as he lifted the hand he clasped to his mouth and kissed it with reverence.

"And that's how I saved the duke's favorite horse from the Spanish guerrillas and the French!" Malcolm laughed heartily. Kate cracked a reluctant smile, and Cora's body vibrated against Adam's as she chuckled at Malcolm's exaggerated story.

Adam sat back in the carriage squabs, feeling more contented than he could remember feeling in his life. Cora was tucked into his side, her bonnet pulled off, her golden head near enough to his that he could easily bend and kiss her on the top of her head. And he had, several times.

The first time, she had looked up at him with startled eyes, and then smiled with a quiet delight. Joy had raced through him, and he'd wanted to kiss her more, all over her cheeks and rose-bud mouth, but thought better of it. They weren't alone.

But he hadn't been able to resist her sweet forehead. He kissed it again, and sat back, his arm holding her close, their bare fingers entwined.

He hadn't felt so warm in days. Years? Her body next to his filled him with a soft glow of happiness. She fit perfectly, her tall frame comfortable in his arms.

Lassitude overtook his limbs. She was safely where she should be, and he could sleep.

Malcolm closed his eyes against the painful joy of the lovers cuddled across from him. The duke had won his lady, despite all the man had done that ought to ruin it.

Kate was beside Malcolm. She hugged the carriage wall, not touching him, self-contained and self-controlled. She was the moon: distant, cold, and untouchable. But still his side burned with heat, like if they touched, he might scorch in her silver flame.

Did she feel it at all? Was she completely unaffected by him? Was his worship all one-sided?

Had he fallen desperately in love with the one woman who resisted him in every way? Rejected him at every turn? This coldly burning, proud beauty. She was mistreated by so many. She was so vulnerable, and so strong.

His heart clenched. How could he ever win her?

The cold rain came down in sheets, blocking the view of breathtaking vistas that should otherwise be opening before them on this route through the Pennines. It drummed against the carriage top, rattled against the glass windows, and, Adam could imagine, whipped into the faces of Charlie and the post boys. The glass fogged, and moisture gathered and ran down it in streaks. The chill and thick dampness made their skin clammy and uncomfortable. Something was leaking.

The horses plodded on in deluged misery, and Cora pushed closer into his side, enough for him to wince as she put pressure on his recently-healed ribs. But he clutched her tightly as well. They were all tense with this weather, and the bumping and rolling motion of the carriage was making his bones ache.

They had to get past this high moorland, and down into Carlisle. Then it would be only ten miles to Gretna Green, where they would be able to rest.

And he would get his answer. He tightened his arm around Cora, and she turned her face into his chest.

Surely—surely!—her answer would be yes.

Sunday, the dowager and Lord Eastham ran afoul of mud, twice.

And then the Great North Road flooded.

They moved forward with agonizing slowness, the waters moving just under the carriage's base, the horses sloshing through up to their knees. Lord Eastham drove white knuckled and tense, staying in the middle of the road, carefully avoiding the ditches to either side he could no longer see.

The light was lowering, the afternoon stretching, soon to evening. The rain had lessened, enough that Cora could see the rolling moorlands about them. The tension in the carriage eased with it.

Adam held her hand still, and over the afternoon they had grown more comfortable with each other than she would have thought possible. She looked over to him as he watched the landscape through his window.

Could she kiss him, there, above his black cravat, just behind his ear?

She sat back. Best not. But she would, soon. After Gretna.

She looked out the window. She had never felt so contented sitting still and traveling before, with her fingers interlaced in Adam's. It was amazing.

They had been descending more than ascending for the last hour, and as she watched, the landscape opened up before them, and they descended faster. They were leaving the Pennines.

The road curved, and they slowed to take it. Then they reached a bridge, like a hundred others they had crossed on their journey. The stone cobbles rattled the carriage.

Cora looked down, past the low bridge wall, at the swollen and fast-moving stream below them. The bridge wasn't that long, nor did it arch far above, but the water looked high, like it might be hitting the bottom of bridge under them.

She looked upstream, following the course of the water with her eyes.

A fast torrent of water appeared above them, roiling, arcing back and forth, overflowing the stream-bed. A tidal wave of dark, muddy water choked with torn branches and debris was racing toward them.

She cried out.

They were in the middle of the bridge.

The water hit.

The horses screamed.

The carriage lifted, tilted, and then it dropped. Water began filling the carriage, swilling through the cracks in the door, pushing in the glass windows. They swirled dizzyingly in the water.

They were rushing downstream!

Water reached her calves, flowed over her half-boots, filled them, soaked her skirts till they were heavy. The water was cold. Everything seemed to happen in slow motion, but the freezing weight of her skirts made it worse. She looked up, and Adam's eyes were wide with horror. Her hand was still clutched in his, and she squeezed with all her might.

Adam lunged for doors, unlatched them, crying, "Malcolm!"

He pushed against them. The pressure of the water outside was keeping them closed. He only had one hand. He refused to let go of Cora. He must not let go!

Malcolm was there, lending his strength, and the doors popped open. One door ripped away, and slammed against the side of the carriage with a shudder. The other was forced shut by the water rushing against it.

They had a way out. He had to get Cora out.

Adam moved forward, clutching her to him. The carriage was tipping toward the door. Not good. "Move back, move back!"

They pushed against the right side, and counter-balanced the carriage. It tipped, and they rolled that way and then back to vertical. They were soaked through, but the door was still open.

They would drown! He had to save them! He needed to be able to move.

He let go of Cora like wrenching out his own heart. "Stay till I'm out," he shouted above roar of the water, "Then follow."

The deluge was swirling, pushing them downstream. He climbed out, clinging to the door frame, searching for something to grab onto once he let go. A tree branch, anything.

The carriage dipped, going over an unseen ridge in the water, and plummeted down the other side in a rush. It dunked him in the water.

The wild current pulled at him, tugged, sucked at him, and then something—a tree branch—slammed into him, and his grip was gone. He was ripped away from the carriage. He tumbled through dark water, swallowing, gulping. There was only water, water everywhere. He was completely out of control, powerless.

Which way was up? He tried to control his panic. His lungs were burning.

He was in the field at Waterloo. He was trapped, buried under the dead, the scorching sun overhead, and mud around, dying of thirst and struggling for breath through broken ribs.

Then his father's hands were around his neck, squeezing off all air, the fetid stench of alcohol filling his nose as he tried to breathe in. Father's red-rimmed eyes bore down on him in mindless rage. His lungs were burning, screaming for air.

He sucked in. Water filled his lungs.

Something solid scraped his side, and he pushed off of it. His head emerged out of the water, and he was breathing! It was the ground. He pushed again, and was able to stand, the water under his knees now, much shallower than it had been further upstream. The force of the stream was less here, more spread out, though still strong. He struggled, but kept his footing. He coughed out water, spewed it out, and sucked in clean air. His lungs burned and rejoiced in relief.

"Adam!" It was Cora's voice. He turned, gasping in air. Through his water-blurred eyes, he saw the carriage was no longer being carried downstream, but was stopped, leaning at a strong angle as the torrent battered against it. It had stuck against an up-cropping of muddy rock. Malcolm had climbed out and was assisting Cora.

Uncontrolled coughing seized him again. He was paralyzed by the wracking of his lungs. He almost slipped; the dark water ate away the mud beneath his boots.

When he could do anything else, he inched forward through the strong current. The horses had washed up in a gully. They neighed in panic, but were cut from their traces and heading to the shore.

Charlie, the postboys, where were they?

Adam watched, helpless, as Malcolm inched Cora and Kate, hand in hand, through the flood. There were people on the shore, men reaching out to them, knee-high in the torrent.

The brown, filthy water surrounded him. There was a deep cleft between him and the opposite shore. He dared not try to cross it. Behind him, a ledge he had gone over cascaded water, making retreat upstream impossible. He was separated from the others, isolated. The current battered him, threatened to overbalance him. There was nothing to hold on to. He would slip and be lost. He focused all his strength on staying upright.

The rescuers created a human chain, and reached the others. Cora, Kate, and Malcolm linked with them, and began to inch toward shore. Cora's face was drawn with tension, and she looked back at him when she should be watching her footing. She slipped, he shouted, she dragged at the others connected to her, dunked, almost covered by the water.

They were able to haul her back. The men on shore pulled them in with their human chain, and she was safe.

Charlie, the two post boys, there they were. They were safe as well, a part of the chain.

They were all safe. Alive. Malcolm and Kate were clinging to each other on the shore. Cora was wide-eyed, staring at him. Only yards separated them, but they were un-traversable.

"Duke! Stay where you are! We'll get a rope out to you!"

It was Charlie.

The men worked, making their chain again, this time anchored by a rope. They inched toward him, finally reaching the chasm, where they could go no further.

"We'll throw you the rope!" The man in front said.

They tossed it. It missed him, too far away to catch. He gritted his teeth and dug in his feet against the pull of the wild water.

They dragged back in the heavy, sodden rope, and tossed again.

There! He caught it. He wrapped it around his wrist three times, grabbed it firmly, and inched forwards.

The chasm, a gap, two feet wide only, lay before him, water cascading down it. He could jump it, if he were on dry ground.

"I'm going for it, gentlemen!"

"Go!" The lead man said. He was a solid farmer, with, Adam hoped, solid strength.

He pushed forward, and tried to jump. And failed. His feet were swept from under him. He went under, felt his body slip, go through the gap, and be yanked forcefully by the arm as the rope caught him, almost pulled his arm out of its socket.

He gritted his teeth, held his breath, and held on, as he was dragged slowly, but relentlessly, out of the torrent.

Strong arms pulled him up, and he was finally on his feet again, supported on either side by men. They helped him, staggering and still coughing, to shore.

And he collapsed there, just breathing, as rain poured down on them.

He'd almost died.

And so had Cora, and all who went with him on this foolhardy trip.

All nature was against him. Mother nature had unleashed her fury on him.

Cora was there, kneeling in the wet grass in her wet skirts.

"Oh, Adam!" She cried. Tears were joining the rain.

He stared up at her. This beautiful young girl. This light, this joy.

He'd dragged her, screaming against his hand, struggling against her bonds, helpless.

Helpless, as he had just been, tumbling out of control through dark water. Helpless, as he lay wounded on the battlefield. Helpless as a child against the strength of his father's rage.

The most horrifying feelings he'd ever experienced.

What had he done?

It was there, dripping, rain running over his bare head, and relief singing in his veins, that Mort blurted, "Marry me, Kate!"

"What?" Her hair was springing from her sodden cap, her bonnet lost. She wiped rain from her eyes and stared at him.

He rushed forward, grabbed her hands. "I love you and I want to marry you, Kate! Please, put me out of this misery!" Her soaked skirts brushed against his knees.

He tried to take her in his arms, but she pulled her hands out of his and pushed him away. "Are you drunk, Mr. Malcolm?"

"Only on relief that we're alive! Life is too short to be apart from you any longer, Kate. And you won't have me any other way. So, please, marry me, Kate!"

He caught her hands again, and held her eyes.

"I want to be with you, Kate. For you, I'll make the sacrifice! I'll tie myself down. Because I know that's what you want, and that's what you deserve, and so I'll do it. Marry me, Kate!"

Her dark eyes were wide, and for a moment he thought her lips trembled, but then they firmed, and she wrenched herself out of his grasp. "You forget yourself, sir!" She moved rapidly away from him. His arms were left bereft, chilled to the bone. A shudder ran through him. "Please, Kate! I—"

She drew herself up, holding her arms tightly around her body. "I ask you to stop this disgraceful display." The cold rain hit her face, and she blinked against it, her expression just as cold. "I have no intention of ever marrying, Mr. Malcolm. And especially—" She stuttered. She was shivering. She was cold!

He took another step toward her, desperately wanting to hold her, to warm her, to warm himself.

"—Especially not to an unprincipled man, womanizing, gambling his wages, wasting his strength in riotous living, Mr. Malcolm!" She spat. "A man such as you takes what he wants and leaves. I will not tie myself to that, Mr. Malcolm." She turned and hurried away.

She reached her lady and the duke, knelt beside them, attended to them. Mort was left standing alone, pummeled and broken.

Chapter Twenty

Farmhouse

SUNDAY, JULY 7, 1816, NIGHT

Cora shook as Kate rubbed her down and clothed her in a borrowed night-rail. She was so cold and tired.

Full dark had fallen. A farmer and his goodwife welcomed them into their home. The kitchen was warm, with a blazing fire in the grate, and the farmhouse was of a good size, prosperous enough to have a maid-of-all-work employed. The family was large, with eight children. "We have nothing fit for a duke and a lady . . ."

"Do not concern yourself about me." The duke had said, standing in the cold rain. "I'm an old soldier. But if you could provide a bed for the lady, that would be most welcome."

The goodwife was plump and kind. She clucked over Cora, wrapped her up and set her before the fire.

"If the lady and her lady?" She paused, taking in Kate.

"My abigail, yes."

"Wouldn't mind sleeping with my daughters, we could move the littlest ones with us, and give the duke and his man the boys' room. The boys can sleep in the stables."

The girls, twelve and fourteen, bobbed curtsies with wide eyes. But the two-year-old looked at Cora in her towels and warm quilt, and climbed in her lap without a by-your-leave.

"Susy, well I never! Don't—that's a lady!" The goodwife scolded when she spotted her forward child.

"That's all right, she is warming me up." Cora had rarely had the chance to be this near a small child. She wrapped Suzy's little body in the blanket, and buried her face in Suzy's dark curls, the smell of child rich and unfamiliar. "Hello Suzy. I'm Cora. And I got dunked in the river today."

She held the warm child close, and felt calmer. She sent another prayer of gratitude heaven-ward that they had survived.

Suzy babbled. Cora had no idea what she was saying. "Mmm-hmm," she encouraged, lassitude stealing over her limbs. "Kate, you need to get warm too." She blinked at her. Kate hadn't gotten dunked, but was thoroughly rained on, and was standing with bare feet, trying to dry her skirts in the fire without taking anything off. "Could we get more blankets for my lady's maid?"

"Yes, my lady."

Cora rested, her eyes getting heavy. The aches in her limbs were calming with the kitchen fire before her, and the small child in her arms. Suzy sucked at her fingers, and soon slept. Cora wanted to join her.

A warm mug was pressed into her hand. "Hot broth, milady. It'll do you good."

She blinked at it. "Thank you." She took a sip. Warmth spread down her chest, into her stomach. Oh, that was good.

A cold draft passed over her face, disturbing the steam from the mug. She looked up. Adam stood in the doorway from outside.

His look was shuttered, his eyes shadowed, brows lowered. A dark presence in the kitchen, bringing his own chill.

"Adam, you're still in your wet clothes! Come, you must get warm! Oh. Do we ladies need to vacate the kitchen so the men can get warm?" Cora became aware of how little she was wearing: a borrowed flannel night-rail, towels, a blanket, thick woolen socks on her feet, and a child on her lap. She ducked her shoulders, pulled sleeping Suzy closer to her stay-less chest, and struggled to keep herself from blushing.

The two eldest girls did blush. They curtsied at the tall, intimidating presence of the duke.

"That would likely be the best plan, milady, iffen you're willing to be moved." The goodwife bustled. "Lucy, take Suzy to her trundle, put it in our room tonight." Lucy obeyed. Cora felt the loss of Suzy's warm weight. She rewrapped the blanket over herself, intensely aware that the borrowed night-rail was too short and her stays were visible among the clothes drying in front of the fire.

"Julie, please show the lady and her maid to the girl's room. The bed is big and comfy there, milady, we hope you all will sleep well there."

Cora blinked, unsure just how many would be sleeping in the same bed with her, a novel experience. As the daughter of a countess, she had never shared a bed before. "I'm sure we will, thank you."

Kate helped her up, and Cora checked her over quickly. Her face was ashen and drawn, and she still hadn't removed her traveling clothes. Cora hoped she was warm enough.

Cora kept hold of the wonderful broth. It was cooling too fast. "Duke, be sure to get some warm broth, it will help you. Is there more for the duke?"

"Of course, my lady, I'll take care of the men now." The goodwife shooed them, but Cora stopped in front of Adam.

His eyes looked haunted, his skin bleached as death. His tightly pressed lips were tinged with blue.

"Will you be all right, Adam? You are too cold!"

He nodded sharply, and moved out of her way, saying nothing. She frowned, but started forward.

"Lady Cora." Adam's voice was gravelly and deep. Cora stopped and looked up at him. He was close enough to speak low to her, his face near to hers. "May I request an audience with you in an hour? We must . . . discuss."

Cora nodded. "Of course, your grace. I may be," she glanced down at her blanket, "under-dressed, though, if that is all right."

He looked pained. "Do not be concerned."

She looked into his eyes. He looked away. "In an hour, then."

And she followed the awkwardly waiting Julie, Kate behind.

"This is the boys' room. And here's the girls'." Fourteen-year-old Julie was losing some shyness. The rooms were interconnected, passing through the boys' to get to the girls'. "And me parents', that's theirs there." A closed door to a bedroom, not a closet, then. Cora swallowed, and accepted seeing the goodman and his wife when they came through later in the evening to get to their own room.

But she was glad to see a screened dressing area with a covered chamber pot. That would make the interconnected rooms less awkward. The farmhouse was clean and neat, and the bed was big. It looked heavenly, no matter how many bodies would be in it tonight.

"Kate, you will get out of those clothes now, I must insist."

Kate finally acquiesced, and donned a borrowed night-rail, one of the goodwife's. It was huge on her, and not quite long enough.

The maid-of-all-work brought up a tray of warmed-over Sunday supper for them, and twelve-year-old Lucy joined them. Cora and Lucy ate on the bed, there not being enough chairs.

A fire had been laid in the fireplace, and as Kate tended to her clothing, Cora told the girls the tale of their wash-out. "He went under! It was the most horrible thing!"

"The duke, and you, my lady? Are you . . . ?" Lucy's eyes were huge and avid.

"We are affianced. He is taking me to Scotland to be married. My mother is following more slowly, she will meet us there." It was even true. Cora needn't blush.

"Oh!" The girls looked at her with wide-eyed amazement.

"He scares me!"

"Lucy, never say that!" Julie shushed her. "He's so handsome. And a duke!"

Cora couldn't help but laugh. "He's a bit scary, isn't he? And very handsome too!" Then she sobered with a shiver. "But he almost drowned today. I tell you, girls, that was the most scared I've been in my life. I almost lost him." She pulled up the blanket, the chill creeping back into her bones.

She tried to lighten the mood again with a smile. "And I haven't had the chance to marry him yet!"

A solid knock hit the door.

"Speak of the devil," Kate said in an under-voice. Cora flashed her a look. Kate's face was grim, but she stood, and opened the door.

And there he was, standing at her bedchamber door. How incredibly improper. Except that he was going to be sleeping on the other side of that door, and she was surrounded by females.

He was wearing a blanket now as well, a nightshirt, and some ill-fitting woolen trousers. And woolen socks, she was pleased to see.

But it was his exposed neck and triangle of upper chest that drew her eye, and made her swallow. She had yet to see him so naked.

She scrambled awkwardly off the bed, and the other females joined her in curtseying. She had to stifle a laugh. So many irregularities.

"It is time for our interview, Adam?"

"Yes, my lady, if you would join me?" His jaw flexed, looking uncomfortable with the circumstances, but he stepped back with a gesture to the boys' room. She suppressed a grin.

"Excuse me, ladies. I must leave you for an interview with my fiancé for a moment." She let the grin come out then, as the girls watched her starry-eyed.

But Kate looked concerned. That was worrying.

Cora frowned as she closed the door behind her. She tried to wipe away that expression as she faced Adam. She kept her eyes off the two beds in the room, and noted the open door to the stairway.

"Malcolm is standing on the stairs to ensure the privacy of this conversation." Adam spoke low. His face was grim, worse than his usual. Cora's body begin to feel cold as she looked at Adam's forbidding face.

"Is something wrong?" she asked, also softly.

Adam grimaced, but said. "How are you? Are you recovered from your ordeal?"

"Yes, I am fine. It is you I am worried about. Are you warm enough?"

"It doesn't matter."

"Of course it does."

He shook his head. "I am here to speak with you about something of greater import."

She closed her mouth, and folded her hands in front of herself. A terrible feeling filled her chest. He was so distant. After finally experiencing a taste of closeness this afternoon, this change was painful. Where had the connection gone?

His jaw worked, and he seemed to gather himself. He kept his gaze to the left of her ear. "Lady Cora, I have been faced today with the reality of my utter failure . . . that I have betrayed every principle I once held dear, the entire lack of honor in my actions. I must, totally, abjectly, apologize to you." He bowed his head.

Cora blinked at him, at a loss.

"My excuses, my justifications, were not just. My calm rationalizations were not rational. What I did to you, in stealing you away, ripping you from your mother, abducting you, binding, gagging you—I was wrong. I should not have . . . I bitterly regret that I . . ." he swallowed. "I desired to marry you, and when she denied me, your mother accused me of being like my father. With my offended pride, I vowed to do as my father would have done, and take what I wanted."

Cora stood still.

"I have striven my entire life to not become like my father, Lady Cora. As I have failed—have plunged with headlong deliberation into failure—I must now endeavor . . ."

"What did he do?" She interrupted him. "You have said he was a bad man. What did he do that his son is so determined to not be as he?"

He took a step back, but she caught his gaze and held it.

"I suppose you have a right to know." He ran his hand through his short-cropped hair. "He was . . . brutal. When drunk, he hit. He beat me, my other siblings, servants who had the misfortune to get in his way. When he was sober, he was almost worse. He punished, and called himself just. He'd lock the girls in their rooms with no candles or fires in the grate in winter for the slightest infraction. He would try to pit Nicolas against me, until I refused, and then he punished me himself. I tried to shield Nicolas, but I was a boy, and did not always manage. Nicolas had a temper like Father . . . but his was quick burning, and he became cheerful as soon as it burned out. I—" He looked at Cora. "When I left for Eton, it was with the greatest relief, and with terrible worry. And when I was grown enough to be able to leave and not come back, I left as quickly as I could."

He stepped closer to Cora. She opened her eyes wide to keep tears at bay, and pressed her lips together to keep them from trembling.

"I've tried to never lift my arm in anger. I've tried to never drink in excess. But then in cold deliberation, I acted intentionally as he would have, and I took you, Lady Cora Winfield." His voice was husky. His eyes burned into hers, but not with passion, but with the need for restitution and forgiveness. "I took your choices. I took your life because I wanted it, and I am sorry."

He looked away, stepped back, and adjusted his loose, ill-fitting clothing. "I cannot undo what I have done, Lady Cora. But I will endeavor to restore my honor and do the right thing from this day onward."

Chill fear gripped her. "What do you intend to do?" Her voice felt dragged out of her.

"I have left neither of us much choice. I will marry you tomorrow when we reach Scotland. It is the only honorable thing I can do. I have ruined you in the eyes of the world, and so I will give my name, my title, my wealth, and what is left of my honor to restore yours."

Cora's stomach clenched and her mouth tightened.

"I will escort you to Edinburgh, and then into the highlands to Blackdale Castle, and also to the Lochelys estate if you wish, so you may look over my holdings, and choose where you want to live. I will make sure you are comfortably settled, and then I will move into a different residence. You will never need fear that I will come near you, or dishonor you with my advances again."

A strangled cry of outrage caught in her throat, but he kept speaking.

"If after a while you prefer to return to England and reside with your mother, I will provide funds and a lady's companion to accompany you back. You will be able to do all and anything you wish, with as many funds as you wish. You will be able to go where you please, a duchess with wealth and whatever else you desire. And I will not approach you. You need never fear for your person again."

Cora watched him, aghast. "Never approach me?"

"I have forced you once. I will not do it again. I will not even touch you, Lady Cora, I sw—swear it."

The cry did come then, ripped out of her. "What? You expect—you think—!"

He drew himself up, every bit the duke in his simple, borrowed garments. "Yes, Lady Cora. This is the best and only way for my honor and yours to both be restored. I have done you a great wrong, and I will restore as much as it is in my power."

"You intend to marry me and then never touch me? If you think—!" She stopped, took a deep breath in, trying to control herself. She glared up at him, keeping tears at bay with anger. "And what of the dukedom, Adam? If you marry but never approach your wife," she bit it out, "you will have no son to inherit."

His mouth twisted. "My brother Jude will doubtless have a legitimate son soon enough. Do not fear for the title."

A headache was building behind her eyes, and her supper had soured in her stomach. "This conversation is . . ." ridiculous, but she stopped herself from saying it. "We are both tired, Adam. I think we ought to both retire, and we'll discuss this further tomorrow."

His mouth worked, but he nodded. "Yes, my lady, if you so wish."

Neither of them moved. She stared at him, his ridiculous, foolish, awful vow ringing in her ears. "You say you will never touch me."

He shook his head. "I will not."

She advanced a step toward him. He swallowed, his mouth downturned and forbidding. She stepped closer still.

He was a tall man standing straight, but she was a tall woman. Had she been shorter, she would not have been able to steal the kiss she had taken this morning.

Surely, he loved her enough that this foolish notion would not stand. Her touch would bring him around, must bring him around. Her kisses, he wouldn't resist them, surely? She must dissolve this foolish resolution with the power of her kiss.

She rose up on her tiptoes again, and kissed his mouth once, twice.

His arms remained at their sides, his mouth did not move against hers. They were dead, cold kisses.

He stepped back, his lips pressed into a straight line. She advanced again—surely they must!—and he retreated. He turned his body, giving her his shoulder.

A stab hit her chest. She stared at his unyielding form with a chill of misery running through her inward parts.

He didn't want her to touch him! Her stomach roiled. Her face flamed. Embarrassed, ashamed.

She was worthless and ugly. Her face drained and cold overtook her body.

Her tears dried in her unbelieving eyes, but an unvoiced sob clogged her throat.

The kisses of last night, the caresses and closeness of today, dried, denied, gone.

Suddenly her body craved his touch more than it had ever hungered for food. Her arms ached for it, and her core cried for it.

She lifted her arms in silent entreaty, stared at his hard face in supplication.

Please, Adam.

He swallowed, and turned his head. The distance between them seemed an unfathomable gulf.

"You are right that we ought to retire. Enough excitement for one day. Lady Cora." He bowed, her body would not respond fast enough to give answering courtesy. He stiffly moved past her, and opened the door to the girls' room.

She stared at it, and forced her lower limbs to respond. Her wool-clad feet skudded against the uneven floorboards, her legs wooden.

Then she rushed through the door. It shut firmly behind her. Kate was standing there, just inside.

The sob finally tore out of Cora's throat, and she threw herself into Kate's arms. "Kate!"

Cora cried.

Rejected. Unwanted. Unloved.

The room arrangements were intolerable. The large gap at the base of the door blocked no sound all.

Adam stood motionless for long seconds, feeling the empty chasm of his stomach, the hard, cold void in his chest. Her sobs came through clearly, each miserable noise feeding the abyss where his heart should be.

Would this be what it would be like, married to her?

The girls asked what was wrong in alarmed voices. Kate soothed, her voice low and indistinguishable.

Cora was a warm, loving creature. Could he deny her, when she wanted to be touched? Could he damn her to an affectionless marriage?

His resolution of the last few hours shook. He had never been whirled about in his emotions like this before. He couldn't stand it.

He couldn't stand this. He couldn't stand to be this close to her, a thin door all that stood in the way of her, her beautiful body, her sweet face, her weeping heart.

He was in an untenable position.

Could he hold her, kiss her, as she'd asked tonight? Marry her on the morrow, then never touch her again?

He had been determined. He had been stalwart. He had been resolute, so sure of his own strength.

He had none.

He turned, and fled past Malcolm on the narrow stairs, almost slipping in the ridiculous stockings.

He roughly pulled on his damp boots, the cold of them seeping into the woolen socks.

Malcolm followed him to the kitchen.

"What was that, your grace?" His demanding, belligerent tone drew a gasp from Molly the maid-of-all-work. Malcolm had been grim and silent since the accident, but now he snarled. "Of all the lily-livered, contemptible—"

Adam refused to look at him. "You may sleep in the first room, Malcolm. I shall be in the barn with the post boys."

And Adam fled.

Cora cried herself to sleep, surrounded by bodies. The bewildered and uncomfortable girls took one side, and Kate and Cora took the other.

There was no way to talk to Kate about what Adam had said without being far too indiscreet in front of the girls, but Kate said, "I heard enough."

Cora tried to control her crying—and her rage. She wanted to kick things, hit things. And scream.

If he thought she would marry him under this ridiculous edict, he had another thought coming!

As the dowager and Lord Eastham drove through the night, a terrible thunderstorm hit, pounding down in impenetrable sheets and close lightning strikes, spooking the horses. They were forced to stop and wait it out at an inn, the dowager near tears of rage and frustration. Lord Eastham was grateful to be able to get some sleep.

Chapter Twenty-One

Gretna Green

MONDAY, JULY 8, 1816, MORNING

Captain Bowden arrived at Gretna Green at daybreak, his hard-ridden hack flagging underneath him. He roused the blacksmith, who scowled to be pulled out of his bed without the promise of a couple to marry and their requisite compensation.

No, no dukes had darkened his door. None by that name.

Captain Bowden smiled. He'd beaten the duke there.

Captain Bowden tipped him, and asked him that if a duke should come, if he could delay till the captain could be notified.

The blacksmith scratched his face with the coin and claimed, "I'm an honest man, and marrying is what I do. If a duke does stand before my anvil, I'll not wait on a captain, if ye see what I mean, begg'n your pardon, sir."

Bowden snorted a laugh. "Fair enough. I'll be diligent then."

He got himself a room at Gretna Green Hall and caught a few hours of sleep before taking up his post outside the blacksmith's.

Cora woke sullen. The girls were talkative. Cora wished she had her customary privacy. Quiet Kate only would be a blessed relief.

Her narcissus was on the dresser. She had thought it was gone forever, washed away in the flood with the carriage.

"Kate, where did this come from?"

"I don't know. I slept though its delivery."

"Those are pretty flowers, milady."

"Thank you. I thought them lost. *Narcissus papyraceusm.*" She held it, and hope and resolution filled her. Foolish masculine notions of honor would be overcome.

She would overcome. She would have Adam as husband, and have his love as well.

Their trunks were discovered in the boys' room outside their door, also having been recovered.

The maid-of-all-work told them, "The water went down, and the men were able to retrieve your things."

Amazingly, they hadn't leaked, though they were water stained. Even Kate's bag had been recovered, though still damp.

It was a quiet ride to Carlisle in a rented post chaise.

Adam was taciturn, with a sharp edge to his voice. Cora was calm. She didn't know how, but she would prevail.

He sat diagonally from her. Mr. Malcolm was across from her.

She watched Adam. He wasn't watching her anymore, so she felt free to turn the tables.

He didn't look well-rested, with darkness under his eyes, and lines between his heavy brows. But his jaw was firm, his nose distinguished. He was handsome, and she wanted to kiss him badly—to smooth away those worry lines, and lift those brows. To bury her face in his neck, and hold his hand.

He turned his head, met her gaze. She held it, refusing to look away.

His eyes were haunted. She gazed deep, feeling her eyes must burn as fiercely as his ever had.

He broke and looked away, jaw clenched.

They went through Carlisle with a quick change of horses, and then it was the final ten miles to the border. Malcolm's eyes looked sunken, and his mouth was held at a grim line. Kate sat still and tense. Cora wanted to pull her feet up and curl into the uncomfortable seat, but she sat properly and straight.

They were all silent.

At the River Esk, she felt a tightness in her neck, a stiffness in her back. Her hands clenched. They passed over it safely. They weren't washed away.

Then they were at the River Sark. A terrible presentiment came over her. She could see the water rising to rush them away again, but it didn't. And then they were in Scotland.

They drove into Gretna Green at a sedate pace. No dash, no runaway elopement here. There was hardly an indication that this small town was the goal of their clandestine trip.

With a tense heart, Cora watched out the window, seeking the famous blacksmith's shop.

There it was, whitewashed, brashly proud in its own humility, and clearly proclaimed. A red-coated figure lounged against the side of the building, bright against the white. Cora stared at him as they drove on past. The soldier lifted his head. She started in recognition, and then pulled back from the window and faced forward, her heart pounding.

It was Captain Bowden.

"What is it, Lady Cora?" Adam had noticed her start.

"Nothing!" Cora flushed. Her mind scattered around in confusion. The captain had seen her. She huffed in frustration. "It's . . ."

"I do believe we are being pursued, your grace." Mr. Malcolm interrupted her. Their hired carriage was equipped with a rear window, and he stared through it, past the women in the forward-facing seat.

Adam leaned forward, and studied the rear window as well. Cora turned her head away with a scowl, and refused to be curious enough to leap up and kneel in her seat to look as well. As much as she wanted to.

"The soldier mounted quickly after we passed him." Malcolm said.

And? Cora wanted to scream. *What is he doing?*

"Who is it?" Adam's voice was calm, almost disinterested.

Cora turned to him with glaring accusation. "It is Captain Bowden.," she snapped. "He saw me."

Adam looked away from her, and sat back, his face a stone mask. His eyes closed, and he took in a deep breath. He raised a black-gloved hand to his face, and released his breath.

Cora saw it, when the tension released, and relief went through him. She saw the moment he let her go.

He wouldn't have to marry her now. She was rescued from him. A gallant soldier was here to make it all right, a hero.

He was rescued from her.

Outrage ripped through her. Rage and misery. Her limbs stiffened, her mouth tightened, and her hands clenched.

Cold took over. She was calm, she was reasonable. Logical, rational. She turned her face to the window again, and saw nothing.

"I wonder how long he's been waiting? We were quite delayed on the road," Mr. Malcolm said.

"Very. It will be surprising if he was the only one to reach here first."

"A few had to have considered we might go another route, or that they missed us. Maybe they are spread along the border like a border guard? Ah, he is overtaking us."

Cora blinked, and focused her eyes as a horseman drew up beside her window. Captain Bowden looked down at her with an eyebrow lifted. She twisted her mouth at him, and didn't open her window. He gave a smile—what was that? Intrigue?—glanced at Malcolm who was looking blandly pleasant, tipped his hat, and urged his mount forward.

"Ho, there, driver!" They could hear him hail Charlie Coachman. "Where are you headed?"

Charlie gave no answer.

But they turned off the main road soon enough, and onto a pleasant lane, Captain Bowden keeping pace.

They arrived at the Gretna Green Hall Inn.

Malcolm exited first, letting down the steps.

Cora watched as Captain Bowden dismounted and strode toward their carriage.

Adam exited.

"Blackdale!" the captain called.

"Captain Bowden." Adam's voice was cold.

Cora wasn't going to allow anything to happen without her. She scooted past Kate, and descended from the steps too fast for anyone to assist her.

"Lady Cora!"

"Captain Bowden." Cora straightened her skirts and curtsied perfunctorily. She wasn't happy to see him. Such trouble he was causing.

He strode up to her, and stood too close. Travel stains were evident on his uniform, but he was clean shaven, and bright eyed. "Are you all right, my lady?" He spoke low and with concern.

Cora frowned. "I am fine, Captain." Must she be courteous? He had made the arduous journey for her, as unwelcome as he was. "Thank you for your concern." She clasped her hands in front of her, putting a barrier between them. "How was your journey?"

"It was smooth. I arrived this morning." He looked uncomfortable. "How was yours?"

Cora snuck a glance at Adam. He was stiff, not looking at them.

"It was . . . fraught. We had several delays."

"Tell me, Captain," Adam said, "are you the only one waiting here?" Adam's voice was cold, almost unconcerned.

"So far, yes. I know several more set out before me, but likely did not take as direct a route."

"Who?" Cora asked. Who else would arrive to complicate things?

Adam narrowed his eyes. "Your pardon, my lady. Let us enter, and bespeak a parlor where we can discuss these matters in private. If you will join us, Captain?"

Bowden raised an eyebrow. "Gladly. I have a room here. Do you intend to stay here, Blackdale?"

"Yes."

"Then I feel I ought to inform you the proprietress doesn't like eloping couples, won't allow them in. She's told me herself." Bowden conveyed this information with a tilt of his head, watching Adam.

The air around them grew frosty. Adam's mouth stopped just short of curling into a sneer. "Madame knows of the Duke of Blackdale. She won't refuse me." He snapped his heels, strode away, and went up the inn's stairs.

Cora rushed to keep up with him. Bowden tried to fall into step with her, and she walked faster to avoid him.

She wasn't letting Adam out of her sight.

The private room secured, and the proprietress properly obeisant to a Scottish duke in her inn, Adam gathered with the others over a light luncheon for their vital communications.

Adam grilled Bowden, and it was worse than they had predicted. The Prince Regent, the Archbishop of Canterbury, and the Duke of Wellington, all applied to! The news was all over London, and soon to be all over Britain.

Lady Cora sat ashen faced, her eyes wide. Adam caught Kate bringing out smelling salts and watching Lady Cora carefully. Malcolm lingered in the corner of the room, hooded eyes watchful.

What type of foolhardy woman was the dowager? To drag out everything about her daughter, before even knowing all the particulars? There was no way to hush it up. Cora had to marry.

And here was her swain, all sparkling teeth and dashing curls, ready to rescue her.

Adam's stomach roiled. Jealousy, hot and flaring, was curdling the tea in his stomach. He pushed the emotion down and ignored it. He rubbed at the ache in his forehead instead, an ache he could acknowledge.

The captain took a sip of his tea. "Now, if you would explain to me, Blackdale, what happened on your end? How did Lady Cora's bonnet come to be left in the mud of Hyde Park? Did you abduct her?"

Adam's teeth clenched. He squeezed his fist and looked away.

"No," Lady Cora said. Adam whipped his head around and stared at her. She was standing. Bowden scrambled to stand as well, setting down his tea cup. Adam rose, on-edge.

"We eloped," she told the captain, barefaced, and with her chin upturned. Bowden was of a height with her, allowing her to look down her elegant nose at him. "My hat unfortunately came to be left behind, leading to these wild accusations." She spun away from him, and walked to the window. Her hands were trembling, Adam noted. She wasn't an accomplished liar; her composure was breaking down.

Would Bowden notice? The soldier's eyebrows had shot up under his over-long dark curls. No, he wasn't fooled.

"If that is so, why are you not married at this time? You didn't stop at the blacksmith's shop."

Was Cora aware how easy it would have been? They had their own witnesses in Kate and Malcolm. As soon as they crossed the river Sark, he could have taken her hand, and declared "I am her husband!"

And if she had answered in kind, they would be married right now. Bound for life, forever linked.

And he would be honor-bound not to touch her. A life of miserable deprivation for them both.

Best not. Better she marry another. This swain would do. Adam must lay out the particulars to him, but without her in the room. "Lady Cora? Would you allow me to speak privately with Captain Bowden?"

"No!" She spat at him. "No, I will not allow."

Adam stiffened.

She spun and glared at Bowden, twisting her hands together. "Why are we not yet married, Captain Bowden? I will tell you! It is because the dear duke," she gestured at Adam, "has had a crisis of conscious. A crisis. Of. Conscious!" She flung out her hands with derision. "He must restore his honor, he says! Which he has wrongly interpreted as him not being able to marry me as a man should."

The headache flared. She was completely unreasonable! Emotional creature! He must fix what he had made wrong!

"Lady Cora," he ground out between clenched teeth. "I respectfully request that you retire to your room and rest. The captain and I have much to discuss."

She stomped up to him, as heavy footed as ever the dowager had stepped, and glared up at him. "To make decisions about my life for me, Adam? Without consulting me? Don't you think you've done enough of that already, Adam Richard Douglas?" Pain flared in his chest. She stung him to the quick, a knife to his heart. Adam closed his eyes and swallowed.

"Let me tell you something, Adam." Her voice had gone soft, she had moved near to him, her face close. Her warm breath caressed his face. "You cannot offer what is not yours to give. You cannot take, and you cannot pass around. My hand is mine. My heart is mine. I will only marry where I will." Her eyes scanned his face. He was frozen, overwhelmed by her closeness, every muscle an agony of tight control. He must not touch her. He must not!

"I know who I will marry, Adam. And if that person denies me, I will marry none." And she kissed him. Her soft lips were like a blow, a blot of lightening that shot through him and paralyzed every part of him. And then she was gone, stepping back and facing Bowden.

"I thank you, Captain, for the consideration and sacrifice of your journey here for my sake. I don't care what Adam tells you; have your private consultation. It will not change my desires, and my will. Good day, sirs."

She pivoted, and exited. Kate gave Adam a cold look as she followed.

He rocked back, and collapsed onto a nearby bench as the door shut behind them, every muscle suddenly incapable of supporting him.

"Well!" Bowden burst out. And he laughed. He lounged back in his couch, a gleaming delight in his eye.

Adam despised him.

"That's the lady you abducted, there! So determined! My congratulations, Blackdale! She's a rare one. Whoever could have guessed, from all her polite timidity in company?" He took a swig of his tea, grimaced at it, and rose fluidly. "We need something stronger. To drink to the happy couple's health." His grin flashed in Adam's direction.

Only the lingering weakness in his limbs kept Adam from throttling him.

"Men are foolish, vain, selfish creatures." Kate shook out a dress with vigor, her voice venomous. "Inconstant. Manipulative."

Cora rolled over on the counterpane, and blinked at Kate. Cora had thrown herself onto the bed as soon as they'd entered her room at the Gretna inn. After that farce of a conference with Adam and Captain Bowden, she had felt an intense need to pound pillows.

But Kate's level of ire was unexpected.

"Pardon me, my lady. I should not speak so. But I also want to knock sense into a man." She bustled around the room, arranging items from the trunk with precise, forceful movements.

"Who? Did Mal—?" Cora stopped herself. Kate had not spoken about her feelings, whether warm or cold, for Mr. Malcolm to Cora. If there was anything between them, it wasn't Cora's business, surely. She bit her tongue.

Kate's mouth was tight, like she was holding in words. They burst out. "He proposed! The daft fool!" She hung up Cora's pelisse, and brushed it forcefully.

Cora caught her exclamation in throat, and clapped her hands over the delighted smile on her mouth. "Kate! Malcolm proposed?"

"Aye, of all the fool things to do. That man, he wouldn't know fidelity and monogamy if it bit him on the . . ." She stopped herself. "Your pardon, my lady."

"You don't like him at all? His proposals aren't welcome then?"

Kate stopped her labor and gave Cora a straight stare. "Did I give any reason for you to think, for anyone to think, that his attention was welcome to me?"

"Well." How awkward this was. She squirmed. She should keep her mouth shut. "It had seemed, at times, that the animosity between you was more flirtatious than biting . . ."

Kate snatched up a pillow from the bed and plumped it roughly.

"And I could tell his interest was genuine, so I thought, and hoped . . ."

"Genuine! That man?" Kate threw the pillow down. "Oh, he's interested, all right. Just as he's interested in any bonny lass. He considers himself a female connoisseur, the braggart."

"I'm sorry he upset you, Kate." Cora buried her face in her pillow.

Mort passed Kate in the hall. She didn't acknowledge him. He turned to watch her walk away, his heart squeezing painfully.

"Kate." It slipped out unbidden. She slowed, but didn't turn. His heart pounded. "I know I did it badly. But I was sincere, I—" He felt like falling at her feet and begging again. That wouldn't help.

She pivoted, her face cold. "Mr. Malcolm. I know you. I have seen you. You're only interested in me because I've denied you."

"No, I—"

"And what would the duke say to this proposition of yours, sir?" An unamused smile lifted one corner of her full lips.

Hope leaped in his chest. "Oh, he's already given permission! Offered a dowry and everything."

"What?" She went stone still.

He perhaps shouldn't have said that. "Ah, yes, he offered, he wants you to be happy and settled, and—"

"How much?" Her dark eyes were flint.

He scrubbed at the back of his neck. "He didn't get specific, just threw it out there, offered it, like a bone or a carrot." He made it worse. Malcolm kicked himself.

"Like a bone, Mr. Malcolm? My hand and a dowry, offered up by the duke?" Her eyes were getting less flinty, turning into a blazing fire that seared him. "A tempting offer. A brilliant match for you, Mr. Malcolm, with the offer of a dowry from a duke for his bastard cousin."

His shoulders curled under the heat of her displeasure. "It was to be nice, just nice, Kate, he was being generous. If you wanted, it could be all for you." He floundered, like a fish.

"If I wanted?" She bit out. She spun and strode away, her back straight and imperious. Mort wilted against the wall, and scrubbed at his face with his hands.

He was an idiot.

Cora pressed the pillow into her face, and shook her head with a groan. She threw the pillow to the other side of the bed, and sat up, moving to the edge, her stockinged feet hanging off.

The room was too quiet. Kate had gone for something or another, Cora hadn't paid attention. She was restless and ill at ease. After three endless days on the road, she should be happy to finally be still.

But instead she was wild and trembly inside.

Trapped. She felt trapped. The air was too close in this room. It was just another box to confine her. She needed to get out into nature, feel the fresh breeze in her face, the sky above, and grass under her feet, no matter the wet.

She nodded her head. A walk. She would take a walk.

She re-donned her warmest clothes and her cloak. Where were her gloves?

That was it. Kate had taken them to launder them, or else seek replacements. The journey had made the pairs Cora had unpresentable.

Oh well, her hands weren't likely to get worse for a bit more weathering. She twitched the ribbons of her bonnet, and left the room.

Chapter Twenty-Two

Swallowed

MONDAY, JULY 8, 1816, AFTERNOON

As Cora passed a maid, she said, "Please tell anyone who might ask that I have gone for a walk."

"Yes, milady," the maid curtseyed and looked at her like she was crazy.

Cora walked outside.

The sky was heavy with clouds, but it was only drizzling. Cora hurried out of the muddy yard, and onto the grass. The grass fields surrounding the inn were bright green with patches of yellowing in lower areas: over-watered by incessant rains, saturated, not draining. The air was fresh and biting. She sucked in, expanding her lungs.

Every step sloshed, but the waterproofing on her dried half-boots held. Her feet stuck in icy mud and she had to pull them out, squelching.

She walked, heading west, past cultivated fields and sheep. The softy rolling hills of the Scottish lowland spread before her, beautiful, but frostbitten. The crops of the farmers here, as all over Britain, were being tried by this horrid, unnatural weather.

She kept walking, wanting action to overcome the thoughts in her brain, to work off her frustration with forceful movement.

She stomped her feet to work through her aggression, but that just made them stick in the mud.

She went around trees and bushes, and avoided streams. She crested the rise of another hill, her breath coming in pants, the cloud of her exhaled breath hitting her in the face as the wind rose.

She heard water running, but couldn't see its source.

She breathed the humid air, the cold cutting into her lungs in a refreshing way.

She took a step over the rise, and two, another.

The ground crumbled underneath her feet. A hole opened beneath her. The earth rose up and swallowed her.

The dowager and Lord Eastham reached the Scotch Corner. They were told a bridge was out in the Pennines, and they had to take the longer road around.

On the Winter Road, another bridge had been destroyed on a main thoroughfare, and the water was too high and fast for a ferry. They had to wait till it went down far enough for a ferryman to venture in.

The dowager stared numbly across the rushing water. Her daughter was only thirty miles away.

Lord Eastham sighed, closed his tired eyes, and took her clenched fist into his. "It will be all right, Theresa."

Kate answered when Adam knocked on Lady Cora's door. "Lady Cora isn't here."

"Where is she?" Adam's brow furled.

"I'm not sure, your grace. I haven't seen her for an hour. She was here when I left, but not when I returned."

"Please locate her if you can."

"She went off an hour or so ago, m'lord, duke, sir." The maid blushed a fiery red, and gulped. "She told me to let anyone asking know she went walking."

"Walking?"

"Yes, your grace. She was dressed for it, warm, with a cloak, and decent boots for a lady, excusing your grace."

"No, thank you for the information." He tipped her with a coin.

"But, no gloves though. Odd that."

A walk. In this cold.

He went to the window. It was raining again. He couldn't see her in the vicinity of the inn. Unease tugged on his chest.

He went to his room, and dressed as warmly as he could. She shouldn't be out there in this weather. What if it started to snow again? Or, worse, sleet?

When he got down to the main floor, and out the doors, he realized she could have gone in any direction.

An ostler was under an awning, and Adam asked him if he had seen the young lady.

"Aye, your grace, she walked off over the fields west some time ago. That direction." He pointed vaguely.

"Thank you."

Adam started walking.

Cora slid and slipped and tried desperately to grab a handhold of anything. There wasn't anything to grab. Clumps of earth, thin roots, rocks, and mud, sliding mud—she was surrounded by flowing, crumbling earth. There was nothing solid, nothing planted all around her.

She was falling.

Her spread out her arms, trying to control her descent.

She was knocked right and then left, the breath forced out of her lungs.

It seemed to go on forever, this fall.

Deeper and deeper she went. Not straight down, but angled, sliding wildly.

Until she hit the ground, sunk into it, and stuck.

The damp earth from above kept falling, hitting her head and shoulders, piling up around her. It was going to bury her alive. She covered her face with one arm, trying to keep a breathing space free of dirt and mud. It wasn't working.

She scrambled forward, working to get on top, to get away from the onslaught. She pushed and crawled, tangled in her mud-coated skirts.

It felt like she was swimming in loose dirt and mud, trying to keep her head above it.

The movement stopped. The mud and falling dirt settled.

She was buried. She turned, rolled, and her face came free. She sucked in a breath.

She stayed there on her back, breathing deeply in and out, her chest and stomach pushing against the dirt that was heavy over her.

She stared up, her eyes wide with shock. She could see the gray sky overhead, a narrow jagged strip of light.

She was surrounded by broken cliffs of ridged soil freshly exposed. It was a pit, twenty or thirty feet deep, and she was at the bottom of it.

The ground had collapsed.

She still heard the water running, loud, near her.

Her whole body rang from the shock of her fall.

Cora stayed still, inhaling and exhaling, and staring at the gray sky overhead.

Was anything broken?

Her hands stung from her attempts to stop her fall, scraped raw, nails ripped.

She evaluated the rest of her as much as she could without moving. Her breathing was labored, the mud on top of her getting heavier with each breath.

She forced herself to move. First an arm, pushing against the heavy soil, then another. Then her legs, trying to find something solid to push against.

Finally, her feet found something rooted, and heavy enough to push up against.

She began to dig herself out.

Adam walked, and walked, and worried. At every rise he searched the horizon for her form.

She couldn't come to harm here, surely? She'd gone in the opposite direction of the Solway Moss, and she, being a lass with an interest in botany, surely would recognize a bog if she came across one, and would stay clear? Unless she forged into it in pursuit of some unique specimen or other. Would she do that? Yes, she very well could be the type of person who would to do that.

The Solway Sands were directly South, and therefore of more concern. The sands were known to become quicksand on occasion, able to catch the unwary.

But the quicksand was usually only a danger to dogs and small children. She was tall and strong, his bonny lass; she'd be able to pull herself out.

Had she curved south?

He spotted a passing farmer, and hailed him. Had he seen a young lady walking?

"Yes sir, she passed this way a half hour ago or so."

Adam kept on.

At odd intervals he spotted a footprint in the soft earth, its feminine shape testifying that she had passed this way, and that he was on the right path.

Though there was no path to speak of.

The rain wasn't heavy, but it was cold. His wool greatcoat and the blue muffler wrapped around his face protected him. He could walk a great long time if he needed to . . . but he worried about Cora.

She wasn't as delicate of a flower as she often appeared, he knew. But this had been a trying few days, and she did have that leg injury.

Cora rested on her hands and knees. The constantly shifting earth wore at her endurance. But she was on top of it all now. She panted, and tried to stand.

The freshly exposed cliff walls surrounded her, rising high above her.

She had no idea how to get out.

Yards over her head were the original edges of the hill, and a gash of open sky.

Could she climb that?

She skidded and slipped over, and attempted to find handholds in the cliff face with her cold-numbed fingers. The earthen walls crumbled and collapsed as she put weight on them.

No.

Best to look for other ways.

Walking unsteadily on the shifting ground, she turned an edge and discovered the source of the water noises.

An underground river, mud brown and swollen, emerged and rushed past three yards from her feet. She could see where its normal track had been overwhelmed. It had compromised the hill she had been standing on until it collapsed.

She was trapped in its chasm.

She investigated all that she could reach, keeping a wide berth between her and the raging water. There was no way out.

She called for help. No answer. She had been isolated when she fell, and nobody had come in response to the noise of the hill collapsing. No one must be near.

It began to rain, sharp cold needles of falling water. She put up her sodden and caked cloak hood, and told herself to stay calm.

Trapped.

Desperation seized her. She chose the cliff-side with the most angle to it, and attempted to climb again.

She managed to make it up three feet before it collapsed under her, making the cliff's sharp angle worse. Her muddy, sodden skirts were not an advantage, but even if she had been wearing breeches, she still wouldn't have been able to get up the unstable cliff-face.

"Help! Help me! Please!"

No answer.

He had been walking what felt like hours, but when he checked his pocket watch, it had only been one and a quarter. The chill was seeping into his bones, centering in an ache in the healed ribs on his right side. His worry for Cora had grown.

He could see no one for miles whenever he crested a hill.

Was she just happening to be in a low area whenever he was high, and vise versa, and so they kept missing each other?

Had she walked this far?

He looked for more footprints, and didn't find any. He wanted to turn back. She couldn't have gone this far. Should he turn back? Or should he start scouring, moving back and forth along the area and try to pick up her trail again?

He turned to the right and walked forward for a while, turned to the left.

And there! Two more of her footprints. Only partials, and starting to be erased by the steady rainfall. He was on the right track.

With a burst of speed, he went up a hill taller than those around, and crested the rise.

He stopped short.

The hill ended in a sharp drop off. The water-logged grasses under his feet hung in a sharply curved slope of sod that tore off into open air and descended into a gorge—a chasm, deep and ragged. The sides were dark and fresh looking. This had happened recently.

He looked along its edges, studied its depths.

There was a strange mud-colored figure at the bottom. The only reason he could discern it at all from its surroundings was that it was rocking back and forth. To comfort itself, or to keep warm. Or both.

A terrible ache seized his chest. "Cora?"

The figure moved, looked up at him. The hood of her earth-soaked cloak fell back, and he could see her face, far below him.

It was Cora! "Oh, my dear sweet love! Are you all right?"

"Adam? Oh, Adam!" Her voice choked and cracked with tears.

"Are you injured?"

"No, not really!" she called back.

"I'll get you out!" He began looking frantically for a way to do it. He didn't have any rope on him. Why didn't he have rope?

Was there another way out?

He stepped closer to the edge, evaluating the area.

And the ground under his feet crumbled.

Cora screamed. Adam let out a yell.

Adam fell, like she had, the ground under him giving way, crumbling into muddy chunks and dirt clods. He slid and tumbled and scrambled for purchase and found none.

He twisted his body wildly in his fall, seeking a way to save himself. He hit the side of the slope with a thunk and let out a scream of pain.

He tumbled, and slid, and finally came to rest several feet from her.

The earth kept coming. Mud, rooty clods, and dirt fell like a wave after him. He would be buried alive!

She ran to him with stumbling and sliding steps, and grabbed his feet, trying to pull him out of the way. She fell to her knees, unable to take him far, and threw her body over him. He let out an "Oomph," but she was able to scramble up his body, and hunch over his head, creating an arc with her back, and putting her side to the onslaught of debris, as she had when she bathed in the ocean, and turned her side against an oncoming wave.

She planted her elbows on the other side of him, and covered her head with her hands.

The wave came, pummeling her, burying them both. She fought against the weight of the world, piled against her back.

It was dark, very dark. Every breath was agony. His ribs were broken, he had felt the crack. His right side, finally healed, was ruined again.

Her breath was in his face. They were sharing their air. There wasn't enough of it. He was suffocating.

He was wet and very, very cold. The earth holding them was sucking out all the warmth from his body.

Except his face, where she lay over him, her body keeping the chill away.

She was gasping, panting. She was suffocating too.

She had been trying to save him. Was saving him, right now.

"Adam." Her voice was low, a bare whisper, but her mouth was next to his ear, her knees pressed into his other.

"Cora, my love." It took all his strength to speak. He wanted to hold her, but his arms were pinned, buried, incapacitated. With all his strength, he struggled to move. The earth entombing him didn't shift.

The soil pressed on his chest, his damaged ribs not supporting the space for his lungs as they should. It was horrible agony.

He let out a groan of misery.

"Oh Adam! Adam, my love, don't move. I'll move, I'll get us out of here."

The earth shifted a small bit.

"I can move a finger." She had a bit of laughter in her voice.

"A finger!" He wanted to laugh, but coughed instead, and groaned at the lancing pain.

"Shhhh," she soothed. "We will be all right. We are together, we are alive. The Lord willing, we will stay that way."

Please, he prayed, *save this lass. She is the brightest, the kindest . . .*

He felt his consciousness slipping, coming back and moving away in waves. He tried to gasp in more air, but it wasn't enough. The pain eased and was gone.

"Adam? Adam!" He was no longer responding. He was barely breathing, a labored rattle.

No!

No, he could not die! He was to be her husband!

She loved him, this foolish man. He had to live, and be with her! There were children they needed to have together.

He could not die here.

Tears filled her eyes, as they hadn't yet this entire ordeal. She didn't bother blinking them away. Tears blocking her vision didn't matter, there was no light to see by.

The weight of the pounds of damp, gripping earth pressed on her back was crushing her, forcing her down. She would smother him if she let her torso sink any further. No, no, this could not happen!

He could not die here, and neither could she.

Determination filled her limbs, and her heart cried out for divine strength.

Lord, your mercy and power, please!

She moved her finger, then her fingers. She would get them out!

She felt with her hand for places that would shift, and found them.

She pushed, she dug, she twisted until her hand broke free to the surface, and she felt cold, fresh air on her palm, and rain hitting her fingers.

Oh, open air! There it was!

She had broken free to the surface. She pushed and shifted the earth. Air rushed into her aching lungs.

Now, to free them.

Protecting Adam while trying to escape was difficult. She concentrated on shifting the earth over him, and getting him uncovered.

The earth slid around her, caving in. She cried out in despair.

It stopped, it stopped. It would be all right. She would get them out.

For hours it felt, she worked. She dug and pushed and shifted with her bare hands. Her nails tore, and bled, and she ignored it. Her hands numbed with cold. When her fingers stopped responding, she wielded her hands as spades.

She finished uncovering Adam's chest, and saw greater freedom in the rise and fall of his ribcage. His breath was stronger, but uneven, with a hitch. She was terribly afraid that meant his ribs had broken again. What would that do to him?

But he was breathing. Short, quick, shallow breaths of pain, but breathing nonetheless.

She worked.

And, finally, they were free.

She stopped her endless scraping in exhaustion and exaltation. They were free!

"Adam, Adam, it's all right now. We will survive this."

She dragged herself on slabbed hands and numb knees to his face, and kissed his mud-covered forehead with filthy lips. She didn't care. She kissed him again and again, on forehead, cheeks, his cleft chin. Dirt rained down on him with her every movement, and the rain washed his face in muddy streaks.

She turned her face to the rain as well, and opened her mouth to it, trying to quench her thirst with pure water.

She kissed him again, this time on his mud-streaked mouth. His lips were pale under the mud, the red bled from them. But his breath came in and out, and his chest rose and fell. She kissed him again, and he gasped and groaned.

"Adam! My love, please wake up. We are free, we are alive."

His arm lifted, and he touched her, his eyes blinking from the falling rain.

"Cora?" he breathed out.

"Yes, Adam."

They lived. She kissed him again.

Chapter Twenty-Three

Found

MONDAY, JULY 8, 1816, AFTERNOON

Kate grabbed Mort's wrist. "Ye daft man, ye listen to me, and ye listen good." A wild shock went through his arm at her touch. He gave her a sharp look. He was listening now.

"I'm fierce worried. They've been gone too long, something is wrong. We need search parties, and we need to get out there, now. But if ye don't come with me, I'll go alone."

Tramping through cold, soggy fields while being rained on was not what he wanted to do this afternoon, or any time. But he wasn't going to let her wander off without him. "All right, all right, I'll set Charlie to getting volunteers together, and we'll go."

"Lady Cora!"

"Your grace! Duke!"

Mort and Kate projected their voices across the landscape whenever they were at the top of the low hills surrounding them. They heard no answer.

The rain came down on them steadily. Mort hefted Kate's bag of supplies over his shoulder and kept his grumbling to himself. He was getting worried as well.

It was July, despite the chill, and the sun was still hours from setting. Small favors.

Mort and Kate trudged in the direction pointed out to them by the ostler, following the duke's fresher trail. The odd feminine footprint was encouraging.

They didn't speak often, but moved easily together. When he didn't spot a water-filled bootprint, she would. He almost tumbled once, and she grabbed him, and kept him upright.

The animosity had calmed between them. They fell into a comfortable rhythm.

They were good together. He knew it.

But if she didn't want him, she didn't want him. His heart ached, but he was determined to accept her desires. He loved her. He wanted her to be happy.

She had crested a rise and was surveying the surrounding countryside with a furled brow, when he couldn't stay silent anymore.

"Kate." She lifted a brow at him. "I need to know." Her face closed off. He held up both hands. "I won't propose again." He forged ahead. "But, what do you want, Kate? If you could have anything, what would you have? What will make you happy?" He was pleading again. He straightened his shoulders, and smoothed the expression from his face.

She relaxed a small amount. "If I could have anything?" She shook her head. "I keep to the realm of possibility." She started walking again.

He followed. "You want to be respectable, and respected. I know that. I honor that. I do!" He responded to her incredulous expression. "And you want to go to kirk on Sundays. What else, Kate?"

"I've my ambitions."

"What are they? Will you tell me, please?"

She was silent for many long seconds. He waited on edge. She let out a huff of a laugh. "I have contemplated a milliner's shop in the village, but that would always be small. Too small. To scale up, I would need to move to Edinburgh, but that would take me far from Mama."

Mort kept silent, but she lifted a brow at him anyway. "You may say that my mother doesn't need me, having a new nursery-full of bairns to watch over, but I need her. She is my anchor. I've been very . . . adrift since Lady Hester married."

Let me be your anchor. He kept his face smooth.

"With the constraint of staying near her, and also wanting to stay in the duke's employ as long as he'll keep me, I've settled on my ambition. It's grand enough even for you, I think." She tilted her chin up at him. "I want to be housekeeper at Blackdale Castle."

He nodded. "Housekeeper of a ducal estate. A worthy goal."

Her cheeks pinked, but she stepped forward again.

His own goal, as lofty and as attainable as hers, was to be butler, and then house steward of the castle. If their ambitions were realized, they would work closely together for the rest of their lives. Would he be able to stand that?

If he stayed near, he'll be able to ensure she gained her ambition. That she was never adrift, but grounded and respected in her life's work. They, neither of them, would have more, but what they would have would be solid.

Yes, he would stay near.

He was full of self-sacrifice today.

Tomorrow, he may crumble and ask to be reassigned to the duke's Edinburg estate, not being able to stand the self-denial any further. But today, he felt equal to the noble cause.

They walked on.

Kate's expression had grown worried again, and she scanned before them sharply. "Have you seen his footprints recently?"

He'd let himself be distracted. "No."

Her mouth tightened. She stopped, and turned, scanning behind them. "We've lost the trail." She gestured to him to come closer. "We must pray."

"Pray?" He blinked at her.

She let out a huff of irritation. "Yes, ye godless man, pray. The Lord only knows where they are."

"Hey! Me mum had me baptized in the kirk, same as you." She wasn't going to insist they kneel, was she? He eyed the sodden ground.

"Good for her, now, join me."

She prayed.

Cora kept her body near him, spread her sodden woolen cloak over them both, and tried to imagine it keeping them warm.

Hours. Surely it was hours. Adam was barely conscious. It was an exercise in endurance. She prayed.

Then she heard, for the second time, blessed voices calling out.

She answered, her voice rough. "Here! Oh, here! Please!"

"Lady Cora!"

The dear faces of Malcolm and Kate, and soon unfamiliar ones from the inn and the village appeared, with ladders and ropes, and help.

They were saved.

Cora wasn't cold anymore. It was amazing. She had been cold for so long that the warmth of the bath, the tea, and the warmed bed seemed almost a dream.

"Adam, how is Adam?"

"The duke is in bed as well, my lady." Kate answered. "His ribs have cracked, so he can't move."

"Cracked, only cracked. Not broken?"

"Yes, the doctor is sure. He says the duke shall heal, as long as an infection does not set in."

"Is he in danger of an infection?"

"He did get one after Waterloo. Pneumonia. It was a dangerous illness, and we feared for him. Hopefully not this time."

Chapter Twenty-Four

Broken

TUESDAY, JULY 9, 1816, MORNING

The next day, Cora was rested, warm, and restless. She bypassed all decorum and entered Adam's room in the inn. She sat by his side as he slept fitfully. He was unresponsive and running a low-grade fever.

She held her narcissus. It was miraculously beginning to thrive, the few remaining blooms beautiful. She crooned to it, and to Adam. She sang sweetly: love songs, songs of sadness, love lost, and songs of joy, lullabies and hymns, all that she could remember. Her voice wasn't strong, but it was light, and had always seemed perfect for crooning to the things she loved.

She bathed his temples with lavender water and held his hand. Kate stayed with her, mending items that needed it. Malcolm was in and out, seeming unable to sit still when his master was in danger.

The physician came and went.

In the deep of night, Kate and Malcolm had fallen asleep, Kate in the trundle bed fully clothed, with a blanket draped over her, and Malcolm in a chair on the other side of the bed.

Cora felt a stupor over-covering her mind, but it was shaken away as Adam stirred. He was sweating.

She was there. She had been there a lot, her voice weaving through Adam's fever dreams. But this wasn't a fever dream, he was sure. For the first time in what felt like days, his mind was sharp and clear.

He remembered when his father had broken his arm. The strike, and his body falling back against the solid armoire in his father's study. The sharp crack and the flaring pain.

He had gotten a fever from that break as well. His mother had visited once as Nurse Anna and Kate watched over him in his sick bed. Mother had stood at the foot of his bed in the nursery, pregnant with her sixth child. He was nine. She hadn't stayed long.

She left him then, and moved to Edinburgh. And more bruises were to come.

After he started at Eton, he'd also started to grow. He stayed at friend's houses every summer he could manage, and eventually, he had gotten taller, too big for his father to push around. Big enough to fight back.

Father had backed off, physically. But never verbally.

Mother had protected that last child, Jude. She had done more for him than she had for her other children. Adam had felt betrayed by that, more than by anything else his mother had failed to do for him.

But he remembered her face more clearly now than he had since that fateful incident, with the startling clarity of an adult mind. The tension around her eyes, the fear and the pain, and drawn look of her face. She'd rubbed her belly; its swelling straining against her loosely tied stays.

A warm hand pressed against his forehead, touched his cheeks. He split his eyelids, looked up with blurry vision.

"Cora?" Her name was a rough croak in his throat.

"Here, you need water." She lifted his head, cradled him, and brought a cup to his lips.

"I dreamed . . . of my mother." She lowered his head, and he grimaced from the pain. "I always thought . . . that she abandoned us, that she abandoned me. When Jude was coming, she left, took the girls, left Nicolas and me at the castle with Father. Precious Jude, the only one she ever protected." His words were a whisper, the old pain remote in that moment. "But your mother said . . . she said that my father beat Mother as well, that she'd heard rumors . . . I had never heard that. I never saw bruises."

Now Kate stood at the other side of the bed. She also touched his forehead. "Oh, aye. He beat her, Lord Adam."

"I never saw . . ."

"Of course he did. Your mother was at the forefront. We tried to shield you, so you didn't know much of what happened, but she almost lost Jude. Her pregnancy troubles, they weren't from natural causes. And after the old duke broke your arm . . . well, he finally agreed to let her leave. She moved to the Edinburgh house with the girls to escape him."

"That was the deal, then?" His voice was stronger. "Leave his heir and his spare to him, and she could leave and take the other children?"

"Yes." Kate answered. "Mother and I stayed to care for you and Lord Nicolas. And when you were both in school, your father made noises insisting your mother come back. Couldn't stand the empty rooms. She refused. So Lady Hester came, became hostess for him at fourteen. She took over being the buffer between you all and your father."

The old memories, they came, dredged up from where he had sunk them deep. Hester crying, cringing, curling into herself. The dark circles under his mother's eyes. Had they not been ill-health, but injury?

Adam had gotten out of there as soon as he could, done anything to avoid being in the same house as his father. They all had, except Hester.

Mother had never allowed him to spend the summer with her in Edinburgh. He hadn't understood.

She had done what she could to protect her youngest children. But she hadn't known what to do to protect him. She had left Adam.

Left Nicolas, with his cheery disposition and tendency to rages as bad as his father's. Left Adam, who grew more silent and more reserved, more controlled and still with every year.

But what could she have done, truly? Adam thought, his heart aching with his adult perspective. Women were subject to their husbands, with little legal recourse, and little help. And children were subject to their fathers.

Lady Cora wrung out a cloth, and wiped the sweat from his forehead. She smoothed the cool cloth over his cheeks, his neck. Her touch was gentle. Her eyes were pained, but her lips held a small smile. An expression of love. He closed his eyes against it.

She was here, in Scotland. She had been put here by a man who had wanted to subject her to himself. He squeezed his eyes in pain and horror at what he had done.

He had forced her.

And what choice did she have? Just as his mother had had little choice, under his father's whims and rages.

Adam thought if he never hurt her, never raised his hand in anger, that he wouldn't be like his father. Such a fool.

He had put her in danger. Twice he had been powerless to save her or save himself. All nature had raged against him, tried to rip them apart, tried to destroy him. What could he do against it?

She refused to marry Bowden. She was in his room. Did she intend to sacrifice herself like Hester had?

He must marry her. But he could never let himself touch her.

The coming years of loneliness gaped before him. Starvation of touch, self-mutilation. He would atone, he would deny them both. Would that appease the violent earth?

Whether it did or not, he would have his honor back. He would not be his father.

He must have slept.

He awoke to moonlight on his face. Cora stood at the window, the curtains open, her body edged in silver.

He could smell her narcissus in the close air of the room, see the outline of the plant next to her on the dresser before the window. Its deep, narcotic scent pulled at him, drugged him, suffused his nostrils and his mind with low, slow sweetness. It was her, untouchable but inescapable. She filled him like heady perfume.

She turned. The silver light outlined her silhouetted form. She was a creature of mysterious darkness and pale brilliance. She came near.

"The moon is full tonight," she said.

"Where are Malcolm and Kate?"

"They're asleep."

He tried to sit up, and fell back with a groan as his cracked ribs sent shooting pain throughout his body.

"Shh." She pressed his shoulder. Her hand, it was on him. She sat on the edge of his bed. The mattress lowered with her weight. He had to force himself not to roll into the indentation. He resisted the urge to curl around her. "Adam?"

He swallowed. "Yes?" He forced himself to inhale.

She lowered her face till it was right above his. He could feel her breath on his lips in the darkness. "I love you, Adam."

She hovered her lips over his, not touching, not moving away. He breathed in her breath. The perfume clung to her, drugged him. A rush of warmth spread over his body from where her breath touched him and expanded downward.

She loved him. It hurt, hearing those words.

He let out a groan of despair, reached up, and cradled her face in his hands. He guided her lips down to his. He kissed her. A wild burning rushed through his body.

No more!

He let go as if he blistered where they had touched, and rolled away. His ribs screamed. He clenched his teeth down on a cry of pain and despair. "No, Cora." His voice was harsh.

There was silence behind him, only his heavy breathing, and the pounding of his heart filling his ears.

Then he heard her stifled sob, the slap of her feet as she ran from the room, and the slam of the door behind her.

In the cool morning light, Mort exited the duke's room, and met Kate in the hall, bringing in a fresh pitcher of water.

In the hours they had attended the duke's bedside together, an ease had developed between them, and a softness had entered her face.

"May I?" He reached out, and lifted her burden from her hands.

"Thank you." She lingered, looking into his eyes. Searching, perhaps?

He looked back. *I love you*. He didn't let it pass his lips again, but mayhap it filled his eyes.

She leaned toward him, reached out a hand, but withdrew, her face clouded with confusion, and retreated.

He watched her walk away with a full heart.

Chapter Twenty-Five

Arrival

Wednesday, July 10, 1816, morning

Adam slurped the beef broth Malcolm spooned into his mouth and grimaced. He felt on edge, and wanted to lash out about the whole situation, but Cora was sitting there on the other side of the bed, watching with eager eyes each mouthful he ingested. He had to keep on good behavior for her. He couldn't snap at every twinge of his ribs, or the horrible blandness of the broth.

She had entered his room this morning fresh and chipper, no signs of their disastrous kiss or her tears on her face. Was she denying it had happened? Counting it a dream?

He knew it had not been a dream.

She had sat by his bedside, chattering cheerfully, until Kate had mercifully convinced her to leave to be properly dressed for the day.

With her gone, Adam had finally been able to relieve himself and at least change his nightshirt with Malcolm's help. He'd cursed under his breath and sent abuses toward the universe and Malcolm for his rough treatment for a full thirty minutes.

But then she'd come back, and he'd had to be on his best behavior once again.

He took yet another sip of the dismal stuff when a clatter and outcry was heard from outside the inn. A carriage had arrived, and a woman aboard was demanding attention with an imperious English voice.

Adam saw Cora jump up with alarm, and knew with a chilled heart that the Dowager Countess of Winfield had finally caught up with them.

Cora's throat tightened in panic. She turned to Adam. He gazed back with cooled, expressionless eyes for one second, and then looked away, his face blank.

Tears of rage threatened to overwhelm Cora's senses. So, that was all he would do, was it? Calmly accept as she was taken away?

Cora turned without a word, and left the room. Her mother had to be faced. Adam was injured. She would try to head off the storm and protect him as much as she could.

She ran to her room down the hall and grabbed up her pelisse, gloves, and bonnet, tying the ribbons as she rushed down the stairs and to the entrance. She paused outside the door to don the pelisse, struggling with the second arm until it was taken up by Kate, who had appeared at her side, and helped her put it on. She turned Cora and did up the buttons, straightened the bonnet ribbons, and gave Cora a solemn nod of support.

Cora felt the rough panic calm some in Kate's solid presence. She wasn't entirely alone in this.

"Thank you, Kate." Cora turned and opened the coaching house's front door, stepping through to the bright day outside.

The Dowager Countess of Winfield commanded an ostler to help her down from the hired carriage she was riding in, and said, "I demand to see the Duke of Blackdale! And my daughter!"

Cora stood at the top of the steps of the inn's entrance, looking down at the scene below. Her mother looked tired and road weary, her clothes stained and creased, as was her face, with deeper frown-lines and circles under her eyes than Cora had ever seen. Her heart went out to her mother, who must have been having a hellish experience. But then she stiffened her spine. She knew what she wanted, and she would have to act with resolution in order to see it to accomplishment.

"Hello, Mama."

"Cora!" Mother stared at her, her eyes wide and mouth tight. Then she let out a wordless cry and rushed toward her. Cora clattered down the steps and they met at the bottom. Mother folded Cora in an embrace, and Cora felt the tension and anguish that coursed through her mother's body.

She wanted to melt in her mother's arms, let go of all her cares and the tension and fright of the last few days. To let her mother take over and make everything right and safe again.

But Cora couldn't afford to do that. She must remain in control if she was to marry the man she wanted. If Mother took over now, Cora would probably never see Adam again.

Mother drew back and clasped Cora's face between her gloved hands. She examined Cora's face. Cora looked at her mother's eyes. They were wet. The dowager countess rarely cried. Cora felt her own eyes get tight with unshed tears. She opened them wide to hold the tears back. She couldn't afford them right now.

Mother frowned and she seemed to remember that they were in public. She drew back and took Cora's hands in hers.

"My love," she said in a quiet voice, "is your name still Winfield?"

Cora squeezed her eyes shut. Oh, to lie. Or to have already clasped hands before witnesses. They had had plenty of time in Gretna Green. But no, this must be faced honestly and dealt with.

She looked her mother in the eyes. "It is."

Her mother swayed with relief. "Oh, thank the heavens, I'm not too late."

Cora looked away, her mouth tightening, and saw Mother's traveling companion for the first time. "Lord Eastham!" He was tired, rumpled, and in need of a shave. He must have been traveling without his valet. Cora stared at him. Another complication.

It was good her mother had been traveling with a gentleman, and not alone. But this also meant Mother intended on Cora's marrying Lord Eastham if she got here on time to see it happen, and for the first time, amazingly, he'd agreed to it.

Lord Eastham bowed low to Cora. "It is good to see you looking well, Lady Cora. I am here to keep my promise."

Ah. The circumstances of that promise flooded Cora's memory. His introducing Adam to her. She had made Lord Eastham agree to take any negative consequences onto himself.

Yes, he was honor-bound to be here, wasn't he?

One more thing she would have to deal with.

"Who is this person, Cora?" Mother drew Cora's gaze back to her, and indicated behind her, where Kate was standing to the side, her hands folded in front of her, the neck of her black gown high, her cap demure.

"This is my lady's maid, Kate Douglas, Mother. She has been with me since . . . since the beginning of this journey."

"Indeed?" Mother's eye brow was up as she stared at Kate, who curtsied low and gracefully and kept her eyes properly downcast. "The entire time?"

"Yes, she was with me in every proper manner." Cora planted her feet onto the ground and stood steady. "Except when she wasn't."

Mother flashed a glance at Cora, who held her gaze.

"Dowager Countess!" The voice of Captain Bowden rang out from the top of the steps. "You have come!" He clattered down the stairs to join them at the bottom, looking fresh and handsome.

"Captain Bowden!" Mother barked. "How long have you been here?" She looked him up and down.

"I arrived a few hours before the Duke made it in. Was here waiting."

An angry joy took over Mother's eyes. "Ha! So I have you to thank for my daughter still being my own!"

"Not entirely, no, my lady." He looked apologetic.

"What?"

Cora noticed the ostlers, several maids, and a few townspeople standing by, watching this interesting group with rapt attention. "Mother, my lord, Captain, let us continue this conversation in a more private place." And without waiting for agreement, she turned, and strode into the inn's grounds, the sodden grass of the lawns sloshing under her feet. She headed for a copse of trees where they could be less observed, and less overheard.

"Lord Eastham came with the dowager."

"What!" Adam paid for his shout with lancing pain through his ribs, and let out a grunt.

Malcolm stood at the window, looking down on the reunion in the courtyard. "Now Captain Bowden has joined them."

Adam couldn't . . . he must. He had to let her go, it would be much better to let her go. And here were the gentlemen who he would be letting her go to. A worse pain ripped at his heart.

He ought to do this properly. He shouldn't let Cora face all this alone. He must be honorable now, as he hadn't been honorable when he had abducted her.

"I need to be out there. Malcolm, help me, I must get dressed and get out there!"

"My lord, you shouldn't move!"

Adam cursed at him. "Get me dressed, man, now!"

Cora reached the copse, and swung around to see that, yes, they had all followed her, though her mother's face was less than pleased. Eastham looked weary and resigned, and Bowden looked like he was enjoying this. Kate was watchful, but placed herself near.

"Is the Duke of Blackdale even here?" Mother demanded.

"Yes, laid up in his room with cracked ribs," Bowden answered. "There was an accident two days ago."

"Carriage accident?" Lord Eastham said, his gaze sharpening at the news.

"There was one," Cora said. "But that was not where he got the injury. He cracked his ribs when trying to rescue me after I fell into a wash out caused by all the rain."

"Cora, how did you get into such a position!" Mother looked horrified.

"I went walking. The ground crumbled beneath my feet." Cora tipped her head, and stared into her mother's eyes. "Adam and I were alone together for several hours in the cold and rain before we were found by Kate and Malcolm, Adam's valet."

Mother's eyes flew up. "Adam?"

"Adam is in his room. I just came from there. He's better, but ought not to be excited."

"His room!"

"I was with my lady in the duke's chambers," Kate said.

"Captain Bowden!" Mother rounded on him.

"I apologize, my lady, but Lady Cora pointedly reminded me when I objected that I have no authority over her. She said she would go where she wished."

"Well!"

"Indeed."

"Did the duke kidnap you?" Mother asked Cora.

"I was going to see him when we met in the park."

"So you did elope with him?" Lord Eastham asked.

"By the time we reached the Scotch Corner, I knew that I wanted to marry him over any other man of my acquaintance."

Lord Eastham shifted impatiently. "Then why are you not wed?"

Cora tried to control the hurt anger roiling underneath her sternum. She looked at Captain Bowden, but he merely smirked at her. She pointed her gaze away from them all, and dragged out the words. "The Duke of Blackdale has had a belated and inconvenient crisis of conscience."

Lord Eastham guffawed.

"In connection with that," now Captain Bowden spoke, "I do think I was instrumental in keeping the duke from laying formal claim to his stolen bride. As he is feeling guilty for acting so dishonorably, me waiting for them in Greta as they arrived was the excuse he needed to back down, as I could offer an alternative to ruin for our lovely kidnapped maiden." He bowed to Cora, looking smug.

Cora glared at him, her mouth twisting.

"Then he is finally being sensible." Mother stepped forward. "As the duke has backed down, you shall soon be able to put this unfortunate circumstance behind you, Cora. Here are two excellent and eligible gentlemen willing to save you from ruin."

"Are they? How noble and self-sacrificing of them." The chill Cora was feeling came through in her voice. "But I am uninterested."

"Yes, we are noble and self-sacrificing, aren't we! And as no lady can accept a marriage that hasn't been formally offered to her, allow me," Captain Bowden stepped forward. "Lady Cora," He gave a low bow, "it would be an honor if you'd agree to be my wife." He looked up at her, and a gave a smirk. Cora glared at him. He stepped back and turned to look expectantly at Lord Eastham.

Lord Eastham gave a long, defeated sigh, straightened, and stepped forward. "Lady Cora," he bowed, "I am willing to offer you the protection of my name and status, if you will accept me as your husband." He closed his mouth, opened it again as if to speak more, then shook his head and gave a small smile, "Loving speeches I can't give, Lady Cora, but I can promise respect and honor, a good position in society, and lands near your mother's. You would not need to be parted from her often."

Cora tightened her mouth, and glanced quickly at Mother, who was staring at her with pleading in her eyes. "Cora, please."

Cora didn't think she had seen her mother beg before, especially not to her. It hurt her heart.

Cora took a deep breath to steel herself. "My lords, I thank you for the honor you've bestowed upon me by your coming here, and your kind offers. I regret to say that I must refuse you both."

Her mother gave a cry of outrage and anguish, but over that, Cora heard her name called.

"Cora!" It was Adam's voice.

Cora's heart leaped in her chest as she turned her head toward the sound of her name. Adam was walking stiffly up to the copse over the wet lawn, dressed with passible neatness with a simply tied white cravat. He was in need of a shave, and his pallid skin looked almost greenish under the dark stubble. His eyes were shadowed with strain, his lips were bloodless, but he was up and walking. Barely.

Malcolm followed discreetly behind.

"Adam, you should not be out of bed!" Cora rushed toward him, wanting to lend her support.

"No, Cora." He held up a hand to stop her. "Please, stay there. I have come to say what I must."

Cora stopped, tension gripping her and holding her rigid. She had kept them outside so that Adam wouldn't be able to join them. She had been trying to protect him, and to prevent him from making things worse. But instead she had just made him exert himself even more to get here.

Adam stood straight, an impressive posture, but his breathing was short and shallow. She could tell he was hurting.

"Dowager Countess," He turned on his heels and bowed stiffly to Mother. Cora could see the corners of his mouth go even whiter at the action. "Lord Eastham, Captain Bowden," he bowed to each in turn.

The noblemen bowed, each in a mocking way. Mother did nothing in response. She stared at him with stiff outrage.

"It is because of my actions that we are all here," Adam said. "I must do what I can to make right what I have destroyed. I must apologize—"

Mother let out an outraged noise, close to a snarl, but Adam continued.

"Apologize, my lady, for the wrong I have done your daughter, and you. I acted dishonorably. I had my reasons—" Adam's gaze was fixed on an empty spot a few feet from him. He did not look at Cora. "But those reasons did not justify my actions. I was wrong. I must do what I can to make it right."

He turned to the gentlemen again. "I must thank you, sirs, for acting so quickly, and at such personal cost, to come to the rescue of Lady Cora. Your actions show that you are honorable men. I have brought dishonor to a virtuous young lady. To alleviate my actions, and to assuage society, it would be best if she were wed immediately. If you would be willing, I abjectly implore you, beg you, to rescue her fully. I know each of you would be a dutiful husband to her. Then she would not be trapped into a marriage with the man who dishonored her, the man who betrayed her.

"Lady Cora is . . ." Adam's voice cracked, and he swallowed visibly, "everything a man could wish for in a wife. She is kind, and gentle, and brave. She will make a loving . . ." he swayed. Cora took another step toward him, but he regained control, and stood still again. "And a lovely bride. She will make one of you the happiest of men. I assure you, my lord, Captain, that she is untouched. I . . . I have not, physically . . . you need not fear that—"

She could listen to this no longer.

"I am not untouched!" Cora burst out. All turned toward her, alarm in their postures, but Cora looked at Adam, who was finally looking back at her, anguish on his face. She lifted her chin, "We have kissed."

The other men let out noises of derision and impatience. Mother hissed with frustration. "Kissed!"

"Only kisses," Adam shook his head. "Just kisses."

"Not only kisses! Three kisses!" Cora strode to him, and stood in front of him, their eyes locked. "Three times you have kissed my lips, Adam. I have counted. Kisses are important." She let an edge of triumph lift her mouth. "And I have kissed yours six times."

His face was drawn, the bones stark under his pale skin, his eyes cloudy with despair. His pale mouth trembled and his breath hitched with every indrawn breath.

She reached up, and took his face in her hands. "Oh, my love."

"I am trying to make things right, Cora." He stared at her with urgency, but didn't move his face out of her hands. "I shouldn't have, I shouldn't . . ."

"Yes, you were wrong, and very, very foolish," Cora ran her hand over his sweating brow, rejoicing that the fever was gone. Rejoicing that she was touching him. "But you did it. It gave me the chance to get to know you. And now I know you very well, Adam Richard Douglas. And I want to marry you. The way to right your wrong is to agree, and marry me."

His breathing came faster, and his breaths shallower. "How can I . . . even dare—" he gasped, "to touch you?"

A smile began to spread over Cora's face. "I will touch you." She took his hand, her other still stroking his rough cheeks. "Until you will dare in return."

She drew his hand up, and brought it to her own cheek, cupping her palm over the back of his hand.

"Oh," he took a shuddering inward breath, deeper than he had taken, and slowly began lowering to his knees with a groan, as if he couldn't stand up any longer. Cora descended with him, till they were both kneeling on the cold ground. The dampness immediately seeped through Cora's pelisse and gown, but she ignored it.

"You want to marry me, Cora?" His eyes were glazed, almost unfocused.

"I do, Adam."

"Even though I kidnapped you, gagged you, was horrid to you? Cora, I was a monster."

"I have chosen to forgive you. Don't ever do it again."

"Never, my solemn oath."

"Good."

Chapter Twenty-Six

Seeds

Wednesday, July 10, 1816, morning

"No! No, Cora, I forbid it!" Mother rushed toward Cora and Adam where they knelt in the wet, yellowed grass, her face contorted.

Cora moved rapidly, extricated herself from Adam's arms, rose to stand over him, close and protective, and turned to face her mother. "Mother!"

Lady Winfield stopped short, staring at her daughter. Cora looked long into her mother's anguished eyes.

"Mother, I have made my choice."

"I am your legal guardian! You don't have a choice to make! You must have my leave!"

"We are in Scotland. Here, I do not need your permission, Mother."

"That was close to being a legal wedding right there," Bowden said. Mother whipped her head to glare at him.

"Yes, with four witnesses even." Lord Eastham settled back on a heel. "A marriage document for us to sign would be a good idea, though not necessary."

Mother's face was turning red with rage. "I will sign no such thing! I will not witness this travesty!"

"I apologize for distressing you, Lady Winfield," Lord Eastham crossed his arms over his chest, "But two witnesses are all that is required, and we do have that, for I would sign it."

"As would I." Bowden said, for once with seriousness in his face.

"You . . . betray me both?" Mother's voice was strained, and she stared at Lord Eastham.

"The lady has stated her choice." Bowden said, "It's a good match. She's getting a duke, don't forget." He eyed her. "I know you'd rather anyone but him at the moment, my lady, but I can imagine nothing worse than an unwilling bride, and she's not going to say yes to either of us now."

Lord Eastham's face softened, "You'd rather a loveless marriage for your daughter, Lady Winfield? She would not be happy with me."

"How could you not love her!"

Eastham softened even more at her outburst. "She is a sweet child, my lady, but the Duke of Blackdale is the man who loves her."

Cora's heart throbbed in her chest. "I'm sorry you are upset, Mother! I'm sorry you do not like it. But I love him. He is a good man, Mother, despite his mistake."

"A good man! To rip my daughter from me!"

Adam struggled to his feet, "I won't, I can't—It's not—"

Cora turned back to him. No, he would not be giving her up just to appease her mother! She felt helplessness seize her, her limbs paralyzed by fear and frustration.

A low voice spoke near her ear. "Say his name, and 'You are my husband'."

It was Kate, unexpectedly standing next to her. Cora gaped up into Kate's dark eyes, and gasped with hope. Could it be that easy?

Kate nodded with a small smile, and stepped back.

Adam was struggling to stand straight, still offering incomplete phrases to her railing mother.

Cora took two steps, and clasped his arms. "Adam Richard Douglas, Duke of Blackdale," she declared. Their eyes locked. She threw all her determination into her voice. "You are my husband!"

At Cora's words, blood rushed past Adam's ears, blocking all sound but the thundering of his heart. His head began to buzz. All existence slowed to her, standing before him. Touching him. The heat of her hands burned where she gripped his arms.

She . . . she said it! What was he to do? What could he do? What else could he do, but what she wanted him to? It was what he wanted to do, with every fiber of his being.

"Cora—Lady Cora Winfield." He gasped in a breath, and surrendered. "You are my wife."

There. Done.

Her smile was the most beautiful thing he had ever seen.

His legs collapsed underneath him, and he sank to his knees again.

Cora vaguely heard outcries from their witnesses, "Oh ho!" from Captain Bowden, a cheer from Mr. Malcolm. A groan of despair from her mother.

She was on the wet grass again, helping Adam—her husband—keep upright as his breathing hitched in pain. But his expression was pure wonder. And she couldn't stop grinning.

Everything was at once sharply clear—the wide sky studded with deep clouds and patches of glorious blue. The sunlight streaming through on bright grass. The cold wetness of her skirts, and the warmth of the sun on her face. The crowd of onlookers they had attracted, additional witnesses to their dramatic wedding.

Every noise seemed muted. Nothing could touch her in her joy. She was married to the man she loved!

Cora hardly noticed when her mother turned her back and walked away, pushing through the cheering crowd.

Somehow, Lord Eastham got them standing, moving, and back into Gretna Hall.

She didn't want to part from Adam, but Kate and Malcolm worked together to convince her that she and the duke both needed to put on dry clothes, "or risk fever and infection again."

Malcolm called her "Duchess," and her mind blanked from shock. Kate led her out of Adam's room, and down the hall to her own on numb feet.

"Your grace," Kate called her, with a small, pleased smile.

Adam's brain wasn't working. But Malcolm successfully bullied him into fresh breeches, and practically poured a hot cup of tea, fortified with a shot of spirits, down his throat.

He was a married man. His lady was his indeed.

As soon as he was dry and warm enough, he straightened his cravat, ignored all pain, and walked stiffly to her room. He knocked.

Kate let him in with wide eyes, and exited, closing the door behind her without being asked.

Cora, freshly dressed and absolutely beautiful, looked at him with parted lips and blushing cheeks.

He took her face in his hands and brought their lips together.

"I love you, Adam, my husband." She smiled at him with brilliant joy, and he gasped in a sharp, indrawn breath as his heart swelled in his aching chest.

"I love you, Cora. My wife."

Mort lingered as the duke entered the new duchess's room. Kate exited, closed the door, and stared at it, her cheeks pinking. He caught her eye, not able to keep the grin off his face. Her blush deepened, but she smiled, clapped a hand over her mouth, and stifled a laugh.

"It's done! We managed it!" he whispered.

She shushed him, and grabbed his hand, pulling him further down the hall, and away from the newlywed's door. His heart pounded. Then—scandalous!—she pulled him into the duke's room and shut the door.

She leaned against it—slumped, she actually slumped—against it, the tension in her body releasing. "They are married!" She covered her face with her hands. "We are safe!"

She took a deep shuddering breath. Then, she sobbed.

His smile and his stomach dropped. "Oh, Kate." He touched her shoulder, and gently drew her toward him. Wonder of wonders, she came. She buried her face in his neck cloth, wrapped her arms around him, and cried. His whole body ached and rejoiced as he held her.

"I've been so afraid!" She hiccupped.

"I know. I've been too. But I was never going to let them take you, my bonny lass, never." He rocked her, stroking her back. "I was going to steal you away, take you to Canada before they could even think 'deportation.'"

She gave a wet, inelegant snort. "Quite defeats the purpose of running away, if you go where they'd send you."

"Not Canada, then? All right, how about back to Brussels? A pretty little house near Waterloo."

That brought a real laugh. "And how would we live, two fugitives on the run?"

"Oh, the duke would owe us, we'd have plenty to live on. I'd make sure we had a note that we could use to draw on his funds before I left."

"So fanciful."

"I dream big."

She gave a hiccupping laugh, and drew away. He reluctantly let her go, his bones bruised from longing for her. She pulled out a handkerchief, and put herself back to rights.

"But we are safe now." She drew herself up, and so did he, each dignified once again.

"Yes, we are."

Her brows creased as she looked down at his neck. "I quite ruined your neck cloth."

"Tis nothing—" His words cut off as she reached out her elegant hand, and touched the cold spot on his neck where her tears had soaked through. Then her fingers were at the knot at his throat, untying it.

"This will never do."

His heart pounded up into his throat and choked off his breathing.

"Where are your fresh?" Her movements were crisp and businesslike, but he might die under her ministrations.

He couldn't speak, so he indicated with his head, and she moved away to fetch a new one from his bag. He gasped in a breath, the blood rushing in his ears.

She came back. She wound the wide, white cloth around his neck, tying it, adjusting his shirt points. He barely had thought enough in his head to raise his chin to make it easier for her.

She smoothed down the lapels of his jacket, and her hands lingered there. He looked down upon her beautiful, dark face, drinking in the arch of her brows, the elegance of her cheekbones, the lush curve of her lips, and deep intelligence in her eyes.

He had no control over his face. What did she see there, when she looked up into his eyes? His naked longing? The deep tenderness that filled his heart?

Her mouth dropped, a look like anguish pinching the corners of her lips down and raising her brows in pain for one second. And then the expression was gone, and she was business-like again. "All better."

And she stepped away, opened the door, and exited so fast he almost staggered.

But before she closed the door, her back toward him, she said softly, "Thank you, Malcolm."

And she was gone.

Lord Eastham's invitation to a late luncheon couldn't be called welcome. But Adam insisted, and she acquiesced.

They had had so few hours alone.

She had been able to increase her number of kisses. She might even lose count soon.

They did need to have a discussion. The problem of her mother ate at her underneath her haze of joy. They needed to work out a plan.

She told Adam her idea, and the concern on his face for her, and his willingness to accept her plan, made her love him even more.

She stood in front of the private parlor door, her stomach a knot, and her hand clasped on Adam's elbow, ready to lend physical support if it proved necessary.

The door opened, and she caught sight of her mother. She was pacing, her face a tight mask. She looked up as they entered, and turned away, but not before Cora saw that her eyes were red.

Cora's stomach dropped, and her bottom lip trembled. She bit down on it.

She greeted the earl and the captain with passable politeness, and made sure Adam sat, stiff but stable, with a pillow at his back, before she turned to her mother.

"Mama."

The dowager countess was at a window, her back resolutely to the room. "Mama. I know you are unhappy. Adam and I—" her mother's back tensed even further at Cora's voicing of his name, "We have been discussing what we might do to make this less painful for you." She paused, hoping for a response, but received none.

Her hands trembled, but she pushed forward. "So we decided to offer, well . . . we know that you do not wish the Averill lands to be neglected. We wish to offer that we will come down from Scotland and spend several weeks with you at the Grange every year."

Her mother's hands were clenched by her sides.

"Every year we can tour the estates, stay connected to the Averill lands, and familiar to the tenants. And you'll be assured that they will be well cared for. You'll be easy, you'll have less need to fear . . . Mama?"

Her mother turned, her face odd, tight, flushed. Her lip threatened to curl into a sneer. Cora shrank back from her.

"A few . . . weeks?" She said through clenched teeth. Her nostrils flared as she sucked in, taking a deep breath. She unclenched her hands one finger at a time, then spread her fingers out from her hands, holding them rigid. She looked at Cora, her eyes burning with leashed fury. "The Season. You will come down for the Season in London every year," she demanded. "And a month beyond at the Grange."

Cora gasped, as did others around the room. "The Season? Mama, that's, that is more than a quarter of the entire year! I couldn't possibly—"

"Two weeks in London, and two at the Grange." Adam's voice resonated through the room. "One month out of every year for you, Lady Winfield."

Cora looked at him. He sat straight and rigid, his hands white-knuckle clenched on his knees, staring at her mother with a tight mouth. Mother didn't look at him.

"April through June in London, and July on the Averill lands. Those are my terms, or I go before the House of Lords, and bring forth my accusations of kidnapping. The duke has admitted to it. I will get this marriage annulled. And I—"

Cora's stomach quivered with suppressed panic.

"Theresa." Lord Eastham spoke. "Theresa, enough."

Her mother whipped to face the earl, her entire body shaking. "Fredrick, I will not stand for this! I cannot—!"

The earl strode over to her, and clasped her upper arms, facing her squarely. They were of a height, and he looked directly into her eyes. "Theresa, that's enough." He softened his tone. "You don't want to lose the affection of your daughter, do you? You want her to be happy, don't you?"

An expression like despair tugged at her mother's mouth. Cora wrapped her arms around herself to keep from flying apart.

"Look at her, she is unhappy." He pointed with his chin toward Cora, and gently turned Mother. Cora's eyes locked with her mother's and her internal shaking increased.

Mother clenched and unclenched her hands, opened her mouth and closed it.

"Hm." The earl took Mother's hand into his own, kissed it, and drew her closer to him. She turned to him, her eyes wide. "Theresa, I propose you come with me for a few minutes. We'll have a quick chat." Lord Eastham put her hand into the crook of his arm, and led her out of the room, tall and straight. The door shut behind them, and Cora listened as their footsteps retreated.

Mother had followed him, had been led. That was . . . most odd.

She stared at the door. Electric, miserable tension raced through her blood with every pulse of her thundering heart. She swayed, suddenly dizzy.

"Duchess." She found Captain Bowden at her side. He gently took her arm, led her to the sofa, and sat her down next to Adam, whose face was white and tense. She collapsed into the back of the couch, and then curled into Adam, burying her face into his shoulder. He took her hand into his.

"Thank you, Bowden." Adam said.

"My pleasure, your grace." A few moments later. "A most interesting development, eh? I'm heartily amused. An excessively handsome couple. She is what, eight, nine years his senior? This has been the most diverting venture into Scotland a man could wish for."

"Forgive me if I do not yet share in your mirth." Adam said in a dry tone.

Captain Bowden laughed long and loud.

Mother and the earl were gone long enough that nervous energy overtook Cora's limbs. She ordered and served tea for Adam and the captain, devoured three biscuits, urged Adam to lay down on the couch—he refused—over sugared her tea, drank it in four gulps, and paced up and down the room five times. There was a flowering houseplant in the window. A rose geranium, *Pelargonium capitatum.* She tended it. There were two yellowing leaves. She plucked them. Tested the soil dryness. Watered it. Ate another biscuit. Was about to demand Adam and she go back to their room—he was becoming whiter and more strained as the hour progressed—when Eastham and her mother finally returned.

Mother's eyes and her cheeks were red, but her face was calm. She moved with less stiffness. Eastham had an unusual uplift to his mouth. They stood arm in arm. Cora blinked at them, tense and off-balance.

Mother's head was high. "Duke, Cora," she said in clipped, controlled tones. "I ask for two weeks in London and one month at the Grange. Accept this arrangement, and I will not pursue charges."

"Ever. The subject will be dropped from now on, and forever." Adam's voice was a demand. Mother looked down her nose at him. Cora clasped her hands to her chest, hope springing in her heart.

"All moneys will be willed to Cora's children. You will not see a ha'penny."

"Good."

Mother's eyes slitted. Adam's gaze remained steady; he held hers without blinking.

"Done." Mother said.

All the tension left Cora's body at once, and a cry escaped her lips. Mother turned to her, her lower lip down with pain. "Cora?" She opened her hands to her.

Cora looked at her, her heart throbbing, and then ran into her mother's arms. "Mama!"

They held each other tightly. Mother rocked her, and peppered her with kisses, as tears of relief ran down Cora's cheeks. "My sweet girl!"

Preparations for a late wedding supper were underway, if the groom would be able to sit up an hour after a few lying on his back recuperating from the ordeals of the day.

Mort smiled with glee and whistled down the hall. His master was married, and the fiendish mother-in-law was being distracted thoroughly by the earl. There was no announcement yet, and he would make no bets on when such an announcement might come from that quarter, but things were looking up.

And there was Kate, glorious Kate. She lifted an eyebrow at him as she passed, and Mort couldn't let her go by without saying something, not when he was in this jubilant mood. "All this wedded bliss, and over there, an anvil so near and neglected. One could make use of it, me thinks."

Kate gave him her pointed, magnificent glare. "I will have none of anvils or elopements for my wedding."

He froze. His stomach jerked and his blood started pumping.

"I want a church, and flowers, and my mother present." Her gaze stabbed him. "I want her crying tears of joy and not despair."

"I—" he swallowed. "I could arrange that." His mind blanked. Was she saying yes? ". . . For your mother to be there, at the kirk, with flowers, and tears, but I can't arrange for the tears to be happy, I can only hope them to be happy, I—Kate!" He was babbling.

"I'll believe that, Mort Malcolm," she enunciated clearly and precisely, "when I see the church, the flowers, my mother, and you, there, on the hour, on the appointed day." She gave a curt nod and strode away.

He stood, dumbfounded. She was getting away.

"What day? Kate! What hour?"

She turned back with parade precision. "The day after the third banns are read from the chapel pulpit, ten o'clock." She gave a curt nod, and was gone.

Malcolm swayed. She'd said yes! She was going to marry him. Chills raced through him, static electricity through his limbs and his chest. He threw up his arms and cried, "She said yes!"

Mr. Yardley, covered in mud, days in need of a shave, and looking a bit savage, dragged himself into Gretna Green. The detour into Newcastle had cost him precious time, as had his hack throwing a shoe miles outside of Carlisle.

He slid off his horse, muscles screaming from the days in the saddle, and stumbled into the blacksmith's.

He emerged having heard an earful. The lady and the duke were married! "Without having had the decency to use me services."

He got himself to Gretna Hall, and Captain Bowden spotted him. "Ha! My good man. You made it. Just in time for a wedding supper."

Mr. Yardley swayed on his feet, and thought about face planting into the mud of the yard and never moving again.

Mort thrilled as Kate pulled him into a secluded closet. Then his heart stilled as he saw the expression on her face.

"I was too hasty, I take it back, I—!"

"Breaking an engagement, Madame? How improper." He caught her up in his arms, and held her. "What is bringing on these chilly feet, my beautiful lass?"

"How can I ever trust you, Malcolm? I've seen you!"

"How long since you've seen me? When did you last see me with another woman?"

"I don't know, I'm sure I haven't seen all of them—!"

"When?" He stroked her face. She shook her head, her mouth pressed together. "I'll tell you the last time I was with another woman. It was in Brussels. Where you saw me with her. Nothing and no one since, I swear to you."

Her beautiful lips parted and her eyes widened. "How can I believe you? How can I believe that? What about Molly?"

That pesky chambermaid in London.

"Nothing happened, she was just boasting. I turned her down. I promise Kate, I will be faithful, I won't falter, and I won't leave. I am yours, body and soul."

"You won't tire of me and wander off? Your hands and your eyes won't wander? Because if you do, and I have tied myself to you before kirk and God, I will hunt you down, I swear it! I will not let you leave me alone and miserable, tied to a deserter and betrayer for life!"

He swallowed as nervous flutters kicked in his stomach, but he pushed them back. If he could have this woman, he was a new man. "I will never do that. I promise you, Kate. Please, I want to marry you."

And he kissed her. Their first.

She melted into him. A bright vista of happiness opened before him, a joyful glimpse of their future life together.

Adam only made it through the second course. His face was drawn, the red seeped out of his lips, and in the mixed company of mother-in-law and three former suiters to his bride, he was completely silent. Cora decided enough was enough, thanked them for joining them, urged them to enjoy the feast, asked for a tray to be sent up to their room, and excused them both.

He had to be dragged out of his seat, but not because he was protesting, but because he was exhausted and in pain.

She got him into bed, assisted by the grinning Malcolm and the blushing Kate. She twinkled a smile at Malcolm as she pushed him out of the room.

Kate helped her undress, and don one of the pretty and prim nightgowns.

"I'm so happy for you," Cora told Kate as she exited.

“Thank you, Duchess. I’m happy for you as well.” Her smile was sweet and slow. Cora’s answering smile was a full toothy grin. A thrill of excitement went through her.

The tray had arrived, and Cora was set to feed a few more morsels of their wedding feast to her husband, but when she turned back to the bed, he was fast asleep.

“Ah well. Later.” She climbed into the bed, and snuggled in, carefully, next to him. She snuck another kiss on his sleeping lips.

He stirred, mumbled, “Love you . . .” and sank deeper into the slumber.

Cora blew out the candle with her heart full of joy.

Saturday, June 28, 1817, evening

It did not matter how unfashionable it was. He was a duke, and he'd dance with his wife every dance if it so pleased him. He claimed each waltz for himself, and a Scottish reel or two.

They twirled around the London ballroom in each other's arms. She was an excellent waltzer, as he had known she would be. A radiant smile suffused her face as they spun.

Lord Eastham passed them, the dowager in his arms, her cheeks flushed. That relationship was still progressing, it appeared, though if either of them could convince the other to attempt matrimony, Adam would be surprised when he heard it.

Adam and Cora had spent the winter at the castle in a warm cocoon of bliss and tenderness. He had hardly noticed as temperatures plummeted, and fear gripped the nation that summer was gone from the world and would never return. Cora's worry over the harsh, lingering winter had been the only mar to their heady first months together.

Blessedly, April 1817 had seen improvement in the weather, and May had seen more. June arrived bright with sunshine and warmth. Summer reappeared, and all the world breathed easier.

The papers were calling 1816 the "Year Without a Summer." Adam would ever look at it as the beginning of his greatest joy.

With summer's arrival came their first obligatory trip down to London.

Before they left, Cora had gone from plant to plant through the gardens and grounds that it had been Adam's pleasure to give to her last summer. She had walked though the Blackdale fields, the landscaped grounds, the succession houses, the brick orangery in the garden, the kitchen garden, and finally through the old conservatory in the castle, checking the welfare of each growing thing and humming sweet-voiced farewells. She had been sad to leave, but she had been there for planting season, and as they left for London, prosperous green covered the dark soil of Blackdale's highland valley.

Cora had been reassured to be leaving her plants in the care of an excellent staff of gardeners. Adam had been only a little surprised when she had won the heart of the curmudgeonly head gardener through a single conversation with him over the differences between Scotch and Melancholy thistles, the varieties of flowering heather, and the exquisiteness of Scottish bluebells. Mr. Muir was now a devoted follower, and would make sure her gardens were cared for as she wished.

Cora had also been reluctant to interrupt her thriving friendship with his sister Hester and her husband Mr. Gilchrist. Cora loved to coo over the new baby, enjoy the antics of the minister's older children, and have afternoon visits with Hester at the manse, cozy with conversation over tea.

Adam had assured Cora they both would be back soon. "Two months, love. And only two weeks trapped in London."

She sighed. "But the week on the road! And the week back! The misery."

"I'll try to make it less miserable. Not traveling through the night will help."

"True." And she'd come in for a kiss.

The trip down from Scotland in easy stages, sleeping in a bed nightly, had been a vast improvement over any mad dash across the countryside. Cora also proved to be one of those high-bred ladies who insisted on bringing her own sheets when staying at inns. He hadn't complained; he relished holding her every night between those sheets.

They'd given Kate and Malcolm their own carriage, loaded with baggage, but the women often traded seats to chat for a few hours. Kate wouldn't be able to make the journey the next year, her first pregnancy just beginning to show. Adam had hopes to curtail next year's trip to London for Cora for a similar reason. Let the dowager come up to Scotland if she wanted to meet her first grandchild. Adam's mouth curled up at the thought.

The waltz ended. He escorted Cora to a seat and left to fetch lemonade. When he returned, it was to see a red-coated officer at her side. Adam had been silently discouraging her former court all week, and annoyance flared that his scowls hadn't been enough to deter this cad from approaching her.

But then he recognized the golden blond head, the too-wide shoulders, and that arrogant stance. He looked around, and spotted Henriette scowling at them from the other side of the ballroom.

His younger brother Jude was in London, and he was standing too close to Adam's wife. Adam's fingers tightened on the glass handles of the lemonade cups. The liquid sloshed over his gloved fingers as he increased the length and speed of his steps.

As he neared, Cora caught his eye. She gave him a quick hold sign with her fan, and continued her conversation with Jude with a polite smile. He approached cautiously, staying out of Jude's periphery, and noticed his brother's stance had changed. His ears were a scarlet to match his uniform.

Adam caught the end of Jude's answer to a question Cora had posed. ". . . Don't know how Miss Diana Ashby is faring, no." He stammered. Adam stood still in amazement.

"Oh, then you'll be happy, I'm sure, to hear she has recently married." Cora smiled with her lips. "Such a joyful occasion, whenever a painful past is overcome to reach a happy future, don't you agree?"

Jude mumbled an answer.

Cora said, "And your child was fostered with the Donne family in Aberdeen. I wanted to be sure to tell you, for I know I would want to know where all my children are. He's four now, and a vibrant little boy, his foster mother writes."

Though Jude's back was to him, Adam saw the moment Jude went from awkward embarrassment to complete astonishment. Yes, she did just speak of your illegitimate child straight to your face, brother. That was Adam's duchess! A grin stretched his lips.

"We have compiled a list of each of your children that we are aware of, and where they are. My mother contributed to it as well. We will happily present a copy to you later. You'll have to let us know if there are any we have missed." She blinked at him sweetly.

His brother, overly handsome and used to his boisterous flirtation getting him anything he wanted, gaped at Cora.

Adam stepped in. "Brother." He curled his lips at him. Jude took a step back, and shut his mouth. "You've met my wife? Let me do it properly. Cora, may I introduce my brother, Major Lord Jude Douglas of His Majesty's Royal Horse Artillery? And brother, it is your honor to meet Cora Winfield Douglas, Duchess of Blackdale. My wife."

"Charmed," Jude gulped.

"Utterly charmed." Cora gave her politest, coldest smile.

Jude hastily bid his leave, claimed his wife was needing him, and escaped.

Adam couldn't keep the grin off his face. "You are a delight," he whispered in his bride's ear. She flashed him a small, triumphant smile.

At the next waltz, he asked, "Shall I sweep you away again, my duchess?"

"Always."

As he took her up in his arms and swirled her around the floor, her bell-like laughter filled the air. He basked in the sun of her smile, and grew warm in the wonder of her love.

Acknowledgments

I want to thank all who helped me with the development of this novel!

Joy Bischoff, for the encouragement and excitement, and my good friend Emily Martha Sorensen, for coming up with an entire series concept for me in the course of one conversation. Thank you so much to the alpha readers who read the first version I let anyone see: Marissa Bischoff, Alejandra Jensen, Jessilyn Stewart Peaslee, Kaki Olsen, and Heather Chapman. I really appreciate your feedback, and hope I managed to fix a few things.

I was surprised at how nerve-wracking it was to send my romance novel to my parents and mother-in-law. Thank you Mom, Dad, and Cynde Greenwood, for reading and for encouraging me. Mom even read it aloud to Dad, then read through again hunting all the typos. I love you all.

Thank you to the beta reading team for great feedback: Rachelle Sorensen, Sotia Chhang, Madeline Jensen, Virginia Johnson, Kinsey Beckett, Donna Stocking, and unexpectedly, Karl Greenwood! Thank you to knowledgeable Karen Pierotti who stepped in last minute to catch geography problems and suggest alternatives to Americanisms. You were a blessing.

Thank you to the sisters who served with me at church: Elaine Butt, Julianna Allred, and Stephanie Albiston. Thank you so much for lightening the load.

Thank you to Emily Chambers for believing in it before I wrote it, Hali Bird and the Cedar Fort board for taking it on the strength of a chapter, and Priscilla Chavez for the beautiful cover. Thanks to Deborah Spencer and Jessica Romrell for their edits.

Thank you to Mary Robinette Kowal, who encouraged authors to take on race and social issues, and represent all types of people in our fiction. I listened, took on the challenge, and hope it turned out well.

Thanks to the teams behind NaNoWriMo. I'd been watching and wanting to participate for years. This was my first NaNo novel, and I ended November 2015 with a beginning and an end, and a stumped middle. But it was awesome.

And thank you to Karl, my wonderful husband. Through all our hardships, I love you so much, and am so grateful to have you.

Thank you!

About the Author

Rebecca J. Greenwood is an author, artist, and designer with a love of stories, especially Regency romances. She grew up in Texas as the oldest of six and studied visual art with a music minor at Brigham Young University. Rebecca lives in Utah with her husband, where she listens to audiobooks, cooks experimentally, has an interest in alternative health, and constantly has a new project in mind. Visit rebeccajgreenwood.com to experience more of her art, writing, and upcoming projects.

Scan to Visit

www.rebeccajgreenwood.com